CON VER GENT 9.0

An Alex Boudreau Adventure

PAUL H. LANDES

Hunter and Gatherer Publishing Company
Davis, California

CONVERGENT 9.0

CON VER GENT
/kən vərjənt/

- *Convergent* comes from the Latin prefix *con-*, meaning together, and the verb *verge*, which means to turn toward.
- tending to move toward one point or to approach each other
- the degree or point where subplots within a story come together

Hunter and Gatherer Publishing Company

Cover design by Robin Walton Designs
and formatting by The Fast Fingers www.thefastfingers.com

ISBN: 978-0-692-44574-7

For more information about this book and other works by the author, visit:
www.paulhlandes.com

"Today is going to be a great day. Do you know why?
Because I am going to make it a great day."

Karen Oatey
1956 – 2015

San Francisco Post

SPECIAL BY STEPH MOORE

A journalist, like a lawyer, stands alone. We have sources to protect, yet privacy is simply an illusion. They are watching us. Who?

We live in a world where our most private information and deepest secrets are mined, collected, disseminated and/or stored all without our knowledge. Governments around the world have created cyber-attack forces to eavesdrop, break encrypted codes, and pilfer trade secrets and even plant false and misleading information. Privacy, as we have known it under the Second Amendment, has been shredded by the very body our founding fathers had vowed to protect us against.

There are times when our government's focus is so broad that it misses traces of data stored within its own limitless databases. How often this happens is open to debate, but we have now learned that if our government had deciphered specific information it had stolen and stored itself, it may have been able to avert a geopolitical crisis of unequalled magnitude.

This is a story of one individual who found that single trace of evidence hidden within the catacombs of the National Security Agency's own classified database. What he or she found and how that data was used to prevent a bio-weapons attack of unparalleled global magnitude, is the subject of this investigative piece. The identity of this person will not be revealed in this article, nor will I under any circumstance disclose his or her identity. What I will say about this person is that, while using wildly unorthodox methods, he or she exhibited supreme courage in protecting us all from two of the world's most powerful countries squaring off and flexing their military might.

Six weeks earlier

CHAPTER 1

To most people, a 22,000 acre ranch is larger than life, well beyond one's wildest dreams, but by Montana standards it's known as a ranchette. Benjamin Hunter had purchased the M & O Ranch six years ago and it served as his personal sanctuary and a link to his upbringing. He had been raised on a sheep ranch on the outskirts of Auckland, New Zealand, and each time he walked the pastures of the M & O Ranch, memories of his childhood flashed before him.

Benjamin's elbows were drilled into the cedar railing that bordered the outside decking of his log-framed home. His head rested on his thumbs and he stared vacantly off in the distance. "If I replaced the cattle with sheep, this sight would be exactly like where I grew up. See the lake over there?" His right hand pointed to the end of the pasture at a crystal blue lake bordered on one side by soaring Ponderosa and Lodgepole Pines. "That was the first thing I did when I bought this ranch. I built that lake as a reminder of where Will and I used to swim almost every day back in New Zealand."

Alex gazed out at the shimmering water. "And what about today? Do you still swim there?"

"Absolutely, it's still a ritual for me every time I come here. Well, in the summer time anyway," Benjamin smiled.

Alex rose from her chair and walked over beside Benjamin. She wrapped an arm around his waist and pulled herself close. Her head spun and her aquamarine eyes sparkled as they scanned the panorama. "It's beautiful, Ben. I can see why you love it here so much. Just how big is this place, anyway?"

Benjamin nodded his approval and smiled. "22,465 acres to be exact or

9,091 hectares in your system. I had it surveyed as soon as I bought it. I don't know why I did that, I just did it." He gave Alex a squeeze. "Wait until you see what I have in store for you. How about we get some warm coats, refill your cup with some more tea and I'll take you on the 25-cent tour?"

"Judging by what I can see from here that tour could take the rest of the day, and then some. I'll make us a couple sandwiches and we'll have lunch down by the lake. And a swim for sure, if it's not too cold for you?" She winked.

Benjamin heated up some water and Alex rustled through the refrigerator grabbing everything she needed to put together a picnic lunch. She hummed a song and in a matter of minutes, sandwiches, apples, bottled waters and two chocolate bars were neatly tucked away in a wicker basket. "Good to go. Do we need anything else?"

Benjamin turned and his eyes met Alex's. For the first time since he had met her, he could see behind the veil of her eyes that had protected her inner thoughts. He saw calm where he had once seen only turbulence and her tenderness was surfacing, softening her steely backbone. He cupped her cheeks, closed his eyes and pulled her in. Their lips met. Everything around them vanished and they became lost in each other's being. Benjamin's fingers combed through Alex's silky black hair and Alex ran her fingers up Benjamin's spine. Their chins touched and Benjamin rubbed the tip of his nose against Alex's. "Hold that thought and we'll continue from right here once we get to the lake."

"How can a girl resist such an offer?"

They reached the back porch and Benjamin held out the picnic basket. "Here, you take this."

Alex grabbed the basket and Benjamin bent down, scooped her up and cradled her in his arms. He feigned a groan. "Hmm, you seem heavier than I remember."

Alex elbowed him. "Or maybe you're losing your strength?"

Benjamin walked down the wood hewn steps to the chipped cedar path. Alex gently swayed in his arms as he strolled toward the lake.

"Stop!" Alex jumped from Benjamin's arms and clamped her hands over his ears. The moment her feet hit the ground a blinding flash and a blast of wind catapulted them forward at freeway speed, whip-slamming them into the ground. A shower of debris and deadly projectiles, sounding something like a mix between heavy rain and falling sand, pelted the ground around them. A burst of white light slapped the back of Alex's eyelids.

Alex lay spread-eagled across Benjamin's legs, moaning like she was in a cocoon of pain. She shook her head and reached over to grab Benjamin. "Are you okay?"

A warm stream of blood trickled through his fingers as he rubbed the back of his head. "I think so. What the..."

They both looked back and jumped to their feet. They stood, carved statues, their fists clenched and glued tightly against their legs.

Less than sixty seconds ago they had stood in the kitchen of the ranch house, alone, lost in each other's world. The same house whose walls had now been blown apart—a soaring fireball, followed by puffs of dark smoke had turned their dreams into a nightmare.

CHAPTER 2

Alex stood silent and watched as Benjamin shone a flashlight on the ground and kicked through the ashes. Clutched tightly in his right hand was a round, tin container, charred and dented. "This is probably all I'll find. I'm sure everything's been destroyed. This is my mom's cookie tin and it was always full of something she'd made for us." Benjamin looked up at the stars and screamed out, "Why? Why? Who the hell would do something like this?" His words were delivered in increasing decibels, climaxing with a loud, "Who, god damnit?"

Benjamin continued kicking through the ashes, the rubble and the scorched debris. "I don't know how many times I've asked myself: hey, if there was a fire, what would I want to grab and run out with?" He turned to Alex. "Have you ever asked yourself that question?"

"I'm sorry, Ben. Maybe tomorrow when it's light we'll have better luck. Let's go back inside. Come on."

"One thing, the most important thing I have, and it's gone—forever." His eyes began to water and his voice cracked. "The only photograph I had left of Will. We were down at the lake and had just finished swimming. Just the two of us… like always… just the two of us."

That night, Benjamin and Alex stayed in the guest house on the M & O Ranch. The police had urged them to stay in town, but Benjamin had been adamant—he wasn't going to be intimidated by anyone. The guest house was set back in the pines a good thousand yards from the scorched embers and glowing ashes of the main house.

Lightening doesn't strike in the same place twice, he reasoned. He had felt the guest house would be the safest place to stay that night and the police had finally relented, but only after Benjamin had agreed that two policemen could patrol the grounds that evening.

Benjamin sat in a leather chair, his arms dangled over the side and his bare feet were propped on a matching leather ottoman. His face was chiseled with sharp features, prominent cheek bones and a deep-set dimple creased the center of his chin. His wavy brown hair was disheveled and his chestnut-brown eyes revealed a man who had seen the passing of time before him. "God, the pounding. My head's going to explode any minute and my ears are still chirping or hissing like flies or mosquitos or whatever. It's constant, it won't go away." He wrapped his hands around his ears.

Alex sat on the floor, her back propped against the wall. She looked parched, as if all the moisture that made her skin glow and made her hair shine had been sucked out of her. "We were lucky. If we'd been any closer to the explosion we wouldn't be here." She raised her arms above her head and stretched, craning her neck from side to side. "Headaches from explosions are called powderheads and yours should go away after another dose of Ibuprofen. First thing tomorrow morning, though, we're driving in to Bozeman to find a doctor and have our ears checked. Mine are ringing too and we may have suffered some inner ear damage. I doubt it, but it's possible."

Benjamin's hands were still wrapped around his head, covering his ears. "That's probably a good idea, because right now I can't get the sound of that explosion out of my mind, or my ears."

"What you felt and heard came from the shockwaves and blast wind. The sudden change in pressure in your inner ear causes you to hear sounds that aren't there. Tinnitus is the official diagnosis, but I don't think we'll end up there. I'm sure this is just temporary, maybe by the morning the sounds will be gone."

Alex pulled one of the throw pillows to her lap and hugged it. "I don't think the local police will have any luck in finding out who did this."

"You might be right, I don't know, but we'll give them some time and keep pressing them. That's about all we can do."

"I'm not sure, yet, but I have an idea who might be behind this; and if I'm right, the police won't find this guy," Alex said.

Benjamin lifted his head, his brows furrowed. "What do you mean—you have an idea?"

"When we were in the Queen Charlotte Islands to find the eagle, I received a text, remember that?" Alex asked.

Benjamin nodded. "I do, I even memorized it. *The greatest trick the devil ever pulled was convincing the world he didn't exist—prepare to meet your maker.*"

Alex pushed up from the floor and began to pace around the room. Her arms wrapped tightly across her chest. "That's it. I tried to trace that text, but I couldn't find its origin. What I suspect, though, is it was sent by a man named Kioshi Nakajima. One of the things I've tried to do over the years is continue to track the people that I stole from. Not all the time, but periodically I'd check in to see where they were. I've always suspected that if any of them ever found out that it was me who ruined their lives they would come after me. That's really the main reason I lived so many years by myself, avoiding relationships. I lost track of Kioshi some time ago. I couldn't find him."

Benjamin leaned forward and began to stand. "Alex, you can't keep blaming—"

Alex stood behind Benjamin's chair and pressed her hands on his shoulders. "There's a lot more to this than I've told you, but I'm almost certain that Kioshi is the guy who blew up your house."

Benjamin leaned back, cocked his head upward and closed his eyes. "I want to find this guy as much as you, Alex, but if you know who he is then let the police handle it. Stay out of it."

"They'll never find him. Kioshi is an international arms dealer, a black market trafficker, a guy who has his hands in dozens of illicit activities." Alex winced from the throbbing pain in her head, and then continued, "He completely vanished shortly after the start of the Afghanistan war, and Intelligence agencies have been looking for him ever since. With the presence of the U.S military in that region, I'm certain he's fled and is holed up in some other obscure place. It's been 14 years since he disappeared."

"Maybe you're overthinking this. The guy could be dead for all you know."

"He's not dead. He's the one responsible for blowing up your house and he's looking for me."

Benjamin clasped his fingers, his knuckles turned white and he let out a long sigh. "Okay... okay, maybe you're right, I don't know, but go ahead and tell me everything and then we'll figure out what to do."

Alex's hands gripped the windowsill and she leaned back. "The two propane tanks near the side of your house caused the explosion, I'm certain of it. Tomorrow, when the spot's cooled down, I'll be able to look around some more. The Fire Marshall knows the tanks exploded and my guess is that's what he'll pin the blame on." A twinge of pain ricocheted from one temple to the other and Alex grimaced.

Benjamin's head jerked forward. "I saw that. Are you sure you're okay? Maybe we should drive into town now and find a doctor."

"I'm fine, I really am. Every once in a while a sonic-like boom goes off inside my head." Her fingers gently massaged her temples. "It doesn't last long. Anyway, I found some steel fragments from the tanks and one of the pieces had a hole in it, maybe six inches, the hole was made from the outside in, meaning something hit the tank and penetrated it. Someone had to have planted an explosive charge near the tanks with the intention of using them to burn your house down."

Benjamin squinted. "Are you sure? The Fire Marshall was pretty clear that it would take several days, probably longer, to sort through the debris and come up with some answers."

"I'm certain that's the cause, and I'm almost certain that the tanks were hit with an RPG that ripped through the metal and caused the explosion."

"Wait a minute, RGP—like the military weapon?"

"RPG—rocket propelled grenade—a Russian made anti-armor weapon. Whoever planted it removed the launcher and placed its warhead under the tank. I'm guessing it was set on a timer. When an RPG ignites, the explosive energy is directed at a copper lining inside which liquifies and is propelled forward. Obviously, if it can penetrate an armored vehicle, it would have no problem shredding the steel of a propane tank."

An RPG!" Benjamin's eyes were now the size of saucers. "How'd you know there was going to be an explosion? You jumped out of my arms a split second before it happened."

"Instinct, that's all," Alex paused and closed her eyes. As a clandestine operative, who for years had lived undercover in the world of corporate espionage, her instinct had served her well. It had become a part of her arsenal, sort of a sixth sense, and she relied heavily on it when the need arose to make an on-the-spot decision. With some people, it was an innate quality—you either had it or you didn't. With others, it was something you eventually recognized and learned to trust. With Alex, there was no difference between conscious thought and instinct. She opened her eyes. "I felt that something was going to happen. I wasn't sure if it was going to be an explosion or not, but I knew it. I knew that something bad was about to happen and I reacted."

"RPG's, explosions, tinnitus, powderheads, how do you know this kind of stuff?" Benjamin asked. "This is too much for me to think about right now."

"We can talk more about it later, but that's my take on all this," Alex replied.

"Jesus, Alex, did you tell any of this to the police?"

"No, not yet. I'll wait until the bomb squad and the Fire Marshall finish their investigations and I'll take a look at their reports to see what they conclude. They won't reach the same conclusion as me, they just won't. The local departments here don't have the expertise and it's a pretty easy way to wrap up a report by simply saying faulty propane tanks caused the explosion."

Benjamin jumped from his chair and with a stiffness difficult to describe, he took three long strides. His hands gripped Alex's shoulders. "I don't like where you're going with this. You're done, finished, no more placing yourself in danger, remember?"

"I am done, but I know this guy, and he has a score to settle with me. He won't stop until he wins. By win, I mean he wants me dead. That's his way of settling the score."

Benjamin tightened his grip. "What'd you do? Why's this guy looking for you after all these years?"

Alex stood up and embraced Ben. After several minutes she pushed away and took a deep breath. "When I stole the uranium from your grandfather I had it routed to my client. The enriched uranium was a weapons-grade isotope, and they intended to use it for humanitarian purposes—cancer detection and treatment, elimination of bacteria in food, for the production of drinking water, all the right things. That was the only reason I agreed to take that job. I never would have become involved if I had known the uranium was going to be used to create weapons. Within a month after my client received the uranium, he contacted me and said it had been stolen and their warehouse had been blown up."

Alex circled the outer edge of the room. She took small, deliberate steps and her hands were clenched, pushing into her chin. "The explosion at my client's warehouse was caused by an RPG. It took me a while to figure that out, but I managed to track things back to Kioshi and I found my client's uranium stashed in a compound in Afghanistan. It struck me as odd, at the time, that only two men were guarding that compound, but it made my job easier. I was able to return the uranium to my client, but what happened at that compound meant that Kioshi would not rest until he found me and killed me."

Alex stopped and turned to Benjamin. "Are you familiar with the samurai warriors and their principal of Kobayashi Maru?"

"Captain James Kirk was the only person to ever win in that type of situation. That much I know, but how does that have anything to do with this Kioshi guy and this whole mess?"

Alex laughed out loud. "Star Trek, I saw those shows too, but that's not what I'm talking about. It's not even close." She stopped, leaned back against the wall and continued, "Kioshi traces his ancestry back to Takeda Nobushige, a samurai leader from the 16th century. Kioshi follows the teachings of the samurai— and not just their religious doctrines of Buddhism and Zen, but in their practice known as *The Way of the Warrior.* To the samurai, the path of the warrior was one of honor, and they emphasized duty to one's master, and loyalty until death. One of the ways they tested a warrior's honor to his master was to put him to a test where he faced a no-win situation. That's what the Kobayashi Maru means to the samurai. Kioshi surrounds himself with people who are entirely loyal to him and would sacrifice their own lives to save his. That makes him even more dangerous. He has people close to him who would risk their own lives to protect him."

Alex pushed away from the wall and walked over to Benjamin. "I'm going to find Kioshi. I have several ideas where to start. This is something I have to do and I have to do it myself."

Benjamin stood still, his eyes fixed on Alex. He turned and walked over to the bookshelf behind her and his fingers brushed across the books' spines. He grabbed a book, pulled it out and cradled it in both hands.

Alex reached out and placed her hand over Benjamin's. With a mere whisper, she spoke, "When I first met your grandfather at his house, he did the exact same thing when he was in thought. He reached in his bookcase and pulled out a book."

The corner of Benjamin's lips rose upward. "I'm sure my grandfather has read every book in his library. Some of them he's probably read many times. With me, it's more like a habit. I've been doing it all my life."

Alex plucked the book from Benjamin's hand and held it out. "*Tempting Fate.* Have you read this one?"

Benjamin shook his head. "Nope."

"Maybe you should. Maybe we both should. Maybe there's something in here that will explain what's going on." Alex stood on her toes and kissed Benjamin on his chin.

"Look," Benjamin raised a hand and continued, "call me old-fashioned, but all my life I've been led to believe that I'm supposed to take care of the woman—of you. This doesn't sit right with me. I don't like it. I'm coming with you."

"Hmm. First times happen all the time."

CHAPTER 3

"Good morning, Miss Moore. It looks like you'll be turning the lights on again this morning. This is turning into a habit with you."

"Yep, I'm afraid so."

"I've already signed you in. Have a good day."

"Thanks, Walter. You, too."

"Stephanie! Hold the door," a commanding voice echoed from the lobby.

Stephanie turned and jammed her hand between the closing doors. "Hi, dad."

Mr. Weintraub stepped inside the elevator. "You want to hit my floor." He draped his overcoat over his arm. "You're making a habit of this. I like that."

"I have some appointments out of the office later, so I'm coming in to get a few things out of the way first."

"You've always been conscientious about your work. Say, why don't we have dinner? You and me. It's been a while since just the two of us have gotten together. Give Susan a call and find out when I have an opening and tell her to book it. We can go to the club. I'm anxious to learn what you've been up to."

The doors opened and Stephanie stepped out of the elevator. "Yeah, okay, I'll give her a call."

■　■　■　■　■

A loud, gruff voice silenced the buzz around the newsroom, "Steph! Get your ass in here!"

Stephanie Moore was smart, stubborn, a raging ball of energy, the opposite of a clothes horse and nearing her one year anniversary as a reporter with the San Francisco Post. She minimized the browser on her monitor and pushed her chair back.

A reporter in the cubicle next to her poked his head around the divider. "It sounds like another whipping. You'd better hurry up."

"Three o'clock feeding time," another voice warned.

Still another whisper, "Don't forget your armor."

Steph reached out, grabbed both door jambs, hung on and leaned forward. "Thirty more minutes, that's all I need, just 30 minutes, Chief."

Cliff "Chief" Upton had been the News Editor at the Post for the past eight years. Before that, he had cut his teeth as a journalist at a handful of papers across the country. He had garnered three Pulitzers, had been recognized by the Society of Professional Journalists countless times and had earned the respect of every journalist, editor and publisher who had ever worked with him. Called "Chief" by those who hung on his coattails and those who envied his position, he was tough, demanding, overbearing, cantankerous, and righteous to most. Over the years, a few had called him fair, nurturing, helpful and the like, but Steph had not been part of that group.

Cliff had a full head of salt and pepper hair and dressed the part of a news editor. He sat hunched over his desk, shuffled through some papers and kept his head buried. "What is it with you, anyway? Why don't you ever get things turned in on time? This isn't some blockbuster, once in a lifetime story you're working on. It's a short piece on the unveiling of some damn statue. Christ, we have hundreds of stories on file about that kinda stuff. Just grab one, rewrite it and get it to me—now!"

"Actually, Chief, I am working on one of those blockbuster type stories—*right now*—and I was going to talk to you about it later today… but… well… do you have a few minutes… say, maybe right now?"

Cliff raised his head, slid his hands together and remained slouched over his desk. "Huh? You're off working on a story without running it by me first? Christ, Steph, just get me the statue copy—now!"

"I will, Chief, I promise you'll have it by the end of the day, no problem. But… well…" she took a deep breath and blurted it out, "I've heard from a reliable source that Agrico was hacked into and some of their files were stolen. Right now, I'm—"

"No, don't tell me, your so called reliable source is Edward Snowden the second, right?"

"Nothing like that, Chief. Last night I was at Americano and the two people sitting right behind me had more than their share of drinks and it was pretty easy to overhear what they were talking about. They both work at Agrico. I think the gal works for the guy, but anyway, just a week ago Agrico's computers were penetrated and some GM files were copied and uploaded. This is a big deal."

Chief grunted and leaned back.

Steph took long, determined strides in a short space and her hands chopped the air. "They have no idea who stole the files. They bantered around all sorts of names and activist groups who are constantly hounding them whenever they announce some new type of genetically modified food product, but they don't know." She stopped, spread her hands on the Chief's desk and leaned forward. "Someone just broke into Agrico's computers and stole information from them. This is dynamite and—"

Chief threw his hands at Steph and leaned back in his chair. "Maybe there's something there, maybe there isn't, but these hacking stories are for the Guardians and the WikiLeaks of the world, not us. Things have changed. This paper gave up on investigative reporting after the McMullen scandal broke. I wish we hadn't, but that's just the facts. Do you remember McMullen? Nah, you couldn't, you didn't know anything about journalism back then. I wasn't here at the time, but I had some journo friends who worked here and that mess really hurt the paper's credibility. McMullen was a good reporter, but he screwed up big time. His story on suicides on the Golden Gate Bridge ran front page, above the fold. Turns out he plagiarized a good part of it. He broke every rule in the book."

Chief covered his mouth and let out a rumbling cough. "You're a cub reporter; you're still getting your feet wet and it's a long way to investigative journalism from where you're sitting now." He looked up and scowled. "At least where you're supposed to be sitting. Anyway, just get me that damn story."

"You're wrong. When the Watergate scandal broke, Woodward was 29 and he'd only been at the Washington Post for a year and Bernstein was, I think, 28. You, yourself, when you were awarded your first Pulitzer were what, 24? Am I right? I'm on this story—it's my story. You need to let me run with it. I know there's something there, I have a hunch."

"I have a hunch," Chief permitted himself a smile. "If I had a dime, hell even a penny, for every time I heard a reporter say that, do you think I'd still be sitting here today? Hunches rarely pan out, especially in today's environment. You need sources, facts, connections, backbone. Get me the statue piece. Forget the other stuff."

Steph flipped a business card across the desk. "Delynn Longo, Manager, Genetic Plant Research. She's my first source and I'm having dinner with her tonight at the same place. I'll get her to open up. I ended up sitting with both of them last night for two hours and 14 minutes. I already know enough facts to know this is a story, a big one. And, no one's ever accused me of not having a backbone. I played goalie in college for our field hockey team and was all conference two years in a row, and," Steph leaned forward and stretched all the way across Chief's desk, "I had the balls to come in here and ask you to let me run with this story. It's mine. I can do this." She exhaled.

Steph stared straight at Chief and waited for his answer. He sat still and pressed his thumbs together. "Come on, give me the go ahead!"

"You have two weeks to come up with something solid, something printable, but whatever you write I'm going to need to run it up the chain before it goes to print. No guarantees and this is going to be a big one for you, you need to let me know everything you're doing—and I mean everything. I want to know what you eat for breakfast, who sits next to you on the bus, everyone you speak to, look at, how much you tipped at a restaurant, websites you visited—everything. One more thing, clean your browser history each time you leave your desk and empty your own trash each night. Got it?"

Steph pushed back from the desk, turned and sprinted—her red hair trailing behind her. "You won't regret this."

"Steph, get your ass back in here!"

Steph's head poked around the door jamb. "Oh, yeah, sorry, and thanks Chief!"

"Your statue story?"

She nodded, "Tonight… for sure… I promise."

CHAPTER 4

"Darts?" Alex rolled her eyes.

"Yep, darts," Benjamin laughed. "Just before I closed on the ranch, Phil and I were fly fishing on the Gallatin River and we drove into Bozeman for dinner. The ranch was called the Pitchfork then, but I couldn't relate to that name. It didn't really click. I wanted to name it something unique, something with a personal meaning to it."

"Pitchfork, sounds like a ranch name to me."

"We'd had a few beers and were playing darts and came up with a game to name the ranch. We each had three darts and we threw with our left hand. I hit 13, Phil hit 15 and we missed the board with our other darts. The thirteenth letter in the alphabet is M and the fifteenth is O. There you have it; M & O Ranch."

Alex tossed her head. "I guess that sounds better than OM or MO."

Benjamin looked at his phone. "That's Phil, hold on a sec."

He stuffed his cell in his pocket. "It looks like he's bringing his new girlfriend over, so we'll get a chance to check her out."

"Phil has a girlfriend? Why am I just learning about this now?" Alex asked.

"Oh, sorry. I forgot to tell you. He told me about her earlier this week and," he shook his head, "with everything happening it just slipped my mind."

"No worries. When will they be here?"

"Five minutes."

Phil Morgan was Benjamin's closest friend. They had met shortly after Benjamin had moved to Mill Valley, and since then, the two connected spirits had spent untold hours together swimming in the icy waters of San Francisco Bay, diving for abalone along California's northern coast and just about anything else that involved the outdoors and some form of friendly competitive wagering. While Benjamin had many friends, Phil was the only friend that he truly trusted.

Alex had grown close to Phil in a unique way. When they had first met, Phil had discovered Alex in the back yard of Benjamin's house, her hands clenching the steel meshed fence that had served as the temporary home to an injured eagle Benjamin had brought home from Canada to help heal. Phil's initial mistrust and borderline hatred for Alex had not been unfounded. Benjamin Hunter was Phil's best friend and Alex had been the person responsible for his disappearance. She had all but admitted so when they had first met. From that day forward, the two had developed a bond that was based on Alex's grit and moxie and Phil's perseverance and unwavering loyalty to his closest friend, Benjamin Hunter.

Alex smiled and headed toward the kitchen. "Five minutes should be just enough time for me to get a pot brewing for our favorite caffeine-aholic."

The Conga drum roll on the front door was Phil's calling card. The eternal nonconformist, Phil refused to ring a doorbell—any doorbell—ever.

Benjamin shouted, "Come on in. Door's open."

Phil marched into the entryway. "Ah... I smell it already." He turned to the lady next to him, looped her arm through his and herded her down the hallway.

Phil and his lady friend entered the kitchen and Phil grabbed Benjamin by the shoulders and gave him a warm bear-hug. He turned to Alex. "You're next." He threw his arms around her waist and lifted her off the ground. "You look just as great as the last time I saw you but," he cocked his head to one side, "it feels like you've put on a pound or two or three."

Alex pinched his arms. "I think I'm entitled to that, don't you?"

Phil lowered Alex to the ground, spun around and stretched out his arm. "Michelle, these are the two I've told you about—Ben and Alex. Guys, meet Michelle Brophy."

Benjamin extended a hand. "Hi, Michelle, it's a pleasure to meet anyone who can put up with this guy for more than half a day."

"You'll get used to their banter. Most of the time they sound like two little kids arguing over who caught the biggest spider, but deep down they're both mature and sensitive men." Alex looked at Phil and raised one brow. "Sometimes that maturity and sensitivity is hidden pretty deep, though." Alex gripped Michelle's arm.

"I'll grab a mug and filler-up," Phil said, "but Michelle here, well she's more granola than me. Caffeine's not on her list of approved drugs, so maybe some tea for her. Decaf, has to be decaf."

"Here, let me pour you both some coffee and you two head out to the porch." Alex waved to Michelle. "We'll heat up some water and meet you out there shortly."

Minutes later, Phil and Benjamin stood on the back porch. Their hands waved in circles and their matching smiles reflected their unique solidarity and kinship.

"I haven't known Phil for all that long, but I think this is a side of him I haven't seen before." Michelle walked over to the window. "You're so right, Alex. They are like two little boys. It's cute."

Alex smiled.

Michelle gazed out the window and off in the distance she saw the two towers of the Golden Gate Bridge jutting through the low creeping fog draping the hillside. Blotches of sunlight flickered through the trees. "This view is absolutely breathtaking. Tell me you never tire of it?"

"That's exactly what I thought the very first time I stood on that porch and saw that same view. It's an invitation to dream and I knock on wood now every time I stand here and look at that sight."

The two chatted nonstop waiting for the water to boil. Michelle had met Phil through an online book club they both had frequented. It had turned out they had the same interest in specific authors and genres and one thing had led to another. They had finally met for coffee at The Depot Bookstore & Cafe in downtown Mill Valley and had really hit it off. "It didn't take us long to figure out we had tons in common and we've been together now every day for the past two weeks."

"Phil's a great guy. A *really* great guy. Oh, he has his oddities, to say the least, but they grow on you. Did you know he never yawns?"

An eyebrow rose. "Never? You're kidding, right?"

Alex rolled her eyes. "If he does, I've never seen it. Anyway, I've learned so much from him and I count myself lucky to have him as a friend."

"I have to tell you, when Phil started telling me about you and Ben and everything you two have been through, I couldn't believe it. I followed everything in the papers and the internet about Ben's disappearance, that virus and everything about you two that I could get my hands on. It's an amazing story. Scary, for sure, but amazing."

"Right now I'm glad it's all behind us. We're both just trying to put our lives back together, but there are still a few leftover pieces to fit in somewhere."

If Alex had wanted to find a woman for Phil to date, Michelle would be the type of person she had hoped she could find for him. Phil was tall, maybe six feet, four inches, and had the typical swimmer's body—V-shaped, lean and defined by muscles and tendons. The creases in his face reflected a man who had spent hours enjoying all the splendors the outdoors had to offer. Michelle was his perfect counterpart. Standing on her toes, the top of her head would probably notch under Phil's chin. Her crystal blue, elfin eyes sparkled beneath her waterfall of wavy auburn hair. Her crowning point was her attire. She shared Phil's taste in clothes—comfort outweighed style.

Michelle stood next to the kitchen counter and pushed up the sleeves on her Bennington College sweatshirt. Her wrists were slender, but her arms had been honed by years of exercise and she looked as toned and fit as someone half her age. Her khaki pants and her sockless ankles peeking out from her tattered sneakers were identical to what Alex had seen Phil wear almost every day.

"So, is this where you're from?"

"Oh no, I haven't been here very long, really. I was a professor at Bennington College in Vermont." She grabbed the front of her sweatshirt. "Can't you tell?"

"That sounds fascinating. I imagine it was hard for you to give that up."

"It probably looks fascinating from the outside, but I became pretty disgruntled with the whole academia life. Not in the same way as Phil; no, my dissatisfaction had more to do with my own professional enrichment and the fact that the administration wouldn't support what I wanted to do. I came out here on vacation and used that time to decide what to do with my life. I had a feeling that this place was something special. You know sometimes things tug at you and pull you toward them and won't let you go? That's what happened to me here, so I went back to Bennington, quit my job and moved out here for a new beginning."

"So what have you found here to stimulate your professional talents? Are you teaching somewhere?"

"I'm through with academia that much I do know. I've been writing a fair amount. I've finished up my last two manuscripts and I've actually started on a secret desire of mine to write a novel. Although, admittedly I haven't accomplished much on that end since I met Phil."

■　■　■　■　■

"And you don't have any idea who did that?"

"None at all." Benjamin shook his head. "The police are looking into it and I talk with them every day, but so far nothing. Alex doesn't think they'll ever find out who did it. Unless a witness shows up who saw somebody setting the bomb or maybe someone who saw a car drive away, she's convinced they'll just close the case and call it an accident."

Phil leaned back against the railing, his fingers tapped a rolling melody. "The RPG thing seems like a long shot to me. Just because she knows somebody who blew up something years ago using the same thing doesn't mean there's a connection. She's stretching that one."

"Maybe, I don't really know, but she describes it as some kind of a signature. Certain bombers, especially serial bombers, tend to use the same type of bombs, wires, trigger mechanisms and all that. With this Kioshi guy, it's RPGs, and she knows of four separate instances where that's what he used. She points out other things too, like the way the wires are crimped, similar use of fragmentation, stuff that I don't really understand, but she does."

Phil turned his mug upside down and grimaced. "Damn, I'm out already. You know," he shot Benjamin a quizzical look, "do you ever wonder about some of the weird things she knows? I do, all the time. She knows about things that I never even knew existed."

Benjamin nodded. "Yeah, that she does. She's convinced, though, that the explosion has something to do with her and… well, she may be right, but we can't live our lives looking back over our shoulders everywhere we go." Benjamin threw his hands in the air. "We'll get to the bottom of this."

Phil paced around the outer edge of the deck; his fist pounded the railing with each step. "What do you mean it has something to do with Alex? I know she's not sitting around waiting for the police to figure things out. What's her angle? What's she going to do?"

"What she does best—find the guy. After it happened she wanted to lie low somewhere, somewhere less obvious than right here, but I'm through with hiding. She had someone sweep the house for bugs and look for bombs and everything was clean so we came back here. She called her mom right after the explosion and she was fine, but she sent someone to Sidi Lahcen, the village where her mom lives in Morocco, to keep an eye on her from a distance."

Phil leaned into the railing. "So what's her plan? I know she has one."

A shoulder shrug. "She's leaving tomorrow and she expects to be gone for about a week. That's all I know."

Phil grimaced. "Well, here we go again, off on another one of Alex's thrill rides."

Benjamin gave a half-smile. "Not this time. She's going off on her own and she doesn't want me or anyone else involved, or to even know what she's up to. She thinks it's safer that way."

"I've heard that one before, but—"

"Anyone need a refill?" Benjamin and Phil turned and saw Alex and Michelle walking out the kitchen door.

"That would be me, for sure." Phil held out his mug.

CHAPTER 5

"**A**idan! Right on time. Thanks for coming." Benjamin wrapped both his hands around the outstretched hand of Aidan Starr and squeezed tight. "Jessica's already here, so let's get at it."

Aidan Starr was a member of GEN's Board of Directors. More importantly, he had been Benjamin's personal attorney and Benjamin had leaned heavily on him over the past few months as he tried to put GEN back together.

Genetic Engineering Nexus, commonly known as GEN, had been formed in 1987 by a group of former employees from Amdel Biosystems. It had been initially funded by government and private grants to decipher the human genome. At GEN's formation, less than 5% of all human genes had been identified; yet, the ability to create protein from human genes had represented potentially huge profits for the biotech industry. By 2004, GEN had been forced to file a Chapter 11 Bankruptcy to preserve its viability. Benjamin had purchased GEN through a court ordered reorganization plan and had devoted his personal resources and time to finding a cure for cystic fibrosis, the disease that had taken his twin brother from him at the tender age of 10.

The three were comfortably seated in the office that had once belonged to Murray Paulson and was now occupied by Benjamin, until he could find a suitable replacement to take over the helm. Benjamin, Aidan Starr, and another board member, Jessica Wasserman, wasted little time in getting down to business.

Benjamin slid a sheet of paper across the table. "I just received this yesterday from the U.S. Patent and Trademark Office and we're now back on schedule and it looks like we'll have our approvals in the next 60 days. Nice job, guys."

"Oh, Ben, that's marvelous news. This happened much quicker than I ever expected." Jessica looked over at Aidan and nodded. "I'll bet you had a hand in this."

Aidan kept a stoic face. "Maybe a finger or two."

Benjamin continued bringing his two trusted board members up to date. Plans were underway to build the new research facility at the Polar Hole in Antarctica. It wouldn't be completed for another four or five years, but Benjamin had started the wheels rolling to assure GEN a front row seat when that facility opened its doors.

Dr. Jessica Wasserman was an Associate Professor of Medicine at Stanford University, specializing in pediatric AIDS. A round woman with flame red hair, she had always been blunt, forceful and her pragmatic mind had kept her focused on the task at hand. Her excitement radiated through her voice. "The possibilities there are endless. You wouldn't believe the countless number of people who've contacted me hoping to get a shot at working down there. Do you really think we'll have the opportunity to work there?"

Benjamin nodded. "I've already been assured by the project's director, Harry Colvin, that we get the pick of the litter. I'm taking him at his word."

"The research that can be done there on gene suppression in a weightless environment will have an immediate impact on how we can cure a whole array of diseases. This is going to be Nobel Prize material for a lot of people," Jessica said.

France and the United States had been appointed as the lead countries to build an international research station at the Polar Hole in Antarctica. In Alex's search for a way to rid Benjamin of the G-16 virus that had been injected into him, the two had discovered the Polar Hole, a vast, unexplored hole containing endless research possibilities for the epigenome community. Buried deep in the ice of Antarctica was a bunker that the Germans had built during the Nazi regime that they had used as a research facility. When Alex and Ben had found the bunker, they had also discovered that the deeper they had traveled into the Polar Hole the less the gravitational pull. Once Benjamin had remained exposed to that near weightless environment for several hours, the G-16 virus had been repressed and silenced—permanently.

The meeting wrapped up in just under an hour and all three felt a sense of relief that GEN was back on track and would soon fulfill its goal—patented and FDA-approved cures for cystic fibrosis.

The day before, Benjamin and Phil had agreed to meet at the Dolphin Club after Benjamin's meeting. Founded in 1877, The Dolphin Club was the oldest swimming and rowing club in San Francisco. The clubhouse sat on the sandy shores of Aquatic Park and Benjamin and Phil had been regular swimmers there whenever Benjamin had been in town. Benjamin had found the solitude of swimming in the icy bay waters invigorating and a way to clear the dead-wood from his often cluttered mind. Phil had always relished the chance to swim with his friend and that day had been like all the others. The last 100 yards had turned into a sprint with the loser vying for the right to pick up the tab for a couple of beers afterwards.

The two walked out the front door of the Club and down the steps to Jefferson Street. "Michelle's busy until later tonight and Alex is out of town so how 'bout I pay off the bet now and I'll buy us a beer over there?" Phil pointed up the hill to the Buena Vista Cafe.

Benjamin elbowed Phil. "I thought you were going to welch on the bet, as usual. Let me throw my gear in my car and then you're on."

"My car's on the way. Let's just throw our stuff in there," Phil countered.

They dropped off their swim gear in Phil's Karmann Ghia and walked up Hyde Street. Just like old times, the two walked stride for stride, laughing, cajoling and taunting the other with identical grins etched across their faces. Benjamin reached for the door to the Buena Vista Cafe when they heard a loud explosion behind them.

They whirled around and saw a cloud of flames billowing from Benjamin's Land Rover, parked below on Jefferson Street. A crescendo—ping, ping, ping—filled Benjamin's ears.

CHAPTER 6

In the Penthouse high atop the Fairmont Hotel on Nob Hill, Alex pushed her chair back and walked over to the window. She slid the curtains open and gazed out. It was late afternoon and she had not taken a break since she had arrived earlier that morning. A low fog crept beneath the Golden Gate Bridge and soon, it would blanket Alcatraz Island for the evening.

It seemed like a lifetime ago when she had sat in that very room and had searched for back doors to GEN's computer system and had penetrated Benjamin's home computer with a Trojan Horse. It had been in that same room that Alex had let the years of guilt she had harbored over the loss of her sister, Christina, spring from the cocoon that had held her ache captive. That night, not so long ago, in that same room, seeds of change had been planted in Alex and she had begun her transformation. That had been the night when she had laid curled up on the floor, sobbing, and alone, and had given her soul to Benjamin.

A knock on the door brought her back to the present. "Room service."

Alex opened the door, and after the server wheeled her food in, she tucked a crisp bill in the palm of his hand and sat down to eat. She took a sip of hot tea and wondered out loud, "This is such a long shot… I don't know… maybe there's another way."

The National Security Agency, commonly referred to as the NSA, was the United States' primary intelligence agency used to gather information to protect its security interests. Public disclosures, beginning in 2013, had put the NSA under public scrutiny both at home and around the globe for what many had perceived as operating a carte blanche, unregulated organization that had freely mined troves of data from innocent and unsuspecting people. The breadth and scope of the NSA's cyber-intelligence activities had been made public by Edward Snowden, an NSA independent contractor with a high level security clearance and a conscience that believed peoples' right to privacy had been violated. Thousands of top secret documents had been leaked to the press and many world leaders had become outraged when they had learned their own communications had been captured by the NSA.

Congressional hearings had been held, independent panels had been formed to investigate the matter and to make recommendations to the President and yet, while the NSA had held fast with its assertions that iron-clad safeguards were in place to protect any improper use of its mined data, nothing had changed. The NSA had continued to operate in near total autonomy and had continued on with no visible changes to its operations.

Alex believed that somewhere in the NSA's stored data she could find information on Kioshi Nakajima. Warrants for his arrest had been issued by six countries and even though his whereabouts had been unknown, for over 14 years, Alex knew he communicated with encrypted messages and his encryption methods changed frequently. Still, she knew that even the most sophisticated cyber security systems, while effective, weren't NSA-proof. If she could hack into the NSA computer network, she was certain she could isolate specific data by region and, *if* she had the time, she would be able to decipher and analyze the data and locate him.

So far, Alex had encountered one roadblock after another. She had run port scans and port sweeps to find any active ports to determine if there had been any known vulnerabilities. None—everything had been locked and protected. Each attempt to insert a Trojan Horse had been rebuffed. She had known that all port scans were routinely logged by IT personnel so she had quickly logged off.

Alex's life, up to now, had been based on a single-minded premise: win—at any cost. She had found the one profession that had allowed her to move about freely and unnoticed, living in complete anonymity. Able to move from shadow to shadow with an array of aliases and disguises, she had been a sought-after operative retained by private individuals and corporations in need of her discreet and professional services. While she had always considered herself a trained agent schooled in the many nuances of corporate espionage, she had known she had really been an emissary of greed, serving clients who had desired nothing more than to control and own what was not theirs.

Alex was good—very good. She was skilled in martial arts, computer sciences, electronic surveillance and explosives, and she had mastered the subtle nuances of seven languages. Her skills had allowed her to move around the world as she had pleased, unnoticed, and to infiltrate corporate or government targets to steal the technology she had been handsomely paid to deliver to her clients. None of this had been without its risks, but Alex seemed to thrive on finding herself in situations that had demanded quick thinking or even creating her own forward-looking technology.

Alex shut down her computer, walked back to the window and leaned forward. Her forehead rested against the cold glass and she closed her eyes. *Think, Alex. There has to be another way.* Her mind raced as she sifted through her knowledge of the NSA and the organization's complex web of divisions and operations.

Alex's first encounter with the NSA had been shortly after she had left the French DGSE and had ventured out on her own. She had been hired by a client to infiltrate the U.S. Embassy in Moscow, so that her client would have access to sensitive trade negotiations that were to take place in that embassy. During that operation, she had encountered an American who had been working at the Embassy and she had learned he had been recruited by the Soviets to pass on secret documents and information. The American, Clayton Pollard, had actually been an agent with the NSA and part of the information he had passed on to the Soviets had detailed some of the inside workings of that Agency. At that time, little had been known about the inner hierarchy or structure of the NSA. Even today, the Agency's structure has not been made public.

Alex had been successful in planting electronic audio surveillance devices within the secured confines of the U.S. Embassy. Her mission had been a success. What had intrigued her the most, though, had been the information she had successfully uploaded from Clayton Pollard's computer—a map to the NSA's inner sanctum. The Signals Intelligence Directorate, known as S3, was the Agency's largest functional directorate. It has three subdivisions. One helped determine the requirements of what the NSA called its customers—other agencies, the president, and the military. The agency's main analytical centers lived there too. The super-secret work of SIGINT, collecting offensive cyber warfare, was also the responsibility of S3, with its many bland-sounding and compartmentalized branches.

Several years later, Alex had read that Clayton Pollard had been captured and arrested. Convicted as a double agent, he had been sentenced to life in prison. Had it not been for his lavish lifestyle, his treasonous actions may very well have gone unnoticed. The Soviets had paid Powell over $2 million which he had foolishly spent on fancy cars and exotic trips.

Alex smiled and threw her arms in the air. "*The TAO, that's it!*" she blurted out. "I've wanted to do this for too long."

The NSA has an elite team of hackers specializing in stealing data from the toughest of targets. The Tailored Access Operations, or TAO, has its own motto: "Getting the Ungettable." The TAO was a branch of SIGINT. Breaking into the TAO computers would be impossible, she knew that, but she had another idea. She could play the same game by their rules. It wasn't going to be easy, but it would be effective. She knew it.

Alex heard the phone ring and ran back to her desk. Next to her computer was a prepaid throw-away cell phone she had purchased to communicate with Benjamin, but only when it was absolutely necessary. *Oh god, what's wrong?*

"Hello, Ben! Is everything alright? Are you okay?"

"Yeah, yeah, everything's fine, but there's been another explosion. Someone blew up my car outside the Dolphin Club. Phil and I were about a block away when it happened. It scared the living hell out of us."

"But you're okay? You're not hurt?"

"No, I'm fine. We're both fine. I just finished going over everything with the police and they're going to contact the Bozeman police and see if this is somehow related. Hell, how can it not be? Two explosions in a week, that's a record for me."

Alex held the phone tightly in one hand and the fingers of her other hand combed through her hair. "Listen, Ben, it's not a good idea for you to go back to Mill Valley. You need to find another place to go until I get back. I'm leaving for Austin and I should be back in two or three days."

"Phil and I already talked about that and I'm going to stay at his place for now. And what's in Austin? What do you know?"

"It's probably a long shot, but I need to go there. One more thing, rent a car, don't drive Phil's. Did the police check his car?"

"No, I don't think so. They didn't say anything about that."

"Call them. Call them right now and have them sweep Phil's car for explosives."

"Okay. Alex, what's going on?"

"We're both in danger and so is anyone around us until I can find this guy. I think it might be a good idea for you to leave and go somewhere you've never been—somewhere no one would suspect you'd go."

"I'll think about it. In the meantime, I plan on being more vigilant. You be careful. I'm sure you're okay, but I still worry about you."

"I'm fine... I really am. Be careful, Ben—I love you."

The instant Alex hung up the phone, she placed a call.

CHAPTER 7

Steph had paid little attention, until now, to the news stories about hackers penetrating large companies that now seemed like daily occurrences. POS malware infecting UPS, Community Health System's loss of 4.5 million patients' records, Fandango, Credit Karma, financial institutions, every day there had been new breaches. She had noticed that a company's initial response after finding out about the hack had been nothing more than talking points laden with inconvenient truths. They all had claimed no one was at risk because of the breach and they had their own security people looking into it. The FBI had looked into each of those breaches, but they had never said a word about anything that had transpired.

The previous night when she had spun her chair around and had slid across the table to where Delynn and her coworker, Adam O'Keeffe, were downing scotch and sodas, she had had no idea what she was doing. Pulling her chair up to the table, she had announced her name and had talked nonstop for the next 10 minutes, spitting out long, drawn out sentences without periods at a tempo that would shock even the most skilled auctioneer. Soon, she had been buying rounds and had edged her way into getting them to open up about Agrico.

She flipped her wrist and looked at her watch. "Ah no, I'm going to be late."

Chandler Mills and Steph were sprawled on the couch filling in the other about their day. Steph had had a couple of short term relationships in college, but she had resigned herself to the fact that she would forever be single. Her sex life had been nonexistent, but she had a long list of friends, male and female, and her social calendar had been crammed with invitations, spontaneous get-togethers and her regular Wednesday night movie group. Serendipity had played a part in Chandler and Steph hooking up six months ago at a wine tasting at Toby Lane Vineyards, and they had been inseparable ever since.

Just three weeks ago, Chandler had moved into Steph's apartment and everything had seemed just right to Steph, maybe even perfect. Chandler was warm and kind and was probably the only person she had ever met who could tolerate her endless quirks. The fact that Chandler wasn't Jewish was one of about a dozen reasons Steph's father didn't approve of her new relationship.

An only child, Steph had given up on her father's approval years ago. It had been a rare occurrence when Hylan Weintraub had made it to one of her grade school plays or recitals and then, only for the closing minutes. He had missed her college graduation entirely and when she had graduated from NYU, even though he had graduated from the same school, had been a Trustee, and had been scheduled to hand out the diplomas to the graduating class, he had cancelled at the last minute. Work—his first family—had beckoned again. It had been at that exact moment that she had dropped the hyphen and the Weintraub name and became known simply as Steph Moore.

Chandler sat up and scowled, "No, not tonight, not again. I thought we were going to have a nice quiet dinner. Come on, Steph!"

"I wish I could—I really do," Steph pleaded.

"You're doing that eye-rolling thing again," Chandler flashed a lips together smile.

Steph turned, ran back and kissed Chandler on the cheek. "I'm sorry—tomorrow, I promise."

Chandler's scowl softened. "I'm going to hold you to it this time."

Steph ran into her bathroom, brushed her teeth, ran a comb through her hair and flew out the door. Moments later she ran back through the door, re-booted her laptop and frantically typed away. She attached a document to an email and hit the 'Send' button. *God*, she thought, *if I'd forgotten about that Chief would have me doing statue articles 'till I'm dead.*

■ ■ ■ ■ ■

The Americano Restaurant and Bar was a hip, after-work watering hole located right on the Embarcadero, with close-up views of the Ferry Building, San Francisco Bay and the Bay Bridge. The leathered barrel chairs on rollers, padded couches, and a classy outdoor heated seating area made it easy for men in suits, women in pencil skirts and tourists toting shopping bags to find the perfect spot to mingle or unwind.

San Francisco had undergone a modern day renaissance with the emergence of dot-com companies relocating to the City. When Twitter had gone public, it had sprouted 1,600 new millionaires and with companies like Pinterest, Square, Yelp and others calling San Francisco home, a financial tsunami of young-minded, techie-nerdocrats had hit the City. New clubs had shot up from Gold Rush era brick warehouses that had been renovated to attract those elite and nouveau-affluent code jockeys. The latest, the 1907 Musto building in San Francisco's historic Barbary Coast district, had been renovated and opened as The Battery, an ultra-private, traditional and invitation-only club. Similar to London's Soho House, it attracted the City's heavy-hitters in tech, the arts, innovation and philanthropy.

The Americano had been where Agrico's up-and-coming alpha geeks, stress puppies, and on occasion, a few gray-matters chose to meet up after work.

"Oh, I'm so sorry, Delynn." Steph pulled out a chair and took a seat. "It's been one of those days that I'd rather forget. Do you ever have those? But, well, here we are."

The waiter refilled Delynn's water glass and she took three, maybe four, large swallows. "I think today would count as one of those. I've been surviving on aspirin all day and I forgot all about our dinner date until

Adam reminded me this afternoon. If I'd known how to get a hold of you I'm sure I'd have cancelled and be curled up in my bed right now. I'm starting to feel a bit better though." She held up her hand and squished her thumb and finger together.

Steph had had those types of days more often than she had cared to remember, but last night she had sensibly nursed her two drinks while acting out her role as a hard-charging party girl from memory. "Fortunately, for me, I started a bit later than you guys, but this morning was still rough. If it's alright with you, I think I'll stick to water tonight, too."

"You have some catching up to do. I'm already half done with my third glass."

Steph lifted her water glass. "Here's to the day after."

Delynn placed her glass back down, slapped her elbows on the edge of the table and leaned forward. "I need to apologize. Last night, Adam and I were way out of line and if any of the work things we blabbed about ever got back to any of our colleagues, we'd be in more trouble than we could handle. You can understand that, right?"

Steph had anticipated this, but she was still uncertain how to respond. As a journalist she took her responsibility seriously. She had taken a graduate on Ethics in Journalism and she knew the Code of Ethics by heart that every journalist had ceremoniously agreed to when they had been hired by the Post. She had it tacked to the wall in her cubicle just in case. Still, sitting across from her, clutching a glass of water with one hand, rubbing a temple with the other and staring right at her, sat someone her own age who could help her crack a big story—a career-making story. Chief had surely faced this same crossroad in his career, as had Woodward, Bernstein and countless others.

"Steph? Please tell me you understand."

The fork in the road was clear. Steph took it. "Last night you never asked me where I worked. How come?"

"Too many scotch and sodas is the obvious answer. I was shit-faced drunk, even by the time you sat down." Delynn brushed her hair back and creased her fingertips in the back of her neck. "No... this isn't good... I'm screwed."

Steph took a breath and let it out without a sound. "Far from it. There's nothing we talked about last night that has left my lips and it never will. I promise. I'm a reporter, Delynn, with the Post, but before you say anything—"

Delynn turned the color of chalk. Her elbows collapsed and her hands trembled. "Before I say anything? I'm not saying another word to you. I can't believe you did that! You have no idea the kind of trouble I'm going to be in now because of you."

Steph reached across the table, but Delynn abruptly pulled both her hands back and threw them to her lap. Steph's shoulders scrunched forward. "Everything you and Adam said last night is safe with me. That might be hard for you to understand right now, but you will. If it ever came down to me having to spend time in jail for not divulging your name, that's exactly what I'd do. I'd rot there before I'd ever mention a source's name—yours or anyone else's. Please, Delynn, you don't have to decide anything right now, but you need to take the time to see all of this from my side."

"Oh god—Adam. He's more paranoid about that place than me. I need to get a hold of him." She pushed her chair back and shot up.

"Wait, Delynn! Please hear what I have to say and if you want me to go with you and tell Adam, I will, but please, you'll want to hear what I have to say. Please... please, sit back down."

"Is everything alright here?" The maître d' towered between the two. "I am so sorry if you've been waiting long. I will personally go and send a waiter right over."

Steph turned her palms up and her eyes darted from Delynn to her chair. "We'll each have a Cobb salad. The sooner the better."

"Yes, madam, two Cobb salads, they're on their way." The maître d' pivoted, clicked his heels and raced toward the kitchen.

"Maybe I should have a drink after all." Delynn sat back down, snapped her napkin and draped it over her lap.

"Thanks, Delynn." Steph took a sip of water. "I get your humor, but I think it best if we both just stick to good old-fashioned water for the rest of the night."

"For the rest of my life should be more like it." Delynn raised a brow. "You set us up, didn't you? You obviously overheard our not-so-private conversation and you moved over to our table to get yourself a story. I'm right, huh?"

Steph nodded. "For the most part, yes, I overheard your conversation and I did want to find out more. I was interested in what you had to say, and I bought way too many drinks. Sorry about that, but it really wasn't until early this morning when some of the things you mentioned jumped right at me. I should've told you last night that I was a reporter and if you'd have asked I would have told you, at least I hope I would've. I've been wrestling with just what to say to you about all this for the entire day."

Delynn's color had returned, but her face still dripped with worry. "Do you have any idea how many memos have circulated around our company in the past year that literally scream out at us? I've signed a confidentiality agreement, just like everyone else. You're sitting on a story that you think may make your career and I'm sitting here knowing mine might be over."

"My aunt was a whistleblower four years ago," Steph said. "She did the right thing and yet, she's still paying a steep price for it today. She ended up settling the issue out of court and I asked her later if she had it to do all over again would she do the same thing. She didn't hesitate. No, no, no, that's what she said. She reported someone who'd been embezzling funds to her immediate supervisor and it was dismissed as something she shouldn't bother with. She went up the chain of command and was rebuffed at every step. Her work environment became a living hell, everyone shunned her, talked behind her back, she had threatening notes stuck to her windshield; you name it, it happened. Someone even slashed her tires in the parking lot. Finally, when she began to have health problems she went out on medical leave. Oh, everything eventually got settled and life went on for her employer, but not for her. She believes she was punished for doing the right thing and that's been holding her back from moving on with her life. Those are hard things to understand, unless you've somehow been a part of it."

"Okay, so you have a heart. Maybe even a conscience, too. Good for you," Delynn said.

"I am so sorry for the wait, ladies. These are on the house and if you should need anything else, I will have my eye out." The waiter set the plates on the table and promptly left.

"My first free meal. Maybe that's a sign of things to come. God, why do you have to be with the Post? Why not some neighborhood weekly that no one bothers to read? What do you do there? I plan on looking up some of your articles, so where should I start?"

Steph chuckled. "Well, here's another moment of truth. You'll be hard pressed to find my name on a byline in more than two or three stories—tops. I have a story that'll be out tomorrow about the unveiling of the Capt. William Alexander Leidesdorff statue as part of Black History Month. The byline for that one, like all the rest, will be San Francisco Post Staff. I cover whatever local, non-important events my editor chooses to throw at me."

Delynn's jaw dropped. "And you've never, I mean *never*, done any investigative reporting?"

Steph shook her head.

"I don't know if I should cry, jump for joy or reach across the table and strangle you. This is getting worse by the minute," Delynn said.

"You're right to have your concerns about all this, but not about me, no way. I graduated magna cum laude from UC Davis, got my Masters in Journalism from NYU where I received the school's highest award—the NYU Journalism Award, and I'm tough as nails. Journalism is nothing more than finding the truth and writing about it in a way that's not only balanced, but making sure that all the parties know what you're doing, up front, no hidden agendas. That's the only way I'm moving forward with this story."

Steph pushed her plate away, brushed her hair back and looked straight ahead. Her hands were spread. "Hear me out first. Let me tell you what I've already learned today and what some of my theories are on this. I have some ideas of my own about why your computers were hacked. You're going to want to hear everything I know at this point and then we can meet again. Nothing has to be decided today—nothing."

Delynn listened intently. Her hand stroked her chin as Steph made her plea. She pulled her napkin from her lap and dabbed at her lips. Dropping the napkin on the table, her red-nailed fingertips drummed on the white tablecloth. "Call me crazy, call me whatever you like, but I have 20 more minutes before I need to be home. What's your angle?"

CHAPTER 8

Phil walked in the front door and over to Benjamin, sprawled out on the couch. His head was propped up on one armrest and his sock-clad feet dangled over the other. "Here you go. These are yours." Phil dropped a small package in Benjamin's lap.

Benjamin held up the package. "What's this?"

"Open it up. You'll see. You've already seen them, but I had them printed up for you. I figured you'd never get around to that one."

Benjamin tore open the flap and pulled out a pack of photos. "Damn, these are the pics you took on the Channel swim. I haven't looked at them since you emailed them to me. These are..." Benjamin pulled a photo out and held it up. "Captain Streeter... and Alison. You had them sign this one?"

"Yep. I'll sign it and we'll get Alex to sign it when we see her and then you'll have a signed photo of your courageous crew."

Three months ago, Benjamin had fulfilled a goal he had set for himself several years earlier—swim across the English Channel. What he hadn't known was it was going to take two attempts to cross the Channel, but cross it he had. Captain Streeter had been escorting channel swimmers for over 10 years and his 37 foot steel trawler, *Suva*, was the perfect boat. The Captain's sister, Alison Streeter was known as the "English Channel Queen," having made 43 official crossings in her career. She had been aboard as an official observer.

The shortest distance across the English Channel was from Shakespeare Beach, Dover, to Cap Gris Nez, the headland halfway between Calais and Boulogne on the French shore. Benjamin had chosen to heed his captain's advice and start the 21 miles swim one hour before high tide.

On his first attempt, the seas had been rough and the Captain had told Benjamin that a successful crossing was not in the cards that day. "Wait for better conditions, mate," he had warned. In spite of the Captain's urgings, Benjamin had chosen to attempt the crossing that day. Six hours into the swim and still short of the midpoint, Phil had convinced Benjamin to call it quits. It had been taking too long for each of Benjamin's feedings and the extra time to complete each feeding had lowered his core body temperature to a dangerous level. The water temperature that day had hovered around a chilly 57 degrees. When they had pulled him onto the boat, his speech had been slurred and his body shook from shivering tremors. He had been on the edge of hypothermia.

Nine days later the conditions had improved, and the Captain proclaimed that they should start the swim that evening—everything was perfect. At 2 am, Benjamin dove from the boat into the icy water and swam ashore. The official English Channel swimming rules require the swimmer to start from the shore and since the boat could only get within 200 yards of the shoreline, the swimmer had to swim this extra 200 yards to get to the start line.

By the time they had been able to see the cliffs of Gap Gris Nez, both Phil and Alex had been certain that Benjamin would make it. His stroke count had remained at a steady 60 to 61 strokes per minute, his feedings, every 30 minutes, had been quick and Benjamin had never lost that inner focus that propelled him forward. At the halfway point he had experienced some shoulder pain and he had taken 600 mg of Ibuprofen, but other than that they had been right on plan and Benjamin had been expected to finish in the next two to three hours.

Michelle rounded the corner and came into the room carrying a tray. "Here are a couple of sandwiches for you two and I cut up some tomatoes and carrots." She placed the tray on the table in front of the couch.

"I marvel at how you did that," Michelle said. "Phil's told me about your swim and I'm just amazed that you can stay in 50-something degree water for over 10 hours. I'll bet you thought about getting out more than once during those final few hours."

Benjamin sat up, grabbed a sandwich and took an oversized bite. "Hmm... good," he muttered.

By the time Benjamin had been within eyesight of Gap Gris Nez, he had less than a mile and a half to go, but for that past hour his pace had slowed considerably. The tide had begun to ebb and Benjamin had to angle his way into a stronger than expected current that had pushed from the north. If he had let the current pull him to the south, he'd have missed the entire coastline of France. Benjamin had asked for a double feeding and Alex had thrown two bottles to him; each had been filled with warm water and saturated with dietary supplements. As he finished up his feeding, the Captain had yelled, "Just stay within eyeshot of my starboard side. I'll be heading you in the right direction. You're going to make it, mate. I feel it in my bones."

That last stretch should have taken less than an hour at Benjamin's regular pace, but because of the tide and current, it had taken him just under three hours. By the time he had crawled out of the water and had clambered over the rocks to dry land, he couldn't stand. He had reached the beach and had collapsed on the sand. Somehow, he had summoned the strength to raise one hand and had given a half fist-pump salute to his crew.

Benjamin sat back on the couch and wiped his mouth with a napkin. "Boy, I didn't realize I was so hungry." He looked at his watch. "Three o'clock, no wonder."

"So, tell me. Did you ever think about getting out during those last few hours? You must have." Michelle sat cross legged on the bamboo wood floor.

"No. Not once. That wasn't going to happen. What I thought about was why I jumped in in the first place."

"Why did you do that? What was so important to you about that swim?" Michelle asked.

"Oh, that's a long story and I'm not too sure it's all that interesting to most people. But, a lot of it was because of my brother... and because of the long training hours I logged with this guy," his head nodded at Phil, "and because Alex was there and after everything I'd just been through it seemed like the perfect thing to do to get my head screwed on straight again. That's the short answer."

"Well, I think the whole thing is amazing. I really do. Someday I want to hear the long answer. Maybe when Alex gets back?" She stood up. "You two need anything else?"

Phil jumped in. "Speaking of Alex, have you heard from her?"

"I got a short text about an hour ago. She said she was leaving Austin. That's it."

"She didn't say where she was going or when she was coming back here? Send her a text—find out."

"I did. I texted her right back, but she hasn't responded." Benjamin quickly glanced at his cell phone.

Phil sat on the floor with his back against the wall and his legs crossed yoga style. "Look, we need to figure things out. We need a plan. I feel like we're just sitting around twiddling our thumbs, waiting for another explosion to happen. Any ideas? Cuz I sure have some."

Benjamin locked his hands behind his head. "I want to hear from Alex first, but I think we should start looking for someplace to go until all this cools down. I don't want your house to end up looking like mine."

"Let's go up the coast. The abalone season ends in a few weeks and we're a pretty poor excuse for a couple of divers. How many dives did we get in this year? Six, maybe seven? Pretty lame. Let's drive up to Gualala."

"Too familiar. Like Alex said, it needs to be someplace new where we wouldn't typically go." Benjamin looked at Michelle and continued, "What do you think? The longer you hang around us the more likely you are to get involved and you're probably best off not getting involved. In fact, I know you're better off staying out of this one."

Michelle smiled. "I've spent most of my life in small towns where the biggest events were the July 4th parade on Main Street and switching our clocks twice a year. Listening to your lives over the past year is all so surreal to me. I can't quite comprehend it all."

"Me neither," Benjamin nodded. "Maybe it's best we think about this a bit and we can talk later, but my gut tells me we should plan on leaving tomorrow morning."

"Agreed," said Phil. "But what Ben says is right, Michelle. You may already be in danger from just hanging around us. Hey, can you run the idea of Michelle coming with us by Alex?"

"Sure, as soon as I hear from her."

"Call her up, leave a message if she doesn't answer."

Benjamin shook his head. "The phone's for emergencies only. If I don't hear back from her by tonight then I'll give her a call, but Michelle," he turned toward her, "I think maybe you should plan on packing a bag."

Phil pushed off the floor, walked over to Benjamin and sat down beside him. He placed a hand on his shoulder. "You need some down time, my friend, and maybe then you'll tell me what's really eating at you." Phil tilted his head. "You look like shit, bud, and your mind's off in some other world."

Benjamin stared straight ahead, his eyes glazed over. "I think it's all about down time, that's what I really need. Alex and I stayed in Paris for a few weeks and dealt with all the hype about Antarctica and then I came back here and started my training. Alex went back to Morocco for about a month and then she went to Paris to close down her apartment. We met a few times in the south of France, but I swam every day and was too focused on my Channel swim to be much company. We had decided to go to Montana and spend whatever time we needed to unwind, to get some alone time and to heal from all this crap. Hopefully start a new chapter in our lives. Now, here I am, totally embroiled again in something that's beyond my wildest imagination. When will this end?" Benjamin turned and looked at Phil. "Tell me, Phil, when will this end?"

"This may be your new life. Alex comes with a big twisted past and from what I've seen of it so far, it may be near impossible to bury it."

"I've thought the same thing, but I love her. I mean I *really* love her. I can't imagine having to go forward without her. It took me years to recover from the loss of Will and I'm afraid that losing Alex would be the same. That's really the main thing we wanted to talk about when we got to

Montana. How do we want to lead our lives together? How could we be sure that Alex's past wouldn't surface and cause these types of problems? How can two people who have led such opposite lives now live their lives together and be happy? I don't know the answer to any of these questions and now I'll have to wait until this storm blows over to hopefully find the answers."

"Hold that thought." Phil stood and raced into the kitchen. When he returned he handed Benjamin a cold bottle of beer. "Here's to a speedy passing of the storm."

Their arms extended and their bottles clinked.

CHAPTER 9

Dell Computers has a unique business plan. It does not warehouse any of its computers; instead, its suppliers store parts in a Dell facility that manufactures its computers only after they have received purchase orders. Dell's build-to-order model lets it receive payment from its customers immediately—through credit cards, either online or over the phone. It pulls the parts directly from its suppliers on-site and builds and ships the product within four days. The company doesn't pay those suppliers until 36 days after it receives payment from the customer. So Dell has achieved a cash-conversion cycle of negative 36 days. Dell's suppliers finance the cost of its operations.

Before leaving San Francisco, Alex had placed an online order to purchase 30 Dell laptops. She had been logged on through a proxy server based in Spain and she had covered her tracks so that the order could not be traced back to San Francisco. The order had been placed in the name of José María Arregi Erostarbe, a political and military leader for a Basque nationalist and separatist group called Euskadi Ta Askatasuna, or ETA. Erostarbe and ETA had been well known terrorist operatives to the international intelligence agencies, but they had posed little threat compared to the major terrorist groups. Recently, ETA had flexed its muscles and had extended its political and military reach to Mali in Northern Africa. This expansion had most likely raised its alert level inside the NSA, but not to the red alert level of more dangerous terrorist groups.

Upon entering the Morton L. Topfer Manufacturing Center in Austin, Texas, Alex's eyes scanned the reception area. Always size up your surroundings, she had learned over the years. She spotted two cameras, one directly above her over the entranceway and the other on the wall to her right. She suspected there were others, but then she recognized the brand. The CrimeEye 125 was state-of-the-art and very expensive. Its pan-tilt-zoom capabilities allowed the camera operator to move the camera in different directions and to make an image larger. Loaded with immigration facial recognition software, the operator could identify any person who was part of a biometrics database. Her mind ticked. Why such an elaborate and expensive system?

Dressed in a navy blue tailored suit that covered a heavily starched white blouse, she folded her hands, rested them on the reception counter and waited patiently. Out of the corner of her eye she saw her reflection in the window and nodded, slightly. Yes, she thought, the dark glasses and the brown shoulder length wig did the trick. She had applied a beige skin foundation to her face to lighten her olive colored skin, had used a clear lip balm, and a birthmark wrapped around her jaw on the left side of her face rounded out her disguise.

Alex heard a soft Texan drawl and she turned to see a woman in her mid-thirties standing in the doorway. "Oh, I'm so sorry; I didn't hear anyone come in. May I help ya?"

Alex's voice mirrored the same drawl, "Yes, I'm Agent Kolb, and I have a search warrant to inspect an order that I understand will be shipped from this facility sometime today." She reached inside her jacket and pulled out a folded piece of paper.

The woman's eyes widened and she stepped back. "Oh dear me, that's a new one on me. Let me get our manager, Mr. Hitchings, and I'm sure he can help ya." She turned and disappeared through the doorway.

That hadn't been the first time Alex had prepared a warrant. A search warrant was a simple document to forge and she had used that ploy dozens of times. To be valid, a search warrant only had three requirements: a magistrate's signature, a description of the place to be searched and a description of the items to be seized. On only one assignment had the validity of her forged warrants been questioned. It had been at the Bank of

America headquarters in Charlotte, North Carolina. The bank had a policy that all warrants had to be first approved by the legal department before they could be honored. When she had been told by a bank officer that she would have to wait until the legal department had issued its stamp of approval, she had deftly changed her request and had exited the bank. Her mission had been delayed, but not scuttled. She had resorted to her usual means of cracking their computer security codes and pirating the source codes she had been after.

"What can I help ya with?" Coming through the side door was a man who could be featured in a cartoon. He had a very short and stocky body coupled with an awkwardly long neck that only brought unwanted attention to his face that resembled a gnarled bone. A few hairs were spread carefully over the top of his head like fiddle strings. "I'm Todd Hitchings, the manager here."

"Yes, Mr. Hitchings, I'm Agent Kolb with the FBI, and I have a search warrant to inspect a shipment that is being delivered to a José María Arregi Erostarbe in Girona, Spain."

Mr. Hitchings took the warrant from Alex, unfolded it and looked at it only long enough to see it had a magistrate's signature. "Looks mighty official to me. Mind telling me what all this is about?"

"It's just Agency protocol, nothing more. Can you show me where I may find the shipment?"

Mr. Hitchings nodded and then turned his head to the side, "Sure thing, follah me."

Mr. Hitchings led Alex into the manufacturing facility and she was immediately taken aback by a blur of synchronized activity. A whir of positive-force ventilators blew dust and grit back out onto the Texas hills, the rush of forklifts plied the factory floor and multiple assembly lines snaked and swerved through the plant like boardwalk roller coasters. Alex stopped and stared at the cavernous facility. "This is the first time I've been inside someplace like this. It's enormous. How do you possibly keep track of everything going on?"

Mr. Hitchings beamed with pride. "We crank out more than 700 machines an hour here. The entire process, from the time a customer places an order to when the finished PC or laptop exits the factory is only four to eight hours. Ya can't beat what we all do here—nobody can."

Alex walked slowly and committed the layout to memory.

"Keep comin'." Mr. Hitchings waved at Alex. "We're almost there."

They stopped in front of a pallet, neatly stacked with 30 individually packaged laptops. A separate delivery ticket was attached to each box. Alex's hand brushed against the boxes as she circled the pallet. "I'd like to take two boxes to a private room so that I can inspect them. Can you show me to a room where I could have some privacy?"

Mr. Hitchings' fingers rubbed his chin and then he looked at the search warrant again. His lips mouthed every word in the warrant. Looking up, he drawled, "Mighty unusual it seems to me, but this piece of paper says ya have the right to open and inspect this here shipment." He waved the warrant. "It's even signed by a judge. So, I'll help ya grab coupla boxes and show ya where ya can do whatever in the heck it is ya do."

Mr. Hitchings led Alex down the side of the warehouse. She stopped at an open door and peered in. "This should do fine. Let's put the boxes down in here."

"I think ya'd be more comfortable in the room I had in mind. It's down a ways more." His chin pointed ahead.

"This should be fine right here. Comfort's not all that important and this won't take long."

They placed the two boxes on a small metal table and Alex escorted Mr. Hitchings out of the room and closed the door. Two walls were lined with shelves stacked with a wide mixture of computer parts, operating manuals, packing material and an assortment of unmarked boxes. Probably parts waiting to be restocked, she thought.

She pulled a box cutter from her side pocket, opened each box and placed the two laptops on the table. She removed each hard drive and reinserted new ones. Rather than open the plastic wrapped power cords, she found two cords on the shelf and within minutes each laptop was booted up. She pulled two flash drives from her pocket and inserted them in the USB outlets.

Under "My Computer," she copied Removable Disk (E:) then opened the C Drive. Scanning down, she right clicked Windows and opened the AppPatch folder. She pasted the Trojan Horse to both the sysmain and the .LNK file. She looked at her watch and less than five minutes had elapsed since she had closed the door. She shut the computers down, put them back in the boxes and resealed them, taking extra care to make sure they did not appear to have been tampered with.

She found Mr. Hitchings waiting outside a few steps down the corridor. They carried the boxes back to the warehouse and placed them on the same pallet. "Thank you sir, you have been most helpful. I appreciate it."

"No problem on my end. I'm going to send this here warrant over to headquarters. I'm sure they'll want to take a look at it. Procedures ya know. Hey, do ya have a card, or somethin', so I can remember your name?"

Alex reached in her coat pocket. "Oh, I'm so sorry. I must've left them in my car. Here, let me just write my name on the back of the warrant." She scribbled Agent Sharon Kolb on the back of the warrant and handed it to Mr. Hitchings.

CHAPTER 10

"Good morning, Elke. Is Chandler in?"

"Hi, Steph. I don't think so, but let me check. Hang on and I'll ask with Kathy."

This was the third time in as many days that Chandler hadn't been in the office. Chandler was rarely out of the office and certainly not for days, or even hours, at a time. Maybe I'm imagining things, she thought. Maybe—

"Nope, Chandler's a no-show today, again. Apparently this is the third day in a row. I'll leave a message that you called."

"Oh, that's okay, don't bother. It was nothing. Thanks, Elke."

＊　＊　＊　＊　＊

Agrico was one of the world's leading manufacturing companies of chemicals, pesticides and herbicides. In the early 1990's it had broadened its manufacturing base and had pioneered the commercialization of transgenic seeds into a multibillion dollar industry. It had promoted those genetically engineered crops, or GM's, as part of a life science revolution that would greatly increase food production throughout the world. That may have turned out to be a half fulfilled promise, but worldwide, 81% of the soybeans and 35% of the feed corn grown had become biotech varieties, with Agrico controlling the lion's share of those markets.

Agrico had not been without its detractors, and assaults on its products had become a common everyday occurrence. Their worldwide manufacturing and research facilities had been harangued by protesters and in major cities throughout the world, particularly in Europe where protests had drawn tens of thousands of people with chants of *I Am Not An Experiment* and *Hold Agrico Accountable*. Those opponents had asserted that by inserting foreign genes into crops, the food had become dangerously allergenic or that it had been a scheme to sell more chemicals. Agrico had countered with countless studies that had concluded that transgenic crops had revealed no health dangers since their inception. The detractors alleged that the technology employed by Agrico and others, had been nothing more than a ploy to dominate the agricultural supply chain and leave farmers dependent on high-priced transgenic seeds.

Agrico had been highly profitable, but its position as the world's lightening rod for the entire GM controversy had left it vulnerable to a wide range of attacks. It had assembled its own army of political consultants, public relations firms, armed security personnel and highly trained computer techs to protect its corporate interests and to ward off certain, but anticipated attacks.

Steph had arrived early at Golden Gate Park, a thousand acre urban public park. She had chosen Elk Glen Lake as the rendezvous point, not just because it was far away from Agrico's headquarters, but the blustery, foggy weather that day would keep the park's inhabitants to a minimum. She zipped her parka up to her neck and pulled the strings on her hood tight; her cheeks were already pink and wisps of crystallized smoke rose with each departing breath. She had spoken with Delynn twice since they had met at Americano, but this would be the first time she would come face to face with Adam. Adam O'Keeffe was an accountant with Agrico and was part of the team that prepared the quarterly and annual corporate reports and the required filings with the Security and Exchange Commission. He had agreed to meet with Steph only after repeated urgings from Delynn and Steph, who knew that his corroboration with Delynn's story would be important.

Steph saw a blue Prius parked on Martin Luther King Jr. Drive. Even wrapped in a calf-length wool coat and a matching hat pulled down over her ears, Steph recognized Delynn exiting the car. Delynn raised her chin as Steph waved both hands in the air.

Steph extended a hand. "Hi, Adam, thanks for coming." She nodded at Delynn.

Adam gripped her hand. "I'm here, but I'm not certain I should be. I wanted to meet with you to plead my case… if you will."

"I understand. I really do and you can plead all you want, but the three of us each want the same thing—the truth."

Adam crammed his hands in his coat pockets and pressed his arms against his side. His Harry Potter glasses overshadowed his small, triangular face and he was disturbingly shaped. He was all legs with a long, slender neck that seemed to start from his waist. "I'm not going to give you any documents or tell you anything that isn't already a matter of public record. Delynn told you that, right?"

"She did and that's fine," Steph replied.

"The only reason I'm even here is because Delynn says she trusts you. Opening my fat mouth the other night at Americano's is the dumbest blunder I've ever made. I wish you hadn't overheard anything, but you did and now I'm involved." Adam reached up and flipped his jacket collar around his neck. "I figure if I stay close to you and keep tabs on what you're doing, that that might be my safest bet."

Steph hunched down the best she could so she was closer to Adam's height. "Keep your friends close and your enemies closer," Steph smiled. "You can stay as close as you want. I'm not going to print anything before first talking to you both. You also have the option of whistleblower statutes that will protect you. You know about that, right?"

"Doubtful," Adam shrugged his shoulders. "Delynn told me about your aunt's experience with that and I read online about other whistleblowers who wished the same thing. I don't want to end up there and frankly, well— Agrico is too damn big to mess with in that way."

"I don't blame you for feeling the way you do, I really don't, but it's an option for you at any time. You don't have to decide on that now."

"Yeah, I know, but I'll see where this route goes," Adam replied.

"Fair enough. Can I start with telling you what I've learned from

Delynn and some of the things I've pieced together on my own? I'd just like to know that we're all on the same page with respect to the facts."

"Sure, let's hear it," Adam replied.

Steph looked around and other than a mother and two children playing on the swing set, the park was deserted. "Let's take a walk and we'll talk. I think my blood will freeze if I stand still much longer."

Steph was flanked by Delynn on one side and Adam on the other. "You two didn't know each other outside of the Agrico work compound. Hey, I looked it up on the internet and it says Agrico has 4,500 employees in the buildings where you guys work and 22,000 worldwide. Is it really that big?"

"It could be. I think I've heard something around those numbers. It's a massive company, that I know," Adam responded.

"Anyway, you two first met each other at Americano's, where I gather some of the Agrico employees meet up for a drink after work. Agrico Aggies I think you called them, Delynn? That's cute, I like it. So, Adam, Delynn told me you overheard her talking with some colleagues about a new rice product that had been in the pipeline to be commercially marketed in the coming year. The product, called Novum Rice, had been genetically modified to contain iron and it's going to be marketed to third world countries where millions of people die annually from sicknesses caused by iron deficiencies in their diet. In fact, there's a large market in the developed countries for that product. Those are the numbers I found in my research. Delynn mentioned that the Novum Rice had been originally developed by Agrico, but because of the overwhelming public outcry over this new product they had moved everything to another company entity. Am I getting things right up to this point?"

"Sounds about right," Delynn replied.

Adam shrugged his shoulders. "Keep going."

"Okay, what really grabbed your attention was when Delynn was talking about a non-profit company called Sustinere Messes Corporation. She said that Sustinere was part of the Agrico corporate umbrella and that Sustinere had taken over the research and development of Novum Rice for roughly the past 10 years." Steph stopped, pinched her chin and nibbled on her lower lip. "Sustinere Messes… do you know how they came up with that name? Any idea what it means? I'm just curious and I couldn't find anything."

"I've asked the same question dozens of times," said Delynn, "and finally, one of Sustinere's researchers told me that it's derived from Latin. *Tenere* in Latin means hold and *sub* means up. *Messis* is also Latin and means harvest or crop so, putting the Latin translations together it loosely means sustainable crops. I thought that was pretty clever."

Steph grinned. "Yeah, it is, thanks. Now, where was I? Oh, yeah, you'd never heard of Sustinere Messes before Delynn had mentioned it to you, right?

"Uh, no, that was the first time."

Steph reached down to tie her shoe. "Just a sec." She stood up and continued down the path. "Okay, Adam, you've been at Agrico for around three years and you work in the accounting department mainly on compliance issues. So, the next day when you showed up for work you poured through the financial records you had access to and you couldn't find any entries remotely related to Sustinere or anything about Novum Rice. Now, you knew that it cost millions of dollars to develop and market new GMs and there was no way that kind of money wouldn't show up somewhere in the financial records. That's when you first began to get worried because if that money had been spent, somehow, or if a mistake had been made, then all of Agrico's SEC filings were in error and there would be hell to pay by someone—probably you. How we doing so far?"

"Pretty good, except I've only been at Agrico for two years and four months, not three years," Adam replied.

"Okay, noted. Thanks. Now, you called Delynn and the two of you met after work that same day back at Americano. You had some questions about Sustinere you wanted to ask her. When you told her you were unable to find any records relating to Sustinere or the development of the Novum Rice, she felt you were mistaken. Delynn talks with people at Sustinere almost daily and she has always believed there was a connection between Sustinere and Agrico."

While Stephanie presented the facts as she knew them, she also kept an eye on a dark gray sedan that had stopped just a few car lengths in front of where she had parked. There was one person sitting in the car, man or woman, she couldn't tell. Keeping one eye on the car, she continued, "It'd been that very night, after you two met at Americano's for the second time that Agrico was hacked. The next day at work, Delynn, and others, spent most of the day with Agrico's IT and security people and a few corporate execs. That's when she first started to put some of the pieces together. Everyone she spoke with that day strutted around with a sense of urgency and all of the questions had to do with Sustinere.

"And that's about it until I crashed your party at Americano's. Both of you had some suspicions about what was going on and you wanted to compare notes." Steph stopped on the path and grabbed each of them by the arm. "Is that the same way you each recall things?"

"For the most part, yes, that's the way I remember it." Delynn took a deep breath and let it slowly escape. "I think I might've suspected something was haywire before the hack, actually. I know about how much our department spends each year, give or take some, and there's no way that money shouldn't show up on the financials anywhere—no way."

Adam nodded his agreement and slid his glasses back up to the bridge of his nose. "We ended up talking again the same night as the hack. Delynn called about an hour after we left Americano and wanted to ask again if I was certain."

"Right," said Delynn, "and he said he was, no doubt about it, and that's when it really hit me that something was going on."

Steph's eyes flickered between the two and finally settled on Adam. "Let's just say that $50 million has been spent on this whole project and—"

Adam interrupted, "They could spend more than that in a year, easily."

"50, 100 million, just pick a number, it probably doesn't matter. I'm not much at accounting, but I sort of remember that everything is coded somehow into various accounts. Who ends up doing that?" Steph asked.

"That's the part of my job that I hate; paper pushing," Delynn responded. "It takes up way too much time, and I always end up dealing with someone in accounting weeks later asking me questions about what I turned in, and why it was coded a certain way, and by then I can't even remember what they're talking about."

"What do you turn in, exactly?" Steph asked.

"Each week I turn in time sheets and expense reports and copies of all the invoices I approved. There's a separate code for everything."

"What are the invoices for?"

"Lots of things, maybe a hundred or so each week. Anything from equipment purchases, supplies, funding requests from Sustinere, vendor invoices, it goes on and on," Delynn said.

Steph raised a brow. "Funding requests from Sustinere? What do you mean?"

"Each month they send in a request for money to fund their operation. I look at it, initial it, and send it on. I don't have anything to do with their budget, I'm sort of—I guess a conduit for them. They send it to me and I pass it on. That's been the procedure since I've been here."

"Has anybody ever questioned you about it?" Steph asked.

Delynn shook her head. "Nope."

"Who codes the Sustinere invoices? Do you do that?" Steph asked.

Delynn nodded. "409. That's the code that I use each time."

Steph looked at Adam. "Does that mean anything to you? 409?"

Adam weighed heavily on the question and answered, "I'd have to look it up, but we don't have many codes in the 400s. They're mostly for miscellaneous things that are too small to account for, but this isn't a small item by any means." His hands were jammed in his pockets; he clenched his fists and his jaw tightened. "Money's being siphoned off and not being accounted for and it's a god-awful amount."

Steph saw the tenseness in Adam's body language. Not only was his jaw tight, but his shoulders stiffened, the creases around his eyes hardened and he rocked, slowly, on his heels. Easy, easy, she thought, now's not the time to push. "That's probably enough for now, I think we all have some things to think about and we can meet again."

Steph reached out and touched Adam on the elbow and through the corner of her eye she saw the gray sedan pull away from the curb, maneuver a tight U-turn and speed down Martin Luther King Jr. Drive. "Are you okay with everything, Adam? We've touched on a few new nerves and I just want to say again, that whatever we talk about isn't going anywhere. Under no circumstances will I divulge to anyone where I got my information. I don't know either of you. Are we square on that?"

Adam's hands were jammed in his pockets and he rocked back and forth on the balls of his feet. "I… I hope so."

CHAPTER 11

"**G**et the door, Ben! I'll be out in a minute," Phil shouted out from the back bedroom.

Ben unlocked the door and turned the knob. "Alex!" He stepped forward and threw his arms around her.

She smiled. "I'm glad to see you're keeping the door locked."

"One can never be too careful around these parts." Ben dropped his hands to her waist. "Come in. I didn't expect to see you so soon."

Alex walked in, slipped her backpack from her shoulder and threw it on a chair. "Where's Phil?"

"He's in the bedroom with Michelle. They'll be right out. Damn, it's great to see you. Tell me, what've you found out?"

Alex leaned back against the kitchen counter. "Enough that I won't be staying long, but I wanted to see how you're doing. Is everything okay here?"

"So far, yeah. No more explosions. We're going to decide this morning where we should go for our next hideaway—"

"That couldn't have been you knocking on the door. I thought people like you just walked through walls." Phil gave Alex his classic bear hug. "I can't wait to hear what you've been up to. Go ahead, spill it."

Alex smiled. "Hi, Michelle. Have these two been behaving? They're treating you okay?"

Michelle pushed a lock of hair from her eyes. "They've had their moments, but I have to tell you, I'm not too sure I was cut out for this type of action. It's all pretty frightening to me."

Phil snuck up behind Michelle and wrapped his arms around her waist. "I'm sure Alex is going to tell us everything's fine now and we can all go on with our lives." He squinted at Alex. "Am I right?"

Alex looked at Phil and then turned her head to Ben.

"Wait a sec," Phil blurted out. "I can tell this might take longer than I hoped. Michelle and I will whip up some breakfast and then we can talk about things."

Other than a few hours of airplane sleep, Alex hadn't rested in two days. When she had arrived back in San Francisco she had found a quiet corner in the United Lounge and had gone back to work. The TAO had responded to Alex's bait. One of the methods utilized by the TAO to gather information had been to intercept computers in transit and divert them to its own 'secret workshops'. There, it would booby-trap their contents with malware or malicious hardware from its extensive library. The computers were returned to transit and once they arrived at their destination and were booted-up, the TAO had remote access to those computers.

As Alex had hoped and had expected, the TAO had intercepted the computer shipment to José María Arregi Erostarbe. She had found herself inside the computer network of that elite task force. Her Trojan Horse had set up a new account and had created its own password. She had safely bypassed the firewalls and once inside the virtual private network, she had unrestricted access to the neatly organized files. The file folders had been created by region and by importance. She had located two primary files on Kioshi, one in the Eastern Asian section and the other in the Western Asian section. Neither of the folders had been earmarked as high priority which had led her to believe that the NSA had no longer been interested in Kioshi or his whereabouts.

Benjamin looked at Alex and his mind flashed to the scene where they had first met. He had just finished a speech to the Stanford University alumni about establishing nonprofit medical foundations. She had introduced herself to him and after a brief exchange she had exited as quickly as she had appeared. Standing at the top of the auditorium, she had turned to look at Benjamin one last time. What he had seen standing there had remained permanently etched in his memory. The sun had shone brightly through the windows just behind her and a shadow had draped a veil over the refined and delicate features of her face. The silhouette that had stood above him had sinuous and subtle curves that had stirred his senses and had aroused his passion. Even now, each time he looked at Alex, he still felt that same tremor that had rippled through his body and that same warmth that had enveloped his core on that first encounter.

"I think I've seen that look before on more than one occasion." Alex placed a finger on her lower lip. "Your red cheeks are a new touch though."

Benjamin grinned. "Busted—you got me." He extended his arms. "Come here."

Phil slid four plates across the kitchen counter. "Come and get it."

Alex winked at Ben. "Hold that thought."

They each sat on a bar stool and devoured their food—scrambled egg whites, toast and hash browns. Phil had his own blend of coffee made by the Death Wish Coffee Company and the beans were certified organic, all fair trade and, more importantly, carried the reputation of being the strongest coffee in the world. Finally, Phil leaned back, pressed both hands on the counter and looked over at Alex. "All right, lady, the floor's all yours. Fill us in."

Alex wiped her mouth and dropped her napkin on the counter. "I'm leaving later today and I'm not really sure how long I'll be gone. At least a week, probably more. In the meantime I think it's a good idea for you all to pack up and find another place to go, like you've been talking about."

Phil spread his hands. "More info, Alex, come on. You must have located that Kioshi guy by now, so where is he and what *exactly* are you planning?"

"I'm fairly certain I've found him, but it'll take me a while to get to him and I'm not sure what I'll do when I do find him. I have a couple of stops to make first, so I have plenty of time to figure things out. That's all I really should tell you at this point."

Benjamin placed a hand on Alex's arm. "You're not going anywhere by yourself. I'm coming along with you."

Phil nodded. "Count me in."

There was no mistaking the shock painted across Michelle's face.

Alex took Benjamin's hand. "This isn't anything like what we just went through. This guy is dangerous and his protective network stretches—probably everywhere. He's halfway around the world, yet he found a way to blow up your ranch house and your car. I can't take the risk that something may happen to you." She looked at Phil. "Or you, I just can't. I need to do this by myself."

Benjamin stood and walked over to the sliding glass door, slid it open and stormed out to the back deck. His fingers wrapped around the railing and he leaned forward. "Damnit, Alex!"

His foot kicked the deck and he spun around. He waved a hand. "Come here."

Standing in front of Benjamin, Alex knew that look. His brows were furrowed, his mouth zipped tight and his chin twitched. "I know what you're thinking and you can't come along. You just can't," Alex said.

"It's the right thing to do. If we're going to be together, like we've planned, I need to be a part of this. All of this," Benjamin waved both hands in the air, "has to do with both of us. Your past is now a part of my here and now. I hope that there'll be a day when this is behind us, but right now it's not. There may be other events or people that surface just like this one and if that happens, we'll deal with it together."

He put his hands on Alex's shoulders and drew her in. "I don't know where you're going, but you're not leaving here without me. I can help. I need to help out on this."

Alex burrowed her head into Benjamin's chest. "If anything ever happened to you, I'd never forgive myself."

"Then you'd better bring me along so you can keep an eye on me."

Alex tapped a fist into Benjamin's chest. "How about you come part way with me? I'm going to London first and as things fall into place, we can decide what to do."

Benjamin smiled. "Turn around, now you have to deal with Phil."

Phil stood angled in the doorway, his arms folded across his chest and his head tilted. "That's right; if Ben's going, I'm going. End of story."

Seated in the living area, Alex started to bring them all up to date on what she had learned. When Alex mentioned she had penetrated the computer network at the NSA, Phil leapt to his feet. "Nooo, tell me you didn't!" He stood in front of Alex, his face inches from hers. "It's one thing for you to break into a bank; you seem to do that all the time, but this? Jesus, Alex, you've read what's been going on with that outfit and you hacked into their computers!"

"There's no trail. There's no need to worry," Alex replied calmly.

"You hack into the NSA and now you're sitting in my house and I'm not supposed to worry? What bridge did you just jump off of?" Phil spun around and headed toward his bedroom. "I'm packing now. Let's get the hell out of here while we still can."

CHAPTER 12

Peering through the tiny square window on the side of the plane, Alex looked down below and saw a pink and orange hue ripple through the clouds as the sun crept over the far horizon. She closed her laptop and slid it across to the soft leather seat next to her. Gently touching Benjamin's arm, she said, "I'm going to talk to Phil about a few things. I'll be right back."

She walked down the aisle, sat in the open seat next to Phil and tapped him on the shoulder. "Phil, we need to talk."

Phil opened his eyes and turned his head. "Ah… now I'll never know how that dream was going to end. Couldn't you have given me a few more minutes?"

Alex whispered, "Sorry about that, but I need to ask you about something."

Phil brought his seat upright and rubbed his eyes. "Okay, now, you have my attention."

"I need to ask you about Michelle. It seems like you two have really hit it off. How well do really know her?"

"Are you probing into my love life?" Phil asked.

"I'm not going there, but seriously, how much do you know about her?"

"Just a sec." Phil waved at the flight attendant. "Could you bring me some more coffee? Just plain black, thanks. Now," he looked back at Alex, "what's your sudden interest in Michelle all about?"

"Satisfy my curiosity. Tell me about her."

Phil's toothy smile said it all. "I'm following in Ben's footsteps. I think I've fallen for her." He shrugged his shoulders, "In fact, I know I have. Yeah,

I know I haven't known her very long, but neither did you guys. In fact, I'll bet I've spent more time with her already than you two have since you first met. When I first met her at the coffee shop we spent the whole afternoon talking about all kinds of things. She's smart, sassy and you gotta admit she doesn't wear on your eyes, at least not mine anyway. I was dreaming about her before you woke me, thank you very much."

"What do you know about her before she moved here? Her family, friends, where she was born, anything like that?"

Phil pressed his shoulders back against the seat. He shot Alex a quizzical look. "Where are you going with this? What are you driving at?"

"I checked the records at Bennington College. And," Alex turned toward Phil, "there's no record of Michelle Brophy ever being on faculty there. In fact, I couldn't find a trace of her anywhere. I'm sorry, but I had to try to find out more about her."

The color drained from Phil's face, his mouth zipped shut and his eyes widened. He stared blankly ahead.

Alex spoke softly, "There may be a perfectly good reason for all this, there probably is. Can you think of any reason why she made up that part of her past about Bennington? What else do you know about her past?"

Phil's mouth was dry, yet he found his tongue, "Uh… whoa… I don't know what to say. This blows me away—totally. There's too much about her that's real for me to believe she's hiding anything. She said she taught political geography at Bennington and we've had some interesting discussions about her work. She knows her stuff; she couldn't have made that up. She just couldn't. You've seen her sweatshirt; it's more tattered and worn than anything I have. She's had that one for a while—bet on it." Phil stroked his chin and leaned back. "When I left, the look in her eyes was real. She's terrified that something's going to happen to me. Last night was the first time we've both said I love you to each other." Phil shook his head. "You must've missed something. You had to."

Alex lightly touched Phil's arm. "Maybe I did. Let's hope so."

CHAPTER 13

Portobello Road went straight through the heart of Notting Hill, a trendy section of London and home to the Portobello Market. Every Friday and Saturday the market sprung to life and hosted not only Europe's largest antique market, but a thousand yards of stalls selling everything from African handicrafts to exotic Caribbean fruits, to mixed bags of fresh vegetables, meats and every goodie or oddity known to man. The outer stalls were lined with expensive boutiques and cafes, tucked under endless rows of blue and red canvas awnings. Many of those cafes were favorite celebrity haunts.

Talkhouse Coffee was a local favorite situated in a dodgy part of Portobello Road. They served Workhouse Coffee and had set the standard for pulling the proper espresso. Large pucks for each pull and just a sprig of nectar filled one-half a demitasse cup with the finest espresso in all of London.

Ben took a sip of espresso and placed his cup on the table. "He's really shaken up and I can't blame him. He's been trying to reach Michelle ever since we landed and he can't get a hold of her. I've never seen him so down."

"I don't like the looks of this. I've tried everything I could think of to find out anything about Michelle; she doesn't exist. I'm certain she's someone else and right now she knows too much about what we're doing," Alex said.

"Maybe, but let's give him some more time and then we'll see."

"In the meantime, I'm going—"

"What gives, here? Are you two vacationing again?" Standing in scruffy white laceless sneakers and wearing what was most likely another of his freebie t-shirts, Devon Briggs stood between Alex and Benjamin, one hand resting on each of their shoulders.

Benjamin stood. "Devon, you're looking no worse for the wear. Great to see you." Benjamin motioned to the chair beside him.

Devon leaned towards Alex. "Well, I have to say I was a bit surprised when you called. I didn't expect to see you again for, well maybe, oh… another five years. Sounds like you're back in business, though. I'm here to help." He took a seat.

Alex had called Devon three days ago. She had needed his help. Devon had created a new program he had dubbed *Back To The Future* and the last Alex had heard, he had run some beta tests, but still had some bugs to iron out. She needed him to have that program operational—*ASAP.*

Devon had been intrigued by a cyber-attack several years ago in which the attackers had installed harmless looking titles on a national website that had been used by people with epilepsy to access current research on their disease. Once the user had clicked the title, they had been exposed to a series of rapidly flashing images, and there had been cases of people having seizures and migraine headaches. At that time, Devon had known that flickering images had been used to develop a multi-colored LED flashlight and when it flashed with a certain sequence of colors, its victim had become nauseous, disoriented, or vomited. Devon had taken that concept and tailored it to a completely different use.

Once Devon had begun looking seriously into the theory of flashing images and mind control, he had discovered that the whole idea had been in use by advertisers and marketing engineers for years. With the introduction of digital television sets and monitors, advertisers had learned how to lull viewers into a mildly hypnotic state. Once hypnotized by the screen flicker, various forms of neuro-linguistic programming cues were introduced to steer the viewer's thoughts, making them either calm or accepting of the product being sold, or openly hostile and uncomfortable with a competitor's product.

Devon had achieved, with limited success, the ability to plant pseudomemories in a subject to make them believe they had actually experienced an event or had known the facts of an event, even if it had never actually happened. He had known the possibilities of such a program in the cyber-espionage world would be unlimited.

"I don't know if back in the business is really true, but I'm glad you're here." Alex poured some tea for Devon and continued, "You look exhausted. Have you been working on your program since I talked to you?"

"Every single second and it's been wicked hard. I shoved everything else aside. You know I've been dying to give this thing a try in the real world. Where are we going? When do we leave?"

"Sorry," Alex pushed her hair back. "You can't come along, not this time."

"Ah, buggers, no… no…. Whatever you're going to do with *Back to the Future*, you'll need to program it for your specific needs and I'm the only one who knows how to do that. You have to bring me along. You *neeeeed* me."

Alex smiled. "I'm sure you're the only one that knows how to program it, but that's why I'm here. You're going to run me through a quick tutorial and I'll figure out what needs to be done at the right time."

Devon scrunched his mouth and his 10 fingers tapped the tabletop. "Pathetic excuse." His fingers played staccato, "That's *really… really* not fair… and you know it."

Alex nodded. "No, it's probably not, but that's the way it has to be. Now, did you bring the program with you?"

Devon reached in his pants' pocket, pulled out a flash drive and slid it across the table to Alex.

"Let me ask you something." Benjamin slid forward in his seat. "Alex explained your program to me, but it doesn't make sense to me. I might be able to believe that over a period of time exposure to certain light images could have an effect on someone, like strobe lights, but I have a hard time believing that you can direct light to accomplish something specific; like erasing part of someone's memory. Seems like science fiction to me."

"Ah, another naysayer. Do you know anything about optogenetics?" Devon asked.

Benjamin shook his head. "Never heard of it."

"It's a new science and it's bang on. It's only come into its own in the past 10 years, maybe less. It's all about flashes of light being used to switch particular neurons in the brain on and off. It's already been used, successfully I might add, to help with pain, addiction, sleep disorders and who knows what else."

"I don't know, I'm a natural skeptic and what bothers me the most is what you're doing hasn't been run through any scientific experiments to prove if it will even work," Benjamin said.

"Au contraire, that's where you're wrong." Devon's head was now bobbing from side to side. "Now, bear with me. Most people think that memory is static, but it isn't, no way, no way. Memory's stored in the hippocampus in the back of your brain and it evolves over time. Right now, as we're talking, your brain is processing everything through your memory, so your memory is changing as we speak. My program doesn't erase parts of someone's memory; it adds false memories that override what is already in one's memory bank. MIT's McGovern Institute for Brain Research, has already proven that false memories can be implanted in mice."

"Yeah, mice, right," Benjamin laughed, "but that's a long way from the human brain."

"Maybe, maybe not. What MIT's studies proved is it's possible to have a defined control over a defined set of cells that lead to the recall of a specific memory. There are guys, some really smart guys, at MIT, Stanford and Cambridge who are convinced that this whole concept is doable on humans. The problem they're facing is the age-old problem all scientists face when they discover a groundbreaking advancement that borders on science fiction—no one believes them. People come out of the woodwork calling it a hoax; these guys are changing the natural order of things or, and here's my favorite one, that's impossible. Impossible, yeah, and the world is flat or there's no life beyond earth."

"Hmm." Benjamin nodded and rubbed the back of his neck. "Okay, so, take me to the next step; how's this going to work? Tell me it's going to work."

"The brain operates on a millisecond timescale, so you need something that can operate that fast. The only things that can operate on that level are light and electricity. The brain already uses electricity to communicate so if you go in and zap part of the brain, you'll be zapping a lot more than just memory. The nifty part about optogenetics is that brain cells don't normally respond to light, so the only ones that respond to light are going to be the ones that you trick to respond to light. What my program does is actually shoot light into the brain, leave neighboring cells intact, and the only ones that will be responsive are the ones in the hippocampus that have been preselected to affect memory. All we're doing is probing the brain on the timescale that it communicates on, and that," Devon tipped his head, "is what makes optogenetics so frickin cool."

"And you really think this is going to work?"

"Oh yeah. This morning I tried it out on a couple friends." Devon puffed out his chest. "I had them each repeat the word 'fleckless' over and over while they watched the screen. In less than a minute and a half the word disappeared from their vocabulary. I shut down the program and opened a new screen with the word fleckless centered in the middle. Neither guy had ever seen the word before. It was awesome."

"That's not exactly scientific proof, but the whole idea seems to make sense and I have no doubt that it works on some level." Benjamin leaned back in his seat, placed his hands on his thighs and looked across at Alex. "I think I'll do some sightseeing while you two figure out the details. Text me when you're done, I want to see Devon again before we leave."

Devon poured himself some more tea. "You won't reconsider? Are you absolutely sure about that?"

"Absolutely."

"Hey, when we talked the other day you were asking me about different ways to re-write hard drives. Did you ever come up with anything?"

80

"I did. That's why I'm here. It worked."

Devon leaned forward. "Splendid. Details, I need details."

"Did you read about the NSA's hacker team called the Equation Group?"

"Oh yeah, that's the name they were dubbed with because those geeks love encryption algorithms and advanced obfuscation methods. I thought that was pretty cool. It's no surprise to me that they're the leader of the pack. What about them?"

"It's not so much about them, but what they created. They found a way to re-write disk drive hardware from most of the major manufacturers. When they do this, a secret storage vault is created on the drive that houses whatever malware they want to infect the computer with. This is so far ahead of anything we've ever heard of and they're even able to avoid detection by military-grade disk wiping and reformatting."

"They'd need a source code from the drive manufacturers to do that and they wouldn't give up those codes to anyone. No frickin way."

Alex tilted her head. "This is the NSA we're talking about and they have an endless talent pool. They have programmers who write their own version of the disk controller firmware from scratch and then they reverse engineer the manufacture's firmware and add it to support their own nefarious intentions. To them, this is simple stuff."

"Wait a minute." Devon looked around and then he leaned forward. "You didn't hack into the NSA did you? Is that what this is about?"

"You don't want to know who I hacked into and that's not really important. What is important is I took what the NSA created and turned it into a two-pronged attack."

"I'm listening," Devon whispered.

"I had a computer that I knew was going to be attacked, so I loaded a new hard drive containing controller firmware that I re-wrote and then—"

"You can't do that without the source code."

"You're right, but I got by that hurdle. I knew the exact hardware configuration of the computer that was going to be attacked, so I found an open source version of the disk drive firmware from a Linux project. The other thing I did is put a worm in the .LNK files that Windows uses to display icons when a USB stick is connected to a computer. As soon as a USB stick is inserted it becomes infected. I'm not certain which method worked, but I ended up inside my target's network and was able to move about like any approved user."

"Frickin brilliant, Alex. Frickin brilliant."

"And that's why you're going to run me through how to program *Back To The Future*."

For the next two hours, Devon and Alex sipped tea, nibbled on crumpets and Devon ran Alex through the inner workings of his new program. As expected, Alex was a quick study and mastered it in little time.

Alex leaned back. "So do you think this will work? I'll be able to erase a part of someone's memory?"

"Not erase, no, but you should be able to plant a false memory in the brain of whoever it is you're after. Actually," Devon lifted both hands and pointed at himself, "only if I come along with you."

Alex gripped her hands together, leaned forward and looked into Devon's eyes. "*Should work* isn't good enough. I'm going to have one chance, and only one, to do what I need to do and get out of there alive. You know that."

Devon's mouth twitched and he stared straight ahead. The twitch had been a trademark of his since birth and the root of endless teasing all through his adolescent years. Even though he gave the appearance of being lost in the moment, Alex knew he was tough as nails and not someone who could be easily riled. He was streetwise—the hard-boiled type. Finally, he looked at Alex and the twitching stopped. "What you're asking me to do is thread a cat through a needle. I can do it, but I need more time."

"I'm leaving in two days and once I'm gone there'll be no contacting me. Two days, Devon, that's it."

Devon's mouth twitched. "Two days is a lifetime compared to what you usually give me."

CHAPTER 14

The cobblestones of the Champs Ellyses, the Eiffel Tower, L'Arc de Triumphe, pedestrians strolling along the sidewalks, cafés with brightly colored umbrellas....

Alex pushed away from the picturesque fixed-glass tinted window where she stood on the 32nd floor of the Tour Monetparnasse. Stay focused, she thought. Stay in control.

From out behind the solid mahogany double doors, stretching to the ceiling, strode Andre Broussard. Even though he had the stature of Napoleon, he marched forward with the confidence of a man twice his size. Standing before Alex, Andre took a half-bow at the waist and then extended both arms. "Alex, what a pleasant surprise. You look exquisite, as usual." He stepped forward to embrace Alex.

"Stop!" Alex straightened her arm and pressed her palm into Andre's chest. "You and I need to talk and then maybe we will have time to exchange pleasantries."

Alex pivoted and started to walk around the room. She had always felt an odd incongruity whenever she had entered Andre's office. She had been certain that he had subconsciously surrounded himself with overpowering opulence as a way to compensate for what nature had failed to give him. As she moved around the room, her hand brushed against *La Dance*, a rare bronze sculpture by Louis-Ernest Barrias; her fingers swept over the leather bound tomes of the French authors Honoré de Balzac, Cyrano de Bergerac and Albert Camus; and her feet slid effortlessly over the rich Persian rugs.

She reached the far end of the office and turned to face Andre. "I won't ask for much of your time today, but I do need to ask you a few questions.

Shall we sit here?" She moved around to the side of a chair that was part of an intimate seating area. She had chosen a seat as far away as possible from Andre's throne of power, the place where he felt the most comfortable—his ornately decorated 18th century mahogany desk centered perfectly on the opposite side of the room.

Andre remained outwardly calm and held his hands out, palms up. "Alex… my dear Alex, there seems to be an edge about you right now. I do not recall seeing that in you before. Rest assured that you may take all the time you desire." Andre took quick, measured steps and walked over to her.

The two longtime friends sat across from each other and Alex was reminded how they shared a competitive spirit that was often fueled by the other. Andre was a master at intimidation and had taught himself to stare endlessly without blinking. His eyes were quick and set deep in his sockets, his lush lashes hiding the whites. His arms rested comfortably on each armrest and a single finger on his right hand tapped against the silk upholstery. He stared straight into Alex's piercing eyes. "What is it? What is troubling you?"

Alex sat across from one of the most powerful men in the world, who directed one of its largest multinational corporations, yet she knew he needed continuous reinforcement through his surroundings to fill the giant shoes he so awkwardly wore. She countered Andre's stare. "The last time we saw each other, you knew I was planning to move into a life of obscurity where I could spend much needed time with my mother and start to plan a real life with Ben. That dream has been short-lived, unfortunately."

Andre interrupted, "Ben, how is Monsieur Hunter? I have tried to contact him numerous times to talk with him about my proposal to partner with GEN, but we have not as yet made contact. He wouldn't by chance be trying to avoid me now, would he?"

"He's been very busy with a number of things. He, too, is trying to get his life back together after everything that has happened." Alex crossed her legs and straightened the collar on her blouse. "I need to find Kioshi Nakajima and I recently found out that the two of you share business interests."

Andre blinked, his back stiffened, his razor sharp voice cracked, "Kioshi? What could you possibly want with that man?"

Alex leaned forward, her voice dropped an octave, "He tried to kill me."

"Mon dieu!" Andre shot out of his chair and began to pace back and forth. The silence was broken only by the measured clicking of his spit and polished black leather shoes against the parquet flooring. He turned toward Alex and swallowed—hard. "How did you ever get involved with such a man? He is not a man to be taken lightly; not by you, not by anyone."

"Come on, there's probably a dozen Kioshis out there that would love to know where I am. Most of them I encountered while working for you. Level with me, where can I find Kioshi? I need to know."

"I wish I knew myself, but I do not—I really don't." Andre sat back down and took a deep breath, then another.

"Your face, you look pale. Are you okay?"

"I've been a bit off color today, but I'm fine." Andre rubbed his cheeks and continued, "No one knows that I have business dealings with that man. How did you find that out?"

"Don't be so sure no one knows. The NSA has intercepted emails between the two of you. There are no specific details outlining your relationship, but they do know that you two have been in contact."

"You are speaking about the United States' NSA? They have this information?"

Alex's eyes bored into Andre. "Yes, they do and now, so do I."

Andre's tapered fingers gripped his tie and gave it a quick tug. He unbuttoned his shirt collar. "This is far worse than I ever imagined." Gritting his teeth, he continued, "I have not seen the man nor heard from him in over three years, at least. When was the last time you saw him?"

"Fifteen years ago," Alex replied.

"I am afraid you would not recognize him, then. When the Afghanistan war broke out, he vanished entirely from sight. Several years later he reemerged a fully changed man. His facial features have completely changed and he began to assemble interests in legitimate companies. For the most part, he does not own these companies, rather he owns the men who control them. I'm afraid that is how I first met him."

"Are you telling me that Kioshi owns part of CS Generale?"

"Non, non, not exactly owns, but we do have an arrangement. He acquired a drug that was in the development stage and he needed a company to complete that development, test it in places where there would be little regulatory interference and then be ready to supply and market the drug when the need arose. There is a huge market potential for this drug and the profits should be enormous. He shares in those profits." Andre's hands were clasped in his lap, his knuckles white. "Does the NSA know about this?"

Alex shook her head. "I'm sure I only know a small part of what the NSA truly knows, so I don't have an answer to your question. If I were you, though, I would assume they know everything and then some."

"Like so many things in my life, I never imagined anything like this could happen." Andre straightened up in his chair and stared directly at Alex. "I believe it is me who needs to ask you for help. You need to help me with this. It could ruin me and everything I have built if any of this were to be discovered. *S'il te plait*, Alex, I need your help on this."

Alex stood upright and walked behind the chair hoping the touch of its raw silk would soothe her inner turmoil. She knew Andre was telling the truth. The NSA files she had seen did not reveal any correspondence between Andre and Kioshi for the past three years. She doubted the agency knew the details of their business relationship, but she couldn't be certain. She had only penetrated the TAO, one of many separate divisions in that vast and sprawling organization.

Alex raised her head, pulled her shoulders back and countered Andre's demand, "At this point, I'm not certain I want to know what hold Kioshi has over you. He obviously has something on you or you could go ahead and terminate whatever business arrangement, as you call it, you have with him. As to the NSA, I can't help you with anything you've already done or even find out if that agency is aware of Kioshi's real involvement with you. They have correspondence—emails—that's all I know. I have to get Kioshi out of my life permanently and if I do that then, maybe, just maybe, he would be out of yours, as well."

Andre's eyes widened, but he wasn't about to cede the field. "I will do whatever I can to help you find Kioshi. You have my word. But you must… *please*… help me in some way and find out how I can best avoid any involvement with the NSA."

"Let's focus on finding Kioshi first." Alex said.

For the next two hours, the two sat at the same conference table they had used on so many past occasions. Alex reviewed all of Andre's email correspondence with Kioshi to see if she could find a pattern. Andre had explained that he moves around frequently trying to avoid any unwanted attention.

Satisfied that she had learned everything she could from Andre, Alex rose. "That should do it and thank you. I still don't know everything I need to, but I certainly know much more than when I came here."

"If I think of anything else, anything at all, I will get a hold of you, and thank you, my dear." Alex accepted his embrace.

"Andre, you didn't!" She walked over to the wall near the double doors and pointed to a painting hanging prominently on the wall. "You specifically told me that you would return this painting to its rightful owner and here it is—in your office. You gave me your *solemn* word that you would return this painting, Andre, remember?"

When Alex had rescued Benjamin from the Koidu plant in Sierra Leone, she had come across a trove of Nazi war relics including a stolen painting by Raphael, *A Portrait of a Young Man*. Most scholars had assumed *A Portrait of a Young Man* had been destroyed during the war. She had given the painting to Andre to return it to the museum in Poland where it had been stolen, knowing full well that he would find some way to profit from it.

Andre's composure had returned and he smiled, "Oh no, no, you are badly mistaken. Shortly after you gave this painting to me I went straight to the Czartoryski Museum in Krakow, myself, as I promised you I would. I took the painting with me and we made a mutual arrangement. They have generously allowed me to hang this painting here, in my office, for one year. That is all—one year. Afterwards, I will return it to them and they will hang it in the new wing they are building just for this painting. I should add that they received a most generous contribution to pay for their museum's new Broussard addition. Gagnant-gagnant, oui?"

"Somehow I think the win-win situation was probably weighted in your favor."

Andre held his hands out. "I am a man of principle; I pay my debts and collect my markers. Now, you and I, we are even."

"Hmm... even... we will see... we will see." Alex turned and headed for the door. "I'll let myself out."

■　■　■　■　■

Alex stood in front of the stone carved Curie Building. A bone-chilling dampness hung in the air penetrating her clothing and stinging her covered skin. Once inside, she felt warm and protected and she rushed up the stairs to the second floor.

She knocked on the mottled teak door and heard the shout, "Entrez," from within.

Alex opened the door. "Hello, Charles."

"Oh no, oh no, not you, no, I will not have anything to do with whatever it is you have come here for." He gave his chair a push and rolled back from his desk. "No, Alexandra, I will not get involved in anything."

"Great to see you too, Charles," Alex said as she entered the room and walked toward Charles. "Do you mind if I have a seat?"

With his wire-rim glasses at the bottom of his nose, Charles placed his index finger on the middle iron piece and pushed them back up to where they belonged. He waved at the chair beside him, "Well, sure... have a seat, but I am still recovering from everything we went through the last time and I am just not cut out to get involved again with the things you do. I hope this is just a social visit."

Charles Diderot and Alex knew each other from graduate school and Charles was now a professor of genetics at the Université de Paris. Just over a year ago, Alex had gone to him to help her determine what she had in the cystic fibrosis files that she had surreptitiously uploaded from GEN. It had been Charles who had concluded that the G-16 virus could search out a specific DNA pattern which made up a specific race of people. The virus could then be altered by its manufacturer to seek out any specified race. All other humans would be immune from that virus. Charles had known that scientists had been researching that specific theory for years, but as far as he had known, no one had come remotely close to perfecting it. The thought that it had become a reality and had rested in the wrong hands had frightened Charles.

Alex smiled, "I'm in Paris just for the day and I wanted to stop by, but I do have some things I would like you to look over for me."

"I don't want to know anything, so don't tell me what you are involved in." Charles fidgeted in his old wooden swivel chair.

Alex raised a hand. "I didn't come here to get you involved in anything. I know how frightened you were when you learned about the G-16 and I don't blame you, but," Alex nodded, "if it hadn't been for you, that virus may very well have been used by its maker. You saved thousands of lives."

"Everything about that virus scared me, and I am so thankful that it was discovered before any harm came about," Charles said

"You and me both." Alex reached in her backpack, pulled out a folder and dropped it on Charles' desk. "I would like you to look at something for me and I promise there's nothing evil or frightening about any of this. It's just a simple vaccine that I'd like you to examine."

Charles tilted back in his chair with such force that he had to catch himself on the edge of his desk to prevent a sure fall. Righting himself, he stared down and began nervously rubbing his hands together. "I think that is what you said the last time. No, I am sorry, but I will not be able to help you out this time."

"Please, just take a look at this and if at any time you decide you don't want anything to do with this, then stop. This folder has the data and specs for the development of a particular vaccine called ProTryX. All I want to know is what the vaccine is intended to be used for. There won't be any need for you to do anything else, I promise."

"May I suggest the obvious, Alexandra? Why not just ask whoever may have created the vaccine what it is for? Surely they would know."

"I wish it was that easy, but it's not. I'm afraid I don't really know who created the vaccine and even though I have some ideas, I still want to get some independent verification."

Charles looked intense. His brows furrowed. "Why am I thinking that there is probably more to this than you are saying? Your friend, Mr. Broussard, certainly his company can figure this out. Have you asked him?"

"This vaccine is being held by CS Generale—that's where I got this file. They may very well know what it is to be used for, but I need to verify it myself." Alex stood up and brushed her fingers through her hair. Clutching the back of her head, she continued, "This vaccine is the cure for some new type of virus. I don't know what the virus is and even if I did, well, remember, you don't want to know anything about this."

Charles was sitting on the front edge of his rickety chair. His head was cocked to one side and he bit down on his lower lip. "Something is going on here, and maybe I do not need to know everything. I do want to help you, but how do I know that I will be safe and this will not turn into another nightmare?"

Alex chose her words carefully, "I have no idea what this vaccine is to be used for, but I do believe that the virus will be deadly and something the world has not yet seen. If I'm right, then this vaccine will save thousands of innocent people and I will need to find a way to deliver it to the right people. If I'm wrong, then there will be nothing for anyone to do."

Charles' glasses again slid down to the tip of his nose and his voice tapered off ever-so-slightly, "Oui, oui, I will look this over and be in touch."

CHAPTER 15

Shakespeare Beach was Great Britain's closest point to mainland Europe. A stretch of coarse sand and rounded shards of rock, the beach was bordered on one side by Shakespeare's Cliff, a composition of chalk with streaks of flint, rising 350 feet. On a clear day, this point was visible from the French shoreline, 21 miles due east. In 1940, reporters had gathered at the top of the cliff and had watched aerial dogfights between the British single-engine Hurricanes and Spitfires and the German Bf 109 squadrons during the Battle of Britain.

Today, there were no signs of aerial clashes above or shrapnel exploding in the distance. It was a rare, cloudless day and the sun's rays glistened on the cresting waves and the twisting and churning white foam that lined the water's edge. Cawing gulls circled overhead and they swooped in and out of the crisp northerly gusts. Their wings were spread, mimicking the threatening aircraft that had appeared so many years ago. The rhythmic sounds reminded Alex of that day, not so long ago at Point Reyes, when those same sounds had offered her safety, reassurance and a new beginning.

After Alex had met with Andre in Paris, she had stopped by the avenue de Paris location of Crédit Agricole where she had opened one of her safe deposit boxes. Pulling out a dark, cylindrical shaped plastic tube from her box, she had spent a few minutes disassembling and reassembling it and examining its parts. Satisfied that everything had been in perfect working order, she had stuffed it in her backpack and had made her return trip to London and then had driven straight out to Dover.

Alex was the first to emerge from the frigid waters of the English Channel. She was wrapped in a thick terrycloth robe drinking hot tea when

Benjamin and Phil first stood, waist deep in the water, and began splashing and shoving. Seated on a rock, she heard their taunts and barbs as the two old friends waded in toward the beach. By the time they were standing on the firm sand, their arms were draped over the other's shoulders and their matching grins masked the verbal barbs they had just slung at the other. Alex adored Phil and whenever she saw the two together she felt their bond. Two souls locked together, feeding off the other and traveling down life's path in perfect harmony in search of their next quest.

Alex tossed them each a towel. "Dry off and have some hot tea. You'll need it in a few minutes."

Benjamin rubbed his head and wrapped the towel around his chest clutching it tightly with his fingers. "You got out a little early. You alright?"

Alex smiled. "I think I was beginning to feel the cold, but I'm fine now. That was just what I needed."

Fully dressed and huddled together on a rock, they polished off the last of the hot tea. "Waaa...." Phil shouted. "It's kicked in. My adrenaline has kicked into overdrive—I love this feeling."

Each of the three diehards, tucked securely behind a rock outcropping to protect them from the wind, had put in countless hours over the years swimming in cold water and they laughed at Phil's outburst. Exposure to cold water causes the blood to flow away from the outer layers of skin to protect the vital organs, leaving a piercing, tingling feeling on one's skin. Overexposure to those types of conditions can lead to hypothermia, but exiting the water before that happens, results in a giddy euphoria that only a hardcore, cold water swimmer can appreciate. Endorphins and adrenaline race to protect the body and shield its pain from the numbness. The result leads to uncontrolled shaking, giddiness and an all-out laugh fest.

"I have a proposal for you guys. Wanna hear it?" Benjamin's body had stopped shaking and the warmth began to return to his bones.

"Fire away. Let's hear it," Phil replied.

"Okay, you just had another taste of swimming in the English Channel so, I'm proposing that you each toss your name into the hat and take the plunge. It'll be a couple years before you get accepted for the swim, so what the hell, why not? Sign up today, both of you!"

They were at it again.

"I've got my sights on another swim, something *way* more challenging," Phil shouted.

"Bullshit!" Benjamin shouted.

"What? Are you calling me out on that?" Phil asked

On camping trips, dive trips, rainy days or just about anytime Phil and Benjamin had some down time together, they played Liars Poker. Like everything else, the games had always been competitive with the loser having to buy a round of beers or maybe a couple rounds. On one of their ventures, during a heated round of Liars Poker, Phil's impromptu answer had sent them reeling to the floor in laughter. That's when Liars Poker had morphed into Bullshit.

Benjamin screamed, "No! I think you're up to something. Ever since I kicked your ass in the last Alcatraz swim you've upped your swim yardage. You're planning to—"

Phil's arms shot up. "Kicked my ass! You cheated. We agreed there would be no drafting and you sucked off my wake for damn near the whole swim."

"Cheated! You know damn well—"

Alex slid across the sand on her knees and knelt before the two fearless swimmers. She grabbed each one by their feet. "Shhh, I have a better idea. Let's go get a couple hours of shut-eye, which we all need, and we'll have dinner tonight at Smugglers. I've already made up my mind on this wager and I'll give you my answer at dinner." She winked at Benjamin.

"Yeah, some shut-eye, I'm up for that." Benjamin stood, returned the wink and looked down at Phil. "How about we meet you around seven at Smugglers? Perfect spot for dinner—good choice."

"Shut-eye my ass. I'm the only one around here that's going to get any sleep right now." Phil grabbed his towel and stood. "I think I'll pass tonight on dinner. You guys go ahead and I'll meet up with you in the morning."

By the time Phil had finished he turned and saw Benjamin carrying Alex piggyback and charging up the wooden stairs.

■   ■   ■   ■   ■

The Smugglers Bar and Restaurant was located in an unassuming building on High Street in the village of St. Margarets-At-Cliffe, just two blocks from the ferry terminal. In the 1700s, the village had been a center of operations in the dark days of smuggling illicit booze. The Smugglers building, like most of the older buildings in the village, had been a prominent point to store barrels of rum.

The quaint interior had all the charm of the typical neighborhood British pub and then some. Local fishermen sat on worn leather strapped bar stools and cozied up to the oval shaped wooden bar that looked like a large beer mash tun. Paper currency from around the world was tacked to the ceiling and photos of the Smugglers' famed skittles and dart teams, both teams to be reckoned with, filled the walls.

Alex and Ben were both famished. They ordered the salmon aurora and the mushrooms a la greque, a couple pints of Guinness and soaked in the ambience. Alex dabbed at her lips with her napkin and said, "You know, Andre asked about you, I think he thinks you're avoiding him."

"That weasel." Benjamin wagged a finger in the air. "The only single regret I have in my life is I didn't flatten that son-of-a-bitch when I first met him at the Lapin Agile."

"Oh sure, slug Andre Broussard while you're in Paris. Where do you think that would've landed you?"

"Okay, point taken, but I'm still finding broken pieces of my life and of GEN scattered around, all thanks to him. I thought we were rid of him. I really did."

"We may be. I have some separate ideas about that, but I did get out of him what I needed."

Benjamin reached for his mug and held it up. "Here's to the

disappearance of Andre." He flashed a movie star smile and emptied his mug.

On her drive out to Dover, Alex had finally put the pieces together that she had artfully pried out of Andre. Kioshi had definitely changed his methods since he had vanished, but his intentions had remained the same. He had surreptitious connections to financial institutions, construction companies, mining companies and a host of others. His long arms now spanned three continents. His interest in a particular international company dealing with pesticides and genetically modified plants had interested her the most.

Alex took a sip of her Guinness. "Around 10 years ago, Kioshi acquired a new drug that was in the early developmental stages. I imagine he acquired that drug the same way Andre acquired so many of the drugs in his stable."

"You mean he stole it?" Benjamin asked.

"Probably. I think that's why he set his sights on Andre to pull him into his clutches. He found out that Andre had done the same thing over the years and that he could be lured into developing the drug simply by seeing the profits at the other end."

"So what's the drug used for?" Benjamin asked.

"Andre isn't certain, but he suspects it's going to be used to fight off a virus that Kioshi is creating. When Andre learns of a new viral outbreak, that's when he'll surface and make the drug available."

"That doesn't make sense. How can you develop an effective drug if you don't know what you're fighting? It's impossible; you'd need to run tests and trials using the virus to prove the drug has any efficacy."

"I thought the same thing, so when I was in Paris I stopped by to see Charles Diderot. Remember him?" Alex asked.

"Isn't he the geneticist at the Sorbonne who helped you on the G-16?" Benjamin replied.

Alex nodded. "I stopped by his office. I don't think he was too happy to see me at first, but—"

Benjamin interrupted, "Weren't you in graduate school with him?"

"I was, but he's still reeling from what happened with the G-16 and was afraid that maybe I stopped by to enlist his services. Anyway, I gave him all the background data on the vaccine and he'll see if he can determine what it is supposed to be used for."

"So, you're saying Kioshi plans to spread a virus and then sell the only drug available as the cure?" Benjamin scratched his neck. "For him to make the kind of money for this all to be worthwhile, that virus would have to reach near epidemic proportions. I'd wager that tens or hundreds of thousands of lives are at stake over this."

Alex shook her head. "That's right."

"We need to go to the authorities—now. This has to be stopped."

"I thought about that, but it won't work," Alex said. "I think he plans to introduce the virus within the next month, at the latest, and it will take the authorities longer than that to get up to speed on everything. Besides, having Kioshi arrested, even convicted, won't solve our problem with him. The man has connections everywhere and he'll be more determined than ever to kill me—us."

"You're certain of this? He really plans to spread that virus to humans? How's he going to do that?"

"No, I'm not certain, but it all seems to fit together brilliantly. Somehow he got inside Agrico and—"

Benjamin interrupted, "Agrico? I'm pretty sure I own stock in that company. I'll check first thing in the morning and if I do, I'm selling it."

Alex continued, "About the same time Kioshi got involved with Agrico, it had developed a genetically modified strain of rice that was fortified with iron. The rice was to be grown in underdeveloped parts of the world where iron deficiency is the norm. It has the potential to save millions of people."

Benjamin reached across the table, took Alex's hands in his and leaned forward. "Where's Kioshi right now? Whatever he's planning on doing we have to stop him."

CHAPTER 16

Steph pulled the wooden spoon from her mouth and licked her lips. Hmm, short a dash of oregano and a clove of garlic. She chopped up a single garlic clove, then added another just to make sure and she tossed them into the marinara sauce giving it one final stir. Steph knew she had absolutely no chance of ever being hired as a chef or short order cook at even the seediest of hash houses. Most of her meals were simple, tasteless concoctions she'd eat on the fly, but there were a handful of recipes that she had mastered and tonight she wanted to have one of her specialty dinners on the table by the time Chandler made an entrance.

She placed an open bottle of Toby Lane Vineyards, 2011 Cabernet Sauvignon on the table, lit two tapered candles and placed them in the center of the table. She retreated back a step. Her flame-red hair was pulled back in a loosely-tied pony tail and a single streak of eyeliner, matching her sky-blue eyes, rimmed her eyelids. With her middle finger, she flicked a dried garlic leaf from her beige peasant blouse and then caught an image of herself in the mirror. She liked what she saw. Her usual attire was either jeans or some old gabardine pants with one of her JC Penny blouses half tucked in and if she hadn't gotten around to doing laundry, which was usually the case, she'd throw on one of her UC Davis Field Hockey sweatshirts. She looked down at her bare feet and wiggled her toes. Neither of her two pairs of shoes would go with her mood that night. Shoeless it would be.

Steph was sitting by the fireplace, mesmerized by the flickering flames, when she heard the door. She jumped up, smoothed her hair one last time just as Chandler entered the room. Chandler placed a grocery sack stuffed with food on the hall table and beamed. "I can't believe you beat me to it. I've been at the store trying to figure out what to make, then I come home to this. It smells absolutely, positively, without a doubt fabulicious." Chandler took a step back. "And look at you! I'd say you have more on your mind than dinner. You're ravishing!"

Moments later the two were tangled in the other's arms. Steph could feel Chandler's heart beat in sync with hers. She lifted her head back, stared into Chandler's flecked brown eyes, their lips brushed, and she whispered, "I didn't make anything for dessert, I figured I'd leave that up to you... you know, you being the creative one and all. Now, hurry up and change and we'll polish this off as soon as possible." Their lips parted, their eyes closed and their mouths opened.

"Not now, pleeeese not now. I should go see who that is."

Chandler dropped an arm and squeezed Stephanie's hip. "That damn phone of yours. Are you sure you don't have some kind of alarm on it to keep me away? Go ahead, check your phone and I'll run and change."

Stephanie picked up her phone, saw the number and put on her work face. "Chief, hi, what's up?"

"I know, I know Chief, I'm supposed to fill you in everyday, but I just walked in the door and I didn't have time to make it back to the office. I'll be the first one there tomorrow, I promise, and I'll fill you in. I think this is turning into something way bigger than I first thought."

Stephanie sat down on the kitchen bar stool and leaned back against the counter. She imagined Chief, sitting in his office with his feet on the desk and fully reclined in his 1970s style oak swivel chair. His tie was half undone and the sleeves of his wrinkled white shirt, never blue or any other color, just plain white, were unevenly rolled up. Her fingers tapped on her knee as she listened to Chief drone on about investigative reporting and the promises she had made to him.

She saw the wax from the candles begin to melt and tiny balls of wax curled over the top. She knew she was in for a long night. After listening to three grunts, four huffs and an untold number of didn't I tell ya's, the phone was silent. She gave in, "No, this is as good a time as any." She walked over to the stove, turned the burner off and let out a deep sigh. "I met with both of my sources today over at Golden Gate Park...."

The candles had burned to nubs and streams of melted wax had pooled and splattered around the base of the brass holders. On the sofa, across the room, Chandler's head rested on a throw-pillow and a half-empty bottle of Toby Lane sat on the floor.

"I'm such an idiot."

CHAPTER 17

Driving up Grand Avenue, Stephanie was oblivious to the rows of Elm trees, the perfectly trimmed, shiny green lawns and the concrete lion statues that protected the brick walkways leading to pillared homes. She had grown up in the enclave of Piedmont, California, in a house full of maids and butlers and a garage full of cars with fancy sounding European names. In the 1920s, Piedmont had been given the nickname The City of Millionaires, and nothing had changed. The town had more nannies than children and enough gardeners to spruce up Golden Gate Park in a single day.

Lung cancer had taken Stephanie's mother from her when she was 12. The memories of her mother remained clear today, like when the two had baked cookies and Stephanie's fingers would scrape every drop from the mixing bowl, or when her mother had rocked her in her arms and hummed softly when she hadn't felt well. There was never a single soccer or field hockey game when her mother hadn't paced the sidelines yelling encouragement to her or loud taunts at the refs, louder than any of the other kids' fathers. It had taken Stephanie years before she could think about her mother without an onslaught of tears streaming down her cheeks. Now, when she thought about her mother, which was always, she could smile and laugh and feel her presence.

Steph's father had raised her the best he could and after her mother had died, he had tried to be around as much as his work had allowed. What had started out as a few family dinners a week and maybe her father showing up for part of a Saturday game, hadn't lasted very long. Work had always seemed to be his excuse. He had been building the family business— for her. She'd thank him someday.

Steph slammed her brakes and skidded to a stop. A soccer ball, followed by a young boy clad in a crisp white soccer jersey, knee length red socks and polished cleats, charged from across the street. A portly black lady trailed behind him and swooped him up with one arm, inches from Steph's front tire. Steph smiled, rolled her window down and hung her head out. "I can remember a day when you'd never let some kid out-run you."

"Lordy!" The lady tightened her grip on the boy and lifted her head. "I am sooo sorry. This boy can wiggle faster than a rattler in a gunny sack. Sometimes I...." She stopped, put the boy down and grabbed the back of his jersey. "I can't believe my eyes! Miss Stephanie, is dat choo? Well of course it choo, I could never forget choo, never."

"Manna," Stephanie's eyes beamed, "you've made my day. I think about you almost every day."

Manna moved around to the side of the car, one hand tethered to the boy. She reached in and clasped Stephanie on her arm with the other. "Look at choo, girl! You's all grown up inta one mighty fine lookin' woman!"

"I'm all grown up, alright." Stephanie clutched Manna's hand. "You look great, although I don't think you ever would have let me run out into the street. You slowing down?"

"Not one ounce, I'm not. This one here, well, he may be more of a rascal than even you was. You's going up to see yur dad? I heard rumblins that you's working for him. I'll bet that makes him proud as a hen with one chicken. Yup, mighty proud indeed."

"No, no, I'm not really working for him. You know me, always got to figure things out on my own."

"You was feisty back then, probably still is." Manna gave Stephanie a squeeze on the arm. "I gotta run, honey, I'm fixin' to get this young boy to his practice. Can't ever be late ta practice. I learned dat from choo. But listen, I don't want choo to be a stranger no longer. No, ya know where I am so I expect choo to come by and tell me all about what choo been up to. Hear me now?"

"I've always heard you, Manna, loud and clear and I will stop by—you can count on it."

Stephanie shook her head and took a deep breath. She couldn't get Manna out of her mind, the woman had meant so much to her, but now she had to focus. She had a job to do. She drove up the tree-lined driveway, pulled the car to a stop and swept her hair back. Her phone rang. She didn't recognize the number. "Steph Moore."

Stephanie's almond-shaped eyes rounded, her brows raised. "That's great news. That's going to be more helpful than you can imagine. I know that was a difficult decision for you, but thank you, thank you, Adam. Pick a place where you want to meet and I can meet you there when I finish up here—say, two hours."

"Sure...sure... I will... I will... I promise... See you soon." The back of Stephanie's head smashed into the headrest and she gave a two fisted hand pump. "Yes, yes."

▪   ▪   ▪   ▪   ▪

Standing in the parlor room, just off the foyer, she rehearsed her lines. She knew what she was going to say, if she was ever given the chance. She wondered if every house in Piedmont had a parlor like this one. Furniture so perfect one was afraid to sit on it and oil paintings with men clad in red hunting outfits riding white horses and chasing a pack of hounds trailing a fox at the end of its rope. Everything in the room was devoid of anything personal. She had always thought these types of rooms were holding cells for those calling on the lord of the manor in hopes that they might take a minute out of their day to speak with the less fortunate.

A voice bellowed from the doorway, "Miss Moore?"

Steph spun around on her heels. "That would be me." She extended a hand.

The man's hands remained stuffed in his pants' pockets. "I'm Eric Cummings." He pulled a hand from his pocket and looked down at a business card. "You're with the Post, I see. I don't answer questions from reporters, so I'm afraid you've wasted your time in coming here."

Steph pulled her hand back and stepped forward. "I haven't asked you any questions."

"I'm sure that's why you're here and I have nothing to say. So—"

"You don't know what I'm going to ask you. Aren't you at least a little curious why I've driven all the way over here to see you?" Steph asked.

"Miss Moore, you obviously know where I work, so you're aware that when any news coverage surfaces about Agrico it's never presented in a favorable way. People in your line of work seem to only want to report mistruths about what we do. For that very reason we have a public relations department that handles press matters. I suggest you contact them. Now, if you don't mind showing yourself out, I have some things I need to take care of." Mr. Cummings stepped back from the doorway, turned and disappeared.

Steph dashed out of the parlor into the foyer. "Will they be able to tell me about why Agrico is funneling hundreds of millions of dollars into Sustinere Messes Corporation? Or about the files that were hacked from your computers just over a week ago?"

Cummings froze, then turned. His head tilted to one side and he leered at Steph over the top of his glasses.

Steph stood firm, her shoulders squared and she returned the glare.

"Hmm." Mr. Cummings walked back to Steph and placed a hand on her back. "Another rumor floating around, I guess. Come, let's go back into the parlor and you can tell me what you *think* is going on."

Eric Cummings was officially Agrico's Senior Vice President of International Row Crops and Vegetables. He had come to Agrico with an MBA from Dartmouth's Tuck School of Business and had excelled through the corporate ranks. Articles in Forbes and Fortune magazines, had called him Agrico's corporate linchpin and the man responsible for what Agrico called its commitment to sustainable agriculture. Before his promotion to his current position, he had served as the President to Agrico Asia.

Mr. Cummings sat with his legs crossed and his arms rested comfortably on the leather padded armrests. He lifted one hand. "Please, have a seat."

"I'm more comfortable if I just lean, if that's okay with you?" She leaned back against a mahogany console table set against the wall, her arms spread and her fingers gripped the edge.

"Fine by me." He shifted in his seat. "I heard something about this a few years back and, of course, it was false then and it's false now. Who's spreading these rumors again?"

He's trying his damnedest not to look guilty, she thought. He pushed his glasses back to the bridge of his nose and his eyes narrowed to match his pressed lips. Showtime. "Why do you think this is just a rumor, Mr. Cummings?"

"Because it's not true, that's what rumors are."

Steph nodded. "Good, then you can help me out here, because I think otherwise."

"Let me start by giving you a few facts, Ms. Moore. In less than 30 years' time, there's not going to be enough food to feed the population on this planet. So companies like Agrico are visionaries and we're working to not just increase the yields to meet these demands, but to improve the lives of farmers and their families all around the world. Let me ask you a question. Have you ever been to any of the Third World countries in Africa or Asia and witnessed some of the conditions those farmers have to deal with?"

"No, I'm sorry to say that my travels have been pretty limited," Steph replied.

Mr. Cummings re-crossed his legs. "Not too long ago, a former British prime minister said that African poverty is a scar on the conscience of the world. He was right and I'm afraid the outlook for that continent's future is dreary, at best. Do you know that by 2020 the continent's food production is expected to be half of its current production? Population growth, drought, disease, refugees, lack of sanitation all contribute to Africa's continued demise. Last year, Zimbabwe and Lesotho lost over 40% of its maize production, their main food staple. That paints a pretty bleak picture, don't you think?" Cummings asked.

Steph nodded, "It sure does."

Cummings raised a hand to his mouth, cleared his throat and

continued, "Asia doesn't fare any better, southeast Asia in particular. Every year the monsoons come and in Bangladesh, for example, the rains can destroy half or more of a local farmers' rice crop. Half a billion people in Asia rely on rice for their daily nutrition. A new, flood resistant rice has been developed that can breathe under water for up to two weeks. This means that many of the local farmers can now produce enough rice to feed their families and have extra grain that they can sell at local markets. There are new and successful ways to help combat hunger and poverty and Agrico is a leading participant in that revolution."

"Hmm, you paint a glowing picture of how Agrico is poised to help these undeveloped countries, but when I poured through your company's sales reports, it looked like less than two-percent of your income was generated by selling to those countries." Steph paused for a reaction from Mr. Cummings. Seeing none, she continued, "Companies like Agrico don't sell seeds to the farmers in those regions because those farmers don't have the money to buy them. They're small, sustainable farmers, who reuse their own seeds and barely end up with enough crops to feed their families. I don't really think Agrico cares much about what goes on in Zimbabwe, Bangladesh or any of the Third World countries."

"You're wrong. Things aren't going to change in those countries overnight, but we're one of the few international companies who are trying to make a difference," Mr. Cummings replied.

"That's all good stuff and I imagine you're pretty proud of all that, so why all the secrecy with Sustinere? Why is all that hidden from any public records?"

"Look, I know all about Sustinere and the Novum Rice they have developed and I applaud them. People think we're trying to corner the international agricultural supply chain, but that's far from the truth. I hope they're successful and those same people will see how these GMs are providing a needed product and that the market is open to everyone."

"So, what you're saying is, Agrico has nothing to do with Sustinere, financial or otherwise?" Steph asked.

"Nothing whatsoever, other than we're cheering them on from the sidelines," Mr. Cummings replied.

"How easy would it be, do you think, to hide a couple hundred million dollars from Agrico's financial records? I mean, suppose someone wanted to funnel money to Sustinere, or to anyone, could that be done without others knowing about it, like, say... you?"

Cummings pushed up from his chair and walked over to Steph. "I've given you an emphatic no to each of your questions. Who's been feeding you this line of crap? Cut to the chase. What's your point?"

"My point?" Steph rose to her full height. "My point, Mr. Cummings, is I don't believe a word you're saying. I've poured through Agrico's 10-Q and 10-R SEC filings and there's nothing in there about the hundreds of millions of dollars Agrico has transferred to Sustinere. I don't know if that money was an investment, a bribe, a cover up or what, but I do know Agrico spent the money. I also know Sustinere is in constant contact with Agrico, and you and I know that the development of the Novum Rice was halted by Agrico about the same time that Sustinere somehow started the same project. Maybe that's a coincidence, but I don't think so. The files that were stolen the other day, they were about Sustinere, nothing else."

She turned away, walked to the window and looked down at the rows of potted plants lining the brick pathway leading to the street. She wasn't certain if she had played out any of this the right way. Had she overplayed her hand? Should she have been more subtle, less forceful? She turned and looked at Eric Cummings. He stood tall, his left hand half clenched. She continued, "I have a deadline to meet and I'm going forward with this story. I've confirmed everything already, but I wanted to give you the chance to comment ahead of time." She turned and walked toward the door. "Thank you for your time, Mr. Cummings."

"Ms. Moore. I don't know what else I can say to you to convince you otherwise, but writing an article about what you're claiming to be true will do your career more harm than good. Trust me; you may want to rethink what you're calling facts. Why don't you come by my office tomorrow and let me show you around. I think you'll like what you see and it'll help you out with your research."

"You're on. I'll call tomorrow and we'll confirm a time."

Walking out the front door, Steph stopped and asked, "Are you planning on retiring soon?"

He laughed, "God, no! Retire and do what? Why do you ask that?"

"Oh nothing, really, but… well, I saw where you've been selling your stock options over the past couple of years and I just figured that maybe you were getting ready to retire. Maybe a new career plan, but I guess I was wrong."

Cummings grabbed the door knob, his knuckles turned white. "My financial advisor thought it best that I diversify my portfolio—that's all."

Steph felt the beady eyes burning on her back. When she reached her car, she looked back—the door to the pillared house had just slammed shut.

CHAPTER 18

Phil would rather walk across a bed of burning coals, crawl through the Sahara and drink sand, or claw his way out of a buried casket than spend 26 hours with his lanky body crammed into an airline seat designed for people half his size—not that he hadn't done so before. He had logged over two dozen flights between San Francisco and the southwest Pacific island of New Guinea while he had been a professor of Anthropology at the University of California at Berkeley. The moment Phil had left academia, he had vowed never again to subject himself to the unavoidable tortures of long distance air travel. He had retreated to his Bolinas home where he had grown his own organic vegetables and grains and often had remained in his eclectic house for days on end without encountering a soul.

"You know, I've always resented the one percent, but now, well, I can sort of see why you want to keep things so exclusive." Phil stood in the aisle with a lopsided grin, one hand resting on the plush leather seat where Benjamin sat, sipping an oaky, dry Chardonnay.

Benjamin returned the smile. "What've I told you all along, bud? There are some comforts that make life just a little bit easier. First class is one of them."

"It must be nice being you." Phil squeezed Benjamin's shoulder and then asked Alex, "I looked at my ticket and it says we won't be returning for three weeks. You really think we'll be there that long?"

Alex placed her tea cup down beside her. "God, I hope not. I'm thinking more like a week, but I booked us all round-trip tickets to avoid airport delays. Whenever you book a one-way ticket you're guaranteed to be pulled from the security check-in, your bags and person searched, and you'll be asked endless and pointless questions by the security personnel. It's been that way since 9/11."

Phil shook his head. "One day, that's all I ask. One day inside that head of yours to see what other mind-numbing bits of information is lodged in those cracks."

Alex chuckled. "When this is over I may just take you up on that. There are all sorts of things I'd like to erase from my brain."

"Well, I'll let you two get back to doing whatever you were doing. Right now I'm going to head back to my seat and figure out how I can enclose that contraption around my seat and see if I can get some sleep." Phil waved a half-hearted salute. "Don't forget to wake me."

Alex turned toward Benjamin. "That's the most relaxed I've seen him since before I talked to him about Michelle."

"Yeah, he told me back at Heathrow he thought the flight might just help him get his mind off Michelle for a little bit. He's pretty consumed over it all."

Alex leaned over and nuzzled her head into Benjamin's shoulder. "I know how he feels. When you were missing, I couldn't think about anything else. I always wondered where you were, were you okay, how long will it be before I find you? It was horrible. I really feel for him."

Benjamin wove his fingers into Alex's and squeezed. "I couldn't be any better than right now. Although, I've gotta admit if I had a choice I'd rather be back at the M & O," he gave another squeeze, "house intact, of course, figuring out what we're going to do for how long forever is."

"Forever... I never imagined that I, Alex Boudreau, would be sitting somewhere with someone like you even contemplating the concept of forever. That's a long time, a *really* long time—I hope."

"It will be if I can just keep you out of trouble," Benjamin said.

"You have your work cut out for you, then."

"May I get either of you a refill, maybe something to eat?" The flight attendant stood, smiling in her crisp, starched blue uniform.

"You know," Benjamin arched his neck, "I think I'm good for now, but maybe in an hour I'd like something to eat." He looked at Alex. "Anything for you?"

Alex burrowed deeper into Benjamin's shoulder. "I have everything I need, right now... right here."

Benjamin glanced up at the flight attendant. "It looks like we're all set for now. Maybe you could bring us a menu in about an hour. She'll be hungry by then—trust me."

London, to Amsterdam, to New Delhi, to Katmandu was the most direct flight plan Alex could arrange, but she needed the time the long flight legs would afford her to sort through the pieces she had on Kioshi. She had even hoped she could get some needed rest because she knew that once they landed at that place called the *Roof of the World*, sleep would fade to a distant memory.

Benjamin, and particularly Phil, had failed in their persistent pleas to try and persuade Alex to fill them in on the details of what she had planned for them. They had arrived at Heathrow totally unaware of their travel destination until Alex had handed them their tickets. Alex had stood by her pat answer, "The less you know, the better off we all are. If something were to happen to one of you, you're better off not knowing too much. It's safer that way." The only hint of their possible destination had been when they were preparing to leave Mill Valley, Alex had said, "Bring your most comfortable hiking boots along; you'll need them."

Alex was still unsure what her exact course of action would be, but she had known from experience that the final details were never really final. She had traveled that not so unfamiliar road before. On an earlier assignment, Alex had found herself in Morelia, Mexico and after a week she had still been unprepared to carry out her mission. She had been hired by a European syndicate involved in the mining and distribution of precious gems. The valuable gems were small and easily concealable and over a period of a couple years the syndicate had determined that nearly $10 million of gems had been stolen from their stockpiles. The syndicate had believed the gems had been stolen by a group of Mexican businessmen shortly before they had terminated their relationship.

What she had learned, however, had shocked even her own conscience and sense of justice. The Mexican businessmen had run a highly sophisticated drug cartel called The Knights Templar and it had been one of the world's largest suppliers of cocaine. The Knights Templar cartel was a Mexican criminal organization that had sprung from a family split within La Familia Michochana. The cartel derived its name from the Templar Order of the Middle Ages which protected Jerusalem, and its hit men had been given commandments to protect the community and keep all activities secret, or their families would be killed.

The Knights Templar had been a major supplier of crack cocaine and methamphetamines to North America, Europe and Australia. Alex had discovered that her own client, the European syndicate, had a direct connection to The Knights Templar's pipeline. Alex had always held personal contempt for the drug cartels that had reaped billions of illegal dollars by preying upon the poor and unassuming. She had justified her own existence by the fact that she had stolen information from rich corporations and governments who had endless proprietary coffers and offshore bank accounts to survive.

When Alex had returned home she had told her client that she had been unable to locate any of the purportedly stolen gems and she had returned her fee, less her expenses. She had prepared a complete dossier detailing The Knights Templar's internal structure, bank accounts, distribution outlets, assets and locations and had it anonymously delivered to Interpol, the Mexican Federales and the U.S. Drug Enforcement Agency. Several years later she had read that arrests had been made and the entire operation of The Knights Templar had been shut down. Its kingpin, Ignacio Coronel Villarreal, had been resting in a federal prison in Miami.

The dead humming of the plane was the only noise and most passengers were fast asleep. Awake, but lost in their thoughts, Benjamin and Alex each imagined being somewhere far away—far from the treacherous, uncertain path they were now headed down. That somewhere was where the past was a blur and the here and now was all that mattered.

A series of beeps brought them back. Alex reached over, pulled her tablet to her lap and saw the light flashing on her screen. "This is strange," she said. "This is a text to a number I rarely use."

She clicked on the text and her eyes widened as she read the message. "Oh god, they have Michelle. They're holding her."

Benjamin bolted upright. "Who? Who's holding her?"

"It doesn't say, *exactly*, but it's Kioshi. I know it.

CHAPTER 19

Katmandu was boisterously noisy, a cacophony of sounds, an aural soundscape.

The night before, the three weary, but still determined travelers had checked into the Hotel Ganesh Himal, a small three star hotel tucked in a residential neighborhood and a 10 minute walk southwest of the chaotic and crowded district of Thamel. Ben had pushed Alex to stay at the Hotel Yak and Yeti where he had stayed a few years earlier when he had come to Nepal for a climbing trip. Located in the center of Thamel, the Hotel Yak and Yeti had been a favorite meeting place for journalists, diplomats and well-heeled trekkers who had opted for luxury and a chance to mingle with like-minded souls in its Pub Wine Bar. Alex had always preferred to stay off the beaten track where she could blend in with the local landscape and avoid the tiger-balm salesmen and tourist barkers.

Alex rose early, quickly showered away her sleep and disappeared into the early morning crowds. She was surrounded by a never-ending stream of honking, colorful public buses and mopeds, all weaving in and out of the hordes of organized pandemonium. The bark of street dogs, the call of temples and the wails of rickshaw drivers angling for customers provided the sound effects for a chaotic and never ending soundtrack. Monkeys were everywhere. They swung on power lines, begged for food, and were perched like gargoyles on building-tops.

She slowed her pace and took a deep breath. It wasn't just the noise that flirted with her senses day and night, it was the teasing smells of the city and, in particular, the piercing spiced scent of street food. Street vendors on each corner served garlic basted *pani puri* and the air was rich with the aroma of curry, cumin, ginger and turmeric.

She opened the rickety door to Yak Mountain and chiming bells announced her entrance. A stout, older man, dressed in homespun wool trousers and a tired looking Patagonia shirt, sat in an overstuffed chair on the side of the room. A gentle smile creased his lower face and dark, deep set eyes revealed a gentle, disciplined man of character. He motioned with his hand. "Good morning. Please, please, come closer and tell me how I may help you. I am Chime Gurung and if you are looking for a mountain guide, you have come to the right place. If you are lost and simply need directions, I would be honored to be of assistance."

Alex walked over to the man and extended her hand. "Good morning to you, too, Mr. Gurung, I am Alex Boudreau. May I have a seat?" She looked down at the tattered chair next to him.

"Of course, but call me Chime. I much prefer that."

Alex, placed her backpack on the floor between her legs, sat down and discreetly scanned the room. The Yak Mountain was not listed as a trekking agency in any of the popular travel guides. It didn't cater to groups seeking to explore the more common trekking routes: Everest Base Camp, The Langtang Region, or the Mt. Kangchenjunga Circuit. Its reputation was based on guiding serious trekkers to the outlying and remote regions rarely frequented by foreigners.

The inside of the shop was cluttered with vintage climbing gear; everything from rows of Chouinard pitons and hammers to Swiss military wooden ice axes to cookware, boot brushes, polish, weapon cleaning tools, extra leather straps, ski wax, and assorted clothing. Even to the true mountaineering aficionado, Yak Mountain was on equal footing with Europe's Messner Mountain Museum or the Matterhorn Museum.

She crossed one leg and folded her hands. "Thank you, Chime. My friends and I are planning to visit the Mustang region and I was told that you might have a reliable guide who knows the area well. We are hoping to find someone who lives there so the guide must not only speak the language and understands the customs, but have personal connections throughout the region."

"Where is your destination, exactly?"

"There's an area between Ghar Gumba and Kekyap Phedi with a cave known as Ritseling. That's our destination."

Alex glimpsed a subtle, but distinct change in Chime's eyes. Her father had often said that a man's eyes revealed his soul and his inner most thoughts and she had honed that skill herself over the years. She had learned that a man revealed much about himself by the way he held his hands, the crook in his neck or the speed and tone with which he spoke his words. He can learn to control those mannerisms and mask his inner feelings, but he cannot control his eyes, the true mirror of his being. She needed to look deeper.

Chime rubbed his chin and his eyes were trained on Alex. "This is a difficult time of year to be trekking in Mustang. Many of the passes are closed and the roads and trails are snow covered or muddy. You may want to reconsider your plans and wait until at least March, at the earliest."

Alex shook her head. "We would like to leave today or tomorrow. I have heard of your agency only by reputation and I was led to believe that you could make these types of arrangements for us. If I am mistaken, I am sorry. Could you recommend another agency we could contact to make these preparations?"

"Ms. Boudreau, I believe that—"

Alex interrupted, "Alex. Please call me Alex. I would like that."

"Alex, then." Chime tilted his head back slightly, but continued to lock stares with Alex. "For whatever your reason, you have chosen to visit an area that until very recently has been closed to all foreigners going back to the days of Marco Polo, many hundreds of years ago. Something tells me that you are not seeking pure adventure there, but rather you have a specific reason to go to such an isolated place during this time of year. Am I right?"

"Doesn't everyone have a specific purpose in mind when they come in here and ask about hiring a guide?" Alex asked.

"We have guided hundreds of people throughout Mustang. We have taken archeologists to visit the Sky Caves, experienced climbers to scale

Annapurna and even Lhotse and countless groups to explore the Kali-Gandaki River. But the area you speak of—not a soul. Why are you so interested in going there?"

Alex unzipped a side pocket on her backpack and pulled out an envelope. She leaned forward and handed it to Chime. "It's very important that the three of us reach our destination as soon as possible and that we have someone with us who can not only guide us, but help us with the local customs once we are there." Alex leaned back in her chair. "The envelope represents half of your payment. The other half will be delivered when we return. Your guide will be paid the same amount and under the same terms."

Chime opened the envelope and stared. His eyelids narrowed and he handed the envelope back to Alex. "This is more money than I see in an entire year, but I cannot accept it under these circumstances. You see, my guides are my family and I cannot risk putting any of them in danger without at least knowing ahead of time the dangers they may face. No amount of money can change that. If you choose to tell me what it is you are seeking at the Ritseling cave, then it is possible I may have someone to help you. Without knowing that, there is nothing I can do."

The aperture flickered and closed in the man's eyes and Alex caught what she was looking for. "Have you heard of a man named Kioshi Nakajima?"

* * * * *

Phil pointed across the street. "That's our spot, right there."

Benjamin saw the plastic sign strung over the entrance—Northfield Café and Jesse James Bar—and he elbowed Phil in the ribs. "Nah, I was angling more for some local flavor; somewhere we can get some potato soup, maybe a roti and a mango lassi."

"Right now I'd like some real coffee and that's gotta be the place. Come on," Phil said.

Before Benjamin could respond, Phil had darted into the street slaloming in and out of the moving and honking cars, mopeds, rickshaws and carts with the skill and speed of a crazed teenaged gamer. Benjamin surveyed the course and jumped in.

Buddha statues sat prominently on benches and rock outcroppings and next to Tibetan ceremonial masks adoring the walls. Multi-colored checkered table cloths covered the tightly packed tables; colorful plants, potted flowers and vines filled the open-aired eatery; and long strands of prayer flags swung from the ceiling and rafters. "See, I told you, this is a perfect spot." Phil opened his menu. "Right here, it says coffee and look there's your mango lassi. You can thank me now."

Half way through their breakfast Benjamin looked down at his phone and read a short text. "That's her. She's on her way over."

Phil gulped down the rest of his coffee and waved at the server, "Another cup, please." He pushed the Nepalese omelet around his plate, unable to eat, his mind fixed on Michelle. A part of him was relieved that Michelle was at least alive and hopefully safe. Another part of him teetered on anger and confusion in not knowing who she really was. Where was she from? Is her name really Michelle? Was this whole thing part of some master plan on her part?

Phil had had less than a handful of serious relationships in his life, but he felt a real connection to Michelle that was different from the others. She gave equilibrium to his life and instilled a calmness in him that he had never before felt. They shared so many common interests, their laughs synchronized in perfect harmony and their arms fit perfectly when draped around the other. But it had been the long periods of silence that had made Phil's heart beat with desire. They could lay wrapped in one another's arms staring endlessly at the ocean or lay toe-to-toe on the sofa reading for hours or watching the world go by without any need to talk.

Ben tapped Phil on the hand. "Hey, did you hear me?"

Phil smirked. "Yeah, yeah, I heard you." He picked at his omelet and continued, "I'm having a real hard time trying to figure out all of this with Michelle. I know you guys haven't said it, but I'm sure you've both thought

Michelle may have some involvement with this Kioshi guy. I don't know what to really think myself, but somehow I believe Michelle and I have something real going on."

Phil pushed his plate away and sat back. "I'm in love with her—plain and simple. I can't believe what a mess this is and—why me? What did I do to deserve this?"

Ben started to laugh.

"What's so damn funny?"

"Remember the night I called you after I'd finally spoken to Alex and she told me all about who she really was? Do you remember that?" Benjamin asked.

"It wasn't night, it was something like four in the morning and yes, I do remember it."

"Well, you and I are two peas in a pod, bud. She duped me good, but that ended up bringing us together. We never would have met otherwise."

"Right, and we wouldn't be here and I'd be back in Marin with Michelle." Phil sighed. "A fine mess you two have gotten me into."

"That's a bit on the harsh side, don't you think? You were very supportive when I told you I was flying off to Paris to sort things out with Alex."

"I wasn't supportive at all. I thought you were crazy, loco, a real nut case. I still do. I told you to get a lawyer, to talk to your PI, to *not* go to Paris, but no, being the stubborn son-of-a-bitch that you are I finally gave in because I knew nothing I could say would change your mind."

"Well, that sounds like you, but that's not my point. I knew then that there was something between Alex and me, something like I had never felt before. I had to follow through on what I felt and you need to do the same thing. If you really love her, you have to follow through on that. When we find her you'll get the answers and if you end up with a broken heart, you know I'll be there to help you glue the pieces back together."

Half of an overripe banana splattered on their table. "What the..." Phil looked up and saw a monkey sitting overhead on the cabana roof chattering away—*ooh ooh ooh eee eee eee aah aah aah.* "Even the monkeys are making fun of me."

A soft accent interrupted, "We're off first thing in the morning, but I have a full itinerary planned for you both today." Alex stood behind Benjamin, leaned over and wrapped her arms around him. "But first, I'm starving. What do you recommend?"

Phil pulled his plate back and picked up his fork. "I was just about to eat myself. Try this, the Nepalese omelet; it's the house specialty." He raised his nose in the air and took a deep whiff. "Smell those spices! You can't find those back home."

When the server arrived, Alex pointed to Phil's plate and motioned she'd have the same. "We leave before daylight tomorrow and I'm told we're in for some real sightseeing. I had a choice between Buddha Air and Shangri-La Airlines. Which one do you think I picked?

Benjamin laughed. "I'm going to go with the one that offers the least services and guarantees us the bumpiest and noisiest ride."

"I think they both fall into that category, but I made reservations on both. Flights around here don't have a reputation for being punctual. I'm hoping we get on Buddha Air because it leaves earlier and I'm told if we're lucky that we'll see the sun light up the peak of Annapurna when it rises from across the valley."

Phil swallowed some food and washed it down with a gulp of coffee. "So come on, tell us the plan. Where are we heading and just exactly what do you have in store for us? If this is going to be like any of the other escapades you've dragged me along on, then I want to know where we're going so I can at least wrap my head around it before we go."

"Tonight at dinner I'll fill both of you in on everything, but first, I have a driver waiting outside who's going to take us on a shopping spree. I have a long list of supplies we'll need to pick up while we're here."

CHAPTER 20

Steph's eyes were closed, she let out a muffled groan and then heard a voice, "You've had an accident, but you're okay, you're going to be fine, I'm here."

The throbbing, over and over and over, pounded her head. A dull, but sharp pain ricocheted and slammed into the sides of her skull. Flashes of blinding light, past events, distant voices, deadlines and ideas all spun round and round in her head, but she couldn't focus. Finally, through the slits of her eyes she saw Chandler, sitting beside her. "Where am I? What happened? Why does my head feel like it's going to explode?"

Chandler's hand caressed Steph's forehead. "The doctor says you'll be okay. Apparently it's nothing serious, but you had a blow to the head and can expect some aches and pains for a couple more days."

"I don't remember anything. What happened? Why am I here?" Steph asked.

"Do you remember pulling into the Grand Mandana gas station on Grand Avenue?" Chandler asked.

Steph took a deep breath and then let out a groan. "God, it even hurts when I breathe. Gas station? What'd you say?"

Chandler slid her fingers across Steph's eye lids. "You should get some rest. There's plenty—"

"Stephanie! You gave me one hell of a scare, but I just talked to the doctor and she said everything will be alright—a few bumps and bruises. You'll be back at it in no time." He stood on the opposite side of the bed from Chandler, his lip curled, "Hello, Chandler."

Chandler looked across the bed. "Hi, Mr. Weintraub. She just woke up a few minutes ago and she's still pretty groggy."

"Well how did this happen?" He was looking down at Stephanie, his hand resting on her arm. "Do you want to talk about it?"

"I talked to the policeman that brought her in. She was at the gas station on Grand Avenue, you know, the Grand Mandana. She must've stopped to get gas." Chandler ignored Mr. Weintraub's scowl. "The gas station attendant saw her lying on the ground with the gas hose still in her car and he called the police. That's about all anybody knows. I guess there were no eyewitnesses, at least nobody has come forward yet."

Mr. Weintraub stood and whisked his fingers across the lapels of his jacket. "What was she doing over there? Do you have any idea, either of you?"

All Chandler could manage was a shoulder shrug. Even though he had never said so, Chandler knew Mr. Weintraub didn't really approve of their relationship. As far as he was concerned, nothing was ever good enough for his little girl.

"What about you, Cliff?" Mr. Weintraub asked.

Chief walked to the foot of the bed and clasped the metal bar with both hands. "She's been working on a story that's taken up a lot her time. I'd bet this has something to do with that."

"What kind of story? I thought she was covering local interest stories. How could those lead to this?" Mr. Weintraub nodded toward his daughter.

Chief had been the one who had called Mr. Weintraub the moment he hung the phone up after talking to Chandler. He hadn't told him anything about what Steph had been working on; only that she had been hit on the head and was in the hospital. Chief and Mr. Weintraub had pulled into the hospital parking lot at the same time and had raced, in tandem, inside to find Steph. "She's moved up a notch, Phil. She came across some information about a computer breach at Agrico and, well you know how stubborn she can be. So I let her run with it and she's been dogging it like a real pro."

Chief couldn't tell whether Mr. Weintraub was going to explode from anger or burst with pride, but he wasn't about to wait and find out. "Look, she's doing a hell of a job on this story. Hell, she does a great job on everything. I don't know what happened, but whatever happened I'm sure she was careful."

"You know, I just want Stephanie to be able—"

"Ohhh…." Steph tried to lift her hands to her head, but didn't appear to have the strength. "Hi, dad… Chief… what… how'd you know I was here?"

"Chandler called Cliff and we came right over. How are you feeling?" Mr. Weintraub asked.

"Like a sparring partner on the short end. I think my head's going to pop any minute."

Mr. Weintraub leaned down, his face inches from Stephanie's and he whispered, "I'll find out who did this, and when I do, they'll pay. Don't you worry about a thing."

Steph let out a long sigh, "It doesn't matter… it doesn't matter."

"The hell it doesn't. Whoever did this isn't getting away with it." Mr. Weintraub's voice echoed in the sterile room. Steph winced.

Mr. Weintraub turned and shot an accusing stare at Chief. "What's going on here? Stephanie's supposed to learn the ropes on running this paper, from the bottom up. That's what I had in mind when she came to work here and it's what she needs to do if she's going to run this paper someday. She hasn't even gotten her feet wet and you've got her running on a story that we have a dozen people better qualified to dog."

"Hold on," Chief squared his shoulders, "She's run with this story with more tenacity than—"

"That's unfair, dad. This is my story and I'm going to do everything it takes to see that… oh god." Steph grimaced and let out a yelp, "My head… let's not do this now."

Mr. Weintraub wrapped his arms around his chest. "We can talk about this later, maybe tomorrow. I'll talk to Cliff about this Agrico story and we'll see if that's something we think you should cover."

Chandler gingerly placed her hand on Stephanie's forehead and turned to Mr. Weintraub, "She really needs to rest. We can sort through all this when she feels better."

A half-grunt. "Perhaps you're right." He reached down and his fingers brushed Stephanie's cheeks. "You're going to be okay, kiddo. Everything will be fine."

CHAPTER 21

Mustang was a cauldron of myth. Ancient, Tibetan script, describes the founding of Lo in 1380 with the defeat of the tribal chieftain, *Demon Black Monkey*. Four hundred years later, Nepal exercised protectorate sovereignty over Lo and it became Mustang, loosely translated from the Tibetan phrase mun tan, meaning fertile plain. Mustang has remained a defender of Tibetan traditions.

The three descended the metal stairs from the twin-engine plane to the dirt landing strip and were greeted by harsh, biting winter winds. The snow-capped peak of Mount Nilgiri, soaring higher than 23,000 feet, shimmered in the thin air and was their first hint of the perilous and unknown hazards they were sure to encounter.

A man dressed in a red, fur-lined polar fleece jacket and knee length fur boots, stood at the bottom of the ramp. His tightly drawn hood highlighted his dark black eyes, thick lashes and brown, leathery skin. His parched lips parted revealing jagged, but pearly white teeth. "Welcome to Jomsom. I am Youten." He handed them the traditional kartas, Tibetan honoring scarves, bowed slightly at the waist and continued, "We have a short walk to Kagbeni where I live." His crooked finger pointed in the direction of Mount Nilgiri. "You may leave your gear here and I have arranged to have it brought into the village."

Benjamin stepped forward, introduced himself and the others. "We're anxious to get going so maybe you could fill us in on when we can leave and how long you think it'll take us to get to Ghar Gumba?"

Youten held his smile. A *mala*, or Buddhist prayer beads, was wrapped around one hand; his fingers scrolled through each of its 108 beads. "First, we walk back to my village and we will have some tea. There will be many details to discuss."

Benjamin nodded. "Fair enough. Let's do it."

The short walk to town turned into a three hour trek where they were pelted with sand and grit from the howling winds. They passed by endless rows of prayer flags fluttering furiously in the wind. As they neared Kagbeni, they walked through fallow fields that would soon be planted with barley, buckwheat, potatoes and peas and they passed by 100 or so goats grazing on the sparse winter grasses, their horns painted for identification.

They entered the white walled village of Kagbeni and followed narrow flagstone streets through a maze lined with white, mud built three story houses. The houses were identical except for the bright red, blue, yellow or green wooden doors anchored in the stone and mud walls. Each house sheltered animals on the ground level and humans climbed to the upper floors by steep wooden ladders. The narrow alleyways burst into sunny squares where women spun wool or washed their raven-black hair at a water tap sprouting from the plaza center.

They stopped at each prayer wheel—and they were everywhere—and each took a spin for good luck.

In the center of the village, in a windswept courtyard, rose an ochre colored monastery built from packed mud and adorned with hundreds of prayer flags. Piles of stone, delicately carved with Buddhist prayers and mantras, had been carefully placed by the faithful.

Youten stopped and motioned to the others. "This is a time of prayer. Please sit and we will pray."

Youten sat cross-legged on the ground and the others mimicked his pose. A hypnotic *ommm* wafted from copper and brass trumpets ceremoniously played by four monks; their burgundy robes seemed to explode in the afternoon sun. The scent of burning juniper filled the air and it seemed as if they were frozen in time, mindful of only the here and now.

Youten rose. "The horn is called a dung-chen and is used as a sound offering to god. Today, there are two important lamas that will be arriving. This is to honor them."

Youten pointed ahead, to the winding streets. "Just a little further—come."

They reached a house that looked like all the others, except for the Yak head mounted over a red wooden door. Youten opened the door and motioned for the group to enter. Inside, on the back wall, an altar bore Buddha images and the Dalai Lama's photograph. Eye-catching yak-butter sculptures covered a shelf and white kartas, ceremonial silk scarves, hung from rafters.

Youten waved a hand. "Please, take a seat and we will have tea and biscuits."

A smiling lady with round, shadowy black eyes served them each steaming bowls of yak-butter tea. She turned and left the room as quickly as she had appeared.

Phil's eyes had been saucer-like since they had departed the plane. "I have never been to a place like this before. It's... I don't know how to describe it... eerily breathtaking, maybe. And I'm not talking about the mountains, or the winds, or the barrenness that define this place, no, there's a feeling of contentment here. Everyone we've seen is happy, their hearts seem to smile; they seem so content, so peaceful."

Youten belted a baritone laugh, "Should it be any other way?"

Phil smiled. "No, it shouldn't, but it's so prevalent here—it's everywhere. I'm not used to it, but I think it could grow on me."

"We have many hard times here, but we are balanced by many good times. It's been this way for hundreds of years. Our harvest this fall was not as plentiful as we need and by the spring we will be very low on food, but the cycle will return and everything will work out."

Benjamin leaned into Alex and whispered, "You've hardly said a word since we left Katmandu. You okay?"

Alex nodded. She wrapped her hands around her bowl, closed her eyes and took a sip. The hot, thick tea was soothing. She whispered back, "I'm missing something. I don't know what it is, but something just doesn't feel right." She opened her eyes and looked at Benjamin. "Maybe I'm just anxious, I don't know."

Benjamin reached over and took her hand and gave it a gentle squeeze. "I still think we need some fire power."

The night before, Alex had filled both Benjamin and Phil in on her plan to find Kioshi and silence him. They had both agreed, reluctantly, to what she had in mind, but not without voicing their strong objections. "The idea of waltzing into someone's compound with the hope of enticing him to look at a computer program designed to plant false memories in his mind seems absurd," Benjamin had said.

"And I'll add to that," Phil had exclaimed. "And not just the fact that your program's never been properly tested, but you want us to come face to face with a known arms dealer who'll obviously be surrounded by an army of trained killers and we're going to be armed with absolutely nothing. It's ludicrous—suicidal."

Alex had remained steadfast. "No guns, no knives, no weapons of any kind."

Youten's fleece jacket hung on a wall peg and he sat contentedly in a wooden slat chair, his feet propped comfortably on a three legged stool. His dark eyes hid behind narrow slits as he looked at Alex. "Chime has told me that your plans are to find a man named Kioshi. When he told me this, I had some concerns—I still do. What is your business with this man?"

Alex watched Youten as he took another sip of tea. When she had met with Chime back in Katmandu, he had several guides available, but after reading their dossiers and discussing each, she had chosen Youten. He was a direct descendant of the notorious Tibetan Khampa warriors, a nomadic clan who had posed a threat to traders' caravans in the centuries past. Over time, those warriors had mysteriously dispersed throughout the region and had assimilated into the local villages. In the 1960s, they had regrouped as guerilla cells to beat back the invading Chinese and to protect the Dalai Lama. The exploits of the Khampa warriors had become part of the lore that had brought life to this harsh land, a place of deep ravines, stinging winds and ancient cave homes. "Yes," Alex had said to Chime, "Youten is the right man to help us."

Now, watching their guide, she was more certain than before that she had made the right choice. "Our business with Kioshi Nakajima is private. I'm sure you can understand our need to keep our interest in him to ourselves and I hope you can respect that."

"Respect is circular. There is no beginning or end, it is shared by all. You are asking me to take you to a man I have not seen, no one has, yet a great deal of mystery clouds his being here. Before he came here it was a rare happening to see a helicopter in our skies, but now, they pass through weekly carrying large cargo containers swinging on ropes. The villagers nearby carry large crates up the steep walls to the Ritseling cave and they return with empty ones. No one knows what is in those crates, but the villagers are paid well and have no reason to ask questions." Youten stopped and took another sip of tea, then placed his bowl down on the table beside him. He cleared his throat and spoke softly, "I believe this man is dangerous and his reasons for being here are not good. I have already agreed to take you there, but I need to know what I should prepare myself for."

Alex's pulse heightened as she listened to Youten. Listening to each word, she knew she was close to finding Kioshi and facing an ominous challenge she hoped she would be ready for. "You are right. I'm in your kingdom, in your home; I should show you equal respect."

Alex began her story. She explained how she had first met Kioshi and how he had resurfaced in her life. Youten listened with interest and parried with questions of his own and Alex had answered with the same candor and honesty shown by her new friend. She had left out many of the details of her past, not wanting to plant any fears in Youten's mind that she shouldn't be trusted.

"It has always been important to me to see that those I guide are safely returned." Youten's knuckled fingers combed through the snarls of his grey beard and he leaned forward. "I have not guided anyone for the reasons you give nor have I guided anyone where the dangers are beyond my control. We will pass through many villages on our trek to Ritseling cave and I can gather people to come with us from each of these villages. There is always strength in numbers and they can help to make sure you are safely returned back here, to my home."

"I appreciate your offer, Youten, very much, but I think it best that we keep our traveling party to a minimum," Alex said.

Youten turned his head. "Nirmala, could you please bring some more tea for our guests?" He looked back at Alex. "We will have one more bowl of tea and then we should leave. I have already picked up your foreigner permits. There is still enough daylight for us to get to Chele and we have a very long journey ahead of us. We will talk more along the way."

CHAPTER 22

The trek from Kagbeni to Ghar Gumba had started with a two day hike up the bed of the Kali-Gandaki River. The river bed has served as a trade route between Tibet and India for over 2,000 years. Flanked by the Annapurna and the Dhaulaghiri ranges towering skyward over 26,000 feet and only 24 miles apart, the Kali-Gandaki River flowed in the deepest gorge in the world. They had followed a flat, worn path covered with an endless mirage of river pebbles and they had scaled steep, crusty rock walls only to descend down knee-shattering steep trails.

After crossing one of the many steel footbridges spanning the river bed, they stopped at a brightly colored Chorten and ducked behind the back side to protect themselves from the blustering winds. Prayer flags snapped and fluttered and grits of sand and dirt whirled in eddies. Benjamin rubbed the back of his neck and took a few swallows from his canteen. "I don't remember the winds being anything close to this when I went to Kangchenjunga a few years back."

"This is like walking into sandpaper," Phil added.

"One of our Sherpa guides in Kangchenjunga had a saying he attributed to Buddha," Benjamin said. "Something like *you cannot travel the path until you have become the path itself.* I never thought much about it, but it's been on my mind most of today. I don't think I want to become anything like this path, especially my ankles. I think I've twisted and turned every tendon and muscle at least twice. These rocks are brutal."

Youten laughed. "So many people take the teachings of Buddha literally. You need to look closer to see what is truly meant."

"So, what does Buddha mean by being the path?" Benjamin asked.

"Many people never achieve their goals because they are unwilling or unaware of what is required to make them possible." Youten chewed on some dry roasted soybeans and continued, "You are strong and I am sure you worked hard to achieve that, but to achieve your desired physical strength, you must also improve your mental strength."

On the second day, they had passed mules with large copper bells draped from their necks and carrying piles of luggage strapped to their backs. They were southern Indian pilgrims on their way to Muktinah, the most sacred Hindu site in Nepal.

Alex had insisted that their caravan be limited to an absolute minimum. She had little need for the usual porters, cooks and kitchen help to accompany them. Youten initially had resisted the idea, thinking they would make better time if they had a full support crew. In the end, their caravan had been reduced to bare-bones and each trekker had been expected to shoulder the burden for the full four days. Alex, Ben and Phil had each carried backpacks stuffed with supplies and three porters had looked after the four tethered horses carrying gear and supplies for their anticipated round trip.

Before they had left Katmandu, they had purchased clothing and gear for their trek: down jackets, thermal hats, socks and gloves, homespun wool pants cut in the traditional Loba style for the colder weather, and more traditional daura's, a double breasted shirt. The had bought sleeping bags, tents, climbing gear, compasses and a small array of cooking gear. They had worn their own personal hiking boots, not willing to risk the certainty of blistered feet that would come from a new pair.

They had arrived late on the third day at the village of Lo Gekar and Youten had been greeted by Kunsang, an elderly monk. Clad in a traditional red robe, his leathery exterior matched the harsh and barren landscape. "Youten, what a surprise to see you this time of year. I usually do not expect trekkers this close to the winter months," Kunsang said.

Youten bowed and held his revered stance. "It is my honor. This was arranged at the last minute by Chime."

Kartas were exchanged and Kunsang introduced himself to the travelers. He bowed to each—one at a time. "It will soon be dark and I am sure you are all weary from your travels. Please, stay here tonight and you can free yourselves of your restless thoughts. Tomorrow you will be stronger for your journey."

Kunsang was the caretaker of Kar Gompa, a 1200-year-old Buddhist monastery and one of the most sacred shrines of Tibetan Buddhism. His family, direct descendants of the Marpa Kagya Tibetan lineage, had been its sole protector and held the keys for 12 centuries.

Kunsang led them down a dirt path lined with poplar trees and he stopped next to a stone wall. "You have passed many of these walls on your journey here. They are mani-walls and they are a sacred part of the Buddhist religion. This wall is over 1200 years old. Look here." Kunsang bent down and pointed at one of the rocks. "You see this? Each rock is carved with the same mantra—*Om mani padme hum.*"

"Om mani padme hum. What does it mean?" Phil asked.

"It is the mantra of Avalokiteshvara and if I translate it into your language correctly, it means hail to the jewel in the lotus. It is the same mantra that is written on each of the prayer wheels you have passed along your path."

Phil swiped his sleeve across his mouth. "What does that mean— the jewel in the lotus? I don't get it."

"The lotus represents wisdom and the jewel compassion. Just as a lotus can exist in muddy water, so to can wisdom exist in an impure world. Make sense?" Kunsang asked.

"You guys have it all figured out, your symbolism, your prayers, your mantras. But on our trek up here, Youten was telling us some of your history and all the different tribes and cultures that've been fighting here for centuries. Do you really feel compassion for those people who've ransacked your villages and tried to force their beliefs on you?"

Kunsang smiled and bowed slightly forward. His jet black hair was tied in the traditional pony tail and it slipped from his shoulder. His fingers routinely flicked it back. "Buddha teaches us not to dwell in the past, do not dream of the future, and concentrate the mind on the present moment. When you live your life with those beliefs, then there is no need to feel anything about what has already happened."

Phil shook his head. "As I'm learning, you guys have an answer for everything and so far it's always been an answer that seems right by me."

Kunsang bowed his head and touched his lips with the tips of his fingers. "Before we enter we must walk around this mani-wall and use it as a time to reflect." His hand motioned in a circle. "Each time you walk around the mani-wall you must begin from the left side and walk around the mani-wall in a counterclockwise direction."

Phil half-raised his hand and then caught himself. "Another question. Why counterclockwise? What happens if we walk the other way?"

"Let me ask you a question. What direction does the earth turn?" Kunsang asked.

A shoulder shrug. "Counterclockwise."

"Buddhist doctrines tell us to always walk in the same way the Earth and Universe rotate," Kunsang said.

Phil laughed and was the first one to fall in line behind Kunsang as they walked around the mani-wall, counterclockwise, each chanting—*Om mani padme hum.*

Inside the tawny colored monastery, was a large white chorten, and painted on the walls and ceiling were some of the best preserved ancient Buddhist art in the world. Rays of sunshine streamed through an opening in a wall and illuminated a portrait of a lama sitting on scattered lotus leaves. Opposite, was a painting depicting the reincarnation of Buddha.

Youten stared at a painting. "Chenrezig," he said and bowed his head in prayer. Lifting his head, he looked at the weary, but determined trekkers. "For Tibetan Buddhists, Chenrezig embodies compassion and Tibetans believe the Dalai Lama was a reincarnation of him."

The group sat in silence at a wooden table on the side of the inner room. They were tired, hungry and their exposed faces were red from the complimentary facial dermabrasion, courtesy of the fierce winds and sand. They sipped from steaming bowls of yak-butter tea and feasted on fragrant chapattis and warm dhal.

Hundreds of flickering butter lamps danced in the hollow room, piercing the darkness. Phil looked around the room. His face was solemn. "People have been lighting candles in here for 1200 years and I'll bet that during that time not once was this place in total darkness. Kinda puts some perspective on where our place is in things, don't you think?"

Youten smiled. "The purpose of these and all candles was best explained by Buddha who said, '*Thousands of candles can be lighted from a single candle, and the life of the single candle will not be shortened. Happiness never decreases by being shared.*'"

"So, you're saying that the candles symbolize the spreading of happiness?" Phil asked.

Youten nodded. "That is one of the many reasons, yes, but there are many others. Buddhists believe that the flame on the candle represents the light of Buddha's teachings and happiness is one of his many teachings. We use candles in our everyday life and during parades and festivals and they serve as a way for us to further our faith. At least once a day, we will isolate ourselves in a quiet room and stare into the flame of the candle, focusing all of our attention on it. As we stare at the flame our minds become enlightened and the worries of everyday life begin to drift away. Many times during this meditation we receive visions, images, and thoughts to guide us."

Phil shook his head. "I used to study tribal cultures in some of the isolated areas of Papua New Guinea. Do you know where that is?"

"No, I have not been outside of these lands except once when I traveled to Katmandu. The outside world is something I am not familiar with," Youten replied.

"I think there are similarities with what you describe in some of Buddha's teachings and the tribal teachings in Papua New Guinea. It's an island in the southwest Pacific Ocean and the Latmul Tribe there has lived the same way and followed the same beliefs for hundreds of years. In the center of each village is a spirit house, a large wooden structure filled with masks, statues and carved figures. They believe the carvings are all inhabited by spirits that help the people meet the challenges of everyday life and they ward off the influences of unfriendly spirits. The villagers pass by the spirit house many times each day and ask the spirits for guidance." Phil paused and then asked, "What would Buddha think of this kind of religious belief?"

A large smile covered Youten's face. "I am sure that Buddha would be most interested in what you speak of. The Dalai Lama has said that one food will not appeal to everybody nor is there one religion or one set of beliefs that will satisfy everyone's needs. As a Buddhist, we rejoice in other peoples' beliefs." Youten sat up, his shoulders pushed back. "You, my friend, I think would be wise to spend some time studying Buddha's way."

"Yeah, I will, for sure. I'm liking this place more and more. Your traditions, your beliefs and the way you lead your lives are inspiring and humbling. I'm marking it down on my to-do list to study Buddhism when I get back home." Phil turned to Benjamin. "What do you think? Pretty interesting stuff, huh?"

Benjamin sat upright on the bench and arched his back. "Boy, I was starved. That really hit the spot. Um, I really wasn't paying attention. What were you talking about?"

Phil bit his lower lip and shook his head. "Nothing, we'll talk about it later."

Benjamin looked over at Youten. "So tomorrow we arrive at Ritseling, right? How long a trek until we'll be there?"

"It will be much steeper than anything we have traveled through to this point. You are all very strong trekkers so, half-a-day, if the conditions are good," Youten replied.

Benjamin reached over and placed a hand on Alex's arm. "You're awfully quiet. You okay?"

Alex was tired and the past few days had exacted a physical toll on her. Her shoulders and back were sore from the weight of the backpack and her mind was tired from anticipatory expectations. She had been weighing the need to take a day's rest before they continued on to Ghar Gumba and then up the steep valley of Ghyung Khola to their final destination—Ritseling, but had decided against it. She had suspected Kioshi had been following their every move from the time they had left Mill Valley until they had arrived in Katmandu. How? She didn't know, but somehow he had been able to trace their steps. He had to know the route they would take to reach Ritseling and he had probably known where they were at that very moment. Rest would have to wait.

Alex brushed her hair back with one hand and returned Benjamin's gaze. "I'm just going over a few last minute items, that's all." She looked across at Phil and then back to Benjamin. "Once we get inside of Ritseling I'm certain we'll be frisked and maybe pushed through a metal detector, so if either of you brought along any detectable items like guns, knives or the like, now's the time to shed them."

One eye caught Phil's feeble attempt to feign innocence and the other zeroed in on Benjamin's furrowed brows. "I thought so. I know you two didn't bring anything into Katmandu, but you spent enough time there without me that you obviously picked up a few things. There's nothing you can't buy in that city, so what did you pick up?"

Benjamin frowned. "I'm still not excited about walking into this guy's place unarmed. He's tried to kill me twice, for Christ's sake."

"And he'll have you killed on the spot if he knows you're armed." Alex lowered her head and raised one brow. "Leave everything here. I want to at least get past the front door."

Benjamin nodded, slowly. "Alright, but I'm not happy about it."

"I don't expect you to be, but it's the right thing." She looked over at Phil. "I have one change in our plans. I'd like you to stay behind once we get to Ritseling and if we don't return by nightfall, then I want you to—"

"No way!" Phil shot up from the wooden bench, his arms flailing. "If Michelle's in there, like you say, then I have to find her. I need to know that she's okay. I'm not staying behind, no way. I didn't come all this way to have you pull that crap on me at the last minute."

"No you didn't, I know that and we'll find Michelle and make sure she's safe. Look Phil, I'm sure Kioshi knows the relationship that the three of us have and I'm afraid he may try to isolate each of us in an effort to force one of us to do something that may not be in our best interest. I don't want to take that risk—you don't either."

"I don't agree, not one bit," Phil shouted.

"I'm sorry, but you need to go along with me on this one."

Alex stood up and moved behind Benjamin, leaned down and kissed him on the cheek. "If you two don't mind I'm going to get some sleep." She glanced over at Youten. "Let's leave before dawn tomorrow. I want to be at Ritseling before noon."

■   ■   ■   ■   ■

"Talk to her Ben, I'm not going along with this one."

"I'm afraid her mind's made up and you know what? I tend to agree with her," Benjamin said.

"Bullshit!"

The two friends walked around the candle lit room, pausing to smell the incense, rub their fingers along one of the many Buddha statues and admire the wood carvings, colored stone plaques, terracotta deities and a tarnished bronze image of Padmasambhava. Benjamin and Phil had known each other for a short span of only seven years, but the two like-minded men had forged a rock-hard relationship that had already been tested to its limits. Less than a year earlier, Benjamin had been kidnapped and held in the Koidu mining plant in the dense jungles of eastern Sierra Leone. His captors had injected him with the G-16 virus and had threatened to activate it if he attempted to escape. Phil had risked his life in rescuing Benjamin from his captors and again when he and Alex had worked tirelessly to find a way to rid him of the virus. Benjamin was certain he would do the same for Phil.

"I know you're worried about Michelle. You're going to find out soon enough if she's okay and more importantly, who she is."

Phil threw his head back. "Do you think I've been duped by her?"

"There's nothing about her that struck me as phony or like she was covering up something, but hey, how would I know? What's your gut telling you?" Benjamin asked.

"My gut? It's been wrenching this whole trek. The closer we get to Ritseling the more my stomach turns and my anxiety level shoots through the roof. I love her. I'm afraid to even think that maybe she's not who I believe she is. That'll blow my mind."

Benjamin draped an arm around Phil's shoulder. "You know, I've been in your shoes more times than I care to remember and each time you were there beside me. I didn't always like what you had to say, but I've always known I could count on you to tell it like you saw it." Benjamin gave a sharp flex of his arm. "Sometimes the truth can be brutal coming from you, but I've always appreciated it. You've been a true friend. I hope someday I can get even with you."

"Well now's your chance." Phil spun out from under Benjamin's arm. "You want to help me out? Okay, I have a favor to ask you—a big one."

"Name it."

"Talk to Alex. Convince her that I need to be with you guys when you go inside Ritseling. There's no way I can sit out there for hours wondering if you've found Michelle, if she's okay and hell, even fretting over whether you guys are okay. Talk to her. Convince her."

"Convince Alex?" Benjamin laughed. "Well, there's always a first time, I guess. Alright, I'll talk to her, but no promises."

CHAPTER 23

When Steph awoke that morning she no longer felt like someone was stabbing her head with hundreds of tiny needles, only a dozen or so. It took her a few minutes to recognize her surroundings and that's when it her—Mr. Cummings had invited her to meet with him at his office. She discarded her hospital gown, threw on her own clothes and stealthily tiptoed past the nurses' station. Minutes later, she stood on the corner, a block from the hospital, hailing a cab.

"Good morning, I'm here to see Mr. Cummings. I'm a little early, but he's expecting me."

A cheerful voice responded, "Certainly, may I tell Mr. Cummings who's here?"

"Stephanie... Steph Moore."

Agrico's reception area was decked out so any visitor knew they were entering the hallows of a behemoth company. On one wall hung a map with small pictures and colored dots pinned in locations where Agrico plied its wares. Each continent, except Antarctica, was covered with multiple pictures and dots.

"Miss Moore? Mr. Cummings will see you now. Please, follow me?"

Steph followed the young aide down the hall and was ushered into a corner office. "Please," the aide pointed to a small seating area near the floor-to-ceiling window that framed San Francisco Bay, "Mr. Cummings asked that you make yourself comfortable and he'll be in very shortly. He's just finishing up a conference call. May I get you some coffee?"

"Coffee, yes, yes, thanks. Oh, wait, forget the coffee. Maybe just a glass of water."

Steph was impressed, but she knew that was the point. The room reminded her of the Beatles song, *I Me Mine*. That song dealt with ego problems and it had been the last song recorded before the Beatles had split-up. She walked around the office and perused the awards that hung like a padded resume; pictures with foreign dignitaries and trinkets from Azerbaijan to Zaire were scattered everywhere. She stopped behind his desk and glanced down at his computer monitor. The idea of taking a quick look crossed her mind, but she thought better of it—the screensaver flashed with random pictures of wheat fields, rice paddies and orange groves. She spotted a brown, thick folder on the corner of the desk. Her eyes darted about and then she picked it up. The white label pasted to the front read Off Balance Sheet Financing - Sustinere. She opened the cover and thumbed through the pages.

"When I asked Miss Hertzler to tell you to make yourself at home I didn't intend that to mean you could pry through my business folders." Eric Cummings held out a hand.

Startled, Steph slammed the folder shut and it slipped from her hands, hit the edge of the desk and landed on the floor—the binding broke and the pages scattered on the floor like a deck of cards in a game of 52 Card Pickup. "Oh, sorry... I was just... here, I'll pick this up." She bent down and reached for the papers.

"Never mind, leave them."

Steph stood up and turned around. "My god, what happened to you? That looks like it has to hurt." Mr. Cummings took a step toward Steph and then stopped—he took a step back, then another. "I just saw you yesterday. Did this just happen?"

"Oh, you mean this?" Steph's fingers lightly brushed the bruise that circled her left eye and ran all the way to her hairline. "It seems somebody doesn't like me very much and... well, I would've been here first thing this morning, but this sorta got in the way. Look, I'm sorry about that," she pointed to the floor, "let me pick this up and I'll—"

"Leave it, right where it is." Mr. Cummings stepped forward and took Steph by the arm. "Let's sit over there."

"Here's your water. I'm sorry it took so long. May I get you anything, Mr. Cummings?" Steph took the glass from his assistant and walked over to the window.

"I'm fine, Diana, thanks." Mr. Cummings sat down across from where Steph stood leaning against the window, her legs crossed. "Sit down, you'd be more comfortable."

"Thanks, but I'd rather stand. I'm more of a leaner than a sitter. I think better this way. I know, kinda odd, but I do." She pressed her shoulders back against the glass. "You promised to show me around. I think you said you'd even help me with my research. So, where shall we start?"

"Why don't we start by you telling me what you want to know and I'll answer the best I can."

"I think I made myself pretty clear when I came to your house. I'd like to know how Agrico can transfer $200 million to Sustinere and it doesn't show up anywhere in your public filings?" Steph turned her palms up. "That's all I want to know."

Mr. Cummings shifted in his chair and folded his hands in his lap. "I don't know where you got that information, Miss Moore, but—"

"Steph, please call me Steph. I prefer that."

"Okay, Steph, I don't think we've transferred that kind of money to Sustinere, but if we did transfer it to them or anyone else for that matter, it would be accurately reflected in our financial statements. That's the way we do business. We're a large multi-national company with a lot of regulations to adhere to and we have an entire department focused on making sure we comply with every single rule and regulation imposed on us by each of the countries where we do business; twenty-seven of them, to be exact." He tugged at his ear and continued, "Where'd you get this information, anyway? Maybe we should start there?"

"I'm a reporter, you know that. Right now I'm just following up on what I believe to be very credible information and if you'd help me get to the bottom of this I'd appreciate it. If not, well... I'll find out eventually. That's what I get paid to do."

"Okay, then, I'll see what I can do. In the meantime," he glanced at his watch, "I have a last minute appointment that came up this morning and I need to attend to it, but I thought that you should get to know what our company is all about. It'll help you to better understand just what we do and why we do it. I've arranged for somebody to give you an inside tour of the place. Of course, we do have areas that are restricted and you won't be able to access those, but you'll get a good feel for who we are and what we do."

Steph folded her arms across her chest. "Does an inside tour include your accounting department?"

"Unfortunately, that's proprietary," Mr. Cummings nodded, "but after you learn more about Agrico and who we are, we'll talk more about the so-called $200 million. Fair enough?"

"The more I can learn the better. But you're not just sending me on a PR tour are you? Because I really have much better—"

The door to Mr. Cummings office was open. "Mr. Cummings? Is now a good time?"

"Ah, Delynn." Mr. Cummings rose from his chair and waved. "Come in."

"I just got your message and I came right down. I hope I'm not too…" her face flushed and her feet riveted to the floor. "I mean, I hope I got the message right. You wanted to see me?"

"I did, and thanks for coming down so promptly. Delynn, this is Stephanie Moore. Miss Moore, this is Delynn Longo. Delynn is the manager of our genetic plant research and I've asked her to show you around. In fact, Delynn is one of our rising stars here at Agrico and you couldn't be in better hands."

Steph pushed away from the window and walked over to Delynn. "Delynn. I love that name. Nice to meet you." She extended her hand.

"And you too, Miss Moore. My pleasure." They clasped hands.

"Steph, please call me Steph."

Delynn nodded—nervously.

"Miss Moore, I mean Steph, is with the San Francisco Post, and she's doing an article on Agrico. I thought it would be a good idea if you showed her around and let her get a feel for the place. The more she knows the better she'll like us. Don't you think?"

"Certainly, I'd be happy to." Delynn turned to Steph. "Do you have anything specific in mind?"

"I do, but I don't think Mr. Cummings will allow me to see some of the things that I'm looking for. I'm told you have," she tilted her head, "what do you call them? Oh, yeah

proprietary things *and* restricted places. I'd like to see some of those, but I guess those are out-of-bounds."

"Listen," Mr. Cummings moved forward and stood between the two women. "We'll have time to go over everything you want in due course—we will. Talk to Diana when you finish up with Delynn and she'll find a time when we can meet again. In the meantime, Delynn will give you the V.I.P. tour. You'll be impressed, I'm sure."

Delynn led Steph down the main hallway, turned right and halfway down the corridor she ducked into a small, empty conference room pulling Steph with her. "My god, what are you doing here? Why didn't you warn me you were coming? I froze in my tracks when I saw you in Mr. Cummings office."

"I'm sorry, Delynn I didn't have time to—"

"And what happened to you?" Delynn's hands covered her gaping mouth. "That looks terrible. Does that… that have anything to do with… you know, this?"

"I ended up on the wrong end of a racquetball, that's all." Steph felt bad about the lie, but she knew the truth would scare Delynn and she'd clam-up. "It's better now, though."

"What were you doing with Mr. Cummings? Does he know what you're after? I sure hope not, because he's shrewd and he's for sure the most powerful exec we have here. If he knew I was involved with you in anyway, he'd can me and make sure no one would hire me again—ever."

"He invited me here. Well, actually I stopped by his house yesterday and that's how I met him."

143

"You went by his house! Oh, god, Steph, what does he know? Does he suspect anything?"

"He doesn't know anything about you knowing me or anything like that—I'm certain." Steph inched closer and lowered her voice, "What he does know is that Agrico has been funding Sustinere. But he hasn't admitted it to me—yet."

"How do you know that if he didn't say anything to you about it?" Delynn asked.

"I picked up a file on his desk that would give me all the answers, but he walked in when I was scanning through it. What I saw though, was enough to convince me I'm on the right track." Steph took two steps back and looked around the room. She took a deep breath and exhaled—slowly. "The file's called Off Balance Sheet Financing – Sustinere. I only saw four or five pages, but his name was everywhere. I think he's the guy who's been authorizing the money transfers."

Delynn's face was flushed, her hands trembled. "We should go and talk somewhere else. I don't like having this conversation in this building."

Delynn stuck her head out into the hallway and looked around. She grabbed Steph's arm and tugged. "Come on. Let's take a walk."

CHAPTER 24

The half day trek from Lo Gekar to Ghar Gumba and finally to the Ritseling cave had taken them through a landscape littered with eerie, empty shells of medieval castles perched on impossibly high peaks. Phil had spoken nonstop and had reinforced in Alex that he was nothing, if not tenacious, hard charging and fiercely loyal. Finally, when she had seen the towering cliffs looming ahead, she had relented. "Okay, we'll go back to the original plan, but there's one condition," she had said.

"Name it," Phil had said.

Alex had smiled. "You see the cliffs up there." She had pointed up ahead to their destination. "You carry my backpack there and you're back on the team."

"God, I thought you'd never give in. You're one tough nut to crack." He had reached over, slid Alex's pack from her shoulders and watched as she shot off ahead leaving a trail of dust in her wake.

They had seen hundreds of caves carved into the hillsides on their trek to Ritseling, so on their arrival they knew what to expect. "It seems like there are more entrances to this place than we've seen in any of the other caves." Phil took a step back. "There has to be some easy way these people got up there."

Benjamin un-shouldered his backpack and dropped it on the ground next to the others. "You sure he's expecting us?"

"He's expecting us. He hasn't made it easy so far and there's no reason he should now." Alex leaned back against the smooth, sandstone face and looked out at the awe-inspiring landscape. She felt dwarfed and humbled by its sheer ruggedness and beauty. "Let's redo our packs and then we'll be off." She pointed a finger straight up.

Phil reached over and picked up the daypack that Alex had pulled from her backpack. "Wheels? What's up with that? Where's your blue backpack you always carry around?"

"I bought this in Katmandu. I sort of liked it and who knows, maybe the wheels will come in handy," Alex replied as she rescued her daypack from Phil.

Phil shook his head and pinched his lower lip. "Nah, I'm not buying it. You're up to something."

Benjamin scanned the slots and the cracks in the sandstone. Most of the entrances were two, maybe three hundred feet up from where they stood. Shouldering small day packs and looking straight up the sandstone walls, Benjamin spoke first, "This won't be as hard as it looks." He pointed to his right. "That seam angles all the way up and there are plenty of holds to get us to the top. This rock's pretty soft and it'll splinter easily." He reached up, grabbed a hold of an outcropping and yanked; the rock crumbled and fell to the ground. "Make sure you test your hand and foot holds first, okay? It can crumble with the lightest touch. I'll go first. Wait until I get to the top and then Alex, you follow, then you, Phil."

Thirty minutes later, the three stood on a ledge and stared at an opening that led back into the cave where they each knew unexpected dangers awaited them. Wooden torches were nailed to the walls casting ominous shadows on the faded, century's old hand-painted murals. Phil stopped and surveyed the murals. "This is amazing, come here."

Phil pointed to a mural. "Look at these animals. Other than possibly the hare over here, they're all domestic animals—a goat, a sheep, a yak. Most ancient paintings depict the wild animals of the area because they believed the paintings would increase the native animal population. I'm guessing that the people who painted these either didn't hunt, which is unlikely, or there wasn't much in the way of wild game here. This was probably their way of trying to increase their own domestic stock."

Benjamin rubbed his fingers across a part of the mural depicting a group of men clustered around a fire. "What do you think's in their mugs?"

"That's an easy one." Phil said. "Most cultures had beer before they had an alphabet."

"A warm English beer sounds pretty good about now. How old are these paintings, do you think?" Benjamin asked.

"I have no way of knowing that. I don't know anything about this region, but Youten told me that these caves are probably 800 years old, maybe older. There's no reason these murals couldn't be that old," Phil said.

"Come on guys. This way," Alex waved a hand, "maybe we can look at those on the way out, but right now we have other things to do."

The two followed Alex's lead with Phil taking one last glance over his shoulder at the murals before they continued into the cave.

Rounding the second bend they came to an oversized steel door that ran from one wall to the other. Phil walked the length of the door, looking up and down. "The door slides to that side." His head nodded to the right. "The tricky part is how to move it."

Alex walked over to the door, looked over her shoulder at them both and said, "Remember, he already knows where we are." Her fist pounded on the door three times.

Moments later and without so much as a squeak, the door slid open. They stepped through into a room that looked more like a finely polished shrine than an ancient cave dwelling. The rock walls and floor were polished to a bright sheen, the quartz and black mica in the sandstone glistened. Electric lights hung overhead and soft, Jōruri music, a Japanese instrumental with roots in the 17th century, filled the room.

Benjamin's jaw dropped. "Not what I expected."

Phil, hunched over from the low ceiling, said, "Me... me neither."

"No chairs and I don't see any doors or any way to get through this room." Alex circled the room, her hand scraping against the wall. "Nothing. I guess at this point we just wait."

The door closed behind them as silently as it had opened.

The air was damp, but fresh. Alex leaned back against the polished wall and she felt her heart pound. She closed her eyes, took slow, deep breaths and willed her nerves to relax. When she opened her eyes she saw Phil pacing back and forth, his nerves fraying with each hurried footfall. Benjamin stood in the middle of the room, his hands combing through the sides of his hair and small beads of sweat puddled on his brows. Alex had always worked alone and she had mastered how to calm her own nerves and how to hone into her surroundings. She knew the importance of keeping her composure and to never telegraph her thoughts or emotions. What she didn't know was how to calm the unraveling nerves of others.

She pushed away from the wall, walked over to Benjamin and took his hand. She gave it a squeeze and grabbed Phil by the arm as he walked by. She spoke softly, "We're all a bit nervous here and rightfully so, but we have to stay focused—it's important." She tugged on Phil's arm. "You have more inner strength than anyone I know. I watched your resolve when we first started looking for Ben and I watched how you handled yourself at Koidu. We're not facing anything like that here. We're really not."

She turned and clenched Benjamin's shoulders. "You've been on the edge of death twice... and you beat it each time. I watched you swim the English Channel and you defied all odds to climb out on the French shore. What we face here is nothing compared to what you've already faced. He's just a guy that we're going to have a discussion with, that's all."

"We should have weapons," Benjamin said.

"We're better off this way. Now, each of you take a deep breath and relax. Keep focused on what we have planned." She threw her hands out, palms up, "Okay?"

Phil took a deep breath, held it and exhaled slowly. He shook his head. "I'm more nervous about Michelle than I am about me—or us."

"I understand. I really do. I felt the exact same way when you and I were looking for Ben, but I felt all along that he was okay and we'd get to him in time. And we did. We'll find Michelle and everything will turn out just the way you want." Alex winked and punched Phil in the arm. "It will."

The corners of Phil's lips began to rise. "Well, you've been right on everything all along so, sure—what the hell—one more time."

Phil threw an arm around Benjamin's neck and pulled him in. "You might have to use some more persuasion on this guy, though. He's more of the silver-spoon type who's not used to fighting his own battles."

"Spoken from a guy who's spent his adult life perched in an ivory tower." Benjamin slipped out from under Phil's grasp and bounced from foot to foot; throwing air punches to the side of Phil's head. "See—floats like a butterfly and stings like a bee. You know who stole that line from me?" Two more quick jabs. "Huh? Do you?"

Just like that the mood had changed and Alex saw the two old friends gain the strength and mettle they needed from the other. Her own nerves had calmed and she felt a sense of relief. She loved it when a plan came together.

"Alex Boudreau." A voice echoed through the room and the three froze, like tin soldiers waiting for a hand to drop and yank them away. "It's been such a long time and I am sorry to keep you waiting. Give me just a few more minutes and I will personally show you what I have in store for you."

CHAPTER 25

Two stout, gorilla-like men escorted the three down a narrow hallway. The men were dressed in traditional black and white Hakamas. The silk Hakamas were stitched with seven pleats, each pleat representing the seven virtues of *bushido*, considered essential to the samurai way. Alex nodded. She was not surprised that Kioshi had retained his deep-rooted samurai beliefs.

They were led into a room and Alex scanned her surroundings, committing every detail to memory. Twice the size of the room where they had waited earlier, it was round with the same polished finish. A large Byzantine marble-topped table rested in the center of the room with eight wooden high-back chairs neatly spaced around it. At the far end of the room were two matching stainless steel doors and hanging prominently in the center of the wall, between the two steel doors and behind the largest chair was an oil portrait of a samurai warrior. Dressed in full regalia, the warrior's eyes were the color of coal, rimmed by a single, thick brow. His sunken face was offset by high, prominent cheekbones. A perfect set of tightly clenched teeth were framed by narrow, thin lips. A Fu Manchu mustache hung inches below his tapered chin and matched his jet black silk-like hair tied in a knot atop his head.

Benjamin stood next to Alex, his arms folded across his chest and his head tilted. "Is that him?"

Alex nodded, "It is, but… he looks different. I can't put my finger on it, but something about him is different." She cocked her head. "Maybe the shape of his face. It seems more angular and his chin looks thinner, more tapered."

As Alex walked around the table, she looked underneath it and under the chairs and she felt the deep-set dark eyes, hanging on the far wall, following her every step. "I'd never forget those eyes, though."

She stopped in front of the portrait. She stared up at the likeness of the man she had not seen in over 15 years and memories of her past unfolded. Alex had never formally met Kioshi, but the man's facial features, smells and expressions had been etched in her memory. Especially his eyes, dark and cold like the breath of a grave; they blocked entry into his soul, yet burned like acid when penetrating his prey.

She had tailed Kioshi for two days before she had executed her plan to return the stolen uranium to her client. Kioshi had a regular entourage of bodyguards and direct access to him had been out of the question. It had been at a small restaurant in Peshawar, Pakistan, where Alex had sat close enough to Kioshi to smell his contempt.

"Let's see where these doors lead. I don't like the idea of just sitting around waiting for that son-of-a-bitch to make his grand entrance." Phil stood to the side of the table, an elbow cocked on the back of a chair. "I can feel it, Michelle's close by. Let's go." He straightened his arm, puffed out his chest and moved toward the door.

"Wait, let's wait a little longer." Alex waved a hand. "This is where Kioshi wanted to meet us and there's nothing in here that looks suspicious or dangerous. Let's wait it out here."

Phil spun around and walked back to Alex. He jammed his hands in his pockets. "Okay… okay, but not too long. I want to find her."

"We all want the same thing and within the next—"

A door opened and a man dressed in the same traditional Hakama stood in the doorway. Tall, slender and old, he was nothing like the muscle-bound goons who had frisked them upon entering the cave. He moved with crisp efficiency and spoke perfect English without a hint of an accent. "Nakajima-san will be in shortly. In the meantime, he has asked that you be seated and make yourselves comfortable. I will see that you are served some tea and if there is anything else you may need, please let me know. My name is Kenji." The man bowed, turned and walked out through the doorway. The door closed automatically.

"Well, there's at least one guy who doesn't pose a threat to us," Benjamin said.

"Maybe our luck's changing." Phil looked at Alex. "Shall we do as we're told and sit?"

Alex nodded. "Grab a seat guys." She looked around the table and pointed. "Ben, why don't you sit there and Phil, you sit across from him. I'll sit over here where I'll have the best view of Kioshi."

Alex sat at one end of the table on the opposite side from where she knew Kioshi would sit. She looked over at Phil, and was relieved he showed no outward signs of nervousness or apprehension. His hands were clenched and rested on the table with his forefingers extended and his thumbs pressed tightly together. His neck turned slowly and his eyelids narrowed as he scanned the room. His face was still flaked with red marks from the biting winds they endured over the past several days. Alex knew that if their success could be determined by the strength of that man's heart and moxie, they would have no problems.

She turned to Ben. He sat erect, shoulders squared, and the beads of sweat that had earlier lined his brows were gone. His arms were folded across his chest and white knuckles gripped his biceps. He looked tense, on edge, but Alex knew that inside he had already summoned the strength to win and the will to remain calm. She had seen it before in him and she saw it again—now.

Finally, the door opened and four women walked through followed by Kenji. The women were dressed in provocative, western clothing and were strikingly beautiful. Alex recognized them for what they were and turned her attention to Kenji who was carrying a tray. "Thank you for bringing us tea," she said.

"Any chance you might have some coffee back there?" Phil pointed at the door.

Kenji bowed. "I am sorry sir, but tea is all we have."

Alex saw Phil hide his disappointment. "Then tea it is, thank you," Phil said.

"Alex Boudreau, in the flesh." The voice floated through the dimly lit cavern as smoothly as a snake through grass. The three turned and saw Kioshi walk through the doorway. One at a time, his eyes laser beamed into each of them until finally his glare landed on Alex. His facial features were identical to the portrait, but he was not the giant of a man portrayed in the painting. Kioshi was no taller than Alex, but his shoulders were broad and his neck thick. He walked around the side of the table and over to where Alex sat. His hands were clasped at his waist. He bowed.

Kioshi turned, walked back to the head of the table, pulled his chair out and sat down. He stroked the strands of his Fu Manchu and spoke, "I have waited for this day for a very long time. Do you know how long it has been?"

Alex returned Kioshi's gaze and noticed that two men had entered the room when she must not have been looking. They were the same height and build as Kioshi and wore identical clothing and Alex guessed that under their Kimonos they were bullnecked and all-around built for power. "We will have plenty of time to discuss our past." She paused and waited for Kioshi to blink, then continued, "Are you going to introduce your two friends to us?" Her eyes moved to the two men who had entered the room unnoticed. Each stood by the side of the doors with their backs facing them, their faces hidden.

Kioshi waved off Alex's request. "In due course."

Alex narrowed her eyes. "I have a business proposition for you, but before I present it, I need to know that Michelle Brophy is here and that she is being well taken care of."

Kioshi smirked. "The American, Michelle, as you call her, is here and enjoying her stay very much. You may take my word on that."

"I hope you don't take this the wrong way, but your *word* doesn't really mean much to me." Alex's instinct was her second sight, her sixth sense, and it was on high alert. "Unless we can see Michelle and know that she is alright, I won't proceed any further with my proposal to you."

Kioshi's hissing laugh echoed off the rock walls. "Look around you. You are in my home, my refuge and the only way out of here is through me." He leaned forward and kept his boiling gaze on Alex. "You are in no position to be making any demands of me."

Alex shook her head. "It's not a demand. I'm merely making a request to you, so that you will show your good faith before we proceed. I'm offering you something very lucrative, but I first need to know that Michelle is here and that she's safe. I'm sure you find this to be a reasonable request."

Kioshi snapped his fingers and the blonde woman walked over to him and bent down. He whispered something in her ear; she turned and walked out of the room. "You will see her shortly. Now, please do not take *this* the wrong way, Alex, but I have a hard time believing that you have come all this way to make me a business proposition." He pushed his narrow chin forward. "What is the true purpose of your visit?"

Alex glanced at Benjamin and Phil and saw they were fixed on Kioshi and his every move. She reached into her backpack and pulled out a lipstick container. She unscrewed the top, removed a flash drive and held it up in her fingertips. "You have an arrangement with Andre Broussard involving a new virus and I—"

Benjamin jerked in his chair, spun toward Alex and yelled, "Andre! You never told me he had anything to do with this. You know I'm not having anything to do with that scumbag."

Alex pushed back in her chair, stared at Benjamin and saw his dagger-like look. Her eyes widened. "As I was saying," she turned her attention back to Kioshi, "I know you have an arrangement with Andre Broussard to produce a vaccine for a new virus you've developed. I have a way to produce the same vaccine for less money and a quicker way for you to get your approvals in the United States. I can make you more money and I'll take less than you had agreed to pay Andre."

Alex flipped the flash drive across the table and it slid to a stop in front of Kioshi. He looked at the blue plastic coated drive, back up at Alex and then he reached down and picked it up. He held it out and stared at it like it was a key to a riddle. At the sound of a finger snap, the raven haired woman walked over to Kioshi. He held out the drive. "Take this and have it scanned for viruses. I'll look at it later."

Benjamin slid his chair down next to Alex and leaned into her. What began as a whisper developed into a loud, venomous rant, "... and you've deceived me again. You've played me for a fool again and I fucking fell for it! Let me repeat it again, so everyone at this table can hear it." His face was now inches away from Alex's and he continued, "There is absolutely no way that GEN will produce any vaccine, antidote or *anything* for Broussard or this guy at the other end of the table. *No fucking way!*"

Kioshi twisted the ends of his Fu Manchu. His eyes were now mere slits and his mouth nothing more than a seam across the bottom half of his face. "Mr. Hunter, I know very little about you, but you have been featured prominently in the news over the past year or so and from what I have read, you went through some rather harrowing times. As a man who himself was infected with deadly virus, I would surmise that you would have a keen interest in developing cures for these types of things. If that is the case, then you and I have several things in common. We should talk about this some more."

"You and I have nothing in common—*not a damn thing!*" Benjamin flung his hands in rage and continued, "People like you always end up getting caught one way or another and I promise you that I'll do everything possible to see that you're exposed and pay for what you're doing."

"I commend you on your noble ideals, Mr. Hunter, but what I have planned is already in motion and neither you, nor anyone else," Kioshi looked at Alex through the corners of his eyes, "can stop things at this point. Time is ticking away and we are down to counting the second hand."

Kioshi's thumb and forefinger stroked his Fu Manchu again and his eyes drilled into Alex. "I will look at your proposal later, assuming you haven't infected it with something and I hold that to be a strong possibility. In the meantime, you have cost me more time and money than I could recover from any proposal you may have for me."

Alex smiled. "You are a very shrewd businessman and I'm sure that missing uranium didn't slow you down for more than a few days; a week at the most."

"You are right, I replaced it quickly and within a few years I had forgotten all about you. Unfortunately, when you surfaced in my business a year ago, I regretted the fact that I had not taken care of you like I wanted to back then. That is a mistake I will not make again."

"What are you talking about, a year ago?" Alex asked.

"The mere mention of one particular virus in this world brings instant panic to the infectious disease community when it hears its name." Kioshi folded his hands and continued, "Russia and the United States have vials of this virus stored in secret locations that really are not all that secret when one starts to snoop around. The Russians are quite unpredictable and tend to overcomplicate much of their military procedures in taking care of things. This makes it too risky to steal anything from them. The Americans are quite the opposite. They are too trusting and their security measures too lax when it comes to protecting vitals secrets. The Russians store this virus at a lab in Novosibirsk where they can keep a close eye on things while the Americans hide it in some out of the way laboratory in the jungles of Brazil thinking no one will be able to find it there. In today's world you can find anything. The trick is to take it without getting caught. The American laboratory in Brazil may have been totally unguarded for what little effort it took me."

"Are you talking about the HCL and the G-16 virus?" Alex fought to remain outwardly cool and not telegraph her surprise. "You have that virus? You were involved down there too?"

"When you exposed the G-16 virus to the world, I expected the Americans to swarm into HCL and lockdown the facility. That is exactly what the Russians would have done. I had a guy working down there for me and he was able to remove a vial of G-16 and a vial of smallpox ahead of the Americans who showed up days later to close down the facility." Kioshi laughed, "He flew halfway around the world carrying a vial of smallpox in his pants' pocket. Imagine that in today's age."

Kioshi looked back at Alex. "That's when I decided I needed to track you down and take care of you once and for all." His teeth glinted.

"So if you have the G-16 virus, you may have the only known supply of that left." Alex said.

Kioshi shrugged his shoulders. "The G-16 virus was a brilliant creation and it has many uses, but it also has its flaws. I'm in the business of selling weapons; I just have different types of weapons now than I did when our paths first crossed. The business of selling Abrams tanks, MAC-10s, Colt M4s, Skyrangers or any military hardware is no longer lucrative. Even the legitimate companies are selling on the black market now and they have cut our profit margins down to next to nothing. Biological weaponry, that is today's market. The G-16 has tremendous potential, but its delivery method is too difficult, too slow to reach thousands at just the right moment. It does have unparalleled backup potential, though."

"Tell me you don't intend to unleash smallpox?" Alex asked with mounting terror.

"Hah, you catch on quickly." Kioshi crowed and sat back. "They stopped vaccinating against smallpox in the mid-70s so anyone born after that time is a likely target. The key to creating my new weapon combines the best features of the G-16 virus with the best features of smallpox. Targets can be identified and hit with pinpoint accuracy. It's brilliant and outright devastating."

Alex sat on the front of her chair, her hands clenched. She made every effort to keep her voice silky and calm. "You can't be serious. How do you know it will even work?"

Kioshi's thick, single brow shot up. "Oh, I am serious, quite serious. I already have more orders than I can fill and the profit margins are better than anything I have ever sold before. The one problem I have is I guarantee everything I sell. I want my customers to be happy, so I need to test things out ahead of time, find my own lab rats, so to speak, and make sure everything works as I planned. My final results are coming in right now so within the next few weeks I will start filling orders. Once that is done, I will sell the vaccine to cure the disease that I helped spread." He sat back and held up his arms. "Rather brilliant, when you think about it."

Alex looked at Phil, his face had lost its color and he was slumped back in his chair. His eyes flashed and then narrowed into mere slits. Opposite him, Ben was locked on Kioshi with a death stare. Alex could see that he had clenched his fists so hard that his nails had dug into his palms and a tiny trickle of blood had dropped to the floor. He was coiled and ready to pounce any second.

Alex smiled. "The brilliant part of your plan is you're going to like my proposal even better than I thought."

Benjamin shot up from his chair sending it crashing to the floor. His stare was as black as midnight. "Alex, you belong in the same place as this asshole and I'm done with this whole charade." A fissure seemed to pass between them.

Before Benjamin could take a step, Kioshi clapped his hands and the two men behind him turned around. They each pointed Ruger 357 magnums in the direction of Benjamin. More startling, the two men were exact clones of Kioshi; their hair, cheekbones, eyes, lips, ears—all identical.

CHAPTER 26

Benjamin sat in his chair, his fingers pressed against his bruised and bloodied cheek.

Kioshi was on his throne, flanked on each side by his matching bodyguards. "In case it is not obvious to you, Mr. Hunter, you nor your friends have any way of leaving here unless I allow it. Those types of outbursts will not help your cause in any way. I trust you understand that now?"

Benjamin had been on the receiving end of two sharp blows from the butts of the Rugers when he had charged Kioshi moments ago. The force from the blows had sent him reeling to the floor and he had been ordered, at gunpoint, to return to his chair. His face was grim and his shoulders slumped, but his eyes focused squarely on Kioshi and reflected the rage boiling within. "The part about leaving, I understand. Why you're doing what you're doing, I don't. It's pure lunacy."

"Lunacy? Perhaps it is, but I would not know. People have called me mad and I take that as a high form of compliment. Madness, you see Mr. Hunter, when it is put to proper use is really the purest form of sanity. You and I look at things differently, that's all."

"Very impressive." Alex sat upright in her chair; her right hand, half-clenched, was fully extended and rested on the table, her left hand was hidden below. "But the rules have now changed. You're going to ask your two goons to leave the room so we can finish our discussion. If you don't, I'll pull the trigger and you'll have no reason to keep your harem girls here any longer."

Kioshi raised his eyebrow, his lower face was etched with an ominous grin. "As clever as always, I see, but this time you have flinched too soon, I am afraid. You have two guns aimed at you and the moment you pull your trigger, a spray of bullets will rip through the heart of you and your friends within seconds. Is that a fair trade?"

Alex's eyes were fixed on Kioshi. "Three people sacrificing their lives to rid the world of you and to save the thousands you intend to kill. I'll make that trade anytime. Now, ask them to leave and we'll make this a win-win for us both."

"Kobayashi Maru. Do you understand its meaning?"

"It has several meanings. You're obviously referring to the samurai meaning, I suppose?" Alex asked.

"That is the only meaning with any true significance. All of my men are put to that test before I deem them worthy of being my true warriors. The two men you killed when you stole my uranium were about to begin Kobayashi Maru when you, unfortunately, intervened. Now, you are placed in a Kobayashi Maru and you must decide whether to use your weapon of choice on me or one of my friends here. Who is the real Kioshi? I am guessing that you have only a single shot."

Kioshi was right, she knew it. Alex's threat to sacrifice her life, along with Benjamin's and Phil's, had been rebuffed and she found herself in Kioshi's Kobayashi Maru. At the sight of Benjamin's jaw shattering, she had reacted out of panic, instead of relying on her hard, calculating and emotionless instinct she had perfected over the years. Without thinking, she had reached down, removed one of the wheels from her daypack and slid the axle—a dark, cylindrical shaped plastic tube—out from the bottom. The cylinder, the same one she had removed from her safe deposit box in Paris, had been a sheath, covering a plastic ballistic knife. Originally designed and manufactured in Russia for the needs of criminals, a ballistic knife was a spring loaded weapon with a detachable blade that ejected with the press of an operating switch or trigger. Alex had modified her ballistic knife using compressed air for propulsion, so it wouldn't run the risk of spring fatigue over time. Not to mention the fact that it would easily avoid detection by even the most sensitive metal detectors.

Alex reached in her backpack and pulled out a flash drive from a separate lipstick container. Holding it in her fingers with the tip of the metal casing exposed through her fingertips, she rose and held up her hand. "This is a remote detonator and once I push it, the plastic C-4 explosives that I left planted in the entrance to this place will ignite and the entrance will be obliterated."

She moved to her left and stood behind Benjamin. The three faces showed no reaction to her threat. Instead, six eyes followed her every step. "I'm sure you have another exit, but the size of the explosion will be seen for miles and the men we have stationed outside have their orders once they see it. They'll fire a Tornado Rocket Launcher and within minutes a salvo of 120 millimeter rockets will pelt this cave and all your expensive decorations. You will be covered by tons of crushed rock. So you see, contrary to what you said, there's still a good use for military hardware."

She kept her ballistic knife pointed at Kioshi and walked along the side of the table. "You're right; you should have killed me years ago when you had the chance. Tell me something, what were the names of your two men that I killed? I have a story about them I want to tell you."

Kioshi's cold eyes stared at Alex and his brick wall persona appeared to harden even more.

Alex moved behind Kioshi and stuck the point of her ballistic knife into the back of his neck. "Tell me their names."

Kioshi bristled. "Ren and Takuma."

"Right, Ren and Takuma." She moved to the side of Kioshi keeping her ballistic knife pointed at him. "Takuma, he was the one with the mustache I think. Is that right?"

Kioshi nodded.

"When you found Takuma you probably thought he died from the bullet hole in his head, but he didn't." Alex stepped to the side and came up behind the bodyguard on Kioshi's right. She stuck the point of her ballistic knife into the back of his neck and continued, "No, Takuma died a very slow death and the bullet hole was nothing more than an afterthought on my part. When he pleaded for his life, he did so in English. I thought that was strange since Japanese was his native tongue and we had conversed in Japanese up to that point. Did you know he spoke English?"

The bodyguard stood rigid and looked straight ahead. Alex pushed the tip of her knife harder into the man's neck puncturing his skin. "Did you?"

"Yes, all of my men speak English."

Alex walked over to the third man and stopped. The moment his eyes locked onto hers, she swung the knife around and aimed it at his heart. "I'm going to walk around behind you and over to that door and I don't want you to move. I don't want you to blink."

The sound of heavy breathing filled the room. When she reached the back of the man, she drilled the knife-point into his neck and her left hand grabbed his wrist and twisted it down. The Ruger fell to the floor. "Now, Kioshi, your charade's over. Like I said earlier, have these two leave the room and we'll continue our business."

CHAPTER 27

The unmasking of the true Kioshi had been a game of wits that Alex had won; neither of the two men she had killed in Pakistan had a mustache nor spoke English. She locked stares with Kioshi, but she knew the Kobayashi Maru was not over. They were in the middle of his fortress and she had no idea what was behind the two steel doors or what other defenses Kioshi had at his fingertips.

Alex walked over to the wall and pulled down one of the samurai swords. She walked back behind the real Kioshi. "Sit down." She pressed the cold steel blade against the back of his neck. "Cloning a couple of lookalikes—very clever. You want to tell me how you did that?"

Kioshi sat erect with his hands folded on the table, his face expressionless. "The ways of the Western World are clouded with unnecessary hurdles that make it far too difficult to blend science and technology to its fullest potential. All I have done is take what was already developed by American scientists and perfected it, using my own laboratory methods free from outside interference." He dropped his chin to his chest and closed his eyes.

Alex pressed the blade of the sword harder. "There's no way to change facial features in adults. I've heard about experiments done with mice to change facial features in the embryonic stage, but as an adult, I don't think so."

"You have obviously been schooled to think as a westerner and not as someone who is not afraid to reach out and try new things. A human's facial features have more than 4,000 small regions of DNA and with just a few genetic tweaks the face can be subtly altered. We know there are thousands of specific non-coding distant-acting enhancers that are working to influence the activity of facial genes. These are short stretches of DNA that act like switches, turning genes on or off." Kioshi put his hands on the table and began to stand.

Alex grabbed Kioshi's shoulder and pushed down. "You're not going anywhere—sit."

Slowly, Kioshi sat back down. "Surely you do not think you can stay here, in this room, much longer? In due course we will have visitors who will clearly side with me."

"I have something special for you in mind. Don't worry about us." Alex glanced at the two steel doors and then back at Kioshi. "First, though, I want to know more about facial alteration. I may be able to buy the fact that minor changes can occur by manipulating the distant-acting enhancers, but only minor ones. Maybe you could change the size of someone's lips or their hairline or even an ear lobe, but you can't alter the existing bone structure. I don't see that as possible."

"But that's the easiest part. You're focused on what I have been talking about and not on what is already known. My two bodyguards were already the same height and close to the same build as me, but all three of us made facial changes so we would look alike. We had facial implants to change those areas we could not modify through gene manipulation. Our chins, cheek bones, jaws and ears were molded with implants to be identical. Everything is done on the inside so there are no visible scars and it heals in no time. The rest of the changes; lips, eyebrows, hair color and hairline, eye lashes and this scar," Kioshi's forefinger traced a scar on his left cheek, "were all done by genetic manipulation."

Phil pounded the table and yelled, "That's enough of this. Where's Michelle!"

Kioshi hissed, "As you can see, I'm in no position to escort you to her."

Alex slid the sword to one side and cut a small gash in the back of Kioshi's neck, piercing his skin. "I think you're going to take us on a tour and lead us to Michelle." She moved a step back and saw droplets of blood trickle down his neck. "That's my version of facial alteration and I have more, lots more, if needed."

Kioshi pointed to the far wall. "If you walk over to that glass panel and touch it, you will see that your friend is quite comfortable."

Phil looked at Alex and she nodded. He rushed over to the glass panel and tapped it with his index finger.

The panel lit brightly showing six grids that appeared to be still-cam shots.

Kioshi spoke, "That is an LED glass screen that operates much the same as any iPhone. On the lower right corner is an interactive menu. Touch it and you can navigate from there."

Phil touched the Menu icon and a list of commands scrolled up.

"Touch 'activate'." Kioshi said.

Phil touched the activate command and the screen came to life and the six grids showed real time cam shots. In the upper left hand corner Michelle appeared, sitting at a table. Phil reached up and swiped the grid and it enlarged to cover the entire screen. Michelle was wearing the same clothes that she wore the last time Phil had seen her. Her hair was pulled back in a ponytail and her face was painted with worry. "I want to see her—*now.*" Phil demanded.

"You can talk to her if you wish. Touch the screen."

Phil touched the screen and a series of commands appeared. He touched 'voice'. "Michelle! Michelle! Are you okay? Can you hear me?"

Michelle's head jerked and her brows widened. "Phil? Is that you? Where are you?" She jumped up and spun around in circles.

"I'm here, right here and I'm going to have you out of there in a few minutes. Are you okay?"

"I'm worried sick about... well, about everything, but yeah, I'm okay. Where are you?"

"I'm here in the cave with Ben and Alex and we'll have you out of there in a sec."

Phil looked at Kioshi. "How do I get there?"

"Wait," Alex interjected, "at least we know she's safe, but we have a few things to get out of the way first." Alex walked over to the screen. "Michelle, this is Alex. We'll get you out of there very soon. We have a couple of things to do first. You'll be okay, just sit tight a little longer." She touched the mute button.

Michelle's head continued to search for the voices in the room and her lips mouthed a string of silent words. Phil stood in front of the screen, slack-jawed.

Alex turned to Kioshi. "I want the flash drive I handed to you earlier and then you and I are going to discuss my business proposal."

She walked over to the table and picked up one of the discarded Rugers, opened the slide and removed the magazine. Seeing it was full, she reinserted it and motioned to Kioshi, "Let's take a walk and show me where I can get it. And remember, I'm right behind you and at this time of day my patience always runs on the thin side."

She prodded Kioshi in his shoulder with the tip of the handgun. "There are cameras everywhere so right now we're being tracked." She looked at Phil and Benjamin. "Both of you walk next to Kioshi and I'll be right behind ready to fire if needed. And Ben," Alex smiled, "great acting job. You almost had me believing you."

"It wasn't hard; really, just the sound of Andre's name can send me off," Benjamin said.

"Yeah, what was that all about?" Phil asked. "You looked like you were really pissed."

"It was Alex's idea. When I talked to her last night about you coming in she finally agreed. She came up with a plan to make it look like she'd duped me again; I'd get mad and that way this asshole might not try and use us against each other." Benjamin rubbed his bruised chin. "This wasn't part of the plan though."

Alex slid her ballistic knife across the table to Benjamin. "You wanted firepower, here you go. Careful of the trigger, it's hypersensitive."

Once they passed through the metal door they walked in formation

166

through a curved hallway. They reached a room where seven people were seated in front of computer monitors. Alex stopped. "Tell these people to sit tight and then we'll keep walking."

Kioshi did as he was told and they proceeded through the room and into another hallway. Alex had sharpened her senses and knew she needed to expect the unexpected. There was no way Kioshi was going to make this easy—no way. She felt the raised hair on her arms bristle against her shirt sleeves. She stopped to listen for noises, whispers—anything. Her eyes darted about and she took quick sniffs with her nose. She heard and felt the air part behind her, but she was too late. A blow to her head sent her crashing to the floor.

CHAPTER 28

lex lay on her side. Her head pounded and she felt leather straps digging into her wrists and ankles. Her right eye opened and she squinted, taking in her surroundings. The room was barren and small, not much bigger than the walk-in closet at her apartment. The walls and floor were crags of unpolished rock and the room was dimly lit by a single light bulb dangling from the ceiling. The steel door had no knob or even hinges on the inside. There was no escape route. She pushed up from the floor, sat back against the cold wall and squeezed her legs to her chest. She dropped her head and rubbed her left eye against her knee; specks of crusty blood rolled down her leg. The harder she pulled and twisted the more the leather straps tightened and dug further into her skin.

Damn, how could I let this happen? She had no recollection of what had occurred or how long she had been in that room. Judging from the dried blood, she knew it had been at least 30 minutes.

Alex wasn't one to sit around. She knew she had to act now before someone came to check on her. She pushed herself to her knees and shook her head to clear the lingering wooziness.

She heard the pinging thud of the door slamming against the rock wall—too late. Two men entered, walked over to her, grabbed her arms and lifted her to her feet. Vice-like grips clenched her forearms. A single nod left no room for bargaining—she knew she had better follow their commands.

The two men led Alex into a room that she thought must be the command center for Kioshi's operations. One wall had three large glass panels that she assumed must be the same interactive LED glass panels she had seen earlier. Two PCs sat on a table and each was flanked by a satellite phone. The men dragged Alex to the center of an oval-shaped black and maroon rug, and one man reached down and slammed his arm into the back of her legs. She buckled and fell to her knees. She heard muffled screams behind her and turned her head. "Are you two alright?" she yelled.

They each nodded, but their narrowed eyes projected the venom that simmered inside. Benjamin and Phil were bound with the same leather straps that held Alex in check and their mouths were gagged with tape.

Alex lurched forward on her knees toward Benjamin and Phil and a hard-soled boot slammed in her chest. The man glared at Alex. "Stay right where you are or the next kick will break a few bones in that pretty face of yours."

Alex knew she could roll to her side and even with her feet bound, she could kick the man's feet out from under him and deliver another kick to his groin. But she was no match for both men. She would have to wait things out for another opportunity. "I just want to make sure my friends are alright, that's all. Ungag them and let me find out for myself."

"Not a chance. You wait right where you are and Nakajima-san will be here soon enough."

Alex's mind raced. *Think, Alex.* Her eyes swept the room and landed on two wakizashi samurai swords mounted on the wall to her left. Even if she could cripple the man next to her, she knew she wouldn't be able to reach a sword in time with her ankles bound before the other man would be on her. She took a deep breath and let it out slowly, silently. No, she'd have to wait this out a little longer.

The door opened and Kioshi stood in the threshold, his arms folded across his chest. His dark, sinister eyes bore into Alex. After a few moments, he grinned and let out a harrowing laugh. "Finally... after all these years... it's time."

He dropped his arms, and with long, purposeful strides he moved toward the wall with the two wakizashi swords. He grabbed one of the swords by its hilt, slid it from the rack and spun around toward Alex. He brandished the sword and took two sharp downward swings, then two more. "This blade is made from a steel called tamahagane, produced from iron sand and used only for samurai swords." He scraped his fingernail across the blade. "It holds the sharpest edge of any sword ever made." His teeth flashed.

Kioshi walked slowly back to Alex and stood several feet in front of her. He pulled a tantō from his belt, leaned forward and placed it on the floor in front of Alex. His steeled eyes looked down at Alex and he waved at the two men standing on each side of her. "You two may go now and leave me alone—to do the honor."

Kioshi's eyes narrowed and his lips pursed. His foot kicked the tantō sword closer to Alex. "That sword is used for *Seppuku*. This is part of the samurai honor code and used by warriors when they knew they were going to fall into the hands of their enemies. You will grab the sword with both hands," Kioshi held an imaginary sword with both hands, "and you will plunge it into your abdomen and move it from left to right—like this." Kioshi thrust his fists into his stomach. "But I am sure you already know how to perform *Seppuku*, am I correct?"

Alex met Kioshi's glare and through the corner of her eyes she watched the two men exit the room and close the door. She needed to take control. "I didn't come here for you to seek revenge, but to offer you a business proposal. If you had seen my proposal, you wouldn't have me kneeling on the floor holding a death sword over me."

"Quite the contrary, I did read your proposal, but I have already rejected it outright. You see, you're too late. I already have everything I need to produce the virus and once that virus is discovered and begins to spread, well, that is when our good friend, Andre, steps in, uses his connections and begins distributing the vaccine worldwide. Governments will be clamoring for it and won't give a damn that it has not been tested on humans. This will be mankind's only choice and the world will come begging. Maybe you could produce the vaccine cheaper and possibly even be more convincing than Andre with those in need of the vaccine, but," Kioshi crouched down on one knee and continued, "there are billions of dollars at stake here and do you really think that saving a few pennies makes any difference to me?" He returned to both feet.

"I can't argue with you about Andre's connections. He has people in his pocket all around the world, but I can use GEN to get you into the U.S. market much quicker than he can. You know that."

Kioshi lowered his sword and ran the tip of the blade up from Alex's stomach, circled her breasts and then ran the tip along the side of her neck. He flipped her hair away from her face. "It is a shame that we could not have known each other under different circumstances. You are a beautiful woman and there is no doubt I would have made you one of my most prized possessions. You would have enjoyed yourself, but now, it is time for you to die—with honor—if you so choose."

"I don't think you fully—"

"Silence!" Kioshi swung the sword over the top of Alex's head and then took one step back. His hands twirled in rapid succession and he spun the sword in circles in front of him. He stepped closer to Alex and cut the leather straps from her wrists.

Alex reached down and wrapped both hands around the hilt of the tantō. Slowly, she lifted the sword up and pressed the tip into her stomach. She looked over at Benjamin and saw the shock wash across his face. His watery, bloodshot eyes bulged from their sockets. She heard the terror in his muffled screams. She looked up at Kioshi and then—lunged—backwards. Her ankles passed over the top of her, she slashed the sword down and cut through the leather ankle binds. She spun and crouched down on her feet.

Kioshi reacted on instinct. He turned, raised the wakizashi to one side and unleashed the blade toward Benjamin's head.

Alex sprung forward, flying in mid-air toward Kioshi. She reached out with her tantō and sliced through his Achilles tendon. Kioshi buckled backwards, let out a curdling shriek as the wakizashi crossed over the top of Benjamin's ducking head.

Kioshi lay sprawled on the floor, a tantō stuck in his back.

Alex uncut the leather straps from Benjamin's and Phil's wrists. Benjamin pushed to his feet and met Alex's embrace. They stood still, tightly wrapped in each other's arms, trembling from the thought that they might not ever have held each other again.

Phil cut the strap from his ankles, walked over to Kioshi and placed a finger on his carotid artery. "This asshole's gone." He stepped over to Alex and Benjamin, wrapped his arms around them and squeezed. "Let's go find Michelle and get the hell out-a-here."

Alex dropped her hands to Benjamin's waist and leaned her head back. She was still trembling. "I'll never forget that look on your face when I stuck that sword into my stomach." She brushed a tear from her eye. "I didn't know what I was going to do, only that I had to find some way to keep you alive."

Benjamin took Alex's face between his hands, bent down and gave her a tender kiss on her nose. He smiled. "Now he's out of our lives. Phil's right, let's get the hell out of here and go home."

Alex stood on her toes and looked at Benjamin. Their eyes closed and their lips met. Phil sliced the leather strap from Benjamin's ankles and said, "There, at least you won't be hobbling out of here. Enough of that, let's get the hell out of here—come on—*now*."

Alex knelt down beside Kioshi and lifted the ponytail from the back of his neck. "We're not done yet. This isn't Kioshi; it's a clone." She threw her shoulders back and stiffened her spine. "With the cameras they have here I suspect we'll see the real Kioshi any second, or at the least another clone. You two go over to those screens and see if you can find a schematic for this place and find us another exit. I'm going to snatch those two hard drives to look at later."

CHAPTER 29

Steph and Chandler were stretched out on the couch, propped up against opposite armrests with their toes massaging the other's feet. Earlier in the week, Chandler had received a promotion at work. Aside from more money and a larger office, the promotion meant extra traveling, two or three times a month, to the company's satellite office in Honolulu. This was the first night the two had been alone since Chandler had received the promotion and as soon as Steph heard the news she opened a bottle of wine and unleashed a bevy of questions—mostly about Hawaii and how she would travel as a stowaway, if necessary, to tag along on some of those trips.

Chandler took the last sip of wine and held the glass in both hands. "What about you? I'm guessing that your day wasn't too shabby either. Anything new on the Agrico story?"

Steph groaned. "I wish I could put everything together, but I can't yet. There's something about this Cummings guy that I can't figure out. The guy's a rock star at Agrico and everybody's in awe of him. You mention his name around his office and people just drool. Chief thinks I'm barking up the wrong tree going after him, but I don't know… I think he's got his hands in the pot."

"Speaking of Chief, I don't know why I keep forgetting to tell you this, but I think he rides our bus," Chandler said.

"No, get out of here, no way. I see him every day and I haven't picked up on anything." Steph smiled, "and my gaybar is always working."

"I never thought anything about it when I met him the first time, but when I was at your office a few weeks ago it hit me. I could tell by—"

The doorbell rang. "You expecting anyone?" Chandler asked.

"Just the food we ordered. That was quick." Steph stood, "I'll get the door."

"Dad. This is… well sorta a surprise. Is something wrong?"

"No, not at all. I was on my way to an engagement not far from here and I thought I'd stop by to see you. Is this a good time?"

"No, I mean yeah, come on in." Steph moved to the side

Mr. Weintraub's eyes swept through the apartment. "This is a nice place. I like what you've done. It looks quite comfortable."

"Most everything you see is Chandler's. I'm kinda surprised, dad, this is the first time you've been here." Steph leaned back against the wall and threaded her fingers together. "Can I get you something? Anything? We don't have much in the fridge, but let me see what I can find."

"No, no, I'm fine. I won't be staying long. I need—"

"Hi, Mr. Weintraub." Chandler came around the corner and eyed Steph. "Here, let me take your coat and you can have a seat over there."

"Thank you, Chandler." Mr. Weintraub handed his overcoat to Chandler, pulled a chair out from the dining table and sat down. "How's everything with you? Are you still working at…. I can't remember the name of the company, but are you still there?"

"Vyodyne and yes, I'm still there. It's working out really well, thanks."

"Chandler was just promoted to Assistant Vice President, so really well is an understatement," Steph beamed.

"Well, that's terrific. I'm sure congratulations are in order."

"I'm glad you came by. We just ordered some take-out that should be here any minute. You're welcome to join us." Steph handed her dad a glass of water and took a seat next to him. "Chinese."

"My favorite." Mr. Weintraub made a feeble attempt at sarcasm and then continued, "I actually wanted to talk to you about work and to see how you'd feel about taking on some new responsibilities."

Steph tilted her head. "I would like to graduate from covering local events, but I was going to finish my Agrico story first and then I was going to talk to Chief about that."

"Cliff's told me you're doing a great job and he thinks you have a real nose for the business. That's quite a compliment coming from him. There's nobody better at running a newsroom than Cliff." Mr. Weintraub spread his thumb and forefinger and rubbed his neck. "I was thinking you'd like to get involved with advertising and circulation. We could use some help there and I think you'd be great at it. It would be good for you. What do you say?"

Steph rolled her eyes. "Sounds like a desk job to me. I think I'll stay put in the newsroom. I know you're not all that excited about me working on the Agrico story, but when I'm done I bet you'll change your mind."

"She's totally consumed with that story. I hardly ever see her anymore," Chandler said.

"You've always had a strong work ethic and that's why I think you should be doing more with your life. There's a lot more to the newspaper business than reporting."

Steph shot up from her seat and turned to her father. "Did you stop by to talk to me as my dad or as my boss?"

His hands parted. "Both. You've earned a promotion from everything I can see. How about it?"

"Hmm." Steph marched into the kitchen, leaned back against the counter and folded her arms across her chest. "My hands are full right now working on this story and when I'm done and it's printed, then... well... I think I might just want to continue with this type of reporting. I'm really enjoying what I'm doing and if I say so myself, I think I'm good at it."

"Listen, Stephanie, you're good at whatever you set your mind to. You always have been, but this investigative reporting is not for you—trust me, I know. It's time for you to start learning the business side of the newspaper. I won't be running this paper forever and I may as well start grooming you to take over things for when that time comes."

"Why don't you just say it, dad? You don't want me to work on the Agrico story anymore. Is that why you stopped by tonight? Are you pulling me from this story?"

"Nobody's pulling you from anything, but you need to give some thought to your future. What you're working on now may be a newsworthy story, but look at you—you were mugged for Christ's sake. I won't have you running around investigating these stories where you put your life in danger. You need to stop what you're doing and move on and do the things that you're expected to do."

"Wow—hold on." Steph's face flushed and her voice cracked, "Just what is it I'm *expected* to do, anyway? Am I expected to work my way up the ranks until I finally sit in your chair? Is that what you expect? How many times have I told you that I don't want to run the Post? Not now, not ever. I love being a reporter and if you won't let me work on my own at the Post and stop trying to turn me into you, then I'm sure I can find another paper to work for."

"Why do you always twist things and act like I'm trying to control you? I've always looked out for your best interests. You know that, and I want nothing more than to see you get the things you've earned and deserve."

"Then let me finish this story and then another one and another one. This is what I want to do with my life right now and there's nothing you can do to change that—nothing."

Mr. Weintraub rose, grabbed his overcoat, draped it over his arm and turned toward Steph. "Life isn't always easy and sometimes the decisions we make aren't always the right ones. I want you to reconsider what I came here to offer you. You're going to regret this if you don't take my offer."

"I've already thought about it and I don't want to change a thing."

"Then think harder." Mr. Weintraub turned and walked out the door.

CHAPTER 30

"We need to go down one level. That ladder should take us there." Phil led Alex and Benjamin through the tunnels and hallways that snaked through the inside of the mountain like a corkscrew. Benjamin and Phil had located a rough schematic of the Ritseling cave that had been used to make the extended improvements by Kioshi's group. To locate Michelle, they had communicated with her through the real time cams and she had provided them with landmarks to, hopefully, lead them to the room where she was being held captive.

"I don't know, Phil, I think we need to go further down this hallway. If I remember correctly, the point where we go down a level is over there at the end," Benjamin pointed a finger.

"You might be right. Let's run to the end and see what's there."

Alex looked behind her, down the corridor and then back again. "This is the third time we've stopped to get our bearings. We're running out of time. We need to find her before they find us. We're too open standing out here."

Benjamin raised a hand and whispered, "Let me check out the end. I'll be right back." He turned and bolted forward.

Reaching the end of the hallway, Benjamin gave a thumbs-up sign. "Come on. This should be it."

One at a time, they descended the steps of the ladder and found themselves on another level of the cave. "This way," Phil said, as he sprinted down the hallway.

Halfway down the corridor they reached another turnoff and Phil knew they were there. They turned right and stopped at the first door on their left. Phil reached down to turn the knob. "Damn, it's locked." He rattled the door.

"Let me look." Alex dropped to her knees and examined the lock. "A Sentex keypad. There's a standard admin-code that will enter the factory-default password."

Alex punched in ***00000099#*. "That should do—"

Phil turned the handle and pushed the door open. He saw Michelle in the corner, her arms tied behind her back and her mouth gagged. "Michelle!" he yelled as he ran into the room, his arms extended, his eyes trained on her.

Seconds later, Phil lay on the floor unconscious. Two men stood in the doorway with menacing grins and guns pointed directly at Alex and Benjamin.

One of the men reached over and pushed the door all the way open and there he was—legs spread shoulder width apart, his hands in front of his chest with the fingers of his left hand wrapped around his tightly clenched fist. His eyes, dark, penetrating and loaded with blood.

Slowly, he slid his left foot and inched forward. "I told you earlier that the only way out of here was through me."

Another step. "Why is it, Alex, that you keep killing my good men?"

Another step. "You have to understand that I cannot allow that to keep happening."

Another step. "You had your chance to die with honor."

One more step and Kioshi stood within striking distance of Alex. "But you chose not to. Now, I have other plans for you; plans that will bring you to your knees and turn your blood to acid."

V shaped creases filled Kioshi's forehead. His muscles tightened. Before Alex could react, he raised his left leg and snapped it to the side. The ball of his foot struck Benjamin in his solar plexus. His leg retracted, he bent at the waist, pivoted on his left foot—

Alex raised her knee and a bullet flew inches from her head and another grazed her calf.

Kioshi's right leg spun around and his heel struck Benjamin in the face. He reloaded—spun again—and again. Benjamin collapsed to the floor.

"Two down. One to go." Kioshi stepped back. "Akio, you stay here and keep an eye on these three. If they give you any reason to kill them, do it. Masato, you will come with me and escort Alex to my chambers."

Masato followed Alex and directed her through the maze of tunnels; Kenji trailed behind. Alex counted her steps and committed them to memory. They had gone up two levels and it seemed to her like they were venturing deeper into the mountainside.

"Open that door and go in," Kenji ordered.

Alex's mind was searching—searching for the right moment, the right clue, and the right time to react. Kenji was armed and he had kept his distance, neutralizing Alex's chances of disarming him. She had witnessed Kioshi's martial arts skills and she knew she would need the element of surprise to successfully overtake him. She reached for the knob and turned it, slowly. She felt the latch give way and she pushed the door open an arm's length. "It would be rude of me to enter first." She turned her head toward Kioshi. "You lead the way and I'll follow."

Kioshi glowered. "Do not press your luck. Open the door, all the way and go in."

Alex did as she was told. The room was similar in size and shape to the room she had been in earlier where she had killed Kioshi's clone, only it was clear that this was Kioshi's personal sanctuary. Centuries of samurai artifacts covered the walls and filled the room: antique Edos, or hand spears; dozens of kabuto helmets; fire costumes; wooden and iron masks. She walked to the middle of the room, stopped and turned. Kioshi entered the room and circled the perimeter. His evil eyes were trained on Alex.

Finally, Kioshi stopped behind the only object in the room that was even close to the 21st century—a solid cherry wood pedestal desk. "You should have carried out the seppuku ritual when you had the chance." Kioshi pulled a pair of handcuffs from the center drawer. "But, since you failed, you will be subject to death by more tortuous and less honorable methods. Is that what you want?"

Alex stood tall, her shoulders squared. "You're making a mistake,

Kioshi. You may very well kill me, like you plan, but this cave will be blasted to smithereens and you along with it if I'm not out of here shortly. Is that what *you* want?"

Kioshi exploded with laughter. "Are you talking about the old man, his three porters and the four horses that are waiting for you outside? That's your army?" His laughter was replaced by a dagger-like stare. "Enough of your nonsense. *Here.*" He threw the handcuffs at Alex and they landed at her feet. "Put those over your wrists and make sure they are pressed tight."

Alex picked up the cuffs. One by one she clamped her wrists. "You can do what you want with me, but the others—leave them out of this. They've done nothing to you. They're here only because of me."

Kioshi stepped from behind the desk and approached Alex. "I am afraid it is not that simple and I think you know that as well as me. The others will be taken care of, you have my word, but not in the way you would hope. You have only yourself to blame for bringing them here."

One final step. Kioshi stood close enough to Alex that she could smell his contempt; that same contempt she had smelled in the small restaurant in Pakistan. "Kneel, now."

Alex remained firm, her eyes planted on Kioshi. "I don't think so. Whatever you plan on doing you'll have to do it while I'm standing."

"Masato, see that our friend kneels so she can receive her proper punishment."

Alex turned her head, but it was too late. Masato swung an Edo that struck her behind her knees and she buckled, falling to the ground. He stood behind Alex, gripped her shoulders and pushed her into a kneeling position. His grip tightened.

Kioshi pulled out a tantō and wrapped both hands around the hilt. He drew the sword to his side, let out a shrill, high-pitched grunt, and swung. The instant Masato released his grip Alex lunged forward, her head smashed into Kioshi's groin and he buckled forward. She rolled on her back, coiled her legs and unleashed a kick to his throat.

Kioshi flew backwards, grasping at his throat and crashed into a set of samurai armor. Alex rolled to her side just as the tip of Masato's spear passed by her ear. A quick scissor kick to Masato's legs dropped him to the floor and Alex yanked the spear from his hands.

Alex jumped to her feet. In one motion, she leveled the spear at Masato, hitting him in his abdomen. She looked up. Kioshi was rushing at her, his tantō swinging from his hand.

Alex crouched down in a horse stance. Her feet were spread wide apart with her toes pointed forward; her thighs were parallel to the floor, her back was arched-up and her fists, tightly clenched, were pressed firmly against her hips. With her eyes trained on her attacker, she moved to her side. Slowly, she began circling the room.

Kioshi swiped down with the blade. Alex lunged to her left. He followed with a backhanded thrust.

"Give it up, Kioshi. Nothing can be gained by you killing me or my friends. Give it up." Alex circled.

Kioshi lunged forward and the blade cut through the air from all directions. Alex moved back, step by step, with each swipe. The instant her back hit the wall she felt the blade tear through her shirt. The sting of bleeding flesh burned through her arm.

Alex leaped to her left, rolled over on her shoulder, sprung to her feet and grabbed an Edo from the wall. Her hands were still cuffed. She held the Edo with both hands and used it as a shield fending off Kioshi's relentless attacks.

The tip of the Edo was sharp, made from the same tamahagane steel as the tantō. Alex thrust the tip forward grazing Kioshi's thigh. Kioshi grabbed the Edo with both hands and his tantō fell to the floor. Pulling tight, the two were locked in combat, twisting, turning—struggling to pull the Edo free.

Kioshi wrapped a leg behind Alex and pushed. She fell backwards. Keeping a firm grip on the Edo, she pulled Kioshi with her to the floor. Crashing hard, they rolled across the floor, exchanging blows with a knee, an elbow, a forearm, until they slammed into the wall. Kioshi's grip loosened and Alex twisted the Edo from his hands. She threw the spear behind her, unleashed her coiled fingers on both hands and struck Kioshi in his thorax. She landed a double-fisted power punch to his diaphragm.

Quickly, she sprang to her feet and ran back toward the doorway where Kioshi had left his gun. She grabbed it from the floor, took a deep breath—then another. Her shirt was stained with blood—she would tend to that later.

Kioshi lay on the floor writhing in pain. Alex stepped on his hand and jammed the barrel of the gun in his temple. She lifted his ponytail and saw the gash on the back of his neck. "The first thing you're going to do is give me the key to these cuffs. The second thing—you're finally going to take a good hard look at that business proposal I came so far to present to you."

Part Two

CHAPTER 31

The Gulfstream G650 had reached its cruising altitude of 30,000 feet and had been traveling at 700 miles per hour toward San Francisco. With a scheduled re-fueling stopover in Seoul, Korea, they had anticipated arriving at the San Francisco airport by 4pm.

This had been the first opportunity in the past six days that anyone had the time not only to sleep, but to think back on what had just happened. When they had exited Ritseling and met with Youten, he had been shocked to see their bloodstained clothing and the cuts and gashes covering Alex and Benjamin. He had been even more stunned when Alex had told him that they would do the return trek in half the time. They wouldn't be stopping each night, but instead would travel through the days and nights until they reached Kagbeni. Youten had restocked their supplies, but he had to go through and discard what was not absolutely essential so they could each carry lighter loads.

In Katmandu, Benjamin had made arrangements to charter a private jet when they arrived in Mumbai. With a range of 7,000 miles and a cruising speed of 700 mph, they would cut two days of travel time off the time it would take for a commercial flight.

Alex sat at a table hunched over her laptop and was searching through the information on the two hard drives she had taken from Kioshi. With four terabytes of data, the process would be time-consuming, a luxury she didn't have. Somewhere in that stream of data, Alex hoped she could find the information that would lead her to uncovering the whereabouts of the virus Kioshi had created. Chills ran up her spine each time she imagined the devastating effects that virus could cause.

Benjamin and Phil had both dozed off before the aircraft had taxied down the runway. Michelle had covered herself with a blanket and nestled her head in Phil's shoulder, but sleep had eluded her. She pulled off the blanket, tucked it around Phil and walked to the galley. She poured two cups of tea, placed them on a tray and made her way to the forward seating area that Alex had commandeered. "Don't you ever sleep?" Michelle asked.

Alex remained focused on her task and her fingers raced across the keyboard. "That's one of my favorite things to do, but it seems that lately I never have any time for it."

Michelle dropped a hand to the seat next to Alex. "Do you mind if I sit down? I can't seem to sleep either."

Alex nodded. "Sure, sit." She locked her fingers, stretched her arms and let out an exaggerated sigh, "Ohhh... I could probably use a break anyway."

Michelle placed the tray on the table next to Alex and sat down. "I brought some tea. Yours is the caffeinated one. I figure you're probably going to need it if you plan on staying up all the way to San Francisco."

"Thanks." Alex lifted the cup to her lips. "This is probably the best tea I can remember in a long while." She gave a half-smile. "I think this is the longest I've seen Phil go without coffee since I've known him. How's he holding up?"

"You are so right. I've never seen anyone, and I mean *never*, drink coffee the way he does. I'd be fueled for liftoff if I drank half as much caffeine." Michelle said.

"You and me both." Alex placed her cup on the table and turned to Michelle. "Now that we're alone, there's something I need to ask you. It's been on my mind since shortly after we first met."

Michelle tilted her head. "Sure, what is it?"

"Have you told Phil yet who you really are?"

Michelle flinched. "You mean that I wasn't a professor at Bennington and that my name isn't really Michelle Brophy? All of that?"

Alex nodded. "All of that—and more."

Michelle leaned back and sighed. "The short answer is no, I've told him bits and pieces, but not everything. I asked him to wait until we get back and can be alone and then I'll tell him everything—I hope." She turned toward Alex. "There's nothing sinister or evil in my past. I'm not a convicted felon or anything like that. I've never even had a parking ticket. I'm dealing with some inner pain and I just haven't gotten through very much of that yet. Is that good enough?"

"I'm not a very trusting person. In fact, my natural inclination is to not trust someone when I first meet them. It's a required trait in my profession. Ben, I love and trust more than anyone I've ever known. Phil and I got off to a rocky start when we first met, but I can tell you in all honesty that there isn't a fickle or untrusting bone in his body. I don't want to see him get hurt. We all have murky, nasty corners down deep in the dark part of our souls. You haven't given me anything to go on that leads me to believe my original hunch about you is incorrect."

"No, I haven't; you're right. I love Phil and I can't believe that I feel this way... so soon." Michelle looked over her shoulder and saw that Phil was still fast asleep. She turned sideways in her seat and curled her legs under her. "My real name is Michelle Holman—that's my married name. I was married for 12 years and the last 10 of those have left me with a scar that may never heal. One day I found the courage and I just walked out. That was nine months ago. I traveled around the country terrified that he would find me, and I never stayed in one place longer than two or three days. By the time I reached Mill Valley I was sick and tired of hiding, of running. I just couldn't do it anymore. I made up a new name, found a quiet place to live and began to have a life all to myself. Now look at me!" She threw a hand up. "So much for a quiet life. I end up being kidnapped, flown halfway around the world and held in some kind of futuristic cave."

"Michelle Holman, is that right?" Alex asked.

Michelle nodded. "Uh-huh."

"Do you mind if I run a trace on you when we get back?"

"I would expect nothing less from you. Be my guest," Michelle replied.

Alex took another sip of tea and then turned to Michelle. Michelle's bloodshot eyes contrasted with her baby blue irises. "What are you running away from? Was your husband abusive? Is that it?"

Michelle buried her head in her knees and spoke softly. "He controlled everything I did—who my friends were, where I went, how I dressed—*everything*. If I didn't do exactly as he said, I'd end up with a black eye or a bruised rib or a swollen jaw, or even all of these at the same time. When he drank, which was most of the time, it was worse—a lot worse. Luckily we didn't have kids. He wanted a house full of kids, but I stayed on birth control and never told him. If he ever knew I had done that I think he would have actually killed me."

"Did you live with this by yourself all that time? There was no one to turn to for help?"

"Huh, right. John Holman, decorated war vet *and* a cop. He knew everyone in town and everyone loved him. No one would've believed me and I mean no one—*really*. John could do no wrong in everyone's eyes and the one time I threatened him with going to the police, he spit in my face and then twisted my arm behind my back, dislocated my shoulder, and threatened me if I ever said anything." A tear rolled down her cheek. "I never brought that up again."

"What about your family, friends or someone who you could've turned to?"

"That's a story for another time." The look on Alex's face made it clear to Michelle that she'd have to explain. "I don't have any parents. They died in a car accident when I was still an infant. I never knew them. My aunt and uncle tried their best, but there wasn't much they could do so I ended up in foster care. Do you have any idea what that's like?"

Alex folded her hands in her lap and shook her head. "I don't."

"I went through six homes; some not so good and some okay. I had two different foster parents that physically abused me and countless foster siblings that teased me, punched me, locked me in the closet and stole things. Oh, don't get me wrong, I know there are a lot of good people out there who sacrifice and give so much to help kids, but I wasn't one of the lucky ones." Michelle gave a half-smile, "It's taken years of therapy to put all this in perspective for me and to start healing from my childhood scars. To answer your question, I learned to distrust everyone when I was growing up, so no, I wasn't going to tell anyone about what was going on."

Alex reached over and placed her hand over Michelle's. "You need to say something to Phil. He'll understand and he'll help you get through this. I'm certain of it. It's obvious to me that he cares a great deal about you."

"I know, I know, and he means the world to me. Before I met Phil I felt like my life was nothing but a long string of yesterdays with no promise for any tomorrows. I'll talk to him and tell him everything, but I don't know how to even start. I'm so afraid that he'll see me as a burden and won't want to have anything to do with me anymore. If I can spend more time with Phil—"

"Hey, I heard my name." Phil leaned across the seat and rubbed the sleep from his eyes. "Whatever you're talking about, I probably need to defend myself."

Alex stood up. "Michelle was telling me some things about you that will forever remain our secret." Her fingers zipped across her lips and she winked at Michelle. "Here, take my seat, I think I'll go back and crawl under the blanket with Ben."

CHAPTER 32

The National Center for Emerging and Zoonotic Infectious Diseases was a large name for an elite task force of scientists and medical professionals charged with preventing and combating infectious diseases both nationally and globally. As part of the United States Centers for Disease Control and Prevention, the CDC, this group of professionals had led the efforts to eradicate the 2014 Ebola outbreak in West Africa, the dengue virus infections that had spread across multiple countries in 2013, and scores of other international outbreaks of infectious diseases, known as Epi-Aids.

Dr. Laura Elsbach ran the Division of Global Migration and Quarantine and had surrounded herself with the best qualified medical professionals as part of an international response team. Three days ago, Dr. Elsbach had dispatched a seven member team of epidemiologists and health workers to Liberia in response to an infectious disease outbreak in that country. Speaking with that team through video conference, Dr. Elsbach flinched when her lead investigator, Dr. James Harrington, conveyed the news to her. "My god, Jim, if you're right about this, we're not even remotely prepared for it, nor is any other agency in the world. This could reach epidemic proportions within the week."

"We've sent samples to you; you'll have them tomorrow," said Dr. Harrington. The audio and visual receptions were hit by patches of delays and static, but his message left no room for misunderstanding. "We'll need the lab there to do a thorough analysis to confirm our field results, but right now, I think we should begin quarantine procedures and vaccinations."

The recent development of a multiplex rapid detection test kit had significantly increased the accuracy of identifying viruses in the field. An antigen-based paper strip was coated with the infected blood and in two to five minutes the paper strip's color could identify the virus.

"Are the symptoms the same in all the patients?" Dr. Elsbach asked.

"The symptoms are clear, Laura, and they're unmistakable: headaches; vomiting; fever; and deep-seated pustules in the same stage of development that spread over the entire body within two to three days. Even without the paper strip ID, I'd reach the same conclusion."

"I have no reason to doubt what you're saying. It must be hell there right now." Laura scribbled a note on her legal pad. "I'll make sure vaccines are sent to you today and I'll do everything I can here to get permission for you to use it. What kind of numbers are we looking at?"

"Hard to say for sure. This is pretty remote and we haven't made a complete assessment, but so far we've identified 46 deaths and 346 more infected. I think the last number is on the conservative side. I'll have better numbers by tomorrow."

"Are these cases isolated or spread around?" Dr. Elsbach asked.

"They're not isolated. We've found deaths in four of Liberia's 15 counties, but there are no reported cases in the populated centers," Jim replied.

"Any idea how this originated?" Dr. Elsbach asked.

Jim shook his head. "None. We just started that process so we'll see."

"What other groups have boots on the ground?" Laura asked. "I did speak to David Kirkwood at the World Health, but I haven't heard from any other groups."

"The Liberian Ministry of Health is cooperating fully, but we haven't given them our assessment yet. The Economic Community of West African States, Medicins San Frontieres, Red Cross, and Samaritan's Purse are the leading groups already here and they're all gearing up to bring in more medical personnel. We have a real shortage of not only health facilities and personnel, but sanitary supplies and basic medications are virtually nil."

Laura Elsbach received both her medical and her master of public health degrees from Northwestern University and completed her Residency in Infectious Medicine at Yale University. She had received numerous awards and honors and had published over 75 scientific articles. Most recently, she had led the epidemiologic investigations on multidrug-resistant tuberculosis and on outbreaks of measles, typhoid and cryptosporidium. Within the CDC, there was no single person more respected or trusted than Dr. Laura Elsbach.

"Let me lay out what we need to do and if anyone disagrees or has anything to add, now's the time to check in. Nothing's set in stone and I'm open to any criticisms or suggestions." Dr. Elsbach looked around the table and then back at the video screen. "I'll contact Liberia's Health Minister to start greasing that wheel, and I'll brief Director Wiser. I'm sure this will require a joint response with the State Department and at some point the President will need to be briefed. Jim, I'll get you everything you need. I want to do everything we can at this point to keep this from reaching anything close to Level One. We're still wiping up things after the last outbreak and no one wants to go through that again. Jim, you'll let me know if you need anything further?"

Jim nodded in agreement. "The sooner you can get us complete medical field teams the better; and," he paused and took a deep breath, "I think I'd like to change that to a request for expanded teams—we'll need them. We have enough P.P.E. for 50 people, but we should up that to 500. Other than that we're good here for now."

"Let's reconvene at oh-nine-hundred tomorrow, but let me know before that if you learn anything new," Dr. Elsbach said.

"That works on our end; thanks, Laura," Jim said.

"If you're right, this could far exceed the Ebola epidemic. We haven't seen any cases of this virus in maybe 40 years. We could be facing our worst nightmare. There are no known cures for—"

Dr. Laura Elsbach's voice cracked and cut off her final word, but to everyone in the room with her and to everyone in Liberia with Dr. Jim Harrington, they needed no clarification—*smallpox.*

CHAPTER 33

Delynn spotted Steph the instant she walked into the coffee shop. "Oh god, that still makes me cringe when I look at you. It looks like it's getting a little better though. Does it still hurt?"

Steph pulled a chair over from another table and gingerly sat down. "It's starting to grow on me so at this point I hardly notice it. I do notice that I get a lot more stares than I used to, though."

"We can meet some other time if you're not up to it," Delynn offered.

"I can still hear things, my brain's working and besides I have a deadline on my cracker story, remember?"

"Okay, but let me get you a coffee first." Delynn pushed her chair back. "I'm buying. What's your pleasure this morning?"

"No caffeine for me today, maybe in a couple days. I'm taking Robaxin for the pain and caffeine is a no-no I'm told, unfortunately. I'm going to call this caffeine-free time my cleansing period," Steph smiled.

Delynn returned the smile, pulled her chair back to the table and wrapped both hands around her mug. "You'll let me know if you want to stop or you're not feeling up to it, okay?"

Steph returned the smile and nodded.

"By the way, this is a great spot, I love it. How'd you pick this place?" Delynn asked.

The House of Coffee on Noriega Street was a mom-and-pop shop on the opposite side of town from Delynn's work and Steph had been there before on several occasions, but never without a coffee mug in her hands. They roasted their own beans and the aroma could waft for several blocks. "I've been here a few times and liked it, and it's far enough away from Agrico that we shouldn't run into anyone you don't want to see," Steph said.

Delynn's head rotated 180 degrees and her eyes landed back on Steph. "So, you said you wanted to talk about Sustinere. Where'd you want to start?"

"I've done some research on Sustinere and Novum Rice and I can't help but think that Agrico is the face behind the mask of Sustinere. Jonathon McPherson—does that name ring a bell?"

"We haven't met, but I talk to him a lot. He's a plant pathologist who runs their development crew and pretty high up there, a senior V.P., I think."

"How about Chris McEwan and Leslie Kennedy?"

"Sure, Chris McEwen is Sustinere's president and Leslie, I talk with frequently. She's their CFO and the person who sends the payment requests to me."

"Sustinere was incorporated 11 years ago and the incorporation was done by a law firm named Becker, Funai and Stubbins. Agrico uses that same firm, although to be fair they use a whole slew of law firms. McPherson, McEwen, Kennedy—they were all Agrico employees who ended up at Sustinere six or seven months after it was formed. When McPherson was at Agrico, he led the development of a new rice strain that I think, but I'm not certain, was the same rice strain that later took on the name Novum Rice. I'm not sure about McEwen's background, but I know that Kennedy used to work directly under Eric Cummings when he was in Manila." Steph arched her back, craned her neck and rolled her shoulders. "I'm still a little stiff. Do you mind if I stand?"

"No, go ahead; but where'd you get this information? Some of this happened a long time ago," Delynn asked.

"It's all public record. It just takes some digging around and I haven't talked to a single person, except you—right now. No one else has helped me put any of this together."

Delynn took a sip of coffee, sat back and bit her lower lip. "I have to believe that Agrico had a sound business decision for doing this. Every decision I've ever been involved with there is discussed and over-discussed and then goes through layers and layers of approvals. That must have been the case with Sustinere. I'll bet anything on that."

"You may be right, but I don't think so. This is all too neatly packaged and a couple hundred million big ones, probably more, is unaccounted for. And it's the money, more than anything that is pushing me toward this conclusion."

"Yeah, but—" Delynn's mouth froze and her shoulders sagged. She slumped down in her chair and stared at Steph.

Finally, Steph broke the silence. "That's point one, but I still need to find out more. I just wanted to see what you thought of my theory and that's all it is at this point, a theory." Steph rubbed her forehead and stretched her eyelids. "Hey, what about the name? Novum in Latin is the number nine. Is that where the name came from?"

"That's it. This is the ninth generation of the rice in its development stage. It started as ûnus and was renamed with each new development. Right now, the rice is ready to go so I doubt there will be a decem."

"Oh, before I forget, I was supposed to meet Adam two days ago after work, but then this happened." She pointed to her black and blue eye. "I've been calling him, but I haven't reached him yet. If you see him today maybe you can ask him to call me. I don't want him to think I somehow flaked on him."

Delynn leaned forward and murmured, "I don't plan on seeing him, but if I do I'll let him know."

Steph walked around to the back of her chair and leaned forward, resting on her forearms. "Okay, now the last thing I want to know about is Novum Rice. If my theory's correct, there must be something pretty special about that rice. Agrico has more products than most supermarkets stock on their shelves, so why would they go to so much trouble to hide what's really going on? I know that Agrico gets picketed almost everywhere they show up and they end up having to spend a lot more money to bring their products to market because of that, but I don't think they'd back down from a fight if they knew the product was going to make them some money—maybe a lot of money. Let's start with you educating me on genetically modified foods and then we'll get specific on the Novum Rice."

Delynn was now sitting upright in her chair; she brushed her hair from her face and nodded. "How much detail do you want? I can talk about this for hours."

Steph pointed at her watch. "If you're planning to get to work on time this morning, you may want to condense it down to about 30 minutes, max."

"Okay, here's the 30 minute version. The skeptics disagree with this, but many, if not most scientists believe that by 2050 we won't have enough food to feed the world's population. That has to do with an increase in population and a decrease in the availability of land, water and energy. The result of this will be that food issues could become as politically destabilizing on a global scale as energy issues are today. That's the first premise that you need to agree with or at least tend to agree with, before we can go to the next step." Delynn turned her hand over, palm up. "Do you agree with this prediction?"

"I have absolutely no idea. But let's just say I do for the sake of you taking me where you want to take me."

"Fair enough. The next thing you need to know is that iron deficiency is the most common and widespread nutritional disorder in the world. Next, you need to know that 2 billion people, over 30% of the world's population, are anemic, due mostly to iron deficiency, and in resource-poor areas, this is frequently intensified by infectious diseases: malaria; HIV/AIDS; hookworm infestation; schistosomiasis, to name a few."

"Are you really serious?" Steph raised her brows. "Those are staggering numbers. I'm a little skeptical about them."

"The numbers *are* staggering, but they're real," Delynn replied. "They're not Agrico's numbers; they're the World Health Organization's, and there's more. Three billion people depend on rice as their primary food source and many of those are in the less developed countries where 250,000 to 500,000 children die every year from iron deficiency. I'm not even counting the millions who die each year from a weakened immune system."

"If that's true, it would seem to me that this would be called an epidemic or pandemic or whatever the word is," Steph conjectured.

"If these numbers were at all reflected in the developed countries, you'd be right. The problem though is this population comes from undeveloped countries mainly in Africa and Asia. As a result, they don't rate as high on the radar scale, unfortunately. Anyway, Novum Rice—it's not a cure-all by any means, but it's the closest thing to it. Two ounces of Novum Rice each day would provide 60% of the daily recommended intake of iron. That can save a lot of lives."

Steph nodded her head and swayed back and forth on her heels as Delynn spoke. "One of the things—well there are a couple—but the first is I've read where some people, even some left-leaning groups like Greenpeace, believe these genetically modified foods only benefit the large multi-nationals, like Agrico, at the expense of the poor farmers and the consumers. It's kinda like if you control the seed, you control the food and then you can control the people."

Delynn huffed. "Far from it, but I can't answer that within my time limit. What I will say, though, is Sustinere will allow the farmers to save and harvest the seeds and replant them, which hasn't always been the case with many of the GMs."

"What about long-term effects, and the fact that this rice really hasn't been tested?" Stephanie asked.

"That's one that gets me every time I hear it. Listen, Novum Rice is stitched with a gene from spinach, lentils, squash and other iron rich foods. So, this isn't some weird manufactured material made in a test tube. Nope, it's really the same thing that's naturally found in beans, carrots, melons, squash and a host of other vegetables."

Steph grasped the back of her chair and took a breath. "You've just given me every reason imaginable to believe that Agrico is up-to-something with this rice. According to you, it's the greatest thing since man invented the wheel, so they'd have no reason to get rid of it—absolutely none." Steph raised a hand and gripped her chin. "One more thing. So far Novum Rice hasn't been planted anywhere except a few test plots in the Philippines, right?"

Delynn nodded.

"So," Steph leaned forward, "why couldn't someone fill a bag up with Novum Rice, put the bag say... I don't know, in a package of Minute Rice or Rice-A-Roni or whatever, and ship it off? Who's going to know what kind of rice is really in that bag?"

"Probably no one. There's no way to oversee something like that that I know of." Delynn rubbed her lower lip. "What are you getting at?"

"I don't really know, but... well, I just find that interesting... you know, the lack of regulation on something like that. It seems like a lot of things could happen."

CHAPTER 34

Steph saw Chandler enter the room, heads turned and she mumbled to herself, "I had no idea this was dress up time." She had been waiting for 15 minutes, but for the first time she scouted out the room and noticed everyone in their finery; men in Brooks Brothers sport coats and women in Saks Fifth Avenue dresses. She couldn't see them, but she suspected that under each table was a closetful of expensive shoes, probably Christian Louboutin, maybe Jimmy Choo, but she was certain she was the only person wearing Lands' End sandals.

Steph slid her chair back, dropped her napkin on the table and stood up. "You look like, like you just stepped out of a magazine—wow."

Chandler reached down and took Steph's hands, leaned forward and gave her a kiss. "And if I didn't know better, I'd swear you thought that maybe we were going to Pizzeria Delfina or even your favorite, Taqueria Vallarta."

"Yeah, I just noticed. I'm definitely underdressed." She threw her hands out. "Who'd a thought a place named Boulevard would have a fancy dress code?"

The corner of Chandler's lips rose. "No problem on my end. It looks like you're actually wearing a freshly cleaned blouse. It's not *ironed*, but it is clean—nice touch."

Disguised with a quirky, but sheepish grin that only she could wear, Steph said, "And don't forget my pants, I wore the gabardine ones and they're almost clean."

Chandler laughed. "I'm just glad we finally have a night together. It's been, what, two weeks since we've had dinner together and had a chance to actually have a real conversation?"

Steph nodded. "At least. It's been crazy between grant reporting time at your place and my schedule which, well it's not so much a schedule as it is a sleep deprivation experiment. I'm beat and could really use some rest." Steph reached across the table and put her hand over Chandler's. "Thanks for putting up with all this. I know it's been hard on you."

"I have something exciting to tell you, but first I have to ask; did you talk to Officer Brandt today, like you promised?" Chandler tapped a fingernail on the table.

"Oh, I forgot, I really did. I'll call tomorrow, but really I don't know what good it'll do. They're never going to find out who did this, so what's the point?"

"The point, is Officer Brandt doesn't believe what happened to you was a random mugging. Your wallet was still on you, your phone was still sitting on the passenger seat and nothing was stolen. He thinks you may have been targeted and he wants to talk to you about that. This is important. Promise me you'll call him first thing in the morning."

Steph raised two hands in a gesture of surrender. "First thing in the morning I'll do it, scout's honor. Now let's move on to cheerier things. You have exciting news, what is it?"

Chandler smiled and her eyes glowed like the Akoya pearls strung around her neck. "It's not really news, but I was thinking earlier today, maybe after the Post runs your masterpiece, but before you're showered with your Pulitzer, we could take a trip. I mean a real trip, like Europe."

"Oh my god, I was thinking the same thing driving over here. Zermatt is stuck on my brain. Are you up for some skiing?"

"I'd love that. I've never been there, but—" Chandler bristled. "No, please tell me that's not your phone—*please.*"

Steph looked at Chandler. Her lips pursed and her eyes sunk as she reached into her purse and pulled out her phone. She saw the caller ID. "It's Chief. I'm sorry; I really didn't think he was going to call until later." She held up a finger, "Wait just a sec."

Chandler nodded, but the slight hint of pink that had earlier highlighted her cheeks had faded.

"Hi, Chief. This is sort of an awkward time; can I call you back later tonight?

"I see, but…

"Nothing really, I…

"Hold on for just a sec."

Steph covered the phone, looked at Chandler and sighed. "I'm sorry. I really am. I have to talk to Chief now so go ahead and order for both of us and I'll just run outside and make this quick."

Chandler's head rocked back and then slowly returned. Her doleful eyes said it all. She gave a half-smile, nodded and her lips mouthed a silent, "Okay."

Outside, Steph stood on the corner of Mission Street and The Embarcadero. The crisp air cut through her windbreaker and she huddled next to the building to shield her from the wind. The work crowd had long departed and the only people strolling the streets were couples either heading home from an early night out, or on their way to a mid-week night on the town. Her thoughts ricocheted between Chandler sitting alone in the restaurant and Chief, who as far as she knew, never left the office.

"Uh-huh… I did not…uh-huh." She held the phone at arm's length and stared at it in disbelief. Chief's voice came through loud and clear. Finally, she pulled the phone back and jammed it against her ear. "Wait… wait…wait just a sec. That's not my problem, that's yours. When I came to work at the Post my dad promised me he'd leave me alone and let me earn my own keep. If he's got you hounding me like a watch dog, then, then you need to tell him *no*. No, Hylan, that's between you and your daughter. I know I'll give him a piece of my mind about this again. It's not fair and it's not what we agreed on."

Steph felt her pulse quicken and she took a deep breath, then another. It sounded to her that she had got her point across to Chief and if she had any chance of making it back to Chandler she needed to redirect the conversation. "Chief, I had a major breakthrough today on the Agrico story. I'm planning on coming in first thing in the morning to talk to you about it, so what do you say I meet you at the office at 7 am sharp and I'll fill you in on everything?"

"Uh-huh… I guess I could… okay, if it's that important that you know now I'll give you the Readers Digest version and I'll meet you at the office first thing in the morning."

Steph really hadn't had the time to process everything that had happened that day. After meeting with Delynn first thing that morning, she had gone home and returned phone calls, replied to an endless stream of emails, finished up two of her regular beat articles—only one had missed the deadline—and she had scrambled to make her appointed dinner date with Chandler.

As she talked to Chief about what she had learned, the facts, the people, the motives and the unknowns began to organize into a neatly recognizable pattern. "Here's the crux in all this: Agrico is the largest producer of genetically modified food products in the world. It's numero uno, the big Kahuna. So, why would they sell a product that fits perfectly into their stable of products to a brand new company and then secretly fund that company's development of that product? They wouldn't unless there was something in it for them, or—and here's what I think's really going on—someone inside Agrico is orchestrating all this without the company's knowledge."

"No, much more than a hunch. I know for a fact that Agrico and Sustinere deal with one another almost daily and forms that are turned into the accounting department are being coded differently. These forms all relate to funding invoices submitted to Agrico by Sustinere. The invoices are paid, but don't show up anywhere in Agrico's financial records.

"Well that's still a mystery, I don't know. I told you I was on my way to meet him after I left Cummings' house. I thought maybe I didn't remember things right, but it was written down in my notebook and even circled. I'll find him.

"No, no concrete ideas about who broke into their computer system, but it has to be related. The only files they lifted relate to payments made to

Sustinere. They didn't take anything relating to product development or anything else. Maybe they couldn't find those files, but I doubt it. If they were able to get inside the system, they'd certainly know how to move around once they were in."

Steph now felt a chill creep into her bones. She zipped up her windbreaker, covering her neck and raised her shoulders. "I have another appointment with Cummings tomorrow and I'll track Adam down, too, and look at the financial records he has that cover payments to Sustinere. Once I look at those records I'm certain I'll find the connection.

"No, I don't have a clue how to read them, but I can have Chandler go through them with me. Financial stuff's right up her alley." Steph glanced at her watch and winced. "I have to go, Chief. I really do. I was having dinner with Chandler when you called and I told her I'd be right back. It's been close to 25 minutes already. She's going to end up hating me if I keep doing this to her. I'll handle my dad and I'll see you first thing tomorrow morning."

Steph was blowing on her hands and rubbing the cold from her fingertips when she entered the restaurant. Sitting at the same table where she and Chandler had sat earlier was an older couple obviously enjoying each other's company. She shook her head and muttered, "Not again."

She felt her phone vibrate in her hand. She looked at the incoming message and opened it. *Zermatt I'm definitely holding you to it* ♥♥

She pivoted and raced out of the restaurant. "How'd I get so lucky?"

CHAPTER 35

The evening rains stopped and the dawn's sunlight broke through the clouds canvassing the Oakland Hills. The treetops were tinged with that promise-of-sunshine color. Outside the panoramic window of Benjamin's Mill Valley home, a rainbow arced from the Marin Headlands over the choppy waters of the Pacific and disappeared before it reached the sandy shores of China Beach.

Sitting at the dining room table, Alex was oblivious to the early morning beauty. She wore a pair of loose fitting khaki shorts and the T-shirt she had pulled from Benjamin's closet hung down to her mid-thighs. Her Powermaster laptop had been custom built for her by the British company Premiergent Hi-Tech. With a one terabyte hard drive i5/i7 turbo boost performance, she had all the power she needed for complex analysis and the capacity to store endless data. Kioshi's two hard drives were connected to a disk enclosure allowing her to communicate with them through her laptop. Her fingers screamed across the keyboard and her eyes were fixed on her monitor.

Since leaving Katmandu, Alex had spent several days trying to find ways to penetrate the Chinese government's computer network; specifically, the Chinese Liberation Army. If she was right, that is where she'd find the information to corroborate what she believed to be Kioshi's plan of attack with his new virus.

She ran port-scans and port-sweeps on the government computers to find any active ports and to determine if there were any known vulnerabilities. There were none. Everything was locked and protected. Her attempts to insert a Trojan Horse were rebuffed. She knew her failure to gain access to the system was due to one of two possibilities. Either the network was private and unconnected to the internet or the Chinese government's system was locked tight with a series of Virtual Private Networks and a separate login and password was needed for each VPN. Either way, she had a possible solution.

Alex had hacked into government systems in the past. A few years back, she had crashed through a supposedly impenetrable firewall and had shut down over 300 computers for a 24-hour period—her target being none other than the United States military. She had used a government military contractor with active government contracts to access the military's computer network.

Alibaba was a Chinese based company that had recently launched the largest public stock offering in the history of the New York Stock Exchange. Alex had learned that it had substantial ties with the government. If she could find an open port in Alibaba's database servers that actively communicated with the government, she could open the port and penetrate the system and have the time to look in the government's network for the files she had hoped to find.

"There's nothing like sleeping in your own bed." Benjamin strolled over to Alex, wrapped his arms around her and kissed her neck. "The only thing better would have been waking up and having you there beside me."

Alex threw her arms behind her and clasped her hands around Benjamin's neck. "If you'd have awakened six hours ago I would have been there."

"You've been down here that long?"

"Close, but not really." Alex slid out from underneath Benjamin's embrace and turned around. "It must've taken me 30 minutes, at least, to find something suitable to wear in your closet." She raised her arms. "Like it?"

"That T-shirt's never looked better." Benjamin took Alex's hand. "The teapot will be singing any minute. Come on, I'll make you some tea and some toast and you can tell me what you've been up to all morning."

Alex sat at the kitchen counter and Benjamin scurried around pouring tea, cooking toast, pulling butter and fresh jam from the refrigerator. He talked nonstop. His grandfather had left several phone messages so he had called him straight away when he climbed out of bed. Denis Wilkinson, Benjamin's grandfather, lived in Australia, and they were the only family either one had left. Benjamin adored his grandfather and admired all that he had accomplished. After Benjamin's ranch house had been destroyed, he had decided that he would go ahead and sell the ranch and not return. He loved the M & O more than anyplace in the world, but he felt he would be haunted by the fact that it had been at that place where he had been inches away from losing Alex. No, he had been dead-set on selling it and moving on. That morning, his grandfather convinced him otherwise. Mimicking grandfather Wilkinson's Australian accent, Benjamin told Alex what had changed his mind. "Thar things about arselves that we leave behind in the places we've been. Only by returning to those places can we agin find those things."

Benjamin leaned forward and drilled his elbows into the counter. "There're a lot of things there I want to go back and find. So, how about we spend a few days hanging around here getting some rest? We can even get a swim or two in at the Dolphin Club and then we'll head out to Montana and start rebuilding the place."

Alex leaned back, curled her bare toes on the edge of the counter and drew her knees to her chest. Her chin burrowed into her knees. "I would love that more than anything, I really would, but there are some things still unfinished and I need to take care of them. I don't know how long it will take, but I need to start now, before it's too late."

"What are you talking about? You said yourself that Kioshi is out of our lives for good. What's changed?"

"I don't think we have to worry about Kioshi anymore, but that's not the problem. Do you remember how he told us he had the smallpox virus and had combined it with the G-16 virus and he was preparing to sell his new concoction to a buyer?"

Benjamin curled his lower lip and nodded.

"He calls this new virus cocktail of his SynAid and he's selling it to the Chinese government. I'm only speculating at this point what their intent is, but if I'm even remotely correct, the consequences of unleashing that virus will throw the world into political mayhem."

"Jesus, Alex, this isn't your problem. You didn't create it and you're taking all this to the extreme. The CIA, the NSA or whoever should be the ones handling this, not you. Let me call around and find the right people to talk to about this."

"I wish it was that easy. I can't just waltz into the CIA and tell them about this. Oh," she waved a hand, "and by the way, I broke into the NSA computer system and stole classified files and oh, by the way, it was me who last year shut down the New York Stock Exchange with the *Loki* virus, remember that? It goes on and on, Ben, and I'd end up being prosecuted by the U.S. Government and, in the meantime, it would take them weeks, at least, to verify what I give them and by then it would be too late. All of this is already in motion. It doesn't look to me that we have weeks."

Benjamin pushed back from the counter and walked over to the kitchen window. As he had done so many times before, he stared out at the twin towers of the Golden Gate Bridge. He often used that view to clear his own muddled thoughts. The rainbow had vanished and sunshine now bathed the two steel towers. Under the bridge's span he watched a cargo ship emerge, heading out to the Pacific shipping lanes. His fingers combed the sides of his hair and he locked his hands behind his neck.

Alex turned and stared at Benjamin. She knew what he was wrestling with and she also knew there was nothing she could do or say. Finally, she dropped her legs to the footrest and swung the stool around. Facing Benjamin, she began, "I know I've promised you I'd stop saying I'm sorry and that I would find a way to put this past of mine behind me. That the past would disappear and we could go on with our lives together. Well, I'm going to say I'm sorry one more time, but this is different. None of this had anything to do directly with my past, but I have a special skill-set that makes me the best person to do what needs to be done. When I learn more, and there's still a great deal more to learn, I'll pass things on to the authorities in my own way."

Alex slid off the stool and walked over next to Benjamin. She leaned her head into the window pane and stretched one arm around Benjamin's waist. "One thing Kioshi said rings true. He said the Russians are too unpredictable and the Americans are too lax and trusting. I wouldn't be able to live with myself if I didn't at least try to stop what I think is about to happen—I couldn't."

The loud Conga drum roll on the front door brought matching smiles to their faces. "Guess who?" Benjamin muttered.

Alex leaned into Benjamin and patted him on his chest. "I'll get the door."

Alex opened the latch on the front door and Phil charged in. He threw his arms up to give Alex a hug and stopped, dropping his hands to her shoulders. His eyelids fluttered and a grin flashed across his face. "You look like you've lost 50 pounds. We need to fatten you up." He drew his hands back, pinched the edges of his T-shirt and said, "Matching T's, I like that, but I'm surprised Ben even kept his."

Alex read the front of Phil's T-shirt, "Lake Berryessa Open Water Swim, 2012. I didn't even know what mine said."

"Well you picked out a good one. I beat him that year. Where is the old fart? I wanna give him a hard time again."

"He's in the kitchen. We're just finishing up breakfast. Come on back."

Benjamin was leaning against the window sill when Phil entered the kitchen. "So you win one race, *one race*, and you think that's such a big deal. One out of what, 30?"

"You need to brush up on your math skills, my friend. Do you want me to go through the list and point out all the swims that you think you won, but didn't?" Phil tossed his newspaper on the kitchen counter and headed for the coffee pot. "Ah, freshly brewed Peets. I knew you guys would be expecting me."

Alex pulled a mug from the shelf and handed it to Phil. "The rest of the pot is all yours."

Filling his mug to the brim, Phil swung the counter stool around and took a seat. He took a gulp and puckered. "Aah… now that's real coffee. It's not up to Death Wish Coffee standards, but at least it's a big upgrade from the Starbucks you used to keep around here." He shot Alex an approving smile and continued, "I didn't want you guys to plan ahead on something without including me, so I came over early. What's up?"

Benjamin looked at Phil, and then nodded towards Alex. "Alex has a few ideas. I'll let her fill you in."

Phil threw a hand up. "I'm all ears. Let's hear it."

Alex walked back to the counter and grabbed her tea. "Where's Michelle? Why isn't she here?"

"Ah, I dropped her off at her place on my way over. She has some things to do back there." He took another gulp of coffee. "She's still shook up over everything and I don't blame her. When we went in her place there were still signs of where those guys broke in and waited for her. We straightened up everything and that helps, but still, it gives you the creeps when you think about it."

"I talked to her a lot on our trek back to Jomsom. A week of captivity when you have no idea what's going on can have some lasting psychological effects," Alex said.

"I'll be staying with her at her place until she feels comfortable and gets through this." Phil locked his heels on the foot rest, dropped his elbows to the counter and folded his hands under his chin. "She told me you guys had a long talk about her past and that you were very supportive of her. Thanks, that meant a lot to her… and me."

Alex nodded and smiled. "I can't believe what she's been through. You'd never know it by talking with her. She's a lot stronger than she thinks. God, I feel guilty for even thinking she may have had connections or involvement with Kioshi."

"You weren't the only one." Phil turned toward Benjamin, "You're guilty on that count, too."

Benjamin leaned back against the window sill, his normal vibrant, spirited reverence for life drained from his eyes. "Yeah, I feel rotten about that."

Phil looked closely at Benjamin whose eyebrows were knitted close together in thought. He turned to Alex and her nose was scrunched and her mouth moved wordlessly. "Did I come at the wrong time? The tension's pretty thick in here."

Benjamin rolled his shoulders. "Well… maybe. We were in the middle of something, but it can wait."

"Hey, I'm sorry. I can take a hint. I'll take off and we'll meet up later. No worries." He grabbed his mug and stood. "I'm taking this along though."

Alex cupped her hand on Phil's arm. "You don't need to go. Sit back down."

Phil looked over at Benjamin for his approval. "Take a load off. You'll want to hear what Alex has to say," Benjamin said.

Alex partially recounted for Phil what she had learned from Kioshi's hard drives, leaving out bits and pieces she had not yet told Benjamin. She didn't believe the Chinese intended to use SynAid to create massive destruction in the world, but instead intended to use it to inflame two super powers whose political relations had been tested to the boiling point over the past year. Until she was certain, she would keep this theory to herself.

"Damn, Alex, does this stuff ever go away?" Phil's hands cut through the air. "You're going to pass this along to the CIA or somebody, right?"

"That's what we were talking about when you got here. One of the things that I'm worried about is—"

Phil interrupted, "Hey, you gotta see this!" He grabbed his paper, leafed through a few pages in the front section, folded it and slid it across to Alex. "I never would have paid attention to something like this before, but there's been a virus outbreak in Liberia. It looks like some scary stuff. The CDC hasn't identified the virus yet, but they've sent a team of scientists over there to check it out."

Alex picked up the newspaper. Her eyes bulged as she read the small, single-columned article in the San Francisco Post. She dropped the paper on the counter. "It's started. My god, it's started already."

CHAPTER 36

The ELWA hospital in Zorzor, Liberia, was a scatter of low yellow-and-red-painted cinder block buildings with rusty metal roofs. That part of Liberia was fertile, hilly country, dotted with small villages, and situated 90 miles southwest of the place where the borders of Sierra Leone, Guinea and Liberia converged. That border area had been the cradle of the 2014 Ebola outbreak and ELWA was now ground zero for Dr. Jim Harrington and his medical response team.

"This is out of control, Laura. It's like we're stuck in the perfect storm and there's no way to right the ship. Without more help this will spread to the populated centers in no time. Three health workers have been infected and we're short of supplies to deal with all this." Dr. Jim Harrington pressed his hands together. "If I knew how to beg, that's what I'd be doing. Let us use the vaccine—now."

Laura was tired, not the weariness brought about from lack of sleep or the fatigue from overstress, but the bone-tired, ragged exhaustion that comes only from living in constant fear. She wore battle scars from working in the trenches and having witnessed firsthand the shattering effects of women dying of cholera in the Dadaab refugee camp in Kenya, and being a first responder when meningitis had broken out in eastern Chad. Never in her lifetime had she anticipated witnessing an outbreak of smallpox, a disease that had not surfaced since the last known case on October 26, 1977.

"I can't, not yet… you know that. We have more tests to run and until then all we can do is focus on containment and quarantine," Dr. Elsbach said. "What do the numbers look like?"

Jim reached for a piece of paper. "Our numbers are outdated as soon as we finish processing them. The last report showed 2,423 deaths and an estimated 3,945 infected, but I'm sure both numbers are higher."

"Are you having any success at all with isolation?" Laura asked.

"Hell no," Jim shouted. "These are nomadic people, you know that. They travel from village to village, forage, trade—it's their way of life and it's impossible to fully contain the population. Already, there are cases across the border in Sierra Leone, and I expect this will reach Monrovia within days if it's not already there."

Laura rubbed her eyes and dropped her head. "Jesus, this is getting worse by the minute."

Jim continued shouting, "So what the hell are we supposed to do? We have angry people attacking our make-shift health centers thinking that because we're dressed in yellow or blue moon suits, for all they know we're responsible for the death of their family members. The worst part is we can't stop their traditions and customs. They believe that they need to wash the bodies of the deceased before they're buried. How the hell do we handle that one? Huh?"

"Come on, from what we know so far, the vaccine won't work. This isn't the standard variola strain of smallpox. When we expose the smallpox virus samples to the vaccine it represses and another virus is activated. We don't know what that virus is yet. We have genomic surveillance teams working around the clock all over the country trying to figure this out." Laura took a deep breath. "As soon as I know something, you'll know it."

"So, we just hang out here in the middle of bum-fuck Egypt and hope and pray that the Liberian guards protecting us from knife-toting mobs don't change their mind and turn on us? I don't like those odds, and obviously the Red Cross didn't either; they pulled out in the middle of last night." Jim Harrington was still suited in his P.P.E., a biohazard outfit consisting of a full-body suit and head covering made of Tyvek fabric, a breathing mask, a plastic face shield with goggles, two pairs of surgical gloves, one pair of rubber gloves, rubber boots and a plastic apron. Buckets of sweat from the sweltering heat and humidity poured out from underneath his face shield. "We need help, Laura. We need help in every conceivable area if we're going to stop this from becoming more than just a localized outbreak. In a few weeks' time this will spread throughout the continent; that's my prediction."

"I'll talk to the Director right now. If we can't get you the help you need in the next 24 hours I'm going to have you and your team pulled. You have my word on that. I don't want any of you to be in more danger than you're already facing." Dr. Elsbach rubbed her hands together nervously and continued, "The Liberian government won't allow the U.S. military inside its borders to help on this, but we need to come up with something right now."

Jim Harrington and Laura Elsbach each stared head-on into their video camera. Not another word was spoken, nor were any needed. They were in full agreement; protect the first responders and health workers on the ground in the next 24 hours or smallpox, an infectious disease originating over 16,000 years ago and responsible for killing over 400,000 Europeans each year during large portions the 18th century and millions more throughout modern times, would again reach pandemic proportions.

CHAPTER 37

A lex had been restless that night and unable to sleep. The SynAid virus was a ticking time bomb and the very moment it was unleashed, the political powers of the world would openly begin their verbal assaults while covertly posturing to take advantage of the situation. The United States and Russia were on a collision course and dozens of other countries would be scrambling to choose sides to protect their own interests.

Alex had been in the dining room for the past three hours trying to find a way to penetrate the computer network of the Chinese Liberation Army. Her suspicions about the Chinese network had been correct—it was a private network. She needed to first access Alibaba's network to find an access point into the Chinese government's network. Alibaba's network had been locked tight with a series of Virtual Private Networks and a separate login and password would be needed for each VPN. She could penetrate the VPNs, but it would take time and the longer she spent attempting to penetrate a system like Alibaba's, the greater the risk of detection.

Each computer on a network has at least one IP address that can be tracked down by skilled IT security personnel. Alex used a separate computer that she would dispose of once she had completed her breach of the Alibaba system. She in no way wanted her penetration to be traced back to her.

To gain access to the inner workings of Alibaba's network, Alex knew she would need access to one of its website application engineer's login information. She needed to spoof the Alibaba VPN server. Using her throw-away computer, she sent emails to a host of application engineers informing them that the system was undergoing routine maintenance and passwords would be changed once the maintenance was completed. She asked the engineers for their username and password to prove their identity and permit them access once the maintenance was completed. There was nothing novel about this ploy. An experienced engineer wouldn't fall for such a trick, but she was hoping her email blast would hit a new and unsuspecting junior engineer.

In the meantime, she attempted to gain access using more traditional methods. She had developed her own network login cracker. Patterned after the THC-Hydra program, she had added new modules and numerous protocols of attack, while enhancing the recovery speed. This was usually a hacker's last resort. If a hacker unleashed this method of attack it meant that the targeted password was almost certainly more complicated than a Social Security number, a pet's name or a birth date. She named this program Hercules, after the slayer of the serpent-like Hydra of Greek mythology. While she waited, she ran Hercules to search for protected login information.

Her phone rang and she immediately recognized the number. "Hello, Charles. I'm so sorry I haven't called you earlier, but I just got back to phone coverage."

"That's all right, Alexandra, I haven't known much until just now, which is why I'm giving you a call. Whoever created this vaccine has really discovered some rather remarkable research that somehow has been overlooked for nearly 40 years."

"Have you been able to determine what the ProTryX vaccine is intended to be used for?"

"Well, yes and no. That vaccine is designed to suppress certain control elements in its targeted viral gene. By doing that, the targeted gene will become inactive and will no longer be a factor," Charles said.

"You mean it will stop a particular virus from spreading?" Alex asked.

"That appears to be the case, but the interesting part is how they developed this vaccine. In the late 1970s, Dr. Gardner, from the University of Glasgow, made a breakthrough discovery that was hotly debated by the leading geneticists of that time. Dr. Gardner created a master switch that would turn off, or inactivate, all latent viruses, not just specific viruses, but *all* latent viruses. He had discovered that certain genes had master switches that could turn distinct gene expression programs on and off. That was real groundbreaking research back then."

Alex gripped her phone tighter. "Wait, you're saying that it's possible to inactivate *all* viruses? If that's the case, then it would be possible to cure all diseases caused by viruses, right?"

"Yes, but the problem with that is there are a number of viruses that are beneficial to us. There are viruses, for example, that only infect bacteria, killing them, but not infecting the human's cells. We call these bacteriophages. They were once studied by the Soviet Union in the 40s as an alternative to antibiotics. Nothing came of it then, but they're being studied again for possible antibiotic uses."

Charles cleared his throat and continued, "When Dr. Gardner made his discovery, it touched off what may have been the first debate about cloning. A lot of people were outraged that scientists wanted to change human functions and there were concerns that the master switch might turn off certain normal genes essential for human life. All of this led to Dr. Gardner's research being shelved. It's a shame when you think about it."

"Okay, so how does that all relate to the ProTryX vaccine?" Alex asked.

"Whoever created that vaccine had obviously found Dr. Gardner's research and tailored it to a specific need. The ProTryX has a promoter switch that seems to be synthetic, or man-made. The same way Dr. Gardner created a master switch for all viruses, the ProTryX developer created a master switch for a specific virus."

"Is ProTryX safe to use?" Alex asked.

"I have no way of knowing that and nothing in the information you provided to me indicates that any clinical trials were run using this vaccine. At this point I don't even know what this vaccine would be used for, but I should be able to determine that shortly."

Alex was nearly certain that ProTryX was to be used to combat the SynAid virus once it was unleashed, but a shred of doubt remained. She debated not telling Charles about the SynAid virus for fear that it would send him into hiding. He had made it perfectly clear he didn't want anything to do with anything similar to the fallout from the G-16 ever again. However, she needed Charles to confirm the last missing piece. "Thank you; you've been more helpful than you'll ever know. I think I might know the purpose behind the ProTryX vaccine." She paused, then continued, "The G-16 virus has surfaced again, but this time it's been altered in an entirely different fashion. It's been combined with smallpox—"

"Mon Dieu! Non. How do you know this? That can't be true. Smallpox has been eradicated, that can't be—it just can't."

Alex continued, "This new virus is called SynAid and the person behind it obtained vials of the G-16 virus and the smallpox virus from the U.S. facility in Brazil; the same place where the G-16 was developed. They're getting ready to unleash it in the U.S. at any point now and I need you to help me out on one more thing; was ProTryX designed to be used for the SynAid virus?"

Silence. Alex imagined Charles slumped over in his chair with a finger tightly curled around the end of his droopy moustache. "Charles, can you help me with that?"

Charles' voice cracked, "Alexandra, the combination of those two viruses is lethal. I don't think there is anything that can be done to prevent a virus like that from spreading once it hits its target—nothing at all."

"What about ProTryX? Can you determine if that would be effective? I think that's its whole purpose."

"I can't reach that conclusion without running tests on the specific virus, the SynAid virus as you call it, but I may be able to see, in theory, if that is the case. I will make a call to a colleague I know at the WHO and go over this with him," Charles added.

"You do that at your own peril. Remember, you didn't want to get involved. That will put you right in the middle of this. If you can do this on your end and let me know, I can take it from there."

"Give me a day to see what I can come up with."

"Great, thanks... thanks, Charles. We'll talk tomorrow."

CHAPTER 38

"Today must be my lucky day. This is a primo spot," Steph said out loud as she backed into a parking space in the 500 block of Cole Street; the heart of the Height Ashbury District.

She closed her car door and walked up the steps of a multi-colored Victorian. Her finger scrolled down the directory bolted to one side of the double doors. "There it is—202." She pushed the buzzer.

Like Steph, Delynn had also been worried about Adam. He hadn't shown up for work and hadn't even bothered to call in. Delynn had concocted a story that Human Resources had bought and it had given her Adam's home address. Steph had volunteered to drive over and find Adam.

She pushed the buzzer for the third time when a middle-aged lady unlocked and opened the front door. She stuck her head out and eyed Steph as if she'd seen her before, but wasn't real happy to see her again. "Usually when someone doesn't answer the bell they're either not home or don't want to see nobody." She pushed the door wide open. "Who you looking for? Maybe I can help? I'm sort of the manager here. My husband and I own the place. And what happened to your face? You don't look much like the fightin' type to me."

"Oh, no, it's not anything like that. Yeah, I know it does look kinda scary and it still hurts some. I was hit with the ball while I was playing racquetball. I still ended up winning though," Steph smiled.

"It's gotta hurt. What can I do for you? Who you looking for?"

Steph pushed back her hair and smiled. "I am… I'm looking for Adam…Adam O'Keeffe. He doesn't seem to be answering and he told me he'd meet me at his place at 9:30, and," she held up her watch, "it's 9:37."

The lady chuckled. "Give the guy some space, missy. He's probably running a little late, that's all."

"No, he told me he'd be here all morning and wouldn't be leaving until around 11:00. He's going into work late today."

"Adam… hmmm, you know, come to think of it, I haven't seen him for a day or two myself. A nice guy and usually very punctual, I'll say that about him. I see him coming and going at almost exactly the same time each day." The lady leaned to her side, her elbow rested on the door handle, her shoulder pushed against the door and the other hand was planted firmly on her hip. "What'd you want to see Adam about? He doesn't get many visitors that I know of. In fact I can't think of nary a one."

"I'm his sister and I got into town last night and we were planning on getting together… here… at his place… this morning." Steph extended a hand. "Oh, I'm so sorry I should have introduced myself earlier, I'm Stephanie."

The lady nodded and gripped Steph's hand. "Nice to meet you, Stephanie and I'm Colleen, Colleen Turner, but most everybody, including Adam, calls me Lila. I prefer that."

"Nice to meet you, too, Lila."

Lila moved away from the door and waved a hand. "You're more than welcome to come on inside to my place. I have a fresh pot brewing and, as I told you, Adam is a real creature of habit. I suspect he'll be back here any minute. I'll leave my front door open, like I always do and you'll spot him when he walks by."

"Thanks. A cup of coffee right now is just what I need."

Fifteen minutes later, Lila led Steph up the stairs to Adam's apartment. Steph had put on the charm and Lila had finally trusted her enough to let her into his apartment.

Lila reached the top of the stairs and stopped. She took several deep breaths and wiped her hand across her forehead. "Whew, I wouldn't want to do this every day. This isn't something I usually do you know. This is a real exception to my rule, but I guess there's no harm in your case, you being his sister and all."

"Oh, don't worry, Adam won't mind and this way I can give him a real sisterly surprise."

Lila pulled her keys from her apron pocket and counted through them, one at a time. "There we go, 202, that's it."

Lila unlocked the door, pushed it open and turned toward Steph. "What's the matter? You look like you just saw a ghost."

Steph raised her arm and pointed a finger. "It's a mess!"

Lila turned and shrieked, "My god, what happened here? I never would've suspected Adam was such a slob."

Steph put a hand on Lila's shoulder. "I'm sure it's not usually like this. Adam's a lot more like Felix Unger than Oscar, but ever since he was little he's had these tantrums. This is what he does. He throws his things around, leaves, and then comes back in a few hours and straightens everything back up."

"Odd."

"Yep, it is. Listen, I'll go ahead and clean things up while I'm waiting for him. It wouldn't be the first time I've done it. And thanks for the coffee… and the company, I enjoyed it." Steph grabbed the door knob. "I'll for sure stop by before I leave and say good-bye, that is if it's okay with you?"

Lila smiled. "Good luck, and yes, I'd love it if you'd knock on my door before you leave."

Steph closed the door and leaned back. Drawers had been emptied, books thrown from the shelves and the mattress had been overturned. On the table, next to the bed, sat Adam's coke-bottle, wire rimmed glasses—the place had been ransacked and Adam was in trouble.

CHAPTER 39

Steph stood outside Chief's office, her knees wobbled and she tried to slow her breathing. Hyperventilation was about to overtake her. Calm down, she thought, just calm down and relax.

She regained her wits and poked her head inside. "Got a minute, Chief?"

He grunted and waved her in.

"What are you waiting for?" He lifted his head and leaned back in his chair. "Well, what'd you want? You asked for a minute and that's about all I got right now."

Steph sat down with a thump and leaned her elbows on her knees. Her head drooped. "I have a problem and I'm not sure what to do, so I wanted to talk this through with you to see what you think."

"If you're having trouble on the home front, you're in the wrong office. I'm betting this has something to do with Agrico. Right?" Chief muttered.

Steph sat up and folded her arms across her chest and drew a deep, ragged breath. "Yeah, it does. One of my sources there is missing; he has been for a couple of days. It's the guy who works in accounting. I was supposed to meet with him right after I left Cummings' house the other day, but, well you know, I ended up in the hospital. No one has heard from him so I stopped by his apartment to see if he was there. I talked the landlady into letting me in. Oh," she grimaced, "I was supposed to stop by her place when I left. Oh boy, anyway, his place was ransacked, everything had been thrown around and searched and there was no sign of him at all."

Chief straightened in his chair. "When were you in his apartment?"

"I left there less than an hour ago. I've been walking around in circles trying to figure out what to do and then I came here."

"Who else knows about this? Have you talked to the police or anyone else?" Chief asked.

Steph shook her head. "That's my problem. I haven't talked to anyone because I promised him I wouldn't divulge anything about our relationship. I promised to protect him no matter what. If I talk to the police I'd have to reveal how we know each other and what I suspect. I really think he's in trouble and it has everything to do with his helping me. Somebody must know what he was doing and it may be connected to the guy that mugged me. The last time I spoke to him he said he'd copied some financial information from some files and he was going to give it to me."

"Oh boy, this is some serious stuff." Chief stood up and walked around to the front of his desk and boosted himself on top. "I can tell this is eating at you. What's your gut telling you about all this? Uh, your instincts?"

"My gut's knotted a million times and it's not speaking to me about any of this. I know the importance of protecting my sources. Believe me I've memorized everything written about that and I know it's a fundamental principle of journalism. On the other hand," she let out a long sigh, "his life could be in danger and I may be able to help. Actually, I know his life is in danger and I can help." Her eyes pleaded with Chief. "What would you do?"

Chief parted his hands in a gesture of uncertainty. "Every good journalist runs into this question at some point and usually a lot more than once. I think you've hit the toughest of the tough ones, though." Chief's hands gripped the edge of his desk and he rocked from side to side, slowly. "It's not my question to answer. It's not black and white and there's no right or wrong here. You're the only one who's talked to him and who knows what he expects from you."

"He's been scared about all this from day one and I've constantly reinforced the fact that I'd protect him no matter what. But if he somehow dies or is seriously hurt, I'd never forgive myself—never. What about you, have you ever faced a situation where you thought you may have to give up your source?"

Chief gave a half-nod, "Oh sure, but nothing like this. I've had the usual brow beating by attorneys and cops, but it was just regular stuff and I didn't cave. You know, maybe you should talk to the police and tell them the guy's missing and you suspect foul play without giving them any of the facts. It might be worth a try."

"I thought about that, but they'd probably treat it as a standard missing person and do nothing. Without them knowing what I know, it'd be a big waste of time."

"You were in his apartment and it was ransacked, so you may want to say something before the cops find something out and go sniffing around on their own. After they talk to the landlady they're going to know all about you being there and then you become a suspect. So, give it a try, talk to the police, tell them you were in his apartment and see if you can push them to do something."

A rapid knock pounded on the office door and Chief yelled out, "I'm tied up, it'll have to wait."

"Real quick," one of Steph's co-reporters said as he stuck his head through the crack. "A guy from Agrico was found dead at his house and they're calling it a suicide at this point. I think he's a big shot and I want to take a camera over there and see what I can find out. Okay?"

Steph spun around, her voice boomed, "Who is it? What's his name?"

"Some guy named Eric Cummings."

CHAPTER 40

The Biological Weapons Convention of 1972 had resulted in the first multilateral disarmament treaty banning the production of an entire category of weapons. Signed by 170 nations, it had prohibited proliferation of all biological and toxin weapons. Unfortunately, the lack of enforcement provisions had limited its real effectiveness.

That Convention had been manipulated by the world's superpowers as a means of gathering public support whenever they had suspected another nation of pressing forward in the development, production or stockpiling of biological weapons. Shortly after the Soviet Union had ratified the Convention, they had constructed a massive research organization for biological weapons, known as Biopreparat. When questioned about the facility, they had insisted it had been used strictly for civilian purposes. In 1979, an anthrax epidemic had broken out near the shores of Lake Baikal at the Biopreparat facility, and had again raised suspicions in the West about Biopreparat being an ongoing research facility for the Soviet Union's proliferation of biological weapons. The Soviets had vehemently defended their civilian research facility alibi and had proclaimed that the epidemic had been caused by tainted meat, nothing else.

Ten years later, a leading Soviet scientist connected to Biopreparat had defected to Great Britain. Vladimir Pasechnik had informed the British, and subsequently the Americans, that the Biopreparat system had been used to develop new genetically-engineered pathogens. The United States, Britain and China had publicly reacted with demanding and tough words, but this had all been overshadowed by the Berlin Wall toppling, the Soviet bloc unraveling and the Cold War winding down. Privately, these same countries had assured the Soviets that there would be no retaliation.

"Eat up; you're going to need some calories if you want to keep this pace up." Benjamin placed a sandwich and sliced oranges next to Alex and took a seat beside her.

"Oh, thanks, you must've read my mind." Alex reached for the sandwich and took a bite.

"You making any progress? I just heard from Phil, and he's sitting on pins and needles right now. I think you have a new convert that may take over your enterprise when you really decide to retire."

Alex laughed. "If he intends to have Michelle in his life, I think his days in the espionage business are over." She looked at Benjamin out of the corners of her eyes. "And mine will be too, as soon as this is over."

"If I had a nickel for every time I've heard that," Benjamin chortled. "Anyway, have you come up with anything?"

Alex nodded. "I finally accessed the computer network in China I was having problems with earlier."

"You mean the Chinese Liberation Army? You said you had problems, so how'd you do it?" Benjamin asked.

"You gave me the idea."

Benjamin cocked his head, "How's that?"

"When we were at the M & O and you were talking about the Chinese company, Alibaba."

Benjamin nodded, "I remember."

"The computer network at the Chinese Liberation Army is as secure, maybe more so, than the NSA's and it's a private system. I tried, but couldn't find a way to get in. I ran across some interesting connections between Alibaba and the Chinese government, so I thought the best way to penetrate the government's computers would be through a friendly system that probably communicates with them on a regular basis or at the least would have a secret server with access."

"Alibaba? They have ties with the government? Huh, that must be the main reason my broker advised me to stay out of that offering."

Alex nodded. "Big ties, but you won't find them in their offering prospectus. The Zhang family has been connected to the Army for half-a-century. Zhang Zhen was the Army's highest ranking general and the one who pushed for the bloody 1989 crackdown in Tiananmen Square. One of his sons is currently a general whose job it is to make sure that the soldiers controlling China's nuclear weapons stay loyal to the Communist Party. His other son is also a general, but he ventured into business and set his wife up as the chairwoman of a telemarketing and pharmaceutical business called Citic 21CN. It's a small company that Alibaba purchased for an inflated price of $170 million and gave them below market options for millions of shares in Alibaba. When Alibaba went public in the U.S. last year, the Zhang family made well over a billion dollars."

"When I read through their prospectus, I saw where they had interests in a number of other Chinese companies, but I didn't see anything about any ties to the government or Party officials," Benjamin said.

"Within the year before they went public, they spent more than $4 billion on acquisitions, including stakes in a Chinese soccer team, a ride-sharing company and a digital-mapping business. All those companies have direct ownership ties to high ranking Party officials." Alex sat back. "I'm sure all that was no coincidence."

"Getting inside Alibaba's system was no different than hacking into most companies. Once I was in, I assumed the interface between Alibaba and the government would raise few suspicions because of their connections."

"How did you end up getting in?" Benjamin asked.

"I was able to spoof Alibaba's VPN server and gain access to their database servers. From there I ran a port sniffer to find an open port to the Chinese government's network. Then—"

"Hold on," Benjamin interrupted, "VPN, port sniffer, you've already lost me."

Alex let out a half-laugh, "None of that's really important anyway. What is important is after I accessed the government's network I ran a port sniffer again and," she looked at Benjamin, "a port sniffer is a way to search for an open port that will allow access, that's it. I found the root DNS server, or the Domain Name Server, and it gave me a list of each computer and router on the network. I used specific keywords like Zhang, SynAid, Nakajima and a few others and I was able to find the Chinese Liberation Army's network. Once I was inside, it was relatively simple to find what I was looking for."

"What about the virus in Liberia? Anything new on that?" Benjamin asked.

Alex finished half her sandwich and wiped her mouth. "Well... actually... no, not really. The U.S. government is being pretty closed-mouthed about this new viral outbreak and I think part of that is because they don't know anything. The CDC has reported 46 deaths in Liberia so far with hundreds of others, maybe more, infected. The WHO has confirmed those numbers and both organizations have sent teams to the infected areas. They're saying the symptoms are all similar and they're suspecting it's the same virus and they've already ruled out the possibility of a bio-attack, but I assume that's fairly routine at this stage."

Benjamin's face hardened. "And you think this is the same virus that Kioshi developed?"

Alex nodded. "SynAid—it has to be," Alex replied. "Did you speak with that reporter from the Post or Jessica yet?"

"Yeah, I did talk with Jessica, and she ended up peppering me with tons of questions trying to figure out what I was really up to. I think she finally bought into the fact that I was just trying to see if there was anything GEN could do to help out. She didn't think there was anyway smallpox could be involved. All known quantities of that virus are safely and securely locked up by the Russians and Americans. That's her take, anyway," Benjamin said.

"I would guess that the Americans know their stockpile of smallpox has been hit, but they certainly aren't going to say anything. The CDC and the WHO are both saying that the symptoms of this virus are similar to smallpox—fever, body aches, then rashes on the arms, legs, mouth and face. Eventually lesions form, scab over and leave a severe scar. If you survive, that is."

"Just how deadly is smallpox?" Benjamin asked.

"Whew... deadly. Typically one-third of those infected end up dead, but in the 20th century alone, nearly 500,000 deaths occurred. It's plenty deadly and, probably more than any virus, it scares the bejesus out of the medical profession."

Alex took a sip of tea and continued, "I'm certain Kioshi is behind this outbreak. He has to be. Before the Chinese will pay him for SynAid, they need to see definitive results that it does in fact work. Remember Kioshi talking about having to make sure the virus is effective before he sells it?"

Benjamin nodded.

"I found out from the hard drives that about a year ago, Kioshi stitched the virus into rice grains and delivered the rice to different locations. I'm not sure where. The timeframe to grow and harvest the rice probably matches this recent outbreak. So if I'm right, then the Chinese will be wiring $100 million to Kioshi any day now, and after Kioshi delivers the virus, they'll wire an additional $150 million. I have Kioshi's banking information that I'll check out, but I imagine by now, he's changed banks."

Benjamin pulled his cell from his back pocket. "I think this is that reporter." He touched the Receive button. "Hello?"

■ ■ ■ ■ ■

Alex heard a familiar beep from her computer. She spun her laptop around and hit the green answer button. "Hello, Devon, nice to see your face. I'm sorry it's taken so long for us to get together, but it's been a madhouse here ever since we got back. Could you slide over to your left a bit? Part of you is out of view."

Devon leaned to the right. "You're killing me over here. I've been bouncing off walls from the time you left and all I got was a text from you saying thanks, everything worked. Everything? Everything never works; you of all people know that." He slid back into full view.

"I know, I know, but in this case everything really did work out—

perfectly. *Back to the Future* might still have some bugs, but I sure couldn't find them. I was able to eventually isolate my target and have him spend time looking at the flashing images. I hope it doesn't matter that I forced him at gunpoint to watch the screen."

"One way or another I was certain you'd get your way, gunpoint or not. Listen," Devon squirmed in his seat and leaned forward, "when you were here I talked to you about having to adjust the flickering rate for the primary colors depending on the light intensity of wherever you were using the program. The flicker fusion rate, remember that?"

Alex nodded. "I used the spectrophotometer and got a reading of 2.89, which was lower than where you and I had set the program. So I slowed the spike timing and oscillatory patterns for the reds and blues."

"By how much? That's important," Devon asked.

Alex grabbed her chin and squeezed. "I can't remember exactly. I think I slowed the patterns by .26 milliseconds. Yeah, I'm pretty sure that was it."

"Oh boy," Devon cringed. "I hope that was the number because if you slowed it any more, then you ended up wasting your time. I told you that you needed me. You should've taken me along."

"I'm sure everything worked out just as we planned." Alex laughed, "By the time I left him he was calling me Kristen and inviting me to join his harem. When I walked out of there he had no idea who I was. This program of yours is miraculous, to say the least."

"Still, you should've taken me along." Devon wagged a finger at Alex. "You owe me one you know? I'm already signed up for the next one, okay?"

"There won't be a next one; that I'm certain of. Anyway, I need to go, I'm in the middle of something, but I'll track you down the next time I'm in London and we'll talk about this further. And thanks, thank you, Devon."

Devon bowed, "My pleasure, ta ta."

CHAPTER 41

Steph arrived at the Buckeye Roadhouse 15 minutes early to make sure they would get the table she had requested. She had chosen the Buckeye as a place to meet, not just because the food was lip-smacking good, but because there had always been enough crowd noise to guarantee their conversation would not be overheard.

The Buckeye Roadhouse had been a staple of Mill Valley since 1937. Housed in a stately country manor with old world charm, the restaurant would be more at home in the vineyards of Provence, than nestled along a side road just a short minute drive from Marin's busiest freeway.

She was promptly seated at the corner table she had requested. She looked over at a group sitting near the polished river rock fireplace and smiled. Someone's birthday, she suspected, or maybe a wedding party. Toasts, backslapping and laughter circled the group and wine and champagne flowed freely.

"Would you care for a drink or maybe—"

Startled out of her thoughts, Steph swung around and her arm swept two water glasses off the table, landing on the backpedaling waiter. "Oh, geez, I'm so sorry. I can be such a klutz at times. Let me help."

"No, no, that's quite alright." The waiter straightened up and folded his hands across his trousers. "I will take care of this in a moment, but first, would you care for something to drink or perhaps an appetizer while you're waiting for the others in your party to arrive?"

Steph smiled sheepishly. "I'll just stick with water for now. I expect my friends will be here any minute. Thanks, though."

An hour and a half ago, when Steph had hung up the phone after talking to Benjamin, she had yelled out to Chandler. "You'll never guess who I'm about to have dinner with!"

After hearing the name, Benjamin Hunter, Chandler had been star-struck. Chandler had been working for the past two years as a financial analyst with Vyodyne, a bio-tech company very similar to GEN, only Vyodyne's focus had been in the area of organ transplant rejection medications. It had been her hope that with a few more years of experience she could move over to GEN where she had felt—no she had known—her talents would be better appreciated. The news about Benjamin, the G-16 virus and the near demise of GEN had been a regular dinner table topic for Steph and Chandler.

"Come on, Steph," Chandler had pleaded, "bring me along. If he really wants to find out what you know about that virus then I can help you out. I'll be your own personal expert."

Steph had resisted Chandler's incessant pleas, but she hadn't been able to figure out what Benjamin was really interested in. Oh sure, he had mentioned he had wanted to talk with her about the virus outbreak in Liberia, but when he had mentioned he would be bringing his friend, Alex Boudreau, along, Steph's newly sprouted investigative reporter antennae had begun receiving mixed signals. She had read about Boudreau as well, and there was no way he would be bringing Alex Boudreau with him if that had been all he had been interested in talking to her about.

"May I suggest the pan-roasted artichoke as a starter? I notice that your bread is gone and you've started in on your friend's water." The waiter stood stiff-shouldered to Steph's side, his head tilted forward as if he was begging her to eat.

Steph pushed the empty bread basket away and gave a half-nod. "That really does sound pretty good." She glanced at her watch—they should've been here by now. "And maybe I'll have a glass of wine after all... Sauvignon Blanc. You pick it."

Her ringtone was turned on low, but she heard the all too familiar ting, ting, ting. It was a text from Delynn. *Did you find Adam? I'm worried sick.*

Oh, god, I forgot to give her a call. She quickly replied and told her she hadn't found him, yet, but she had some ideas. She'd call her later that night.

The party celebrating near the rock fireplace had departed and a new group of revelers had already finished their first course. She took the last sip of her second glass of wine and let out an audible sigh. I wouldn't suspect someone like him to be 45 minutes late without at least calling.

She pulled her phone from her purse and checked her messages—nothing. Searching her call log she saw Benjamin's number and tapped once. When she heard the voicemail message she hung up.

Needing some air to collect her thoughts, Steph slid across her seat and stepped into the aisle just in time to catch the outstretched leg of the charging waiter. Four entrees and four drinks hurled forward, tumbling in mid-air and crashing smack in the center of a neighboring table. Shrimp gumbo, pasta primavera, steak Diane and a mushroom soufflé dripped down the fronts of two heavily starched shirts and two expensive and stylish gowns.

Standing outside the Buckeye, waiting for the valet to bring her car around, she chuckled to herself. I'll never be able to show my face in there again. She dialed Chandler's number, but after five or six rings her voice mail came on. Steph looked at her phone, one brow lowered. She's always answered her cell. That's just not like her, not at all.

CHAPTER 42

Benjamin sat at his desk in the den sorting through piles of his mail when he heard a soft-spoken accent, "I really can't go anywhere looking like this."

He looked up and saw Alex standing in the doorway, her arms framed the doorjambs and she leaned forward. "What do you think?"

"I think you look positively ravishing and you'll turn heads wherever we go. I particularly like your shirt."

Alex wore a pair of her old jeans with a frayed tear in one knee and a blue pinstriped linen shirt she had pulled from Benjamin's closet. The sleeves were rolled up to just below her elbows, the bottom hem was tightly knotted, but the shoulder seams fell to her biceps. "Well the baggy look is about all I can do for now. I don't have any clothes with me to go out for dinner or to go anywhere where I'm not trying to disguise myself."

Benjamin walked around the side of his desk, reached out and took Alex's hands. "This is Mill Valley, not Paris, and I think that shirt's never looked better."

Alex punched Benjamin in the shoulder. "Nice try, but… well, is there someplace we can stop along the way where I can buy something a bit closer to my size?"

Benjamin jerked his head to the side. "The doorbell? It couldn't be Phil. How about you see who's at the door and I should be done here in a few minutes. I know just the spot for you to pick out everything you need."

Alex turned to leave and Benjamin swatted her rear-end. "The pants fit perfectly."

Benjamin finished sorting through his mail and strolled out of the den. He looked down the hallway. "Alex, we better get going. Where are you?"

He walked down the hallway and into the foyer. "What's going on? Can I help you guys?"

Alex pivoted on her heels and Benjamin cringed. He had seen that look before. "Ben, this is the FBI and there's been a terrible mistake."

The man closest to Alex stepped forward and held out a piece of paper. The other three stared at Benjamin. "Mr. Hunter, I'm Agent Guzman with the FBI and I have a warrant for the arrest of Diana Shaffner." He held the warrant out. She needs to come with us—*now.*"

"Diana Shaffner?" As he squinted and stepped back, Benjamin saw the panic in Alex's eyes and he looked back at the agent. "She's right; this is some kind of mistake. She's not the person you're looking for. What's this about?"

"The easiest way to handle this, Mr. Hunter, is for Ms. Shaffner to come with us and you can talk with her after we process the paper work at headquarters," Agent Guzman said.

Benjamin looked at Alex, "Where's your passport? I'll go get it and show these guys that they're wrong."

Alex looked terrified. Her body was stiff and she looked down at the floor. She didn't look at or answer Benjamin.

"Alex! Your passport. Where is it?" Benjamin shouted.

Without looking up, Alex whispered, "It's not here. I... I don't know where it is."

Benjamin snatched the warrant from the agent's hand and unfolded it. His brows rose higher as he read each word. *Money laundering, bulk cash smuggling, tax evasion, interstate transportation of narcotics, violations of the Economic Espionage Act, conspiracy to....* He crumpled the warrant and threw it on the ground. "This is bullshit. You guys have the wrong person." He pulled his cell from his pocket. "I'm calling my lawyer and we'll get this straightened out."

Agent Guzman placed a hand on Benjamin's arm. "Go ahead and call your lawyer, she's going to need one, probably a good one, but right now I'm placing her under arrest." He motioned to the other agents and they stepped

235

forward in front of Alex. "You have the right to remain silent. Anything you say can and will be used against you in a court of law...."

Alex's arms were twisted behind her—cold steel cuffs crimped her wrists.

CHAPTER 43

Benjamin stood hunched over his desk and his fingers plucked away at the keyboard. His mind shifted into overdrive as he sifted through the events and facts trying to figure out who could have done this. Who is Diana Shaffner? Why do they think Alex is her? This was some huge mistake or maybe she was set up—but by whom and why? He knew it was possible for anyone to create a warrant with all the bells and whistles of authenticity. Alex had done so herself weeks back when she hacked the NSA's computers. Warrants didn't require stamps or seals and oftentimes, in cases of exigent circumstances, they're not even signed by a judge. The approval could be given over the phone and the warrant would be valid.

Benjamin grabbed his cell and dialed. After two rings a breathy, matter-of-fact voice answered, "Law offices of Starr and Schickman."

"This is Benjamin Hunter and I need to speak with Aidan Starr. Tell him it's urgent—very urgent."

Before Benjamin could exhale his second deep breath, Mr. Starr was on the line. "Ben, what a coincidence, I was just about to call you. I received—"

"Hold on, Aidan, the FBI just arrested Alex. I know you don't handle these types of cases, but I need your help. I need to get her out of there—now."

"Whoa, what do you mean, Alex has been arrested? For what? Where is she now?"

"Four agents came to the house around 15 minutes ago with an arrest warrant. I'll scan it and send you a copy. The warrant is for somebody named Diana Shaffner, and they think Alex is her. She's accused of money laundering and a host of other bullshit charges. It all happened so fast there was nothing we could do. They left here about five minutes ago; they cuffed her and they're taking her in. I asked them where they were taking her, but they wouldn't say; only that they were taking her into custody and she'd be booked on the charges."

"Ben, I don't know, I'm not—"

"Damn it! Just tell me you're going to help get Alex out of there or find me someone who can. I'm not leaving her in jail for one minute. I'll post whatever bail is needed."

"I'm stunned, blown away by this. Are you sure they were FBI Agents? Where are you now? Are you sure this wasn't a hoax of some kind? And who's Diana Shaffner?"

"This is no hoax. The guys who came here were real, the warrant's real, I think, and Alex is in a shit-load of trouble. I don't know who the hell Diana Shaffner is. I'm at my house right now and this is where they arrested her."

"You must've showed them Alex's ID to prove she wasn't that person?" Aidan asked.

"I tried, but Alex just gave me a blank stare and didn't respond."

Aidan Starr's voice lost the silvery cadence that greeted Ben and he continued in a sotto voce tone, "You've run into nothing but a string of trouble ever since you met Alex. Wait; hear me out before you say anything. I know you have feelings for her and I certainly know how loyal you can be to your friends, but, in light of her past, maybe there's something to all this?"

"Don't even go there. She's been framed, this is all a mistake and this is pure bullshit. Are you going to help me or not? I don't have the time for any lectures right now."

"Of course I'll help, but this is an area of the law that I know very little about. I do know someone I can call to see if she'll handle this. Give me a minute, hold on."

Benjamin rubbed the back of his neck as he waited, the phone crammed between his ear and shoulder. This is a total setup. When's this going to end? For a brief moment, he thought about his life before Alex had burst onto the scene and, at times, turned his everyday existence into a tormented hell.

"Okay, I just spoke to Gloria Santora and she's on her way over to my office right now. As soon as I get a copy of the warrant from you, Gloria and I will go over to the FBI headquarters, find Alex and get to the bottom of this. I hope you're right and this is nothing more than a mistake. How are you feeling? Are you okay?" Aidan asked.

Ben heard the loud drum roll on the front door, but ignored it. "I'm scared as hell and worried about Alex. You'll have the warrant within the minute and you'll call me the second you learn anything, right? I want to come over and see Alex myself and get her the hell out of there."

"Yeah, you'll be my first call and if anything else comes to mind make sure you call me," Aidan replied.

Ben dropped his cell on the desk and collapsed in the chair. He leaned all the way back, his eyes closed and his hands white-knuckled the armrests. He played mental ping pong with Alex's obvious set-up and the SynAid virus which was ticking forward toward its undisclosed, but highly public target. He sat on the edge of time; again trying to weave a future in spite of Alex's tangled past. His thoughts settled on Alex. From what he knew about her past, there could be any number of marks out there who would want to frame her. God knows even he wanted to bury her at one point. Kioshi was his first suspect and although Benjamin did not rule him out, he felt he needed to look in other corners to see if any of those faded footsteps may have returned. From what Alex had told him on several occasions, it was an easy task to frame someone by placing untraced money in their bank accounts or by creating a criminal record. Alex had done so herself.

"There you are! What's going on?" Phil charged into the den with Michelle trailing close in his wake. He stood inches from Benjamin, his face painted white from fear. "We passed Alex on the way over here and she was in the back seat of a black sedan. It didn't look good. What the hell's happening?"

"Phil!" In a single motion, Ben slammed his feet to the ground, pushed up from the chair and threw his arms in the air. "Alex was arrested!"

By the time Benjamin had finished bringing Phil and Michelle up to speed on the afternoon's events, Phil had downed his second cup of coffee and was pacing across the kitchen floor. He sucked in air and turned to Benjamin. "We can't just wait around for Starr to call—no way—*absolutely*—no way."

"Yeah, yeah, but, I don't know what to do." Benjamin raised his head and looked at them both. His stomach felt like a twisted chamois cloth and his heart pounded in his throat. "I don't know what to do."

Phil slammed his mug on the counter. "Let's go to the FBI headquarters. It beats waiting around here and by the time we get there maybe Starr will have found out something."

Phil waved a hand at Benjamin. "Come on, let's go."

"Wait," Michelle grabbed Phil's arm. "Ben, do you have a copy of the arrest warrant here?"

"Yeah, it's in the scanner on my desk, in the den. Why?"

"Let me take a look at it first. I'll be right back." She turned and disappeared down the hall.

Phil cocked his head toward Benjamin. "It seems we now have a lawyer in our group."

"Huh?" Benjamin's brows curled. "What do you mean?"

"Well, when Michelle told me about her past and her asshole husband, she also filled me in on her career. When she graduated from law school, Duke, I think, she started working for a high powered Wall Street firm doing mostly corporate stuff, but she wasn't happy there. After she met John, she decided to pack it up and make the move to small town, USA. She had a part-time law practice for a while handling whatever walked through the door." Phil sat down on a high backed stool and locked his heels on the footrest. "Doesn't hurt to let her take a look at the warrant and then let's get out of here."

CHAPTER 44

The Federal Bureau of Investigation was located in the federal building on the outer fringes of San Francisco's seedy, but newly gentrified Tenderloin District. Even before Dashiell Hammett had popularized it in The Maltese Falcon, the Tenderloin had been San Francisco's illicit crime neighborhood. The FBI's San Francisco field office was a full-scale operation, where they handled their own interrogations, bookings, incarcerations and field activities.

Opened in 1911, the San Francisco office became one of the Agency's nine divisional headquarters and had been responsible for cracking some of America's most noteworthy cases: the kidnapping of Patty Hearst by the Symbionese Liberation Army; the murder of Congressman Leo Ryan as part of the Jonestown massacre in Guyana, South America; and it had identified Ted Kaczynski as the Unabomber.

An hour earlier, Benjamin, Phil and Michelle had passed through the metal detectors and security area of the FBI headquarters and had taken the elevator to the 13th floor, where they had been led into a small waiting room. They had been told that Aidan Starr and Gloria Santora were with their client, Diana Shaffner, and word would be passed to them that the three would be waiting downstairs when they finished.

"I can't believe this is happening. It's total bullshit." Benjamin leaned back against the wall, his left leg was bent and the sole of his shoe bored into the wall. The knuckles of his clenched fists rubbed against each other. He gazed off into the distance as if waiting for a bus. For the first time, he felt with nauseating clarity what it was like to breathe through Alex's lungs and to see the dangerous barricades through her eyes. Alex had faced impossible situations dozens of times in her life and she had trained herself to use her own fear and instincts to her advantage. To Alex, there was no difference between conscious thought and instinct. Benjamin couldn't shake the fact that somewhere in this very building, Alex was being held against her will for something she in no way had done. That thought sliced into his gut.

"It's been over an hour. I'm going to go find someone who can tell us what the hell's going on." Phil jumped to his feet.

"Wait!" Michelle uncrossed her legs and leaned forward. "An hour isn't very long considering the circumstances. It would take at least that long to book her into the system, and my guess is that the two lawyers haven't spent much time with her at this point. Ben's already sent a text that we're here. Let's give it a little more time. There's nothing we can do—there really isn't."

Phil turned. "Yeah, you're probably right, but I hate doing nothing, it rubs me the wrong way. If Alex were here she'd have us all moving in different directions and we wouldn't just be sitting around."

"We'll figure out what to do when we know more. In the meantime, sit down and try to relax." Michelle patted the seat next to her. "Please."

Phil sat back down, leaned forward, drilled his elbows into his thighs, locked his hands behind his neck, shook his head and let out a groan. "Like I said, I hate sitting around doing nothing."

"Ben." Aidan and Gloria walked into the room. "We just finished up with Alex."

Benjamin lifted his head and shot off the wall. "How is she? When's she getting out of here?"

Aidan looked over at Gloria, who spoke, "It's not that simple. Let's all go outside. It's better we talk somewhere other than here."

A block down the street from the federal building, the five formed a tight huddle on the sidewalk. The night fog was advancing under full sail, the street lamps shrouded by the gray mist.

"First, we won't be getting her out tonight and it may take a while to schedule an arraignment," Gloria explained. "My guess is the DA will be asking for no bail, but we have some good arguments to counter that, I think. The problem is—"

"What?" Benjamin interrupted, nearly shouting. "No bail, that's preposterous. They can't do that—can they?"

"They can, but let's not worry about that now." Gloria inched closer. "The real problem right now is Alex doesn't want to talk about the charges against her—"

Benjamin interrupted, again, "They have the wrong person. Don't they know that? Didn't she tell you that?"

"They've already run her prints and they match with Diana Shaffner's. They're convinced they're holding the right person. Alex didn't want to talk about that or anything else. All she's interested in is relaying some information to you." Gloria turned her head, "Are you Michelle, Michelle Holman?"

Michelle nodded.

"Alex told us you're a lawyer and she wants you as part of her defense team. Once you're onboard, she'll talk to you," Gloria said.

"I'm not that kind of lawyer, I'm really not. I'll help in any way I can, but I can't defend her."

"We can talk about that later, but right now Alex wants her cell phone. She says there's some information on it that will help her case and she's asked that you bring it to her. You probably already know this, but no phones of any kind are allowed inside the interrogation room. We're hoping that maybe you can get Alex to open up and tell you what's on her phone that's so important. We can check it out later. For some reason she wants it tonight."

Gloria looked at Benjamin. "Have the Feds searched your house or contacted you since Alex's arrest?"

Benjamin shook his head, "No."

Gloria continued, "Good, but expect them shortly. Alex has asked that you remove her laptop from your house and put it somewhere for safekeeping. Somehow she thinks she's going to need it very soon, but I assure you that she won't have any access to it before the Feds have had a chance to look through it. If you want to remove it from your house that's fine, but I need to advise you that if the police have a warrant or ask you directly about her computer, you need to hand it over to them. If you're more comfortable you can direct them to me if they ask you any questions. Any idea what's on her laptop that she's so concerned about?"

Benjamin's face was now calm, but wistful, like someone watching a receding shoreline. His voice was controlled. "Her laptop is like an appendage to her. It goes everywhere she goes. I assume she just wants to make sure she has access to it as soon as she gets out." Benjamin raised a hand, palm up. "What about the charges? They're bogus. Didn't she tell you who she thinks set her up?"

Gloria shook her head. "Like I said, she didn't want to talk about any of that, and I find that pretty peculiar. In fact, I don't think I've ever had a client who has refused to talk to me about anything relating to their charges. They don't always tell me the truth, but they talk to me. Aidan and I talked to Agent Guzman and he was forthcoming about what the Agency knows. Alex wasn't a target of any investigation until very recently. The Agency received an anonymous tip with detailed information; account numbers; wire transfer information; and everything needed for them to act quickly. It didn't take them long to verify all the information and they moved in right away. Apparently, their information also showed Alex to be a flight risk. From point to point, this is probably the quickest arrest I've ever heard of."

Aidan put his hand on Benjamin's shoulder. "These are serious charges and it doesn't look like Alex will be going anywhere soon. Gloria's a good lawyer, the best; you wouldn't want anyone else handling this case but her." Aidan gripped tighter and continued, "It's going to be difficult if Alex won't cooperate. Do you have any idea who may have set her up or how any of this could've happened?"

"I may have some ideas, but I need to talk to her first," Benjamin replied. "When can I see her?"

"That may take a while. I'll talk to the DA tomorrow and I'll ask him, but I don't think Alex will be permitted access to anyone right now, other than her lawyers. That's pretty standard," Gloria said.

Benjamin took a breath, then another. "This is all too much for me to take right now. I just can't believe this has happened. She didn't do anything, I know it... I know it. I'll fill you in on everything I know, but first let's take care of the cell phone issue. It's back at my house." Benjamin looked at Phil. "You come with me; we'll get it and her laptop and come right back here. Michelle, you should stay here and work out whatever you need to with Aidan and Gloria so that you can get in to see Alex tonight. Maybe you can get her to open up when you see her. She needs to help us if we're going to be able to help her."

CHAPTER 45

"You what?" Delynn stared at Steph, owl-eyed. "I should've known something was going to happen. Now the police are involved and everything will come out. I'm royally screwed now—royally."

"You won't be any part of the police investigation. Listen, I wrestled with what to do, I really did, but I know that Adam's life is in danger and I needed to do whatever I could to help him. I didn't say anything to the police about you, and I left out my involvement with the Agrico story. As far as the police know, I met Adam a few weeks ago and when he didn't answer any of my calls I went over to his apartment to see if he was okay, end of story," Steph explained.

"End of story? Hardly! First, they kidnapped Adam and I'm going to be the next to go, that's where this story ends." Delynn hunched forward and lowered her voice to a stage whisper. "What do you think I should do? I mean, I'm probably in danger... oh, hell I'm sure I'm in danger and I'm terrified. Why'd you have to go to the cops? That's going to backfire, I know it will."

"I've really struggled with what to do about this. You know, I think it's kinda hollowed me out a little." Steph paused, took a deep breath and continued, "If it was you and not Adam that was missing, what would you want me to do? I know I've promised to protect you both and I have, but I really believe Adam would've wanted me to go to the police and I believe you'd want me to do the same thing."

"What I want is to have nothing to do with any of this anymore. I'm scared out of my wits; I can't sleep, work, eat or do anything, but worry."

"I understand how you feel, I honestly do, but you need to pull yourself together." Steph reached across and grabbed Delynn's forearms. "Right now, Delynn, right now."

Delynn threw a terrified glance at the door. "What was that? Did you hear it?"

Moments later, Chandler came around the corner. "Oh," her face flushed. "I didn't know you were going to be here."

"Yeah, I'm working at home this afternoon," Steph replied. "Delynn, this is Chandler, my partner."

"Nice to meet you, Chandler," Delynn smiled.

"You too." Chandler curled her lip and stood rock-still.

"Since when did they start casual day at Vyodyne?" Steph asked.

"This," Chandler ran her hands down the sides of her jeans. "I'm moving some boxes today, that's all."

"I thought you had an investor meeting today?" Steph asked.

"Cancelled," Chandler said. "Sorry I can't stay, but I'm in a hurry. I'll grab a few things from my room and then I'll get out of your way." Chandler darted into her room.

With a blank, perplexed stare, Steph eyed Chandler as she dashed from the room and headed toward the bedroom. Finally, she turned to Delynn. "Sorry about that. So, where were we?"

Delynn's lips turned up in what passed for a half-smile. I'm a wreck." She threw her trembling hands out in a ceding gesture. "Like you couldn't tell? I'm sorry I shouldn't be taking any of this out on you. You did the right thing, and I'm worried about Adam, too. What'd the police say they were going to do?"

"They'll check out his apartment, ask around the neighborhood to see if anyone saw anything, and, well, the usual stuff. I have to think, though, that unless they can find some clues in his apartment, it's going to be a real long shot."

"You'll let me know if there's anything I can do, won't you?" Delynn asked.

"Absolutely. While we're playing truth or dare, I should tell you that I didn't get this bruise playing racquetball. I was hit over the head by somebody right after I left Cummings' house a few days ago. I didn't see anybody, but I think there's a good chance that whoever hit me has something to do with Adam's disappearance."

"If you're trying to freak me out all over again, it's working. I didn't really buy your racquetball story, but I thought I'd be prying into your personal life if I said anything." Delynn stood up. "I need a glass of water. Can I get you anything?"

"I'm good, thanks. The glasses are in the cabinet to the left of the sink," Steph said.

Chandler came around the corner toting a gym bag and caught Steph's doubting glare. "I needed to pick up a few things. I'll probably go to the gym after work and be home after that."

"What's going on? I didn't really buy your excuse last night about why you didn't call me back and I don't think I've ever seen you come home during the day." Steph stood up. "What is it?"

"Nothing, nothing at all." Chandler smiled, walked over to Steph and squeezed her hand. "We can talk later when I get home, but I'm already late."

Steph's face weighed heavy with doubt as she watched Chandler go out the front door.

Returning to the living room, Delynn sat back down and ran a hand across the linen upholstery. "I need to ask you something. None of the furniture here is anything like I would have suspected you'd pick out. It's... well, it has more of the feminine touch."

Steph shook her head and tried to bring herself back to the present. "Really? You don't think the floral couch reflects my taste in furniture?"

"No more than the figurine lamps, the soft pastels or the frilly throw pillows. Oh, don't get me wrong, I like everything in here, it just isn't what I expected," Delynn said.

"It surprised me too. All of this is Chandler's. Before she moved in the only things I had in this room were two beanbag chairs. I did get to keep one of them. It's stuffed in the corner over there."

Delynn saw the beanbag chair and chuckled. "Now *that's* what I expected."

"Yep, that's me. Oh, one more thing, and then I need to get back at it. What's the scuttlebutt going around your office over Cummings? That had to surprise a lot of people."

"Oh gosh, you wouldn't believe the place. Mr. Cummings was an icon there, everybody admired him. We're all in shock. I can't believe what happened; I mean why would someone like him want to commit suicide?" Delynn shook her head. "It just doesn't make sense. I was in a meeting with him the day before it happened and he seemed like his normal self; he moved the meeting right along, made sure everybody was on board, told a few jokes. He was the usual, friendly, upbeat, Mr. Cummings."

"Is anything floating around about Sustinere? Have you heard anything?" Steph asked.

"No, but I doubt very many people know anything about Sustinere. It seems like that was Mr. Cummings' personal baby. I haven't heard a thing other than what I've already told you."

Steph picked up her phone. "I'm sorry, Delynn, but I have to look at some of these messages and get some things done, but thanks for coming over. One last thing, why don't you think about taking some time off? Go somewhere, anywhere, but just get out of the area. I'm sure you'll feel a lot better."

Delynn rose and started for the front door. "I'll let myself out, and thanks. You know, I feel better already. It's been a long time since I've taken any time off, but with everything happening at work and all, this probably isn't a very good time. I think I'm better off just doing my normal everyday stuff, don't you think?"

"Normal?" Steph laughed. "Normal isn't something I've ever been very good at; it's something I seem to always be running away from."

Delynn opened the door. "Oh, you startled me." She clutched the knob with both hands.

"I'm sorry. Ms. Moore?" a man asked.

"No, I was just leaving." Delynn pointed a finger at Steph behind her.

"I'm Steph Moore. What can I help you with?"

"I'm Detective Pence with the San Francisco Police Department. I wonder if I could have a few minutes of your time to talk about Adam O'Keeffe."

CHAPTER 46

Steph and Delynn stood stock-still, muscles tensed, and they held their breath.

"It's actually good news. We found Mr. O'Keeffe and he's going to be fine."

They exhaled.

Detective Pence continued, "He's under observation at San Francisco General. He has a few cuts and some bruises, but nothing serious. Like I said, he's going to be fine."

"Oh, thank god," Delynn cried out. "He's safe... he's safe. Where'd you find him? What happened?"

"He was held in a small room inside a warehouse on Beale Street, but no one was there when we entered the place. By the looks of things, whoever was holding him was planning on coming back. We have the place staked out, so if they come back, we'll get them."

"I do have some questions for you, Ms. Moore." Detective Pence paused and looked at Delynn, "Who are you?"

"Delynn Longo, I work with Adam."

"Maybe you can both help us find out who was behind this? Can we sit down somewhere?" Detective Pence asked.

Detective Dan Pence sat at the dining room table and scribbled a few notes on his notepad. He slid a pack of papers across the table to Steph. "We found this in the room where Mr. O'Keeffe was being held. The name Steph is written in the upper corner and underlined a couple times. Any chance this might refer to you?"

Steph held up the papers and Delynn peered over her shoulder. "It might be… I'm not sure, but yeah, probably." She looked across the table at Detective Pence. "When will we be able to see Adam?"

"Probably tomorrow. He's going to be okay, but the hospital wants to keep him overnight for observation." The detective dropped his pen on his pad and scratched his cheek. "That appears to be an accounting ledger for a company called Sustinere. Do you have any reason to think that this had anything to do with Mr. O'Keeffe's kidnapping?"

The terrified look etched across Delynn's face told Steph she needed to tread with caution. "Before I answer that, I'd like to talk with Delynn—in private."

"Why's that?" The detective bit his lower lip and then continued, "It's a lot easier if you just tell me what you know. We still haven't caught Mr. O'Keeffe's kidnappers and it's important in cases like these to follow through on all leads as quickly as possible. The passage of time is never our ally."

"You already know I'm a reporter for the Post." Steph paused and met the detective's gaze. "There are a few things I'm not at liberty to talk about with you or anyone else, but if I can have a few minutes with Delynn, then maybe I can be of some help."

Detective Pence nodded. "I'll wait in the hall and make a few calls. Let me know when you're ready."

The instant the front door closed, Delynn shot up from her chair. "Do you know what this is?" She grabbed the papers. "This is a complete accounting ledger for Sustinere for the past five years. This will lead the police to Agrico, and once they start asking questions there, it'll be pretty easy for the higher-ups to figure out that Adam and I have been leaking info. We're through, finished, kaput. My god," she wrapped her hands around the back of her neck and squeezed.

"Don't write your obituary yet. I have another idea, but I need to know that you'll go along with it. If you won't, then I'll keep my mouth shut." Steph rose and placed her hand on Delynn's arm. "Adam's going to be okay, that's the important thing. But whoever kidnapped him is still out there and we don't know what Adam may have told them. It's probably a good idea to have the police on our side right now."

"You're doing it again," Delynn said.

"What? What am I doing again?"

"You're going to talk me into doing something that I'm just too scared to do. This whole thing frightens me to no end and yes, I'm afraid for my own life right now—see!" She held out her trembling hand.

"Let me tell you what I have in mind and then you can decide. How's that?" Steph asked.

Back at the dining room table with Detective Pence, Delynn had regained her composure and was prepared to go along with Steph's plan.

"Okay," Steph started. "We both want to cooperate in any way we can to help you find the people who are responsible for Adam's disappearance, but we're going to need some assurances from you first."

"What type of assurances are you talking about?" Detective Pence asked.

"The kind where you have to agree not to divulge some of the information we disclose to you here today. Both Adam and Delynn have been working with me on a story, and if their employer knew about their involvement with me, they'd both lose their jobs and maybe more. Delynn doesn't want to take that risk and I'm not going to talk about anything she doesn't want disclosed. If you can promise, somehow, to protect both Delynn and Adam, then I think we have some information that can help you."

"Do either of you have any involvement with Mr. O'Keeffe's kidnapping? Because if you do, I can't do anything, but take you down to the station for questioning," Detective Pence cautioned.

"No, we're not involved," Steph asserted.

"Miss Moore," Detective Pence looked up and continued, "there's an open case with the Oakland PD where you were assaulted and battered. Does that incident have anything to do with Mr. O'Keeffe?"

"I don't know the answer to that…maybe, but how'd you know about that?" Steph asked.

"When you reported that Mr. O'Keeffe was missing we ran a check on you. We do that with anybody connected with any case." Detective Pence dropped his forearms to the table and leaned forward. "If you in no way have any criminal involvement in this case or you have information that could possibly help in finding the perpetrators, all I can promise is I'll do everything I can to protect where that information came from. That's the best I can do. I have my superiors to report to and I'll be working with the DA's office on this. I can't keep information from them. If they ask, I tell them."

Steph saw Delynn nod her approval. "Okay." Steph reached for the stack of papers. "I was on my way over to meet with Adam so he could go over these with me, but that's when I was ambushed, so I never made it. I haven't seen or talked with Adam since then. He was planning on showing me some things that he thought made it pretty clear that Agrico was covering up its involvement with Sustinere."

Detective Pence raised a brow. "Are you saying that Agrico may somehow be involved with this?"

"I don't know if they are or aren't, but I suspect they could be. Adam's entire apartment was ransacked. They were looking for something—and these papers were the only things taken from his apartment that you found with him, right?"

Detective Pence nodded. "If Agrico is involved that's going to move this investigation up another level. The Chief of Police, the DA and the corporate crime unit will need to be in on this. I can't do much to help you if that happens."

"Agrico's not involved as a company. I don't think they have any knowledge about Sustinere or their investment of $200 million in that company. I suspect it's been the work of one or two people, but I'm not sure why they were doing this behind Agrico's back."

"$200 million? Are you saying Agrico invested that kind of money and doesn't even know about it?" The detective rubbed his brow.

"That's what I'm saying." Steph rose from her chair. "Who wants some water?" She turned toward the kitchen and then stopped. "Detective, I have a proposal for you."

Seated back at the table, Steph gulped down half a glass of water and looked at the detective. "Adam's disappearance is part of a much larger scheme. I don't know everything yet, but from what I know there should be enough to keep you busy for a long time. Do you promise to keep me in the loop if I tell you everything I know? I'm investigating this as a story and hope to get it out in a matter of days. I don't want any of this going to any other paper."

"Another unusual request, Ms. Moore, I'll—"

"Call me Steph, assuming we're going to be working together."

Detective Pence leaned back in his chair, folded his hands and pressed them into the edge of the table. "I don't know any reporters, Ms. Moore, so I don't expect I'll be talking to any unless they're involved in this, much like you, apparently. So, I don't think that'll be a problem. Like I said earlier, I need to keep others involved in this investigation in the loop and fill them in on anything I learn." He opened his hands. "Does that work?"

Steph gave a half-smile. "Almost. Look, I'll have my story printed within the next few days and I'm not willing to risk getting scooped." She shook her head, "I can talk to you after my story comes out if that's the only way to handle things."

Detective Pence huffed. "And I could take you down to headquarters right now for obstructing our investigation and continue this questioning."

"You could, but you won't learn anything from me that I haven't already told you. The Post has some pretty good lawyers that I'm sure will be able to buy the time I need."

Detective Pence tapped his pen on the table. Finally, he spoke, "I'll tell you what I can do. Right now I'm only interested in finding Mr. O'Keeffe's kidnappers. If I learn anything further during this investigation I suppose it could wait for a few days."

"And you'll let me know if you've learned anything beyond what I've told you before you talk to anyone?" Steph asked.

Detective Pence nodded. "That's the deal, Ms. Moore."

"Steph, remember? Now that we're working together on this, just call me Steph, okay?"

"Alright, what do you have?" Detective Pence reached for his notepad.

Steph looked over at Delynn. "You wanna tell him what you told me earlier today? I think that's going to be the underlying basis of my story."

Delynn cleared her throat and her eyes darted back and forth between Steph and Detective Pence. "Early this morning I received a call from the person I usually deal with at Sustinere. She said they haven't received the funding on their last request and they'll need it to make payroll and some other expenses. She sounded pretty worried and asked if I could check into it. I don't really know where the payment requests go after I get them and pass them on to someone in accounting, so I went and talked to that person. She said she had no idea where it was. Anything that comes to her that's coded to account 409, she sends directly to Mr. Cummings."

"You know about Eric Cummings?" Steph asked.

"The Agrico exec who committed suicide? That guy?" Detective Pence asked.

"Yep, that guy." Steph leaned forward, "I think you'll find Adam's kidnappers are connected to Cummings' death. Cummings is knee deep in the Sustinere funding and he's been doing it without Agrico's knowledge. My being whacked on the head, Adam's disappearance and Cummings's death are all related—you can bank on it."

Detective Pence bit his lower lip and his wide-set eyes narrowed. "You'll have your two days, like I promised, but I'm going to need some help on this one."

256

CHAPTER 47

Alex sat still on a wooden chair, her head motionless, but her eyes moved about the room like a miner searching for a vein of ore. This was the same room where she had met with Aidan and Gloria earlier and she needed to know that nothing had changed. She saw the lens for a 2.8mm dome camera mounted in the corner opposite her, and while she knew that procedures required it to be turned off once her attorney entered the room, she also knew that she had to be careful. Right now eyes were trained on her every move, and although she hadn't spotted it, she knew a microphone had to be hidden somewhere.

Dressed in orange scrubs and wearing standard issue flip-flops, her identity had been stripped from her. The numbers 92338, her new identity, were imprinted on the back of her scrubs. This was the first time Alex had ever been arrested or incarcerated. Her meticulous attention to even the minutest of details had always protected her from suspicion and had allowed her to avoid having her tracks uncovered. Still, she had always known the possibility existed that she could someday make a mistake and sit where she now sat.

A guard entered the room. Seconds later Michelle followed. "Thank you." Michelle watched the guard leave and close the door. She double checked to make sure the door was securely shut.

Alex pressed her hands on the table and stood. "Thanks for coming. The first thing I need to know is how is Ben doing."

"Worried sick. We all are." Michelle stepped over to the table and leaned across. "I don't know if I'm supposed to hug you or shake your hand. That's how inexperienced I am with all this."

"I'm just glad you came. Did you bring my phone?"

"No; no phones of any kind are allowed in here. I left it out in the car." Michelle laid her briefcase on the table.

"We'll talk about that later, but right now I need to tell you a few things. Please, sit... sit down," Alex insisted.

Michelle sat down, folded her hands and rested them on her briefcase. "What's going on, Alex— or should I say Diana? Your fingerprints match with Diana Shaffner. I guess you've been told that. Why didn't you talk to your real lawyers when they were in here? I told you I'm a lawyer, but I'm not the kind you need. You need somebody way above my pay grade if you want to see the light of day again. From what Gloria told us, there's a strong possibility you may be held without bail." Michelle leaned across the table, "You really need to cooperate with Gloria and Aidan."

"Has Phil or Ben told you anything about the SynAid virus—the virus that Kioshi created?" Alex asked.

"No and I'm not sure I want to know. What I want is for you to open up and tell me, and specifically Gloria and Aidan, what's going on. How did you get set up and who are you, really?"

"The SynAid virus is about—"

Michelle slammed a fist into her briefcase. "I don't give a damn about any virus! I care about finding out what happened. I care about how Ben and Phil are feeling right now and what they're going through. I care about getting you out of here." She sat back and glared. "Do you remember the talk we had on the plane where you told me if I didn't open up to you about my past then you'd continue to mistrust me? Well, I opened up. Now, it's your turn: talk to me—or I walk."

Michelle's stare was unwavering, but not intrusive. Finally, Alex spoke, "Before I tell you why I'm here I need to first tell you that in less than 72 hours an event will occur that will shape the world's geopolitical climate for years to come. It could very likely be in the form of a world war, but in any case hundreds of thousands of innocent people will die. My focus right now is to make sure that we stop this from happening. I can't do that sitting in here," Alex's chin jutted forward. "Can I go on?"

Michelle looked like a turtle without a shell. Phil had told her about Alex and had even given her a few examples of how Alex had wreaked havoc on peoples' lives, all for the sake of stealing corporate assets for her clients. Alex had shared similar stories with her and by now, Michelle was well aware of Alex's past, but she had also seen the look in Alex's eyes when she had talked about Ben, how much she had loved him and how she so desperately had wanted to put her past behind her and start over with a clean slate. That look had been real, Michelle knew it.

When Michelle had made the decision to seek refuge somewhere, anywhere, far away from her abusive husband, she had known that decision would impact the rest of her life. She had hoped and prayed it had been the right decision. Now, she had to adjudicate another emotional battle raging inside her and the outcome would be another life altering decision. Which Alex was sitting across from her? Was it the one who had left a trail of shattered ambitions and broken dreams behind her, or the one who had sought redemption from her past and had so desperately wanted to start over?

Michelle closed her eyes, held them shut and then opened them— wide. "Okay," she nodded, "start from the beginning."

Alex explained how the SynAid virus had already been tested in Liberia and already hundreds, probably more, had been killed. That was only the beginning. Using Kioshi's hard drives, she had pieced together his plan, and to confirm her suspicions she had hacked into the computer network of China's People's Liberation Army. It was there that she had discovered China's real motive.

"China has a systematic plan in place to become the global hegemon and it believes that to achieve that, it must first become the leading economic, political and military power in its own region. It's set its sights on reducing the power and influence of Russia; its primary regional competitor. China is quite content for the time being to sit back and allow the U.S. to patrol and protect the world's shipping lanes, to use its own military prowess to protect the world's energy supplies and to suppress insurgencies. All of that allows China to focus its attention and resources elsewhere." Alex paused and brushed her hands through her hair, then continued, "China plans to unleash SynAid here, in America, and it will look like the Russians planted it. It's not hard to figure out what would happen next."

Alex slid her chair forward and leaned across the table. "Do you have some paper and a pen in your briefcase? If you do, then pull them out."

With a quizzical look, Michelle pulled paper and a pen from her briefcase and slid them across the table to Alex.

Alex scribbled a note on the paper, turned it around and pushed it toward Michelle.

The color from Michelle's face drained as she read the note.

> *Assume they're listening. Anything important we'll put in writing. I can't stop this if I'm sitting in here. I have way to break out without anyone knowing how or where I'm going. That's why I need my phone. I can access program that will alter room's security cameras giving me time to escape. I only need few minutes. Can I count on your help?*

"Oh boy," Michelle sighed. Alex reached across the table, tapped Michelle on the arm and then turned her hands—thumbs up.

Michelle scribbled a note and passed it to Alex.

> *You want me to aid and abet in your escape? You know I'll get disbarred and end up here myself.*

Alex shook her head as she wrote.

> *You won't get disbarred. You'll probably get a medal for this :)*

Michelle's eyes drooped and she turned pale.

*My husband, he'll track me down. I can't take that life
anymore. Sorry, I can't.*

Alex passed a note to Michelle and held her hand.

*You're not alone anymore. Phil will never let anyone harm
you again—ever. You know that. Ben and I will be there
too. You don't need to be scared of him ever again.*

Michelle sat in silence. She bit her lower lip and rubbed her hands
together, slowly. She closed her eyes, shook her head and muttered, "I can't."

"This is not about you or me, Ben, Phil, your husband or anyone we
know," Alex blurted out. "It's about hundreds of thousands of innocent lives
that will be lost if we do nothing."

Michelle swallowed hard and then brushed a tear from her cheek.
"Okay."

Continuing with a series of handwritten notes, Alex began to lay out
her plan. Inside Michelle's notebook was a binder that Alex explained could
be used to hide her cell phone.

*Cut a hole in middle of binder large enough to hold phone.
Put phone in, close it and come right back. They won't
check your personal papers, but if they try, tell them it's
privileged, they can't look at it.*

*Call Ben, tell him to meet me front of Dolphin Club, bring
laptop and backpack. Turn on laptop now, leave it on.
Then send blank text to my phone, don't write anything,
just send blank text.*

Michele put the binder back in her briefcase, closed the latch and stared blankly at the briefcase. Alex could tell that inside, Michelle was still waging a battle against uncertainty and despair. Alex leaned forward and calmly whispered, "I know what I'm doing—I do."

"I sure hope I'm right about you because I'm going to do everything I can to help you."

"Thanks." Alex raised a finger, "One more thing." She hurriedly scribbled another note:

> *When you return we'll spend a few minutes, then you leave room. Tell guard you return in 10 minutes. You're going to restroom and then need to make private phone call. Come back, I'll be gone, act surprised, mad. Demand they tell you where I am. Get it?"*

Michelle nodded as she wrote out a note.

> *What are you going to do with the phone? If you make calls they'll know.*

Alex wrote another note and as she handed it to Michelle, she rolled her eyes at the ceiling panels above.

> *Laptop has program to override digital camera. Phone can start program. When you leave, I walk around table for several minutes. When override camera, it plays same scene of me walking around table. Then I exit.*

Michelle grabbed her briefcase and stood. "God help me if I'm wrong." She turned and walked out the door.

CHAPTER 48

At 1 a.m. Benjamin had no problem finding a parking space on Jefferson Avenue. He had been pacing back and forth on the sidewalk between the Dolphin Club and the neighboring South End Rowing Club. At each turn, he had scoured the landscape hoping to spot Alex, but for the past half hour the only activity he had seen had been two men walking west on Beach Street and one couple who had stopped to peer out at Aquatic Park. They had soon disappeared into a veil of fog. The place was deserted.

Each step Benjamin took was weighted with anxiety and suspicion. Michelle had given Benjamin a complete rundown on her meeting with Alex, but he knew there had to be more to her plan than she had let on—there always was. Why had she been operating under a different name? Why hadn't he questioned her more about the SynAid virus? Was this all part of some ongoing scheme and he was being used as a pawn—again? All he could do at that point was wait and hope that Alex would show up—with answers.

"Ben."

At the sound of the accented whisper, Benjamin spun around. Alex stepped out of the darkness and onto the dimly lit sidewalk. She raced and grabbed Benjamin's hand. "Follow me," she said.

At the entrance to the Hyde Street Pier, a wooden dory provided the cover she was looking for. Taking Benjamin's hand again, she led him behind the dory and spoke softly, "Thanks for coming. I have little time to explain things, but right now everything is okay. I think this will all work." She gazed into Benjamin's eyes and her fingers brushed across his face. "Are you okay? I'm so sorry I couldn't let you know what was going on, but I just couldn't."

Benjamin grabbed Alex's wrist and yanked her hand from his face. A single finger wagged as he spoke, "Unless I can get some honest answers from you, now—*right now*—I'm going to turn around and walk out of here—*for good.*"

Alex recoiled and stood limp kneed. Her eyes met Benjamin's, but she was rewarded with a look as black as midnight. "Ben… what is it? What's wrong? Everything's alright, I… I don't understand."

"You don't understand? Damn it, Alex!" His voice was like thunderbolts of anger and his tone was punctuated with rage. "I can't take this secrecy of yours any longer. Either you're going to tell me what's going on *now* or I'm done. Do you have any idea what it's like to see someone you love handcuffed and driven away in a police car and you're left wondering what the hell just happened? Do you? No, of course not, why would you?"

"I'm sorry—really sorry. I haven't told you what's going on because it's safer that way, for you, not me. I don't want you to get all wrapped in any of this," she threw her hands up in the air, "or anything that has to do with parts of my past. I'm not trying to deceive you or hurt you. I just want to protect you."

"You can't just tether me to a leash and let me loose whenever it damn well pleases you. Friends don't do that and people who love each other sure as hell don't do it. And you don't want me to get mixed up in your past? Are you kidding me? Step back for a minute and count all the things that have happened to me since I've met you. I've been a part of your past since the day we met. If you haven't figured out by now that I'm on your side then you never will. This relationship won't work."

"You can't mean that." Alex's jaw dropped and she reached out to Benjamin.

"Don't touch me, not now. I meant every word of what I said. I've thought about this a number of times, but I always figured that whatever was going on would be over and we could forget about it and move on. But you know what? It just keeps going, on and on, one thing after another. It never ends, Alex, it never ends."

Shadows and creases carved by the twin blades of raw emotion and brutal honesty covered Benjamin's face. He shrugged. "Remember when we sat in Youten's house and he talked about respect and how it was circular? Did any of that sink in? Well, the same thing is true with love and you just don't get it, any of it. This isn't about who's protecting whom... no... no, it's about caring how the other person feels, being honest about your own feelings and trusting each other." He stared down at Alex. "It's a two way street and you haven't always been willing to travel that road in the same direction with me. Maybe you're not able to... I don't really know... and I'm beginning to not give a damn."

Alex's eyes filled with water, one slow, painful tear slipped out and rolled down her cheek. Her heart raced and Benjamin's words played over and over and over again in her mind. Finally, her lips formed a gentle, wistful smile. "You are so right... so right. I've kept you in the dark so many times and each time you've been there for me, supporting me, loving me, encouraging me. I haven't consciously kept things from you to hurt you, but that's what I've done and... I'm sorry, I'm so sorry for that."

Alex held her breath and swallowed hard. Benjamin's rants and her pleas were replaced by noiseless static. She imagined Benjamin's heart pounding against his chest and she wanted to reach out and pull him in, close... closer. "Say something... please say something... *anything*." She paused and it felt like the world had paused with her.

Benjamin stood tall, his shoulders squared and his arms stiff. His eyes were narrow slits and he looked downward, straight at Alex. The loud silence was deafening. He reached out and curled his fingers around her shoulders. "I have your laptop and backpack in my car." He smiled and lifted his arms.

Alex jumped up and threw her arms around Benjamin. She wanted to freeze that moment, for time to stand still and to forever remember how she felt at that very instant. In her soft accent, she whispered, "Thank you... thank you."

Finally, Benjamin pulled back, but kept Alex in his embrace. "First, before we get your laptop from my car, I want to know where you're going."

"I'm going to rent a car and drive to Lake Tahoe. Once I'm there I'm not really sure where I'll go, but I'll figure that out."

"Let me drive you. You already know I'm coming with you, wherever you're going. And I do know my way around Tahoe."

Alex smiled. "I wouldn't have it any other way."

"Wait." Alex tugged on Benjamin. "We need to get your car back to your place. The Feds will be looking for you and if your car's gone they may just put things together. You drive your car back—"

"Phil's in my car right now. There was no way he wasn't coming with me and we figured it might be a good idea to have another set of eyes here, just in case. He can drive my car back."

Alex chuckled. "I might have known he'd be here. Let's go say hi."

Phil spotted the two walking out from the night shadows and he bolted out of the car. "Diana Shaffner? Who the hell is that? You've got some 'splaining to do, Alex—Diana—whoever you are. Come on, spill it."

"Do I, now?" Alex gave Phil a warm hug and then continued, "I'll tell you everything in due course, but first I have a job for you."

"I'll bet. Are you sure I can handle it?"

"I'm sure." Alex smiled and continued, "Drive Ben's car back to his place and then stay there. I'm sure the Feds will be showing up shortly looking for him. Tell them you're not sure where he went. You usually stay at his place when he leaves and he said he'd be gone for a few days. If they press you, then say you think he might have gone up to Tahoe, but you really don't know."

Phil looked at Benjamin and then back at Alex. "Where're you guys going, anyway? What's up?"

"Can you get Ben's car back and stay at his place for a few days?" Alex asked.

"Of course. But come on—you can't just leave me hanging," Phil pleaded.

Benjamin spoke, "This is the last time *anyone* will be left hanging, I promise you that. But she's right, stay at my house. There's a cell phone on my desk. I don't remember the brand, but it's one of those throw-away types she bought that isn't registered to anyone and can't be traced. Take that phone and I'll call you. I'll keep you in the loop."

"I'm not happy about this, but I'll do it." He nodded at Benjamin, "You'd better call."

"Expect it."

"And Phil," Alex raised a brow, "please tell Michelle thanks and let her know she made the right decision. Everything will work out. It really will."

■　　■　　■　　■　　■

They took a cab to SFO, rented a blue Ford Fusion and Benjamin drove while Alex buried her head in her laptop. She needed some time to check on a few things first and then she would fill Benjamin in on everything.

She checked for updates on the SynAid virus and the death rate in Liberia had already soared into the thousands. $100 million had been deposited into several of Kioshi's bank accounts and had been immediately wired out to a handful of offshore accounts. She was now certain, more than ever, that she was on the right track.

Passing through Auburn, Alex asked, "How much longer?"

Benjamin had both hands on the steering wheel and had set the cruise control at precisely 60 mph. "If I could speed up maybe an hour and a half, but at this speed, tack on another 15 minutes."

"The extra time won't matter. Remember, we don't want to attract any attention."

"At this hour I don't think that's an issue." Benjamin reached over and cupped his hand around Alex's knee. "Can I ask you one question, now?"

"Sure, ask away."

"Who's Diana Shaffner? Tell me, what's that all about?"

Alex reached down and patted her backpack. "She's one of about a dozen aliases I have stashed away in here. I have passports, drivers' licenses, credit cards and everything I need to take on a new identity: Swiss, Algerian, Australian, Pakistani, and others. Diana is one of my American identities."

"Yeah, but even the fingerprints matched yours. That's not possible."

"I created Diana Shaffner about six years ago, as a precaution, just in case something like this ever arose. If I was arrested I didn't want the information to get back to my mother, for one, and I certainly didn't want the news out that Alex Boudreau was arrested. That could draw the attention of a lot of people who would want to find me."

"But the fingerprints—how'd they match yours?"

"Simple, I altered the records at the FBI, Interpol, and a handful of national police agencies so that Alex Boudreau became Diana Shaffner. It really wasn't that difficult. You won't find any Alex Boudreau prints anywhere in law enforcements' databases. I don't exist."

"So what do we do once we get to Tahoe and what do you expect to find there?" Benjamin asked.

Alex reached across and rubbed the back of Benjamin's neck. "You only had one question, remember?

Benjamin smiled. "This is part B."

"No, I've told you enough for now. You'll know more soon—very soon."

Benjamin slammed on the breaks and the car skidded to a screeching stop. "Do you want to rethink that answer?"

Alex blanched. "I do… I very much do." She took a deep breath. "I set-up the whole arrest thing because I needed a way…."

CHAPTER 49

Phil arrived back at Benjamin's house in the early morning and found Michelle waiting for him, as arranged. They were both too anxious to sleep and they spent the rest of the early morning hours conjecturing on what Alex had really been up to. Phil had spent enough time with Alex to know that whatever it was, it was complicated *and* dangerous. The woman had a knack for finding trouble that seemed to creep in from all sides. He had suspected it had to have something to do with the SynAid virus and from what he had learned from Alex about that virus, it was lethal with no probable cure, other than possibly the vaccine that Andre controlled.

That morning was overcast, pregnant with unspent rain. Behind the clouds, the sun began to creep over the Oakland Hills and the fog began its seaward retreat. Alcatraz prepared for another day of rain and wind and in less than an hour they would see the full splendor of the Golden Gate Bridge, which at this hour was already packed with commuters heading into the city. Phil was tapping his fingers against Benjamin's throw away cell phone when he suddenly pivoted around. "Michelle! We can't just sit here anymore; we can't, no way. I'm going to call Ben and make him tell me what the hell's going on."

"And I think you've had enough caffeine to give everyone in Mill Valley a lifetime buzz." She reached over and pulled Phil's mug toward her. "Let's give this a little more time. If we don't hear from him by say, noon, then sure, give him a call."

"Noon! Why's that always such a magical hour to everyone? What are we going to do until then? I'm going out of my mind."

Michelle stood up, walked over to the refrigerator and opened the door. "I'll make us some breakfast and then let's take a walk. It's beautiful here, you can show me around." She winked.

"Yeah… well, I guess I am pretty hungry. Damn, the doorbell. That must be the Feds. I'll get the door and you come out in a few minutes. I'll probably need a good lawyer by my side."

Phil opened the door to an empty porch. He stepped outside.

"Hi, I'm looking for Mr. Hunter. Is he home?" A voice filtered up through the rhododendrons lining the side of the front porch.

"Hey, what are you doing down there?" Phil asked.

"Oh, hi, after I rang the doorbell I saw the flowers on these plants and I wanted to get a good whiff. What do you call these?"

"If you're looking for Mr. Hunter, he's not here and I don't expect him back for a few days. Mind telling me who you are?"

Walking out from the side of the porch, Steph looked up. "I'm Stephanie Moore, but just call me Steph. Mr. Hunter was supposed to meet me last night at the Buckeye, but he was a no-show. I've been calling him and calling him, but he never answers. I was in the neighborhood anyway, so I thought I'd just stop by."

"He left last night, but I'll let him know you came by. Stephanie Moore, right?"

"Yeah, that's right only it's Steph, remember?" Reaching the top step, Steph stuck out her hand. "Nice to meet you, Mister…" she tilted her head.

"Phil… Phil Morgan."

"Does Mr. Hunter have a habit of asking to meet someone and then just leave them stranded? That's not very polite and I would've thought that someone in his… well, his position would know better."

A puzzled look filled Phil's face. "He asked you to meet him? What was that all about?"

Steph saw Michelle come through the foyer and walk out to the porch. "Oh hi, I'm Steph Moore." She extended her hand. "I came by to see Mr. Hunter, but Mr. Morgan tells me he's not here."

Michelle stood beside Phil and gripped Steph's outstretched hand. "Nope, he's gone."

"It looks like this will be a long day for me." Steph reached in her pocket, pulled out a business card and handed it to Phil. "Maybe you can ask him to call me when he gets back. I know he wanted to talk to me about the viral outbreak in Liberia and I have some new information I thought he might be interested in."

Phil looked at the card. "The Post, huh? Are you the one who wrote that article about the outbreak in Liberia a couple days ago?"

"The one and only, but I'd hardly call that much of an article. I just pieced together a few snippets of information I pulled off the wires. It was just a filler piece. Somehow I think this may turn into something bigger. I hope so; my gut's telling me that there's a lot more to this story than I've found out about so far. What do you think?" she fished.

Phil rubbed her business card between his fingers. "So tell me, Stephanie, you said—"

"Oh, please, call me Steph, remember? It's a lot less formal and as you can see I'm not really the formal type." Her hands swooped down the front of the JC Penny blouse which was half tucked into her faded and frayed blue jeans.

"Okay, Steph it is. You said you had some new information on this virus. Do you mind telling us? We've been looking for some kind of update since your story came out, but there isn't much coverage on this. It seems like a pretty big story to me."

"Boy, don't I agree, Mr. Morgan—"

"Phil," he pointed to Michelle, "and this is Michelle."

"Well, if you've been following this then you probably already know that the death toll is into the thousands and rising fast. They haven't officially identified the virus yet, but there are a few who are making noises that this may be some strain of that G-16 virus." Steph's upper teeth bit down on her lower lip waiting for a reaction. Seeing none, she continued, "I was kinda hoping that's why Mr. Hunter wanted to talk to me because, well, you know, that's the virus that he and that Alex... what's her last name?"

"Boudreau," Phil replied.

"Yeah, that's it, Alex Boudreau. In fact, she was supposed to come along with Mr. Hunter last night. Is she here? Maybe I can talk to her?"

"Nope, I'm not sure where Alex is, but I'd like to chat with you some more about this. I think I read somewhere that the virus may have been introduced into that region through some rice crops. This is all so intriguing to me and maybe I...," Phil looked at Michelle, "I mean we, can try to track Ben down later today. Hey, why don't you come on in? We were just about to start some breakfast. You're welcome to join us."

"A good old fashioned hot cup of coffee sure would hit the spot."

Phil smiled. "That we have plenty of." He swung an arm toward the door.

As they walked back inside they heard the sound of cars pulling up the driveway. Michelle recognized Agent Guzman exiting the driver's side of the lead car and charging forward; a slight limp marking his steps. The others followed behind him and it was obvious from their matching black sedans with tinted windows and their charcoal gray suits, striped ties and hefty strides that they were all Feds.

Agent Guzman reached the top of the steps with one other man at his side. The others stood below eyeing their surroundings. Agent Guzman was physically fit. His head went straight to his broad shoulders and he stood tall and proud. His skin was the color of burnt molasses and he had piercing, narrow eyes, the kind that can bury a stare in a person while still seeing everything around him. He tipped his hat and nodded. "Good morning, Ms. Holman. I hope you're about to tell me where your client is now and save us all a lot of trouble."

Michelle stepped forward. "I wish I knew, but if you'd done your job in the first place I could be spending my time having your trumped-up charges dismissed instead of having to wait around for my client to contact me."

"Has she contacted you?"

"You know I'm not going to answer that." Michelle folded her arms across her chest.

"No, but you will very soon." Agent Guzman's eyes were as piercing as splintered concrete. "We found out that you're not admitted to the California Bar, so technically you're not able to represent Shaffner. In fact you shouldn't have been alone with her last night. You can bet we're looking into possible recriminations for that move."

"I'm a member of the Vermont Bar and Ms. Santora will have the court approve my admission for this case first thing this morning. You'd be much better off spending your time finding out who set up my client, than wasting precious hours dealing with my bar admission status."

"Don't worry about our time. We're doing just fine." Agent Guzman reached into his coat pocket, pulled out a folded piece of paper, and handed it to Michelle. "It's all in order."

Agent Guzman nodded to the men below, "Let's get going guys."

A steady stream of agents raced up the stairs and within seconds they had fanned out and the house became a hive of activity.

"What do you think you'll find here? You won't find my client or anything even remotely connected to your bogus charges in this house."

"You never know 'til you try. Is Mr. Hunter here? I need to speak with him."

Michelle covered her mouth and coughed. "He's not. How long do you expect this search will take?"

Agent Guzman ignored Michelle's question and looked at Phil. "Who are you? Are you a friend of Mr. Hunter?"

"I'm Phil Morgan," he replied, "and yeah, we're friends. I'm staying here for a few days until he gets back."

"Back from where? Where'd he go?"

Phil shrugged his shoulders. "Don't know. He asked if I could stay at his place for a few days. That's about all I know."

Agent Guzman looked Phil up and down like he was casing the joint. "Do you have any idea where he mighta gone? It's kinda important that I speak with him."

Phil rubbed his chin. "No, I'm not sure. It just snowed up in the mountains, maybe he went to Tahoe to ski or maybe… maybe he went up to Sea Ranch to get away. I'm afraid I'm clueless on that point."

Agent Guzman spied Steph in the far corner of the porch. "And who might you be?"

When the agents had stormed up the front steps, Steph had sidled over to the corner where she had hoped she would be within earshot, but out of sight. She took one step forward. "I'm Stephanie Moore. I stopped by just before you got here to see if I could meet with Mr. Hunter, but… well, as you know, he's not here."

"I see. What'd you stop by to talk to him about?" Detective Guzman asked.

"I'm a reporter, with the Post and I was just hoping I could get an interview with him. Nothing major, just thought he'd be an interesting person to interview."

Agent Guzman turned and took two steps down the stairs, then stopped and turned his head. "We'll be in touch." He smiled and descended the remaining stairs. Halfway to his car he stopped again. He walked over to Benjamin's parked car. He placed the palm of his hand on the hood, turned toward the house and yelled, "This is the same kind of car that Mr. Hunter had that was blown up a few weeks ago. Is this his new car?"

Phil yelled back, "Same kind a car, just newer."

"Nice car." Agent Guzman ran his fingers along the trim. "Seems odd that he's gone for a few days, yet his car's parked right here. Don't you think?"

"Nah, not really. A friend probably drove. It's not unusual."

"Uh-huh. My agents will be a while and if either of you should hear from Mr. Hunter, you'll tell him to get in touch with me, okay?"

"Sure thing, we'll do that," Phil yelled back.

"Is there always this much activity around here? What's going on, anyway?" Steph had now slipped out from the corner shadows and stood in the morning light in front of Phil and Michelle.

"Beats me," Phil said. He turned and threw a hand in the air. "I think you'll have to take a rain check on that coffee. I'm afraid it's going to be crowded inside for a while. I'll call you; I do want to talk with you more about that virus."

"Oh sure, that's fine, I understand." Steph paused long enough to look inside the house and saw fingerprint powder dusting the drawers, door knobs and light switches. She snapped her shoulders back. "You know I may be a reporter, but that doesn't mean that everything you tell me I'll print for everyone to read. You can talk to me off the record and maybe I can help. It's pretty obvious to me that something is happening around here and you might want to have a friendly reporter around to make sure this is covered fairly and honestly. This looks like the kind of story that a lot of news people would jump at and maybe turn into some kind of sensationalized circus, if you know what I mean. That's not me, really. Maybe I should stick around a little longer."

Michelle eyed Steph curiously. "Thanks, Steph, but this is nothing more than a big mistake. Trust me, there's no story here."

CHAPTER 50

The news room was buzzing by the time Steph arrived that morning. She booted up her computer and looked around her cubicle. Her papers, pads, pencils and even the crumpled wads of meaningless paper in her waste basket had been systematically arranged so that she would be able to tell if anyone had rifled through anything. Satisfied that everything was kosher, she sat down and poured through the recent wire services looking for anything she could find on the FBI's arrest records for the night before—nothing.

She leaned forward, grabbed a fistful of hair and sighed. She knew she was on to something; something big, she was close, she knew it, but what? A hand clamped down on her shoulder. She stiffened and swiveled around in her chair. "Chief! Oh damn you scared the shit out of me!" She finally took a breath and then recognized the look on his face. "I was just about to see if you were in and bring you up to date." She sprouted a whimsical smile, "Got a few minutes?"

Chief tapped his watch with his fingers and then frowned. "Didn't I say I wanted to know everything you did? Maybe I should have added—*when you did it*, not a day later."

"Yeah, but I didn't have time to get a hold of you—"

His frown deepened and his head jerked. "In my office—*now!*"

Chief thumbed through a stack of phone messages taking the time to grumble, wince or moan at each one. Even though the day was just starting, he already looked as if he'd skipped breakfast and forgot to shower. "Sit down." He pointed to the chair opposite him.

"Uh, I'll just stand, as usual. You know—"

"Yeah, I do know. I also know that your dad, our publisher, I might add, has put me in charge of making sure you're physically able to come into work each day. I don't like that part of my job, not one bit, but I guess I should've known as much when I agreed that you could come to work for me." He slammed his fist on the table. "Never again, Steph!" The veins in his forehead throbbed. "Capiche?"

Her mouth opened, but her tongue was stuck in the back of her throat. She rubbed her face and took a deep breath, then another. "I'm... I'm so sorry. I've had so much swirling around in my head that I just... well, I just forgot to call my dad, but I will. It's all my fault and it won't happen again. Scout's honor." She raised a hand and three fingers stood at attention.

Chief mumbled to himself and then leaned fully back in his chair and propped both feet on his desk. "What happened with Hunter last night? What'd you learn?"

She felt as if she was 16 again and had just passed the dress code inspection at her prep school, which really hadn't happened all that often. She began to pace back and forth and her hands punctuated each word. "Not a thing, he was a no show. I waited for maybe 45 minutes and then I started to call him to see what was up, but his phone went right to messaging. "So," she pivoted around and leaned over the desk and continued, "I dropped by his house this morning and I met some interesting people—very interesting."

Chief was staring out the window and his hands jammed in duet on his thighs. Steph continued, "You're not even listening to me. Did you hear what I just said?"

Chief's head turned, he looked at Steph and then he rested his head against the back of his chair and stared up at the ceiling. His lips flapped as he exhaled. "Today I have two sit-downs with the editorial board, three op-eds to edit, we still have news holes to fill before today's print deadline; Carson, Middleton and Janis have pitches to make to me, and then there's the endless string of emails and phone messages to answer. So, as you can see, I don't have the luxury to focus on one thing at a time. It's called multitasking. Now," he waved a hand in a circle, "keep going. I'm sure there's more."

"Well," she rolled her shoulders back and continued, "Mr. Hunter wasn't there, but the FBI showed up en masse with a search warrant for his house."

"And you were there when they came?" Chief didn't bat an eye.

"Yeah, I was talking to a guy named Phil Morgan, he's a friend of Hunter's and he was staying at the house and a lady named Michelle... something, I can't remember her last name, but that's not important now. Apparently someone was arrested last night by the FBI and I'm guessing that Hunter knows this person and that's probably why the FBI was there with its warrant this morning. I don't know what they were searching for, but from where I was standing I could tell that they were dusting the place and obviously tearing it apart looking for something."

"Jesus, Steph." Chief threw his legs to the floor, slid his chair up to his desk and hunched forward. "You don't know somebody's last name who you talked to; you don't know who was arrested; you don't know where Hunter is and you don't know what the FBI was looking for?" He wrenched his fists. "What *do* you know? You're supposed to be a reporter, right?"

"Are you kidding me?" She was now stretched across the desk, her feet off the floor and her face was inches from his. "That's totally unfair." She pushed herself back off the desk and stood determined, her shoulders squared and her thumbs looped in her belt. "Read between the lines. Benjamin Hunter is a pretty prominent figure around here. Someone he knows was arrested, by the FBI no less, and nobody really knows where he is right now. No, I don't know all the facts, but I'll tell you what I do know. This virus story has hit a nerve with Hunter and I got some pretty good information out of that Morgan guy. You know what he told me?" She paused and waited.

"Keep going."

"He said he read that the virus may have spread through some rice that was planted in Liberia. You know what? He couldn't have read anything

278

like that because the CDC, the WHO and everyone involved is saying they don't know anything at this point, it's too early. So Morgan knows something which means that Hunter probably knows something and that's why he wanted to talk to me in the first place. Before the FBI showed up, Morgan had invited me in for breakfast, so I don't think I'll face any roadblocks by calling Morgan up and throwing some questions at him." She paused, sat down and pressed her feet into the edge of the desk top. "Do I have your interest now?"

"How 'bout taking your feet off my desk?" A single finger scratched his temple. "Hmm… so, do you think there's any connection to that G-16 virus that Hunter was involved with last year? God that guy has really been put through the ringer, hasn't he?"

"Probably, yeah, probably. On the other hand, when you think about what he's been through maybe he gets paranoid about any so-called unknown virus and he just wanted to find out what I knew. My money's not on that theory though. He knows something about what's going on." She nodded and continued, "I've been racking my brain and even though I can't put the pieces together yet, I think that somehow Agrico's involved in this. I really do."

"Agrico? That seems like a stretch. What's your angle there?"

Steph lit up like a pinball machine. "I know you're not big on hunches, but that's what this is—a hunch—and there's more to it. They're bad people, Chief, not everyone, but there's something going on there that doesn't pass the sniff test. They've hidden a few hundred million dollars from their financials and that's not chump change, even to them. I'm thinking there's a connection here between Agrico, rice, the virus and maybe Hunter."

"If you're right, and you're starting to convince me, then you're going to need some help on this." Chief punched the intercom button, "Leslie, find Murray and have him come in here—now."

"Nnnno! No way, Chief! This is my story and Murray is arrogant, repulsive, pushy, a kiss-ass and if he didn't have spell check he'd be illiterate. No, I'll delete all my notes and become a waitress before I work with him on this or anything."

Chief grunted. "Murray's damn good, and at least I'll know what you're up to."

"Damn it, no! This is my story and I'm not sharing it with anybody, especially Murray. I don't need any help." Steph glared at Chief, her brows furrowed. "Look at what I've found out in the past few days—all by myself. I can put the pieces together and I will, you'll see."

Murray knocked on Chief's door and entered in full stride. "You looking for me, Chief?" He stopped, straightened his tie and matted the side of his hair. His beady eyes darted about and finally landed on Steph; a skeletal smile flashed across his face.

Chief turned his attention to Murray, but he knew that Steph had planted her feet in the ground and was prepared to unleash a biting verbal assault any second. He clasped his hands. "Nah, forget it. I changed my mind. Get back to what you were doing."

"Sure thing." He turned to leave and then stopped, flashing a lopsided grin. "But, I was going to track you down later anyway, I just found out that a lady by the name of Dianna Shaffner was arrested last night at Benjamin Hunter's house—you know that guy who was involved in the whole Antarctica thing a year or so ago? Anyway, no one seems to know who she—"

Steph snapped, "Where'd you find that out?"

Murray gave Steph a quick once-over; a cocky edge trimmed his voice, "Sources." He looked back at Chief. "I'm going to look into this further and see if there's more to this. There has to be."

Steph held her anger in check and glared at Murray. "I don't know who your sources are or how you really found this out, but—"

"Hold everything." Chief stood and pushed his shirtsleeves up. "Murray, thanks for the info, and if there's anything else you've learned about this then pass it on to Steph. She's been working this story even before the arrest and I want her to stay on it. Got it?"

"Yeah, sure thing, if that's what you want," Murray threw his hands out, "but I could be a big help here."

"You already have, thanks," Chief replied.

As soon as Murray closed the door behind him a cold shiver ran up Steph's spine. "That guy gives me the creeps. I can't believe you actually like him."

"Listen, the guy produces and you're going to have to go and talk to him and find out what he knows. Other than that, this is your story to run with, so no more screw ups. Got it? And if you don't keep me posted on everything you're doing, when you do it, then I'll have to bring Murray onboard. Got it?"

Chief heard a knock on his door. "Scram, I'm busy," he yelled.

Another knock and the door flew open. "Since you're both here, this won't take long." Mr. Weintraub entered and took a minute to look at Chief and Steph. His eyes landed on Steph. He stood tall. "As of right now, you're no longer working on the Agrico story."

He turned toward Chief. "Stephanie is to go back to working on whatever you had her working on before she got carried away with that piece. If you want someone else to finish up the story, that's your call."

"What! You can't do that!" Steph clenched her fists and hardened her stare. "I'm close to having everything wrapped up and I'll have the story written in a few days. I'm finishing it."

"As the publisher of this paper I have every right to remove anyone I damn well please. That includes you. You're off the Agrico piece as of this minute."

"No, as of this minute I quit. I'll write the story for another paper."

CHAPTER 51

The CDC headquarters in Atlanta had become the command center for a fast moving public relations holocaust. Until Dr. Elsbach and her team could scientifically determine the specific diagnosis of the disease behind the outbreak in Liberia, they had been sticking to the standard tagline narrative that everything was under control and the viral disease had been contained. No mention of smallpox had been made in any public statement.

The WHO had been patient, and had agreed to cooperate with the CDC and keep any mention of smallpox out of the public spectrum. Until it was known with certainty how to combat the disease, silence would be the course of action. That blueprint, however, was about to be shredded. Every international news agency had encamped outside the WHO and the CDC headquarters and had been pressing for more specifics. They had already written that there had to be more to the story than had been relayed to the public—a great deal more.

In a sunlit room that had recently been known as the War Room, Dr. Elsbach was just concluding a meeting with several of her colleagues. A team of scientists had met regularly in the War Room to plan and direct elements of the human defense against Ebola. Now the War Room had been commissioned to serve as the command center for the latest viral attack—smallpox.

Dr. Thomas Wiser, the Director of the CDC, stayed behind and when the last person left the room, he turned and faced Dr. Elsbach. "Laura, I need to know when you'll have something conclusive on this whole issue." The Director not only had to have the skills and qualifications to carry out the CDC's stated mission, but the political acumen to referee the everyday partisan scrimmages. "I'm not able to hold out much longer. The pressure to give more detailed explanations on what's happening has pushed me to the brink."

"At this point, I have no idea when we'll have conclusive evidence. Soon, I hope—very soon." Dr. Elsbach stood behind a chair, leaned forward and planted her forearms onto the seatback. "The smallpox virus runs its natural course unless it comes in contact with the AMCAM vaccine. At that point the smallpox virus is repressed and a completely different virus becomes dominant. We're still trying to isolate and map it."

"It sounds similar to what we discovered during the Ebola outbreak." Dr. Wiser sat stiff jawed in his chair, his fingers clenched and his thumbs jutting upwards. "What'd we find there, something close to 300 genetic changes from previous Ebola sequencing?"

"This is different, totally different," Laura replied. "The Ebola mutations still left us with the characteristics of Ebola. In this case, when the smallpox gene mutates, it becomes secondary to a new, more virulent virus that we haven't been able to identify. We're sequencing it now, but I don't know when we'll have an answer."

"We're going to have to go public with this. You've seen the press encampment outside, and the WHO won't wait any longer. They don't have the same political constraints we have and the White House is screaming for answers. I've got to make a statement," Dr. Wiser said.

"Please, Tom, we need more time," Laura pleaded. "As soon as the name smallpox leaves your lips, Liberia will erupt, you know that. The situation there is already perilous and at least until we have troops there to protect our own people we can't say anything. I've promised Jim I'll get help to him or I'm pulling him and his team. I'll pull them now if you're planning any type of statement like that."

Dr. Wiser leaned back and nodded, slowly. "I'll wait, but only until troops arrive which should be today."

"Oh, that's great news. How'd you work that out?"

"I didn't. State and DoD worked it out with the Liberian Ministry. We'll have enough troops to secure the roads in and out of Monrovia, the ports and railways. Liberia wants the primary emphasis to be protecting the population centers and I can't disagree with that. Jim and the rest of the health workers will have the full protection of the U.S. military and patrol units will cover as many of the roads as possible."

Laura breathed a heavy sigh of relief, "Thank god. Thanks, Tom. I can't tell you what a relief that is."

"Just a sec." Tom punched the intercom button. "Yes, Nicole?"

"I have Dr. Harrington on the phone for Dr. Elsbach. I told him she was in a meeting with you, but he insisted. He said it couldn't wait."

Tom looked at Laura and they each took a deep breath. "Put him through."

■　■　■　■　■

"It's worse than that, Laura. Eight health care workers who arrived two days ago from Denmark have been infected with something different. It's not smallpox, the symptoms are different and they accelerate at a much faster pace."

"Slow down. You're saying that there appears to be an entirely separate virus there?" Laura asked.

"It doesn't appear to be, there *is* an entirely separate virus spreading over here and it's more virulent. It spreads much quicker than smallpox."

"Where are the infected people now? Are they isolated?" Laura asked.

"We had them isolated, but they were airlifted out of here a few hours ago. I have no idea what this is," Jim replied

"What are the symptoms?"

"It moves fast. In a period of only two days, their skin bruised, blistered and then literally peeled off. Dark blood began to flow from their eyes, ears and nose and they vomited black sludge. By the time they left here, they were still alive, but based on the rate of progression they could be dead by the time they land."

"And they're the only people showing those symptoms now? Are there any others?"

"None that we're aware of. I spoke to the person that's running their facility and he said they were an experienced crew; followed all the standard protocol as far as he knows. They were vaccinated against smallpox before they came here. Everyone's shocked at—"

"Wait a minute," Laura interrupted. "You said they were vaccinated before they came. Do you know what type of vaccine? That's important."

"I don't, but they came from Denmark, so the closest location with a known supply of smallpox vaccine is the WHO in Switzerland. That'd be my guess. Why does that matter?"

CHAPTER 52

Other than announcing the death toll, the CDC had been unnaturally quiet in releasing any vital details about the Liberian viral outbreak. A year earlier, after the CDC had sent a response team to West Africa during that region's Ebola outbreak, they had, within a single day, publicly announced the virus strain and its potential for spreading. During that same outbreak, the CDC had employed, for the first time, an Epi Info viral hemorrhagic fever application. The CDC had christened that new contact tracing open-source software program the *Swiss Army Knife* for field-deployed epidemiologists. With uncanny speed and accuracy, the program had aided in finding everyone that had been exposed to that contagious disease.

With the enormous resources available to the CDC there had to be a reason they had not released more information to the public. Alex had reached the conclusion that the CDC had been sitting on information for one simple reason: its release would cause panic, not only in West Africa, but worldwide. The SynAid virus had been released and its effects were proving to be as predicted—devastating and uncontrollable.

"We have to let the CDC know about the SynAid virus right now. The more I read about what's happening in Liberia, the more convinced I am that it's SynAid and the CDC is withholding information either because they're uncertain about the virus…" Alex winced, "or they know exactly what it is and don't know how to control it." She turned to Benjamin, "How much further to Tahoe?"

Benjamin exited the freeway and headed south on Highway 267 toward Lake Tahoe. "Twenty minutes to the lake and another 10 to the hotel."

"I'm going to call Andre and have him send off the vaccine." Alex reached over and placed her hand on Benjamin's knee. "Hear me out on this first, it's important, okay?"

Benjamin bristled at the sound of Andre's name. "Call him, do whatever you want with him, but keep him far away from me."

"You won't have to deal with him, but I want him to get the vaccine to the CDC and send samples to GEN along with the manufacturing specs—"

"What did I just say?" Benjamin glowered. "I'll have nothing to do with that guy so, why are you doing this? Why get GEN involved?"

"If it hasn't happened already, it will very soon; the SynAid virus is about to be released in the United States and what is happening in Liberia will happen here, only far worse. GEN is better positioned to offer help with the vaccine." Alex spun around in her seat and pulled a leg up to her chest. "If SynAid spreads here, like it has in Liberia, and the U.S. believes the Russians are behind it, what do you think will happen?"

There was no need for Benjamin to respond. He white-knuckled the steering wheel, bit the inside of his lower lip and narrowed his eyes. His face was distorted—terror stricken.

*   *   *   *   *

"Alex, thank god you called. I have been worried sick about you. Are you okay? Did you find Kioshi?"

The quiver in Andre's voice was genuine, but when it reduced itself to a mere whisper at the mention of Kioshi's name, she also knew he was trembling for his own safety. "The vaccine, have you done anything with it yet?" Alex asked.

"I have been at a total loss as to what I should do. I have talked with people I know at the WHO and even though they're saying very little, I am convinced that the virus in Liberia is what this vaccine was intended for," Andre replied.

"I'm certain as well, but I need to know, have you told anyone about the vaccine or sent it to anyone?" Alex asked.

"No, other than you and me and a few people here at CS Generale, no one is aware of the vaccine," Andre replied.

"I need you to ship a small quantity to GEN along with the manufacturing specs, and send the rest of your supply to the CDC. I will take care of alerting them. How much of the vaccine do you have on hand?"

"Wait—I can't send the vaccine to the CDC or anyone. You of all people know the consequences I would face from Kioshi. No, I am going to the WHO and discuss the vaccine with them. If I am able to convince them that it will work, they can help me with the distribution."

Alex knew that Andre would balk at her request. "Forget Kioshi. He's no longer an issue and there are hundreds of thousands of innocent lives at stake and you're sitting on their only hope. Send it and send it now."

Alex imagined Andre somewhere in his office pacing back and forth. She had seen it dozens of times before. His manicured fingers wrapped around the nape of his neck, his eyes dancing from one corner to the next and a cold sweat hemorrhaging between his shoulder blades. She wanted to play this out longer, make him thrash about in the prison of his own addiction, the pools of his own sweat, but finally, in a low whisper, Andre broke the edgy silence, "Tell me what you know about Kioshi? Did you find him?"

"Kioshi is a non-issue. He won't be contacting you, but even if he does he won't have any recollection of you or your so called business relationship. Andre, you need to send the vaccine off—*now*."

"What are you talking about, he won't remember me? That's preposterous, we have met on a handful occasions; of course he will remember me."

"Listen to me, Kioshi is behind the outbreak in Liberia and he is planning something that will kill far more people in the world than are now at risk there. He has absolutely no idea who you are or what you have, you need to believe me on that and trust me—it's the absolute truth. I've taken care of that myself. The vaccine you have needs to be tested and if it in fact can stop this outbreak, it will save hundreds of thousands of lives. The vaccine needs to be in the hands of the right people—*now*."

Slow, rhythmic breathing was all Alex heard. She felt she was drowning in slow motion. Finally, she screamed, "Andre! Do it!"

"Alright, I will do as you ask. You have never failed me in the past, but I do have strong reservations. I will keep a small amount of the vaccine here and I will immediately begin to make more in case you are somehow wrong."

"Thanks. Send it today," Alex breathed a quick sigh of relief.

"As you know, this vaccine costs a great deal to manufacture and its value is worth millions of dollars in profits. If Kioshi is truly out of my life as you say, then I would propose a fair split with GEN for its participation. Shall we say 20 percent of the profits?"

"Shameless. To you this is simply about money, isn't it? I just told you that Kioshi is out of your life and the only thing you can think about now is the money you stand to make." In a cool, raw tone, she added, "For once, do the right thing because it's the right thing to do."

CHAPTER 53

D r. Elsbach hung up the phone, leaned back and took a deep breath. Since the smallpox outbreak in Liberia, she had worked nonstop, and she was beginning to feel that the outbreak was steamrolling out of control. The latest casualty report on her desk sent shockwaves through her spine and her hands had trembled when she had first read it.

The 9/11 terrorist attacks had rapidly changed the way the United States had moved forward to protect itself against future attacks. At that time, Dr. Elsbach had felt the government had been throwing caution to the wind by ignoring standard scientific protocol in order to prepare itself. AMCAM3000, Arestvyr and a host of other drugs had all been approved for future use even though none of them had ever been tested on humans. She had presented her fears to Congressional Subcommittees, but they had gone unheeded.

Dr. Tom Wiser pushed open the office door and walked in. "What is it?"

"You better sit down; you're not going to like this." Laura reached for the bound folder in the middle of her desk.

"Judging by the tone of your voice from your message, I figured as much." Dr. Wiser took a seat.

Laura held up the report. "This is the latest casualty report from Liberia. It's about six hours old so I'm sure things have gotten even worse." She slid the report across her desk. "Before you look at it, we've finished sequencing the smallpox virus and… and it's bad, real bad. The smallpox virus, itself is the same virus we've stockpiled here, nothing unusual about it. But," she looked straight at Dr. Wiser, "the G-16 virus and a gene from the *Thermus aquaticus* bacteria have been stitched to it. This is a terrorist attack, Tom, and we've positioned ourselves right in the middle of it and we're completely unarmed."

Dr. Wiser's shoulders dropped and his neck bowed. "A terrorist attack... are you sure? God, no." He closed his eyes, "God, no."

"One hundred twenty-four U.S. servicemen in Liberia have already contracted the virus and have the G-16 symptoms; within the entire region that number is much higher." Laura leaned back in her chair. "There are two common threads here; each of these people had already been inoculated with AMCAM and they're all Caucasian—no African Americans, no nothing, just Caucasians."

Dr. Wiser had weaved his way through the political juggernaut to become the Director of the CDC, in large part because he could handle the unexpected with tact, poise and fortitude. He pushed up from his chair and stood. When he had walked into Dr. Elsbach's office moments ago, he had done so with the same swagger and buoyant demeanor he had worn for years with confidence and respect. Now, he stood, rooted to the floor, the creases in his forehead V'd. He shook his head, "I knew this would happen... it was only a matter of time. The G-16, you're sure?"

Laura nodded, "A hundred percent. We've sequenced it and the symptoms match."

"Who knows about this?" Dr. Wiser asked.

"Just this room. Jim hasn't been told about G-16, so it's just us." Laura bit her lip. "I'm pulling Jim and everyone else out now. I wanted to tell you first."

"Wait, let's talk this through. If we pull out then every organization and NPO will be right behind us." Dr. Wiser sat back in his chair, crossed his legs and pumped his fists. "Do you have any idea who's behind this?"

Laura shook her head, "No."

"What do you make of the fact that just Caucasians are contracting this and... well, how'd the military suffer these casualties? They haven't been directly involved with the health centers, they're only supposed to be on the periphery," Dr. Wiser asked.

"My best guess is that the G-16 has been manipulated to seek out those cell receptors on the specific combination of targeted gene cells that are found predominantly in Caucasians. Remember, that's the whole purpose of that virus. There are 16 genes that determine a particular race and that virus targets specific combinations of those genes."

"Yeah, but I thought we cleared out HCL and brought the remaining G-16 and smallpox samples back here. How could someone have gotten a hold of those?"

"I don't know, but they did."

"What are we doing about treating our servicemen? I'm going to need to alert DoD about this and advise them on the proper protocol."

"We have them all quarantined, but everyone over there who has taken AMCAM is at risk." Laura said. "We'll need to somehow move everyone not yet infected to an area where they'll be safe and we need to do it now, and in a manner that won't alarm everyone over there."

"Damn, Laura, how'd this happen? How'd our servicemen get caught up in the middle of all this?"

"I have some ideas and I've ordered some tests to see if I'm right," Laura replied. "Do you remember after 9/11 everyone was rushing around trying to put plans together to prepare for any possible future attack? I remember, and every standard protocol was ignored back then. The first two years after 9/11, 1.8 million servicemen were given the smallpox vaccine. That was essentially anyone who might be required to go overseas. Then, after AMCAM was approved, the military inoculated close to the same number of servicemen again. Each of the 124 servicemen that have been infected with the G-16 has been inoculated with AMCAM; the Dutch and Medicins San Frontieres healthcare workers were inoculated with AMCAM. So far, these are the only people that have contracted the G-16."

"So every one of our troops over there is at risk?" Dr. Wiser asked.

Laura nodded. "And every one of our troops here. And the thousands of healthcare workers across the country who've also been inoculated with AMCAM."

Dr. Wiser slumped down in his chair. "We owe you a big thank you. I remember when I started here, our overseas workers were going to be vaccinated with AMCAM, but you fought hard to have that overturned. If you hadn't done that, Jim and all the others over there would be at a greater risk than they already are."

Laura took a deep breath, "Thanks, but right now my main concern is if somehow this virus shows up here, thousands… hundreds of thousands… maybe more would die, and there is no known cure—none."

"Excuse me, Dr. Elsbach." A stocky woman pushed open the office door and peered in. "I'm sorry to interrupt, but there's a truckload of boxes that have arrived for you and this package has your name on it. I thought it might be important."

Dr. Elsbach reached out and grabbed the package. "There's no return address. Has this been checked out by security?"

The woman nodded.

"And the boxes—you say there's a whole truck load?" Laura stood and handed the package to Dr. Wiser. "Why don't you take a look at this and I'll go down to the loading area."

CHAPTER 54

Alex stood on the balcony and looked out over Lake Tahoe's crystal blue waters for the first time. She inhaled the crisp, pine-scented air and captured its lung-seizing freshness. The full moon cast a cold breath of light over the lake's mirrored surface. A fresh layer of snow had fallen and weighed heavily on the surrounding Jeffrey and Sugar pines. She had hoped that just a few minutes of standing and gazing at that natural beauty would ease the tightness in her muscles and the sea of anxiety swelling deep within. It hadn't.

Benjamin stuck his head through the opening of the glass sliding door. "It's the best I could find at this hour, but it should keep us going for a while. Come in and eat up. I have some hot coffee too."

Alex picked through the box full of food. "I'll stick with coffee for now."

"Nachos, hot dogs, donuts, hey—it's the 7-11 early morning special. Lots of people exist on this stuff. You're not interested?"

"Thanks, but I'll pass." Alex took a sip of coffee and leaned back against a small writing table on the side of the room. "We're in the wrong place. I know it."

Benjamin raised a brow. "What do you mean?"

"I've already explained that I think the Chinese government intends to stoke the fire between the U.S. and Russia by unleashing the SynAid virus here in the States and make it look like the Russians are behind it. I'm still certain of that."

"Yeah, but China would only be hurting themselves. They're the biggest holder of U.S. debt and they'd lose billions if the U. S. and Russia had a confrontation like you're talking about. During the Cuban Missile Crisis, the dollar lost over 20 percent of its value in one day. I'll bet this would be worse."

"Come here, let me show you something." Alex booted up her laptop, scrolled through her bookmarks and opened a file. "Here's more proof. Nine months ago, China held 1.32 trillion dollars of U.S. treasuries, and since then they've sold close to 12 percent of their short term holdings, which is more than they've ever sold since they started buying U.S securities. China hasn't been a buyer of any other securities in the world market so they're accumulating cash. Why would they be doing that? It's simple. They've been ratcheting up their sales during this nine-month period and just before the U.S. accuses Russia of planting the virus, they'll dump more U.S. securities and those securities will take a nose-dive when the U.S and Russia start flexing their muscles. China controls the real facts behind the SynAid virus so at some point, it can provide proof that the virus was planted by a terrorist group, not the Russians and they'll start buying U.S. securities again. Sure they'll lose billions in the short term, but they'll more than make up for it once they become buyers again."

"Yeah, okay, that's a big risk on China's part, but since they do control the facts, maybe it's not such a risk."

"And they become the white knight. They increase their stature within the region and throughout the world, which is their whole purpose."

"Shrewd." Benjamin grabbed another hot dog. "What makes you think we're in the wrong place?"

"I first thought they wanted to duplicate the 1979 anthrax epidemic in the Soviet Union that the Soviets covered up. Remember going over that?"

"Sure," Benjamin nodded, "it was somewhere around Lake Baikal and that's how you made the tie-in to Tahoe. Seems logical to me."

"Logical, yes, but it doesn't work. The SynAid virus isn't airborne; it's contracted through physical contact with bodily secretions. I thought initially that they were going to put the virus in the lake and it would spread from there. That's what I thought the tie-in was, but I was wrong. There's no doubt the virus could live in the water here, but it would take too much time for it to enter the human food chain and spread. Sure, eating fish or even swimming in the lake could infect humans and the virus would start to spread, but it would spread at a very slow rate. The Chinese are looking to make an immediate impact while there are real tensions between the U.S. and Russia. No, to make the impact the Chinese are looking for, the outbreak needs to be quick and much larger, much more dramatic."

"I'm with you so far, but that puts us back at square one. They could make that impact in dozens, if not hundreds of places," Benjamin declared.

"Not exactly. The documents I retrieved from the Chinese were very specific in saying they planned to duplicate the Lake Baikal outbreak. Lake Baikal and Lake Tahoe have too many similarities to have it happen anywhere else. The best way they could duplicate the Soviet outbreak would be by infecting meat with the virus. Remember the Soviets claimed the outbreak was caused by tainted meat? That's the link—but it does leave us cold with respect to where. I imagine there are dozens or more commercial cattle operations within a hundred miles of here."

Benjamin polished off the last of the 7-11 hot dogs and wiped some mustard from his lips. "There's not as many as you might think. Before I bought the M & O I looked around Northern California and Nevada for a spread and it turns out there aren't many cattle operations around here. There are a couple in Nevada nearby, just east of Sparks and Carson City, but they're pretty small. Anyway, with the drought going on, the hay production in the higher country is well below normal, so any cattle in this area would've already been shipped to lower elevations to feed for the winter."

"So they'd be shipped to California somewhere?" Alex asked.

"That'd be my guess. I can check on it in a few hours when everyone else gets up."

"Good idea." Alex pushed away from the table, walked over to the window and slid the curtains open. "So this is the lake you swam, from that end all the way up here?"

"Followed the Nevada side the whole way."

"Twenty-one miles?"

"Yep, give or take."

"Incredible." She turned around and looked at Benjamin. "If you had to guess, where would you say there's a cattle operation around here large enough to make a big impact and I mean a really obvious impact?"

"The biggest operation anywhere around here is Harris Ranch; that would definitely make the kind of impact you're looking for, but it's not really that close," Benjamin replied.

"Where is it?"

"Fresno County off of I-5, maybe a five or six hour drive from here. They have somewhere in the neighborhood of 100,000 head and they process nearly every day. It's a big operation." Benjamin nodded. "It's the ideal spot for someone wanting to create the perfect wave you're talking about."

"Harris Ranch… Harris Ranch…." Alex folded her arms across her chest and squeezed. Her eyes squinted shut, she grit her teeth and then it hit her—her eyes widened, "Fú léi sī nuò. How did I ever miss that? Mùchǎng." She spun around. "What time is it? When could we be at Harris Ranch?"

Benjamin looked at his watch and mentally clicked away at the math. "If we left now, probably noonish. Why? That's a long way from here and it doesn't really tie into your Lake Baikal theory."

"Mùchǎng in Chinese means ranch. At the time when I first looked at the documents from China, I didn't make the connection, it seemed out of context, but now I do, and Fú léi sī nuò, I had no idea what that meant. Fresno, it translates to Fresno, or something very close to that." Alex began throwing items in her backpack. "Let's get out of here—now. We need to get there as soon as possible."

"There's an airport at South Shore and Harris Ranch has an airport. I'm sure we can rent a plane and be there in a few hours. Except—" Benjamin stopped and clenched a fist, "you're a fugitive and I guess that makes me one so we'd probably have a group waiting for us as soon as we landed."

Alex smiled and held up her backpack. "Someone else can rent the plane. There are plenty of options in here." She shouldered her backpack.

CHAPTER 55

"Mr. Hunter, Mr. Hunter... wait up."

Benjamin turned and saw a man charging down the center of the parking lot toward him. Each step was marked by a slight limp, but it didn't slow his pace. He raised a hand and gave Benjamin a quick wave.

"We've met before, right?" Benjamin asked like he knew the man, but couldn't make the connection.

"Yeah, we met at your house when I arrested Diana Shaffner, remember? I've been looking for you since then, but I guess you've been gone." The man extended a hand. "Agent Guzman, FBI. If you don't mind, I have a few questions I'd like to ask you." He tipped his hat. "It shouldn't take long."

Benjamin gripped Agent Guzman's hand and held it firmly. "What's this about?"

Agent Guzman flipped his jacket collar around his neck and hunched his shoulders. "Seems kinda cold today. It's no big deal, but how about we go inside. I promise I won't take much of your time."

Benjamin shrugged. "Agent... sorry, what'd you say your name was again?"

"Rulon Guzman." He reached in his side pocket, pulled out a business card and handed it to Benjamin. "You know most people think that being an FBI agent is sorta like it is on the TV shows and in the movies, but it's nothing like that. Most of the time we end up following empty leads and writing up reports. Not very glamorous."

"Agent Guzman, I've been gone for a few days and I'm just getting to the office and I really need to get caught up on some things. Why don't we get together first thing tomorrow morning? I'll meet you right here."

"Yeah, I know what you mean. This has been one of those days for me too." Agent Guzman scratched the back of his neck. "I met your friend yesterday, Morgan, Phil Morgan. A nice guy, he was very helpful. He told me you might have gone to Tahoe with some friends to do some skiing. How come Mr. Morgan didn't go with you?"

"Look, I'm sorry you came all the way down here, but I really have some things I need to do. If you want to meet me here tomorrow, fine, otherwise have a good day." Benjamin turned and headed to the door.

"Okay, I guess this will have to wait, but I thought you'd be interested in what we found out about Diana..." His words were delivered in increasing decibels, climaxing with a loud, "Shaffner."

Benjamin stopped, reeled around, dropped his chin and sized up Agent Guzman. "If this really won't take very long, why don't you come in now?"

GEN's office was an old brick industrial warehouse in Alameda that had been converted to the company's specific needs. Benjamin's office was located at the far end of the building. After having coffee brought in, Benjamin sat down behind his desk. He pushed stacks of papers and mail aside and dropped his forearms to the desk. "So, I can give you a few minutes. I don't know if I can be of much help, but I'll do what I can."

Agent Guzman was leaning back against the edge of a small conference table. "There doesn't seem to be much in your office in the way of personal stuff. I guess you haven't been here all that long, huh?"

"Not really. I'm looking for someone to run the company, so there's no reason to make myself too comfortable," Benjamin replied.

"I remember reading everything in the news about GEN and its CEO being in some kinda trouble... the virus... that was it. That must've been pretty tough for you to deal with."

Benjamin nodded, "Yeah it was, I'm still dealing with the fallout from all that. So, what can I help you with?"

"Do you mind if I take a seat there?" He pointed to a chair in front of Benjamin's desk.

Benjamin waved a hand.

Agent Guzman sat down and pulled out a notebook. "I always like to take notes so I can keep things straight." He flipped to an empty page. "We've been trying to find Shaffner since she escaped. I guess you know about that? Caused some of us some real embarrassment."

"You arrested the wrong person, detective. Her name's not Shaffner."

"Uh-huh. So you heard she escaped?"

"Yeah, I heard."

"When did you find out about that?"

Benjamin's lips turned up in what passed as a smile. "My best friend's girlfriend is her attorney, remember?"

"I didn't know that. I saw both of them together at your place, but I didn't put that together." He scribbled some notes in his notebook and looked back up. "Did you run into Shaffner while you were in Tahoe?"

Benjamin leaned back in his chair, folded his hands in his lap and shook his head, "No. I have no idea where she is, if that's what you're driving at."

"Well, I know you were there and I know you two are friends so I thought that maybe you ran into her." He paused, expecting a reaction. Seeing none, he continued, "We received a tip late last night to have agents at Lake Tahoe today. Don't know who sent the tip, but it said that's where Shaffner would be and more specifics would follow. Does that make any sense to you?"

"I already said I don't know where she is, so if that's it, I can't help you." Benjamin slid a stack of papers to the center of his desk. "I need to get some things done. Sorry for your trouble."

With a loud grunt, Agent Guzman pushed up from his chair. "No trouble at all. You've helped me more than you know." He turned and headed toward the door. Reaching for the knob he stopped. His head turned. "Maybe there's one more thing you could help me with."

Agent Guzman tucked his notebook under his arm and stuffed his hands in his pockets. "How was the traffic coming back from Tahoe? You did drive back today, right?"

"Stop and go in the usual places, but not bad. Why do you ask that?"

"Part of our job, as you know, is to check under every rock and look in every corner. We're pretty good at it; don't usually miss much, but every once in a while we just don't catch a thing or two. Any chance you might know an Alexandria Pancini?"

Benjamin shrugged his shoulders. "That's another no."

"Huh, I thought maybe you would. We checked around with the airports and she and another guy rented a plane and pilot early this morning from South Shore. We showed the guy at the airport Shaffner's picture and he was pretty certain it was her."

Agent Guzman took slow, deliberate steps toward Benjamin. "The plane flew from South Shore to Harris Ranch and then up to the Oakland airport and then the plane went back to South Shore." He stopped in front of Benjamin's desk. "Two passengers left on the plane and it returned empty. The way I see it, one passenger got off at Harris Ranch and the other one at Oakland."

He planted his hands on the desk and leaned forward. "You wanna think that through again? You sure you don't know where she is?"

CHAPTER 56

Harris Ranch was located in the San Joaquin Valley, right in the center of California. Noted for being the largest cattle operation on the West Coast of the United States, few people knew that another 14,000 acres were devoted to 35 different types of fruits and vegetables.

Before landing at the airport, the plane had circled the area and Benjamin had pointed out the feed lots, slaughter house and packaging plant.

Alex had checked into the Harris Ranch Hotel and then had scouted out the immediate area. Two years ago, an arsonist had burned 14 cattle trucks, and as a result, the ranch operation had hired full-time security personnel to protect against any further assaults on its operations.

Back in her hotel room, she placed a call to Charles Diderot in Paris. "Charles, hello, it's Alexandra Boudreau. How are you?"

"Hello, Alexandra, I am sorry I haven't gotten back to you, but I am having some difficulty in identifying the specific target of the ProTryX vaccine. I really have no idea if I will be able to draw any conclusions."

"That's okay; I think at this point it may not matter. I know you've been following the outbreak in Liberia and I'm fairly certain that the virus causing all the problems over there is SynAid."

"No one has identified the virus yet, how do you know that?" Charles asked.

"The person who created the virus is using Liberia as its testing ground. Once the outbreak became public they knew the virus would be successful and it has now been sold to a government. I'm not going to tell you which government, you don't want to know, but they intend to release the virus in the United States—soon, very soon."

"Oh mon Dieu! I am following everything I can about the Liberian outbreak and no one has identified the specific virus. Some people have been inoculated with the smallpox vaccine as a precaution, but the specific virus is unknown at this point. That can't be true."

"Come on, Charles, has there ever been a viral outbreak anywhere where the WHO or the CDC didn't identify the virus, and even the source of the virus, within a matter of a day or two? No, there hasn't and either they really don't know or they're holding back saying anything because of the panic that would set in. I think it's the latter."

"Logic doesn't always prevail in matters like this and I have to believe whatever they are doing they have good reason," Charles asserted.

"The first thing I—"

"Wait, this is important. Several hours ago, the WHO announced the source of the virus. It came from rice grown in a small village near the Sierra Leone border. They have samples of the rice, but what is puzzling is it is red rice, not brown or white."

"Why would that matter?" Alex asked.

"Asians and most Africans prefer white rice and no one has identified any red rice being grown anywhere in that region except that one village. They're trying to determine where the rice came from."

Alex stood up and walked over to the window and leaned back. "Tell me something, to cook rice you need to boil it first and then simmer it. What would happen to the G-16 virus and the smallpox virus if they were boiled? I seem to recall that viruses can't withstand extreme heat. Wouldn't that destroy the SynAid virus?"

Alex sat tight and listened to the silence. She envisioned Charles sitting in his office cluttered with piles of paper, pushing his oversized glasses back up to the bridge of his nose. "An interesting point, but solvable. The smallpox virus is not heat resistant and as far as I can recall neither is the G-16. If this new virus was injected into rice and eventually cooked it would die out. There may be certain seeds which withstand the heat just as a matter of probability, but in theory they would all be destroyed."

"So what you're saying is it couldn't have been the rice?"

"Not necessarily. New viruses are being discovered all the time and with so many of us being concerned with climate change, there are some trying to find ways to make food staples resistant to drought and heat. The Thermal Biology Institute at Montana State University made the first interesting discovery in this area, back in 1967. They discovered a new bacterium called *Thermus aquaticus* in the geyser basin of Yellowstone National Park. At the time, that bacterium was able to survive at temperatures of up to 70 degrees Celsius. They found that that particular bacterium copied its own genetic information with a thermostable enzyme, DNA polymerase, in order to survive and replicate. It is now possible to create synthetic viruses that can withstand heat up to the boiling temperatures and even greater. Do you see where I'm going with this?"

"I think I do. Basically you can add a heat resistant synthetic enzyme to any virus and the byproduct will be able to withstand temperatures up to a certain point. How long would it take to find out if that's the case with the SynAid virus?"

"Genetic sequencing for most anything can be completed in a matter of a couple days. If what you believe is true, that this new SynAid virus is the cause of the Liberian outbreak, then we must get this information to the CDC and the WHO immediately. I don't know if you are aware of the latest death numbers, but they are staggering, and are projected to double every two to three weeks."

"I don't know what the current numbers are, and I'm not sure I want to right now. I believe the ProTryX vaccine is effective against the SynAid virus and I've had it sent to the CDC along with the other information I know. They should have it by now."

"Alexandra, I know I did not want to get involved in this, but if you are correct about ProTryX, then I have to do something. I am going to call my colleague at the WHO and go over this with him."

Alex glanced at her watch. "I think that's a good idea. It's going to be dark here soon and I have a few things to finish up, so I have to go. Thanks, Charles, I'll talk to you soon."

■　■　■　■　■

Alex was now back in her element—the mission, the solving of the puzzle, and then the sting. She enjoyed the puzzle best. That was the creative part of the hunt—the time her intellect entwined with her intuition. That was when her adrenaline was highest. The rush of uncovering the key was addictive to her and she knew she was close.

She threw a jacket over her shoulder and headed out the door. An hour of sunlight was left and she had several loose ends to tie up before she expected the action to begin.

Walking along the side of the pool toward the parking lot, she inhaled the citric smell of ripened oranges and admired the lavender, fuchsia and crimson blossoms of the bougainvillea plants.

"They say tonight will be star-studded and to me the stars are like the trees in the forest, alive and breathing. And they're watching us. What do you think?"

The drawn out Kyushu accent froze Alex in her tracks. She turned slowly and spotted a man leaning against a palm tree; a hat pulled forward shaded his face. "Words from Haruki Murakami, one of my favorite authors. I imagine that describes a typical night in Montana, am I right?" He pushed his hat back.

"To himself everyone is immortal; he may know that he is going to die, but he can never know that he is dead. Words from Samuel Butler, one of my favorite authors." Alex replied.

Kioshi pushed away from the tree, took several steps toward Alex and stopped. His eyes cut into her like Scorpio rising. "You must think that I am a fool and that you are the master." He shook his head in disgust. "Your idea of planting false memories in my mind and erasing others has sound reasoning behind it. I, too, have played around with that idea and like you, I have had little success. The flicker rates to produce the precise images to distort one's perception and make them responsive to suggestions, only works on people who have an innate willingness to accept distortions of logic or reality. I am one of the few subjects who is not susceptible to this technique. I am sorry, but you lose."

"At this point it makes very little difference to me whether you remember me or not. I know about your arrangement with the Chinese government, Liberia and your plans to unleash the SynAid virus right here. If I know that, then you can be sure others do as well."

Kioshi huffed belligerently, "I see your blood still boils, but it is too late for you now. You had your chance to die with honor, but now, since we are here in the western world, I will use other means. Look up at the second floor balcony to your left; the palm tree straight ahead on your right and then look directly above you. Then look at your heart."

Alex stood tall and deflected Kioshi's vicious stare with one of her own. Slowly, her stare moved from left to right and then dropped to her chest—three red dots circled her heart.

CHAPTER 57

Small flecks of light squeezed through the crack in the rubber seal at the bottom of the roll-up door. Alex lay in the back of the truck, her legs pulled to her chest and her arms bound at the wrists behind her thighs. With each bump, she rolled to her side like a beach ball, unable to hold steady or protect herself from slamming into the metal siding on one side and stuffed burlap sacks on the other. She had begun counting the seconds the moment the truck first pulled away and she listened intently to each shift in the gears and each passing car. When they came to a stop she guessed they had driven about 15 minutes, but she had no idea in which direction.

She heard creaking hinges as cab doors opened and the clunk of metal when they were slammed shut. Voices of two, maybe three men were outside near the front of the truck. She recognized the language, Japanese, but the sound was too faint, too jumbled to understand. She closed her eyes, slowed her breathing and heightened her senses. She heard the distinctive Kyushu dialect from the far southern tip of the country, the same dialect as Kioshi's.

Two more doors opened and slammed in the distance followed by the bellowing voice of Kioshi. He must have driven separately. She struggled to free herself, but her wrists were bound tight and she couldn't pry her legs through her arms. Think, Alex, think.

The metal roll-up door screeched open and light poured in. Alex rolled to her side and saw two men step on the rear bumper and jump inside the truck. Within seconds, a hood was placed over her head and she was dragged outside and dropped to the ground.

Kioshi yelled, in English, to one of the men, "Go ahead and get it warmed up and we will throw her in when you are ready." He looked at one of the men standing next to Alex. "Hiroki, see that our friend here is delivered as promised. The sooner I have her out of my life the better."

Kioshi took two steps and stood over Alex. "I am so sorry I will not be able to make the trip with you, but it is a short one and I have other, more important matters to attend to." Alex's hood was yanked off and she saw the pearly white smile of Kioshi leering over her. Behind her she heard the sound of pft-pft-pft, faster and faster and then the whoosh of air being beaten into submission. "I regret that I didn't kill you years ago, but at least you ended up with a few more years. I hope you made the most of them."

Kioshi kicked Alex in the ribs, then turned and walked purposely back to his car.

"Come on lady, we're going for a ride." The same two men reached down, wrapped their cement-like hands around her arms and yanked her off the ground. She turned and clicked a mental image of Kioshi's white Accord. The two men carried her over to the helicopter and slammed her into the back. Her feet dangled over the edge of the seat, her upper body was pulled forward and her arms were wrapped around her legs, her wrists tightly bound. She felt the pins and needles crawl up her legs, a sharp pain in her back and a throbbing in her chest. Her blood flow was being cut off and soon, she knew she would pass out.

Two men slid in and wedged their bodies into the cramped space on each side of Alex. She knew the helicopter, a stripped down version of the Eurocopter B3, the same chopper that had made the first landing on the summit of Mt. Everest and was part of the French Gendarmerie Nationale's standard fleet. The chopper lifted off the ground and headed west.

The man crammed up against Alex on her left nudged her with his elbow. "Nakajima-san has told us that you killed two of his men some years back. We did not know those men, but even so, they are our brothers and it is an honor for us to avenge their deaths."

"Hiroki, right?" The man's eyes narrowed as he stared at Alex. "Kioshi, and now you, talk about honor. Is it honorable for you to kill all those people in Liberia? Is it honorable for you to plant a deadly virus here and kill thousands more?" Alex turned her head and looked at the man. "There is no honor in that, only cowardice."

A fist slammed into her jaw and she felt the pain shoot through the middle of her brain. "I do not want to have to do that again, but I will. I want you alert and conscious when we get to where we are going." He thrust his face closer to Alex, teeth flashing.

Out the side, through the open doors, Alex spotted the peaks of the coastal mountain range below. The Pacific Ocean loomed in the near distance. "Let me guess," Alex said. "Someone's going for a swim."

An indignant grunt, "Nakajima-san was right, you are a clever one."

"This is your last chance to do what's right. After you throw me overboard I'll come back and track you down, just like—"

From the other side a fist drilled into her diaphragm and her lungs collapsed. She sucked empty gulps of air and felt her head twirling round, round and around. The pins and needles now covered her legs and clawed up the edges of her spine. Time was running out and she knew it. She could feel her lungs beginning to expand, but directly below her, she saw the white-capped waters of the Pacific Ocean.

"There's a ship off to our left, maybe you can drop me off there if it's not too much trouble?" Out of the corners of her eyes she saw each man lift his chin, squint and look to the left. Her feet were pressed against the front seat. She pushed—hard. Her body rolled back, she twisted to the side, planted her feet in Hiroki's rib cage, and slammed her head back into the face of the other man—and pushed.

The force of Alex's kick sent Hiroki sliding out the open door. He disappeared from the cabin, but his outstretched fingertips grabbed hold of the landing skids. His legs dangled in the wind.

Alex spun around. She kicked her foot out, landing square in the other man's larynx. He buckled forward. She planted both feet into his waist and pushed. His screams faded as he disappeared below.

Alex sidled over to the opening on her right. Lying on her back she began rubbing the rope that bound her wrists against the metal edge of the door opening.

The pilot in the front turned his head, saw what Alex had done and immediately jammed the left anti-torque pedal all the way down to the floor. The tail rotor accelerated and the helicopter began to spin around its tail axis— faster and faster with each rotation.

The force of the spin slammed Alex to the edge of the door opening. She locked her feet on one side and her head on the other. She pressed down harder and rubbed the rope against the metal edge.

With each change in the pitch of the rotor blades, the helicopter rose and fell as it continued to spin around. Alex felt the frayed edges of the rope—she pressed harder.

Hiroki had pulled himself up onto the landing skids and was climbing back inside. The centrifugal force was pulling him back into the helicopter and pushing Alex out. The rope snapped. Alex untwisted the rope from her wrists and pulled herself back inside.

Hiroki reached across, grabbed Alex with one hand and pulled her toward him. He wrapped an arm around her neck and squeezed.

Alex couldn't breathe. She was immobilized by Hiroki's grip. She thrust her right palm upward into his nose and heard the sound of shattering cartilage.

The instant Alex felt Hiroki's grip loosen around her neck, she slammed her head back and heard the sound of skull against skull. She threw his arm from her neck and spun around just in time to duck and miss a clenched fist.

She grabbed his forearm, threw her shoulder into his upper arm, planted her feet and pushed. Hiroki flew forward into the front seat, careened off the pilot and landed on the cyclic control stick.

The helicopter's nose fell and it plunged downward, still spinning and spinning around its vertical axis.

Alex landed a hard blow to the head of the pilot and he buckled.

Grabbing Hiroki by the collar, she threw him to the side and wrapped both her hands around the control stick and pulled—hard.

The helicopter leveled out and skimmed across the top of the ocean; the whir of the blades parted the water as Alex climbed into the pilot's seat.

Making sure her two passengers were out cold and would stay that way, she lifted the bird upward and turned east.

■　　■　　■　　■　　■

Alex pushed the helicopter to its maximum speed, whirling back toward Harris Ranch. Once she saw her destination in the distance, she brought the chopper down to near ground level.

Within two thousand yards of her mark she could make out the silhouette of the truck; the same truck she had been thrown in earlier. Standing on the side of the truck, a group of men were huddled together, staring in her direction.

One thousand yards—she knew that was her target—straight ahead. She dropped the helicopter down lower; the landing skids grazed the brush.

Five hundred yards—the men scattered in all directions, waving their hands, yelling, screaming.

Three hundred… two hundred… one hundred yards…. The helicopter crashed into the truck and erupted into a fireball of flames.

CHAPTER 58

Stephanie had written a draft of her article and was waiting in Chief's office while he read through it. She flinched each time Chief grunted, looked up at her with a cheeky smirk or waved his pencil like he wanted to slash every word he had just read.

She still had a few items to double check and she needed confirmation from several sources, but she knew her story would rock Agrico's boardroom and possibly redirect the debate over genetically modified foods. It was a good story, she knew it and all she needed was Chief's approval.

This was the first time she had taken a moment to look around Chief's office. Leaning against a credenza, her eyes landed on his first Pulitzer Prize. His story, The Devil's Playground, chronicled lucrative enterprises run by gangs at New York City's Rikers Island Correctional Facility and detailed how the guards had not only turned a blind eye to this activity, but had actively participated in it.

"Not bad, Steph. We'll polish up a few things, but this is pretty good." Chief leaned back in his chair and drilled the heels of his shoes on the top of his desk. "Damn good. I'd sure like to be a fly on the wall over at Agrico when they read this."

Steph pushed away from the credenza and seemed to float across the room. She landed in front of Chief's desk. "I knew it. Oh, I can polish things up, no problem, but I wanted you to see what I've got. I'll finish it up tonight or first thing in the morning at the latest, for sure."

Chief tilted his head, "Are you sure you don't want to reconsider coming back to work here? Let me take this to your dad and show him what you've done. This is damn good stuff. Things will work out and this will be an above the fold story with your name."

"I appreciate your sticking by me and helping me with all this. I know you've stuck your neck out and you didn't have to." Steph folded her arms across her chest. "I'm not coming back here now, or in the future. It just doesn't work for me to be under my dad's thumbs."

"Yeah, your dad, he can be gruff at times, but he's trying his damndest to look after your best interests. I really think that."

"My dad, gruff? I don't think so. No, he's hard-headed, self-absorbed and insensitive, but gruff, nah, that's not him. Everyone thinks you're the gruff one."

"Me?" Chief pointed his fingers at himself, "I'm gruff? And who's everyone?"

"Gruff in a good way. It just means you always tell it like you see it and that's the way I like it. So, I'm not coming back, you can bank on that."

"I understand, but the door's open. If you change your mind, I'll help."

"My heels are dug in on this one and besides, have you ever known me to change my mind?"

The corner of his lips rose, "Nope, not a once."

"Okay, I'll have this to you by the crack of dawn and you'll have until the end of the day to tell me you'll run the story, otherwise I'll shop it around. That was our deal."

Chief nodded his approval. "That it was."

Steph spread her legs, leaned forward and grabbed the edge of Chief's desk. "Since you don't have any comments, I'm going to go ahead and get—"

"Whoa, hold on a minute, young lady, I got a question or two." Chief clutched Steph's article in his raised hand. "The part about GMs needing more regulation, don't you think that opens up an entirely different area than what you're addressing here? I mean you may be on to something, but I'm not too sure it should be part of this piece."

"You're wrong, it's perfect for this piece because if I'm right," she shot Chief a quick glance and started to pace in front of the desk, "and I know I am, then it's the perfect lead in for my follow-up."

"Follow-up? Let's wrap-up this one first, okay?"

"Look, I know Agrico as a company didn't have any knowledge of what was going on with Sustinere, but that's not the point, because all they or any other company need to do is set up a non-profit anywhere in the world to give the appearance that other companies are playing in their arena. It takes some heat off them, but they still reap the profits."

Steph stopped her pacing, laid her hands back on Chief's desk and leaned forward. "Look at what's going on in Liberia and the viral outbreak there. The CDC has announced that the virus originated from some rice grown in the region, but they've been pretty hush-hush in saying anything more. Do you know how easy it would be for any terrorist group to insert a virus into a grain of corn, soybean, rice or anything like that? Pretty simple and then they sell it in the marketplace and boom, whatever they planted spreads. That's what I mean by regulation. I'm not taking a stand here on whether GMs are good or bad, although I have my own opinions on that, but I do think there needs to be a set of international rules governing the packaging and distribution of food seeds and a way to oversee and enforce those rules. What if that's exactly what happened in Liberia?"

"Well, Liberia may be a stretch at this point, but I'm not saying I disagree with you. I just think it detracts from what you've uncovered at Agrico. The fact that a company can spend that kind of money and not even know about it is chilling. This is great stuff, stick to the facts you have and don't make this an op-ed piece."

"I have facts to back all that up and I'll have—" Steph pulled her phone from her pocket. "I have to take this; it's part of my story."

She leaned back against the credenza. "Hello, Mr. Morgan? Hi, thanks so much for calling me back. I guess Mr. Hunter's still not back cuz he hasn't returned my calls, but I did want to talk to you.

"Uh-huh... sure... no actually, I wanted to ask you something. When I met you the other day we started to talk about the virus in Africa, but we never finished. I'm sort of wrapping up a follow-up story on that and you mentioned you'd heard that the virus may have originated from some rice over there. What can you tell me about that?

"Uh-huh… and who was it that told you that?"

Steph looked over at Chief and caught his inquisitive look. She nodded back. "No, of course I understand, but since I'm trying to get my story out now I just thought maybe I'd talk to you first. So, let me see if I got this all straight; you heard the virus originated from some rice that was grown in the region and you're certain that the source has direct access to that information, but you don't want to say anything further right now. Is that about right, Mr. Morgan?"

Steph's fingers twirled around the ends of her hair. She listened intently. "Sure, I can wait, no problem," Steph responded. "I don't want to print anything without verifying its accuracy and if you don't want me to say anything, I won't. So, I'll just say it's from a reliable, but undisclosed source. Is that okay?"

"Oh yeah, that's great, really, thanks. You'll help me with this further when you can?

"Okay, perfect, Mr. Morgan and—

"Oh yeah, Phil, right and thanks so much. I'll get in touch with you if I come across anything new."

Steph dropped the phone back in her pants' pocket, puffed out her chest, closed her eyes and exhaled—long and slow. "I'm getting awfully close to confirming what I need to print in my next story, don't you think?"

Chief dropped one leg to the ground and slapped his knee. "Well played, Steph." He pulled his other leg from the top of the desk, leaned forward in his chair and squawked, "What are you waitin' for? Get me a finished copy."

CHAPTER 59

Two black sedans skidded to a stop on the dirt road sending thick swirls of dust into the night sky. Agent Guzman exited the lead car and was followed by half dozen other agents. He barked out orders, "Get a fire crew out here now—hurry on it. Call the locals and have them set up roadblocks on every road leading out of here. I want the men who left here caught and brought in. Get the locals a description of Shaffner. Grab flashlights, spread out and see what you can find."

They had arrived just minutes after Alex had crashed the helicopter into the truck and flames still spiraled upward turning the cool night air into a blast furnace. Less than 50 feet from the explosion, hundreds of terror stricken cattle huddled in the far corner of a feedlot.

"Agent Guzman, we found these two men tied and gagged by the shed over there." The agent pointed behind him in the direction of the feedlot. "They saw everything that happened. You'll want to hear what they have to say."

"Are you two alright?" Agent Guzman asked.

"We're pretty shook-up and pretty lucky." One man rubbed the rope burns on his wrists and the other was brushing dirt from his tangled hair. "We saw the whole thing."

"What were you guys doing out here? Do you work for Harris Ranch?" Agent Guzman asked.

"We're part of the security for the ranch and this is part of our usual rounds. There were eight men when we drove up and even before we could ask them any questions they'd tied our wrists, gagged us and threw us over there in front of the feed shed. We didn't recognize any of them, but as soon as they left us they started throwing grain into the feed bins and that's when we saw the helicopter flying right at us."

"We saw that chopper flying low to the ground and it looked like the crash was intentional. Do you have any idea who was flying it?" Agent Guzman asked.

The man shook his head. "Nah, It was the damndest thing I've ever seen. It kept getting lower and lower and then everyone started running and yelling about that woman or something like that and then it just crashed into the truck. It sure looked intentional."

"A woman? Do you think it was a woman flying the chopper?" Agent Guzman asked.

"That's the impression I got, but I couldn't tell you one way or another. It all happened so fast. It was just a blur," the man replied.

A stream of fire trucks arrived, unloaded gear and rolled out their hoses. With a measured, crisp efficiency, the firemen spread out and set about containing the blaze.

"We need to talk. I was hoping you'd be here."

Agent Guzman spun around and stood slack-jawed. "Shaffner! What the hell?"

Alex limped toward Agent Guzman. Her face was scraped and cut and blood dripped from her shredded blouse. Her blue jeans were torn on one side and pieces of shrubbery were matted in her hair. "I have a lot to fill you in on, but first, put out an APB to apprehend a white Honda Accord, California license number 7ERE475. That's the guy you want and he just drove out of here before the crash."

"What are you talking about?" He motioned behind him. "Roger, Stu, cuff her."

Two agents moved behind Alex. She offered no resistance as they pulled her arms behind her back and slapped cuffs on her wrists. "Kioshi Nakajima, check him out and if you don't have anything on him then check with the NSA, they know his whole story. I suggest you quarantine the cattle too. The rice they threw in the feedlot is laced with the same virus that's spreading throughout Liberia. I'm sure you've heard of that? Gather all the rice grains you can in the feedlot and send them off to be tested."

Agent Guzman flipped the front brim of his hat up and stood gaping at Alex in disbelief. "I don't know what you're talking about, but we're hauling your ass back into custody—*now*. You've caused enough trouble. Put her in the back, Roger, and keep an eye on her."

"Listen to me! Why do you think you're even here? Why do you think you went to Tahoe? Why am I walking right up to you if I've done what you think I've done?" Alex took a step forward and squared her shoulders. "Most guys like you are looking for a smoking gun and I handed you a bazooka. I've been the one tipping you off all along because I wanted you here when I found these guys. One of the reasons I crashed that chopper was so you could see the flames and get here." Alex took a step forward and continued, "Find Nakajima, I've led you right to him and quarantine the cattle or you're going to have a viral outbreak here that's more deadly than anything you could ever imagine."

Agent Guzman huffed. "That was you that crashed the chopper? How the hell did you survive?"

"I jumped a few hundred yards out," Alex replied. "Come on; put an alert out on Nakajima before you lose him."

Agent Guzman caught the eye of the agent to his side. "Go ahead, put out the alert." He eyed Alex with curious suspicion. "There's something about you that I just don't get. I can't put my finger on it, but we have a plane at the airport here and you'll be flying back with me. I want to know your story—the whole story."

CHAPTER 60

Steph and Chandler drove into the front entryway of the Buckeye Roadhouse, pulled to a stop and exited their car. After pocketing the valet ticket, they walked up the winding stairway. "Wait," Chandler grabbed Steph by the arm. "What's going on? You hardly said a word driving over here and now you're charging up the steps as if I don't exist. What gives?"

"What gives?" Steph swung around, jammed her hands in her pockets and her eyes shot darts. "Why don't *you* tell *me* what gives?"

A shoulder shrug. "I don't understand. What's bugging you anyway?"

Steph took a step forward. "Are you seeing someone?"

"What!"

"Are you seeing someone? Yes or no!"

"What on earth are you talking about? Why would you even ask such a thing?"

"This past week you haven't been yourself. You don't answer your cell, which you always answer. You're not in your office when you tell me you were; you're showing up late to things using lame excuses. Do you want me to go on? Because I can."

"I'm not seeing anyone." Chandler shook her head and attempted a thin-lipped smile although it looked more like she had swallowed her tongue. "I'm so sorry that's what you think. I love you and I would never, ever, step out on you."

"Then what have you been doing? Why all the secrecy?" Steph's voice softened.

"Do you know what tomorrow is?"

"Friday."

"No, I mean what's so special about tomorrow?"

Steph's grim face melted. "My birthday?"

"Right! I've been planning a surprise party for you and it hasn't been all that easy to keep you at bay while I made all the plans. I so much wanted it to be a surprise."

"Oh my god, what a dufus. You wouldn't believe all the things that've raced through my mind. A surprise party? I think that'll be a first for me."

"Do you think you can act surprised tomorrow?"

"Believe me, it won't be an act."

Inside the restaurant, a couple sat against the wall perusing a menu and the maître d' stood stiff-armed at his stand, head down. As Steph and Chandler approached the maître d', he raised his head and gasped, "Oh, dear me, it's you."

"Hi," Steph grinned. "I wasn't sure that you'd remember me, but... well, it looks like you do." She squinted and gave a half-smile. "I'm really sorry about the other night, I'm not... well... I'm not usually such a klutz—really."

The maître d' looked at his reservation list and took a step back. "I'm so sorry, but it looks like we're completely full tonight. I would suggest you call ahead for reservations the next time you wish to dine here."

"I'm pretty sure we have reservations. It's probably under Hunter. We're meeting him here."

The maître d' raised a hand to the side of his face. "Mr. Hunter? You mean... Mr. Benjamin Hunter?"

Steph pushed her shoulders back and nodded. "Yep, that would be him. Is he here?"

The maître d' cleared his throat. "Yes, he is. Mr. Hunter and Ms. Boudreau were seated just minutes ago. Please, let me show you both to their table."

"Mr. Hunter, your party has arrived. I will make sure the waiter comes right over." The maître d' held a chair out as Steph took her seat.

Benjamin pushed his chair back and stood. "I take it you're Stephanie?"

"I am and it's nice to finally meet you." She gripped Benjamin's extended a hand. "Well, actually I prefer Steph and this is my partner, Chandler Mills."

Benjamin introduced Alex and sat back down.

Alex patted Steph on the arm. "I owe you a huge thank you for that timely piece you wrote. If it hadn't been for your article, I'd probably still be sitting in a cell."

"Mr. Hunter told me about that when we talked on the phone. I'm glad I could help, but really, I had no idea that the Novum Rice had anything to do with anything other than money being embezzled from Agrico," Steph said.

"How did you run across all that in the first place?" Alex asked.

"I was in the right place at the right time." Steph picked up her napkin, gave it a quick snap and dropped it to her lap. "I had some inside help, but what really puzzled me the most was why Agrico spun off the Novum Rice to begin with. Did you know that almost all of the seeds sold to the developing countries are purchased by public agencies or nonprofit organizations that are organized to promote sustainable farming? That's because the farmers in those countries can't afford to buy seeds."

"If most of the rice is consumed in developing countries, like you said, then how do companies make a profit?" Alex asked. "It would seem that their real profit would have to come from the developed countries."

"Exactly, and that's the beauty of the Novum Rice," Steph replied. "It has a real value in providing additional iron to peoples' diet and health conscious consumers look for those types of products. I think Novum Rice would be accepted here for that very reason, plus, it has the added advantage of being red rice which is considered more of a delicacy than the normal white rice."

"So I've heard. You seemed to focus on Eric Cummings as being the one who embezzled the funds. Do you have any idea why he was doing that?" Alex asked.

Steph shook her head, "No, not yet. He was well thought of by everyone in the industry and had a very successful career. A police officer I know, who's working the case, has told me that Cummings had several off-shore bank accounts with big seven and eight figure balances. He hasn't been able to get the banks to release any information yet, but from what they found at his house, deposits were made into those accounts from other off-shore accounts." Steph looked around and leaned forward. "He wasn't doing this alone," she nodded. "There had to be others involved."

"Do you have any ideas on that front," Alex asked.

"Cummings' death wasn't a suicide as originally thought. He was found on a couch in his den with a half-empty vial of phenobarbital spilled beside him. The coroner found where he'd been hit on the back of his head and it didn't leave a visible mark on the outside, but he found bleeding on the inside. Also, there was a needle mark between his toes and thallium was found in his system."

"It sounds like you're already on to your next story." Alex reached in her purse, pulled out a flash drive and slid it across the table to Steph. "You'll find everything you need right there connecting Kioshi Nakajima to the Novum Rice developed by Sustinere and even some correspondence between Nakajima and Eric Cummings. This should tie together some of your loose pieces."

"Whoa…." Steph picked up the drive and looked at it like it was a rare diamond. "Are you serious? Oh, of course you are, but where'd you get this?"

Alex smiled. "Somehow I think you and I were looking for the same thing, but let's just say that I have interesting ways of acquiring what I'm looking for. After you take a look at that, I think it will be pretty clear to you where much of it came from."

"So if that Kioshi character that you ran into and Cummings are connected, do you think that somehow Novum Rice has anything to do with the virus outbreak in Liberia? I know the CDC announced that they suspect the outbreak was caused by tainted rice. Maybe a coincidence?" Steph asked.

Alex shook her head. "No coincidence. Kioshi Nakajima was the mastermind behind all this. At the time the Novum Rice was first being developed, he lured Eric Cummings in with some false promises and before long Cummings was in so deep there was no turning back. Nakajima developed a new virus that is a combination of smallpox and the G-16 virus. Do you know about the G-16?"

"Oh yeah, Chandler and I read everything about what was going on with you, Mr. Hunter, and everything you went through. But, from what we read, I thought the G-16 virus was safely controlled and there was no danger of it being used. I guess that was wrong, huh?"

"I'm not sure anything is every safely controlled," Benjamin interjected. "Smallpox was stored safely for some 40 years, but that Nakajima guy found a way to get a hold of it and the G-16."

"Good evening," the waiter arrived at the table and looked around. "Would you care for a drink at this time or perhaps an appetizer? We have—" At the sight of Steph he took a step backwards. "Hello again, Miss..., I see that... that you're back... again." Slowly, he appeared to shake the memory from his head and continued, "Or perhaps you'd prefer a bottle of wine?"

Benjamin looked across at Steph and Chandler. "I was thinking of ordering a bottle of wine. Would that be okay with you two or would you like something else?"

Steph nodded, "Wine would be great. Whatever you pick will be fine with us."

"Okay then," Benjamin pointed at a selection on the wine list, "we'll try a bottle of this. I've never tried it before, but I've heard good things about it. What do you think? Any good?"

"Excellent choice, sir." The waiter took the wine list from Benjamin's outstretched hand. "The Toby Lane Cabernet is one of our finest and the 2012 was just released a few months ago. I'm sure you'll enjoy it."

"Oh my god, Toby Lane, I don't believe it," Steph said. "That's where Chandler and I met and it's our favorite wine. We were there for a wine tasting... what was it? Six months ago? Yeah, six months."

"Seven and a half, actually," Chandler added.

Benjamin raised his water glass. "Perfect, when the wine arrives we'll have a toast to Toby Lane and the two of you meeting."

After Steph clinked her glass, took a sip of water and placed her glass back down, she looked back at Alex. "Ms. Boudreau, you—"

"Alex, like you I prefer the shortened version," Alex said.

"Yeah, I guess we each have one of those names that really just sorta confuse people."

Alex laughed. "I have a few of those names, but right now I'm going to be Alex, just plain Alex."

"So, Alex," Steph started, "do you think there's a possibility that the smallpox, G-16 virus combination you mentioned could be the virus in Liberia? I mean, so far the CDC hasn't really identified the specific virus, which I think is kinda odd, don't you?"

"They know what it is by now. I've sent everything to the CDC and I would suspect that they've verified it all," Alex paused and took a sip of water. "In a couple of days I'll be turning over all of this information to the FBI. Do you think that will give you enough of a head start to break this story under your name?"

"Really? Oh yeah, I'll get right on this and two days is… well that's plenty of time. And thanks, I owe you big time."

Steph reached over and put her hand on Chandler's arm. "We should to go, I—"

Chandler's half-smile told Stephanie that tonight was not a work night. Tonight was their night to be out and nothing better ruin that. Steph gave a couple quick squeezes on Chandler's arm and continued, "What I mean is as soon as we're done here, and we have all the time in the world, I'll get started. In the meantime, how about I bring up the fact that Chandler here has been dying to work for GEN, so if either of you have any connections over there that she could talk to…."

CHAPTER 61

Walking out of the restaurant, Chandler looped her arm through Steph's. "I can't believe I'm really going to get an interview at GEN—a real interview. Do you know what this means?"

"Yeah, there go my Hawaii trips," Steph chortled.

"Don't go cancelling our Zermatt trip. I'm almost done packing."

Steph stopped, tightened her arm and cringed. "That's my dad... and Chief."

Chandler nodded.

"What are they doing here? Oh boy, I knew I was going to have to face this at some point. I guess it's time to get this out of the way."

Mr. Weintraub looked up and spotted Steph. The corners of his lips rose with each step. "Hello, Stephanie. I didn't expect to see you here, but I'm glad you are. You haven't returned my calls and I've wanted to talk to you since your news piece came out."

"Yeah, sorry I haven't gotten back to you. I've been busy. But you know what?" She pushed her shoulders back, "I figured you wanted to talk to me about coming back to the Post and I'm not ready for that conversation." She nodded, "Hi, Chief."

"That was a great article, Stephanie. It's probably generated more buzz for the Post than anything we've published in the last year, maybe longer. You can thank Cliff for giving me a well-deserved brow-beating and convincing me to run your story. For the record, Cliff was pretty hard on me about taking you off that story. He was right. I never should've done that, and I'm sorry. If you want to come back to the Post, you can do that anytime—on your terms, not mine. If you don't want to come back, I'll respect that and support whatever you choose to do."

"Thanks, dad. I appreciate that, I do, but I haven't really thought about what I'm going to do next. Chandler and I are leaving for Zermatt in three days and when we get back, I'll start sorting through some options. I still have some unfinished details I need to follow up on for the Agrico story."

"While you're looking at your options, I hope you'll consider this." Mr. Weintraub held out a folded piece of paper. "Here, read this. If you're interested, it's your story, either for the Post or wherever you want to take it."

Mr. Weintraub reached over and draped a hand on Chief's shoulder. "Cliff suggested I talk to you about it and I couldn't agree more. It's yours, if you want it."

"Check it out, Steph," Chief said. "I'm certain it's something you'll want to dirty your fingers with and you'd be damn good at it. But, I insist you wait until after your vacation."

Steph smiled. "No worries there. Nothing will be getting in the way of this trip." She took the paper and held it in her hand. "This wouldn't have anything to do with my follow-up on Agrico, would it?"

"What do you know about harvesting organs on the black market?" Mr. Weintraub asked.

"What do you mean?" Steph replied.

"How about a Chinese group called Falun Gong. Have you heard of them?" Chief asked.

"Or Nuestra Familia?" Mr. Weintraub asked.

Steph cocked her head and looked at Chandler. She shrugged her shoulders and returned her attention to her dad and Chief. "Hold on. Where're you going with this? Is this some kinda pop quiz?"

Mr. Weintraub eyed Chief with a half-wink. "Do you remember my friend, Gabriel Bick, with the Department of Corrections?"

"Sure, I went to high school with his son, Todd. I remember him."

"He's asked me to look into a problem they've uncovered. It seems one of the prison gangs here has a connection with China's 610 Office. Are you familiar with it, the 610 Office?"

Steph shook her head.

"It's a Chinese security agency set up for the sole purpose of eradicating a particular dissident group in its country." Mr. Weintraub said.

"How does Mr. Bick know about this?" Steph asked.

"Kites," Chief replied. "They're written messages passed among inmate members and eventually to members and associates outside the prison system. They intercepted a series of kites and it led to the connection with the 610 Office."

"This sounds like it should be your story. You're the one who uncovered the gang enterprises at Rikers Island."

"This is bigger than Rikers, way bigger." Chief said. "Falun Gong is the dissident organization targeted by the 610 Office. They've already killed over 64,000 of its members. Do you know how they kill them, and why?"

"I've never heard of any of this before." Steph replied.

"Each of these people died as a result of their organs being harvested and sold in the commercial organ transplant market. The California gang is attempting to wedge its way into the business of harvesting organs and selling them on the black market." Chief said.

Steph held her clasped fingers against her lips, took a deep breath and exhaled, loudly. "Why are you telling me this?"

"It's not just kidneys and livers," Mr. Weintraub added. "Even collagen from the executed organ donors is used in everyday over-the-counter facial creams. It's a big market."

"Facial creams? You mean moisturizers, cleansers, sunscreens? "What brands?" Chandler asked.

"Don't know the specific brands, but I've been told it's not all that uncommon." Chief replied.

"I find all of this numbing. It gives me the chills to even think about it." Steph stared at Chief, "You're saying that Falun Gong kills these people by removing their organs? So they just bleed to death? I can't believe it."

"Believe it." Chief replied.

Steph bit her lower lip and threw her arms around her chest. She had a list of questions she wanted to blurt out, not the least of which was why is this happening? Why can't it be stopped? She reached down and gripped the railing. "Why me? I mean, this is an important story and it—

"You're the best. You've proven it." Mr. Weintraub interrupted. "Besides you speak Spanish and that gives you a real edge."

"Spanish?" Steph asked. "Yeah, I do, but I don't speak Chinese."

"Nuestra Familia is a Latino prison gang. Do you know who they are?" Mr. Weintraub asked.

"No, I've never heard of them, the 610 Office, Falun Gong or any of this. Killing innocent people by harvesting their organs, and selling them on the black market—it's atrocious. Why is this even being allowed to happen?" Steph rubbed her hands together. Her voice softened, "This needs to be stopped."

Mr. Weintraub and Chief nodded in unison. "The paper I gave you," Mr. Weintraub paused and shook his head, then continued, "it lays out everything in greater detail."

Not a word was spoken. The buzzing of car engines from the nearby freeway filled the silence. Finally, Steph looked at Chandler. She couldn't tell if Chandler shared the same atrocity and rage over this inhumanity or if she simply dreaded the possibility that their vacation was about to be cancelled. She nudged closer to Chandler. "Nothing is going to stand in the way of Chandler and me going skiing. Can I give you an answer in two weeks when I return?"

"This has been going on for years. Another couple of weeks won't hurt," Mr. Weintraub beamed with pride.

Driving out of the Buckeye parking lot, Steph looked back at the restaurant. Standing in the same place where she had left them, her dad and Chief watched them pull away. She couldn't tell if it was a grin or a smirk that covered their lower faces. She started to unfolded the piece of paper. "Maybe I should read this now? What do you think?"

CHAPTER 62

The sounds of nail guns, diesel generators, construction workers and power saws were muffled by the rustling of tree tops swaying in the warm, southerly breeze. It was an early spring and the ground had thawed. Dwarf Larkspur, Indian Paintbrush and Fairyslippers sprouted through the thick carpet of green grasses.

Alex sat on a blanket with her legs pulled to her chest and her chin cradled between her knees. For the first time in a long, long time, her thoughts ran in slow motion. She had no need to do anything, but gaze out over the glistening, cerulean waters and listen to the symphony of restless birds and animals preparing for yet another day's harvest.

"Hey, let me see your phone for a sec." Benjamin extended a hand.

"My phone? Sure." Alex pulled her phone from her coat pocket and handed it to Benjamin.

Benjamin walked out from beneath the tree-topped canopy where they had been sitting and down to the edge of the lake. He cocked his arm, looked back at Alex and grinned. Seconds later, in the middle of the lake, ripples of concentric circles surrounded the splash.

"What was that all about?" Alex leapt to her feet and threw her arms in the air. "I can't believe you just did that! I have a lifetime of information on that phone."

Benjamin reached in his pocket, pulled out a small box and handed it to Alex. "I don't think you'll need that phone anymore. Go ahead, open it up."

Alex pulled the flap out and turned the box upside down. "Okay, you bought me a new phone, but I can't retrieve some of the things that were on my other phone. Some of that information is—"

Benjamin pressed a finger against his lips, "Shhh. This is my way of saying that the past life of Alex Boudreau is now officially over. From now on there's no more running around the world or even saving the world. You and I are going to make a life together, right here or anyplace else we decide to." He glanced up at the construction site. "I'm sure those guys will have the house rebuilt before the winter comes and I'd like nothing more than to spend our first Christmas together, right here, you and me."

Benjamin took the phone from Alex's hand. "Here, look at this." He opened up the phone's contacts. "These are the only numbers I programmed into your phone and these are the only people *anywhere* that have your new phone number." He held the phone in front of Alex.

"Well I'm glad your name's in there. Phil, okay, I like that, my mother… oh dear I was supposed to call her a few days ago and it totally slipped my mind. I'll call her right now."

Benjamin grabbed Alex by hand. "Why not wait until tomorrow and then you can tell her yourself—in person."

Alex smiled, suspiciously. "What do you mean—exactly—by tomorrow?"

"She's flying here tomorrow and she can stay as long as you want her to."

"No," Alex shook her head, "there's no way she'd fly this far—no way. She hasn't been on a plane in years and, well she just wouldn't fly this far."

"I know now where you got your stubborn streak. You're mom's a tough one and it took some coaxing, but she's coming. Phil and Michelle flew over to get her and they'll all be here tomorrow. By the way," Benjamin threw his arms around Alex, "she softened up a little when she figured out that I'm Alexandra's man she met in America. Just exactly what does your mom know about me?"

Alex zipped a finger across her lips. "I'm not saying a word. You're going to have to figure that one out for yourself."

Benjamin reached out and took Alex's hand. "I want to show you something."

They walked along the shore of the lake and Benjamin pointed out the grey-green leaves of the Lupine, coated with delicate, silvery hairs. He pulled the seeds from a pod and explained how they had been a major food staple of the American Indians in the region. Above, he pointed to a flock of Canadian Geese migrating to the Canadian wetlands to the north. "Those birds pick a mate when they're two years old and they stay together for their entire life," he explained.

They stopped at the headwaters of the lake where a mountain stream took pause from its meandering journey to give birth to the lake's tranquil waters. Alex drew a deep breath and held it. She rolled her shoulders forward and felt her muscles relax and her mind slow. She slowly exhaled. "Do you think it's going to work out?"

"What do you mean?" Benjamin asked.

"I mean us, you and me. Do you really think we can share a life together without my past surfacing again and sending us into chaos?"

Benjamin smiled and ran the tips of his fingers along his lips. "Let me put it this way," he began. "Before this stream reached this spot, it had stretches of rippling white water and it pounded boulders and ripped at the banks as it rushed its way down steep mountain slopes. What we learn is a river never dwells in the past. Look over there and listen." He pointed to the far side of the stream and continued, "When you hear the water lapping over those rocks, when are you hearing it? In the past or the future? Neither. The river teaches us to live where it lives; exist where it exists and play where it plays—in the here and now."

TO BE CONT.I..N..U...E...D......

ACKNOWLEDGEMENTS

Whew! Writing this book has been exhilarating, but numbing. I knew that each book would present a new challenge, but I also thought, somehow, it would become easier. Wrong!

I am fortunate to have friends who have helped me in so many ways and I have met new friends along the way who have willingly shared their unique talents with me. Without this type of help, it would be near impossible to write a reality-based work of fiction.

Dr. Murray Gardner has worked tirelessly with me since I began this journey. He has spent untold hours with me, either before or after our typical 10 am swim practice, showering me with articles to expand my imagination and discussing many of the cockeyed ideas I, somehow, thought plausible. His expertise in genetic engineering, among so many other fields, has been key in helping me write about a very technical subject in a way that is understandable to us all.

Another fellow swimmer and my dive buddy, Bob Upshaw, has been there at all hours responding to my ideas and helping me understand the cyber world. Walks on the beaches, a beer or two at his place and countless emails and phone conversations have helped to create some forward thinking cyber-attack tools that I think even the NSA would be proud to have in their arsenal.

Sgt. Daniel Powell of the Davis Police Department has once again stepped forward to lend his guiding hand. You would never think it would be so easy to make a firearm, or a deadly bomb, with simple items we all have in our homes. I know I never did. Dan is a true expert in his field and it's been my pleasure to get to know him.

My brother-in-law, Dr. John Holman (not the same character in this story by any means) spent the time to educate me on the development of vaccines. I have a long way to go, but John's patience, expertise and ideas were instrumental in helping me tackle this subject.

Genetically modified foods is an enormously explosive political issue in many parts of the world. I must admit I had my own beliefs before I started delving into this subject. Another lane mate, Dr. Pam Ronald, is, without stretching the truth one bit, a top expert in this field—bar none. It's been nothing but my pleasure to work with someone who emanates such a passion for her chosen field. Thanks to Pam, I've gained a much better understanding of this subject and it's definitely something I want to pursue in my future writing.

The Mustang region of Nepal is an area steeped in history that until very recently was out-of-bounds to foreigners. Candy Kolb, a friend since the dark ages of junior high school, just happens to live in Katmandu and another friend, Sandra Sigrist, was on her way to Mustang for a trek when I developed the idea of using Nepal. How fortuitous is that? You two helped me more than you'll ever know. धन्यवाद एक लाख. As I write this, Nepal was just hit by a 7.8-magnatude earthquake that has killed thousands and the country will take years to recover. Please keep this in mind if you are considering making a charitable contribution of any kind in the coming months.

There's really nothing more important than having people read my drafts as I progress along in the story. As a writer, it's easy to get absorbed in what I'm writing and I need some people to slap me back to reality. I lucked out in this area with no-holds-barred, Diana Connolly, tell-it-like-it-is, Bill Henderson and my wife, Kristen Rogers, who's never had a problem telling me I can improve. Really, this is such an important part of producing a final product that I'm unabashedly proud of and I owe a big shout out to you three.

Nancy Roberts, what can I say? From the moment you said "yes" to editing my writing, you've done nothing but inspire me to do all the things

ACKNOWLEDGEMENTS

I can to become a better writer. I know there's the comma-thing still hanging out there between us, but I wouldn't have completed three books without your guidance, insight and your own creativity. I vow to make the next book easier on you!

My wife, Kristen, was a beta reader for me, but she has been much more than that. She has supported and encouraged me to continue on with this journey and the truth is, this journey has been far from easy. My normal affable self can sometimes, well maybe a lot of times, morph into a grumpy curmudgeon lost in my own dimension. Your patience, love, understanding and untiring nudging have been my rock and I count myself lucky the day I met you.

Moose... Moose. He's been by my side every page of the way and he's never criticized me once. What more can someone ask in a dog?

To you, my readers, a huge thank you for your comments, ideas, and criticisms, and of course for buying my books :). I value each and every one of you and thank you for your support. May I ask that after reading this story, to please post an honest review on your favorite site? Reviews are not only helpful to me, but they may just entice another reader to join me in this wild adventure.